MARVELOUS GEOMETRY

MARVELOUS GEOMETRY

NARRATIVE AND METAFICTION IN MODERN FAIRY TALE

JESSICA TIFFIN

WAYNE STATE UNIVERSITY PRESS
DETROIT

13 12 11 10 09   5 4 3 2 1

Library of Congress Cataloging-in-Publication Data

Tiffin, Jessica, 1969–
    Marvelous geometry : narrative and metafiction in modern fairy tale / Jessica Tiffin.
        p. cm. — (Series in fairy-tale studies)
    Includes bibliographical references (p. 235) and index.
    ISBN 978-0-8143-3262-7 (pbk. : alk. paper)
    1. Fairy tales—History and criticism. 2. Fairy tales in literature. 3. Fairy tales in motion
pictures. I. Title.
    PN3437.T47 2009
    398.2—dc22   2008039516

Published with the assistance of a fund established by Thelma Gray James of Wayne State University
for the publication of folklore and English studies.

Typeset by Keata Brewer, E. T. Lowe Publishing Company
Composed in Scala and ITC Anna

CONTENTS

ACKNOWLEDGMENTS

Eternal thanks to Lesley Marx, who has been an invaluable source of support, encouragement, advice and meticulous reading over many years, as well as dealing with adverbs above and beyond the call of duty. I am also deeply grateful to Cristina Bacchilega for recommending the manuscript for publication, and to her, Don Haase, and all my readers for useful and challenging input during the revision process. As always, family and friends have offered support, discussion, and occasional exhortation where necessary.

This research was made possible by Research Scholarships and Research Associateships from the University of Cape Town, as well as a grant from the National Research Foundation of South Africa. I am also grateful for funding from the Mellon Foundation during the revision process.

This book is dedicated to the memory of my grandfather, Frank Voisey Collins, to whose library and love of literature I owe my interest in magical narrative.

The fairy tale prefers to speak of clothing and golden or silver armour rather than of bodies, not just because they are made of exquisite, shining materials, but because clothing and armour are artificial creations, because the structure, the geometry, of the raiment is further from nature, nearer the spirit, more abstract than the plasticity of the body. —MAX LÜTHI

I like the geometrically patterned flowers best. . . . More than the ones that aim at realism, at looking real . . . —A. S. BYATT

1

TELLING THEORETICAL TALES

There exists, finally, a form of the marvellous in the pure
state which . . . has no distinct frontiers. . . . We note, in
passing, how arbitrary the old distinction was between
form and content: the event, which traditionally belonged
to "content," here becomes a "formal" element. The fairy
tale is only one of the varieties of the marvellous. What
distinguishes the fairy tale is a certain kind of writing. . . .
—Todorov 53–54

Within the development of Western literary and media
forms and narratives across the twentieth century and into the twenty-
first is a recurring and powerful thread of fairy tale. The traditional narratives of folklore, refracted through the literary developments of earlier
centuries and into the literary and popular forms of a more technological age, have retained a relevance which demonstrates their power and
endurance as a cultural artifact. Fairy tale's ability to mutate and recreate itself over time and context is reflected in the plethora of contemporary fairy-tale fictions: not only literary re-explorations of the tale as
short prose form but also excursions into the novel, poetry, the comic
book, and live-action and animated film and television. The ideological implications of this continuing popularity are complex and at times
problematical, given fairy tale's peculiarly coherent surface and its ability to give a deeply satisfying and utopian gloss to assumptions about
society, power, and gender which are often profoundly reactionary. The
form's continued currency relies on a kind of structural recognition:

on the ability of fairy-tale narratives to retain their characteristic shape and function despite a changing social context and their cross-pollination with a diverse range of narratives. Fairy tales signal their particular nature and function through highly encoded structures, a complex interaction of characteristics and content which nonetheless operates with a simple and holistic effect to create a sense of nostalgic familiarity. This quality of recognition not only tends to elide those ideological elements of the tale which are no longer relevant to contemporary society, it also affirms the integrity and identifiability of fairy-tale content within other forms.

To focus on the structural operation of fairy tale before its fascinating ideological byways may be seen as potentially problematical, however. While the structural study of folklore and fairy tale is in many ways based on the work of Vladimir Propp and the Russian formalists, the advent of postmodernism and poststructuralism has rendered structuralist accounts of narrative both incomplete and somewhat unfashionable. Stephen Benson's account of the intersections between narrative theory and folklore in *Cycles of Influence* comments at the outset that "enquiry into the workings of narrative has moved away from, indeed critiqued, the search for deep structures and abstract, essential geometries, in favour of . . . non-geometric conceptions of narrative space, including the possibilities of interactivity" (17). In a postmodern landscape the notion of a unified, universal structure to any form of text, whether literary, cultural, or even human, has given way to an interest in demonstrating such structures to be artificial constructions rather than universal abstractions. Certainly it is not my intention in this inquiry to offer any sort of wholly structuralist account of modern fairy tale, or to deny the complexities of more recent theoretical approaches which recognize the dizzying ideological interactions of text and context and the essentially shifting and historically constructed nature of meaning. Nonetheless, while acknowledging the importance of structure within the context of a broader semiotic whole, I am interested in the extent to which fairy tale's functioning in modern contexts nonetheless invokes a notion of geometric form which self-consciously presents itself in precisely those fixed terms recognized by structuralist analysis. More particularly, this reference to a solid and structurally rigid notion of fairy-tale meaning becomes, in the hands of the more self-conscious modern fairy-tale writers, essentially oppositional; the somewhat utopian notion of structure is invoked only to be explored and disrupted, either playfully or radically, or both. Italo Calvino points to precisely this tendency when he refers to the literature's inevitable tendency to "feel unsatisfied with its own traditionalism and start planning out new ways of looking at the written word until it completely overturns the matrix which it had followed up till then" ("Narrative Form as Combinative Process" 95). At the same time, however, this play is paradoxical; radical inquiry and reinterpretation notwithstanding, the structures of fairy tale must be invoked with sufficient power to be recognizable, to identify the text as fairy tale within the context of the structural tradition.

In characterizing fairy tale by the element of recognition, of course I make a point which can be easily extended to almost any form of strongly generic storytelling, since structure is one of the strongest features of genre. John Cawelti's seminal work on formula narrative argues for a careful balance between "the different pleasures and uses of novelty and familiarity" in popular literature (1). Genres such as Gothic horror, the romance, or the detective story rely on their interaction with their generic traditions for the construction of meaning in any individual text. In this sense genre narratives cannot exist in isolation, but in fact engage, through both adherence to and departure from genre norms, in continual dialogue with the history and pre-existing body of work which constitutes their genre. More than the simple shape of a text, narrative structure becomes a powerful tradition, a set of codes which is continually invoked, rediscovered, and recreated with the telling of every new version, and which thus relies on a self-consciousness about textuality which moves the narrative into the realm of the postmodern narrative technique of metafiction. Recognition is central to this process; the production of narrative comes to rest not only in an interaction with genre traditions but also in a reciprocal relationship between the producer and the receiver of the tale, between the tale-teller and audience, in a shared understanding of the parameters and characteristics of the narrative. In this formulation fairy tale becomes simply one of the oldest and most strongly marked of narrative structures, whose interaction with its own traditions has a large body of exemplars to invoke and an equally wide range of readers familiar with its rules. This is particularly relevant to any study of postmodern fairy tale in particular, because the self-consciousness of metafictional play rests on the foundation of a generic structure which is especially prone to self-conscious situation of its own texts within a highly structured tradition, even before contemporary writers begin their postmodern deconstructions.

Above all, what fairy tale thus offers as a generic tradition is a level of self-awareness, a deliberate and conscious construction of itself within a set of codes recognized by both writer and reader. Again, this self-consciousness could apply equally to any genre text; in the case of fairy tale, however, the self-aware invocation of structure has another layer of self-consciousness which inheres in its deliberate refusal of mimesis. Recognition of fairy tale relies on its striking motifs and circumscribed and predictable plot structures, and also on its status as a marvelous form. Fairy-tale narratives deny reality not only in their calm acceptance of the magical but also in their refusal to provide any sort of realistic detail or conventional causal logic to the worlds they describe. In their deliberate problematization of reality they thus further demonstrate some aspects of metafictional writing. Recognition of this potential can be found even in the classic forms which predate postmodern play; in the nineteenth century, Victorian writers used fairy tale to interrogate linguistic meaning, writing original tales which deconstructed their own expectations. This inherent correlation between structure and self-consciousness perhaps explains the extent to which fairy tale has become the favored playground of many postmodern writers in the late twentieth century. The tendency toward the dissolution, uncertainty, and collapse of narrative authority under the postmodern gaze seems a strange companion to the highly structured, formalized, and patterned conventions of the fairy-tale form, the "marvelous geometry" of my title. In fact, however, many postmodern writers are fascinated by structure precisely because its complexity offers such a rich field for self-conscious exploration and deconstruction. Fairy tale itself, even before its transformation by modern rewrites, exhibits a self-awareness about narrative and a specifically problematized relationship with reality which seems peculiarly suited to the reflexiveness and self-interrogation of postmodernism, as well as to postmodernism's fascination with narrative structure. At the same time the structures of fairy tale operate nostalgically, as part of postmodernism's ongoing dialogue with history and interrogation of meaning.

Along with this tendency to metafictional awareness in a literary sense, fairy tale's development within the cultural expressions of the twentieth and twenty-first centuries adds new layering to its self-conscious employment. In particular it may also be seen as occurring within a tradition of fantastic or marvelous literature which has strengthened dramatically in the last century. In a post-Tolkien cultural setting, magical narrative has found a huge following—one which, however, tends toward the popular rather than the literary. The intersections between fairy tale and popular literature hearken back to the roots of fairy tale itself, in the earliest oral folk narratives which were communally owned by a culture at large. Thus, in tandem with the literary use of fairy tale as a response to some aspects of postmodernism, there is a movement to reassert and recapture the power of the fairy-tale narrative as a tool which reflects the experience of a community in the context of mass literature rather than intellectual literature which is often perceived as elitist. Fantasy and romance writers have seized upon the fairy tale as a popular medium, one which offers the consolation and fulfillment of desire which characterizes fantasy romance writing, or which allows the interrogation of culture within a familiar and recognizable matrix. Even further along the scale, film, and particularly the consumer-orientated productions of Hollywood, also offers a radical rewriting of fairy tale as folklore, an appropriation of a communal and nonwritten medium to present tale as commodity in a purely commercial sense.

> ### A Certain Kind of Writing: Recognizing Fairy Tale
>
> Fairy tales have been defined in so many ways that it boggles the mind to think that they can be categorised as a genre. —Jack Zipes, *Oxford Companion* xv

If metafictional play with fairy tale requires recognition, then it is important to establish precisely how fairy tale is identified, how it is different from any other kind of narrative. I wish to begin with Tzvetan Todorov's apparently vague assertion that "what distinguishes the fairy tale is a certain kind of writing . . ." (54). This is not as vague as it might seem; he argues that the form depends for its identity not on the status of the marvelous within it, but on a clearly recognizable overall effect which is constructed through a number of characteristics, including tone, form, structure, pattern, and motif. Any fairy tale, from Madame d'Aulnoy to Disney, signals itself clearly as fairy tale through attributes which are ultimately a matter of what I shall define as *texture* rather than simple form and pattern. J. R. R. Tolkien says that it is "precisely the colouring, the atmosphere, the unclassifiable individual details of a story, and above all the general purport that informs with life the undissected bones of the plot, that really count" (18). Both Tolkien and Todorov seem decided on the instant recognizability of fairy tale, but a little vague on how this identification is made; the truth is that the means by which fairy tale identifies itself to the reader are strangely complex, despite the simplicity of the response which makes it obvious that a particular narrative is or is not a fairy tale. Alan Dundes's useful essay "Texture, Text, and Content" notes that the student of folklore is likely to achieve a notion of how a genre is defined by reading numerous examples, and quotes Archer Taylor in a similar vein to Tolkien and Todorov: "An incommunicable quality tells us this sentence is proverbial and that one is not" (Taylor in Dundes, 21). This is, as Dundes points out, hardly useful, yet, like

Tolkien's and Todorov's assertions, it underlines the impossibility of defining fairy tale through any single factor. Instead, a constellation of central characteristics creates an overall, instantly recognizable *effect*.

Dundes deals specifically with the notion of texture, but defines it in terms of language: "In most of the genres (and all those of a verbal nature), the texture is the language, the specific phonemes and morphemes employed. Thus in verbal forms of folklore, textural features are linguistic features" (22). This is useful in that some aspects of folkloric tale-telling definitely depend on a characteristic sparsity and simplicity of language, yet it denies the textural effect of characteristics Dundes would identify as "text": structure, motif, and pattern, which are as integral to the "feel" of fairy tale as is the language. In insisting on the intertwined import of text and texture, I follow Todorov's insistence that "the old distinction . . . between form and content" is essentially arbitrary: "the event, which traditionally belonged to 'content', here becomes a 'formal' element" (53). Dundes's argument that "texture" in folkloric expression is untranslatable to a different language further separates it from "text," which at the level of plot or story is perfectly translatable (23). My use of *texture* here thus differs slightly from that of Dundes, in that I argue that texture in the sense of a characteristic, instantly recognizable feel or style, is recognizable on the level of structure and content as much as language. This distinction becomes particularly important in dealing with literary and, especially, postmodern fairy tale; a good example is Angela Carter, who manages to write a sumptuously textured Gothic fairy tale which denies the classic fairy-tale linguistic simplicity without losing its ability to invoke the universality, pattern, and symbol which are equally a part of fairy-tale texture.

Carter's writing also demonstrates particularly well the extent to which the content-based aspects of fairy-tale texture in some ways rely not only on simplicity but also on a self-conscious and playful invocation of the unreal, not only in its inclusion of the marvelous or the magical but also in its denial of the more cluttered texture of realism or realistic logic, what A. S. Byatt refers to as "the peculiarly flat, unadorned nature of the true tale" ("Happy Ever After"). In this analysis, as suggested by the "marvelous" geometry of my title, I am also interested in the specific functioning of fairy tale as magical narrative, as one more layer in its self-conscious play. The strength of the fairy-tale tradition as an exemplary framework for new texts lies not only in the structural qualities of its characteristic texture but also in its deliberate and strongly coded tendency to situate its narratives at some distance from reality. While the magical—enchantment, transformation, curses, spells, and magical objects or creatures—is an unquestioned aspect of many fairy-tale narratives, not all fairy tales are necessarily magical narratives. Even those that are not explicitly magical, however, retain the classic fairy-tale logic; event, psychology, and cause and effect are deliberately unrealistic and nonmimetic, mostly because they are subordinate to the expectations of narrative shape and outcome rather than internal motivation. This particular aspect of unreality in fairy tale is important for my discussion, since the invocation of the unreal is a self-consciously literary act which powerfully highlights the potential even in classic fairy tale for metafictional play.

In identifying fairy tale by texture, I am thus invoking a range of characteristics which rely heavily on clean lines, deliberate patterning and a geometry of structure and motif, but also include style, voice, and some aspects of content and mimetic approach. This attribute of texture, rather than language or motif, renders a fairy tale intrinsically familiar and identifiable even through literary manipulation, and it is precisely this quality of identifiability which allows the form to provide such a rich ground for metafictional play. However, Todorov's identification of fairy tale by "a certain kind of writing" is in some ways problematical, particularly for postmodern literary forms, since it presupposes that, beyond a certain point, disruption of texture by narrative play—especially the inclusion of other, non-fairy-tale elements—may compromise the narrative's operation as fairy tale. Roger Sale notes that "everyone seems instinctively agreed on what the term includes and excludes, even though fairy tales blend easily into related kinds, like myths, legends, romances, realistic folk fables, and cautionary tales" (23). Despite this tendency to generic mixing, however, to a large extent fairy tales tend to retain their central characteristic of recognizability despite the adulteration of their texture with that of other forms. Thus Margaret Atwood's "Bluebeard's Egg," while couched entirely as a realist story exploring a marriage relationship, sustains the reference to the "Bluebeard" narrative through inclusion of the story's distinct motifs, despite the radical difference in language and tone. Propp, while discussing at length the kinds of modifications an oral teller may make to a tale, concludes that literary substitutions are not easily accepted: "the fairy tale possesses such resistance that other genres shatter against it: they do not readily blend. If a clash takes place, the fairy tale wins" ("Fairy Tale Transformations" 107). In fact, the mixing of fairy tale with other genres is not about clash as much as it is about diffusion, reinforcement, and echo; the ability of fairy tale to find convivial company in genres as disparate as horror, science fiction, and radical postmodern literature points rather emphatically toward its status as an archaic and familiar form whose patterns and textures underlie more forms of storytelling than might at first be apparent.

The prevalence of fairy-tale texture through the postmodern multiplicity of form and genre is in some ways a problematical concept, in that my definition of *texture* seems specific and hence exclusive; how can it be maintained through the complexities of metafictional play? While it is very much the case that some modern fairy-tale texts reproduce a purer and more faithful fairy-tale texture than do others, Propp's notion of the resilience of fairy-tale character nonetheless applies. The strength of *texture* as a defining term relies precisely in its complexity and hence, in some ways, *lack* of definition; in invoking such disparate elements as language, structure, pattern, motif, and nonmimetic representation, the possibility exists that a modern fairy tale may well acknowledge and reproduce some characteristics while self-consciously choosing to reject or modify others. Elizabeth Wanning Harries gives a useful definition; her study *Twice Upon a Time* insists throughout on the sophistication and density of apparently simple fairy-tale narrative, a complexity she locates through a historical account of the development of fairy-tale voice. She distinguishes between "compact" and "complex" fairy tales; both are valid representatives of the genre, but, where compact versions work through "carefully constructed simplicity" which operates as "an implicit guarantee of their traditional and authentic status," complex tales "are complex in their reimaginings of well-known and more conventional fairy-tale patterns and motifs" (16–17). Her definition is interesting in that, while distinguishing between classic fairy tale and more modern reinterpretations, the notion of "carefully constructed simplicity" in classic tale acknowledges the complexity and layering, and therefore the resilience to adaptation, of the apparently simple form. Twentieth- and twenty-first-century adult fairy tale tends to fall into Harries's "complex" category, but I would still argue that it necessarily depends on a recognition and invocation as well as a deconstruction of this deceptively "simple" texture.

To return, then, to my title: fairy tale operates as marvelous geometry in its provision of highly encoded and recognizable qualities of structure and pattern *and* in its deliberate and self-conscious distancing of itself from realistic representation, whether in logic and detail or in its operation as magical narrative. These two aspects of its characteristic texture are central to my argument, and require discussion in more depth.

GEOMETRY: PATTERN AND STRUCTURE

To refer to a "geometry" of fairy tale suggests a notion of structure and logic akin to the mathematical, but more importantly it presupposes a set of internal relationships: rules, harmonies, and proportions. In his essay "Narrative Form as a Combinative Process," Calvino refers to primitive narrative as offering "a kind of geometry of story-telling" which depends on "a set of balances and correlatives" (93). Folklore is characterized in this account as an almost mechanistic process in which the whole is constructed through the constitution of already-existing, standardized elements into an overall pattern with qualities of symmetric harmony. This construction is mirrored, although to a less obvious extent, in other kinds of literature, where he argues that a discovery of underlying geometric shape is curiously consoling (97). The patterns of fairy tale are instantly recognizable and familiar: things come in threes, and the old woman who talks to the eldest son as he sets out on his quest will be there to say exactly the same thing to the second and third. The narratives follow clearly defined paths of character, event, and device which impose upon the tale a regular structure and form. Common patterns include the definition of protagonists (the third son or daughter is significant, the first two are foolish, evil, or ugly, while the third is beautiful and good); the incidence of repetition (tests failed by the first two protagonists and completed successfully by the third); or the occurrence of magical artifacts as essential and completely unexplained plot devices (a comb thrown behind you always turns into a hedge, or a mirror into a lake). Such elements are clichés of fairy-tale form—any child could tell you what should be present in a fairy tale, and even how such things should be arranged.

The presence of such patterns in fairy tale and folklore is the key focus in the work of theorists such as Vladimir Propp, Claude Lévi-Strauss, and the Finnish folklorist Antti Aarne, whose system of classification (the Aarne-Thompson index) allows tales to be identified by a type number which describes the tale's elements and functions. Propp's approach is slightly different, relying on internal function rather than an external identification of type. He states categorically that "fairy tales exhibit thirty-one functions" and "in all, the fairy tale knows about one hundred and fifty elements or constituents. Each of these elements can be labelled according to its bearing on the sequence of action" ("Fairy Tale Transformations" 95). The approaches of Propp and Aarne are interesting for my argument more because of their testimony to the importance of pattern and repetition than to any intrinsic meaning in the definition of those patterns. Calvino dismisses the Finnish school represented by Aarne as simply one more in a long list of partial attempts to understand the fairy tale: "a system similar to that used for the classification of coleoptera, which, in their cataloging process, reduced findings to algebraic sigla of the Type-Index and Motif-Index" (*Italian Folk Tales* xvii). Despite the flurry of critical bickering over the nature and legitimacy of such classifications, Arne's system no doubt provides a useful tool for the anthropological and sociological study of folklore. The literary student is perhaps better off simply accepting these technical treatments of pattern as evidence of the essential fact of its existence.

As I have suggested above, this strong sense of structure is vital to the enactment of any fairy tale, classic or modern. Each fairy-tale text is intertextual, created within the context of the structures of the genre understood through its other exemplars. In this focus on the notion of system some correlation can clearly be found to structuralist thinking, particularly in the notion of meaning as a relationship of elements: the individual utterance has significance only in interaction with the system to which it refers. This approach is important for my argument in that the theoretical stance follows fairy tale's tendencies in reference to its own structures. John Sturrock's discussion of structuralism notes the importance of Lévi-Strauss's ideas about symbols, whose "meaning at each occurrence is fixed by the place they occupy within the economy of that particular myth. This is . . . to allow the system itself as it were to dictate the meaning to you" (11). This is precisely how fairy tale works, not only in its insistence on the importance of meaning within a structure of meaning but also in its tendency, along with structuralism, to ignore or elide the historical and ideological processes which have created the system. Instead, the system is taken for granted at the moment of its operation. This is the process Cristina Bacchilega has called fairy tale's "ideological paradox or 'trick' . . . that magic which seeks to conceal the struggling interests which produce it" (*Postmodern Fairy Tales* 7). Paradoxically, while the deconstruction of fairy tale under postmodernism offers the most extreme interrogation of this ideological illusion, self-consciousness about the imposition of structure and its imposition of values can be found as early as the nineteenth century.

Structuralism is basically disinterested in the roots and historical development which have created the systems it explores, but any analysis of fairy tale in the twenty-first century cannot afford a similar disinterest. Even leaving aside the ideological implications of fairy tale's sociohistorical place in culture over time, the importance of pattern and repetition are themselves historically rooted. It is perhaps in its insistence on pattern that fairy tale comes closest to its mythological origins; critics such as Mircea Eliade link the repetitive motifs of fairy tale to primitive religious expression, "ritual motifs which still survive in the religious institutions of primitive peoples" (196). Propp follows the same process of identification, stating that "we can establish several types of relationship between the fairy tale and [primitive] religion. The first is a direct genetic dependency" ("Fairy Tale Transformations" 99). Conceptually, Eliade argues that myth and fairy tale exist on different planes of meaning, differentiated by varying levels of "man's behaviour to the sacred": "Now, it is not always true that the tale shows a 'desacralisation' of the mythical world. It would be more correct to speak of a camouflage of mythical motifs and characters; instead of 'desacralisation' it would be better to say 'rank-loss of the sacred'" (200). The patterns of fairy tale, then, are akin to the patterns of religious myth, holding that extra sense of magical or mystical significance despite their expression in a domesticated format. The increased mythic significance of the narrative is important in that it becomes one of the techniques with which fairy tale entrenches its own structural presuppositions. Thus Calvino argues for the power of mythic storytelling not only to infuse a narrative with significance but also to insist on the shape of the narrative according to mythic archetypes. In his words, "myth forces the exercises of repetition on fables. It obliges the fable to retrace its own steps" ("Narrative Form as a Combinative Process").

The mythic structures of fairy tale are also patterns which reflect, in an expression charged with significance, the patterns of daily existence, the essential human experiences. Eliade states:

> Though in the West the tale has long since become a literature of diversion . . . or of escape . . . it still presents the structure of an infinitely serious and responsible adventure, for in the last analysis it is reducible to an initiatory scenario: again and again we find initiatory ordeals (battles with the monster, apparently insurmountable obstacles, riddles to be solved, impossible tasks, etc) . . . But its content proper refers to a terrifyingly serious reality: initiation, that is, passing, by way of a symbolic death and resurrection, from ignorance and immaturity to the spiritual age of the adult. (201)

The recognition of fairy-tale pattern thus becomes not only a structural recognition or an evocation of primitive ritual repetitions but also a psychological one: the patterns evoked by fairy tale are profoundly linked to human development and consciousness. This perhaps goes some way toward explaining the continuing appeal of fairy tale, its use again and again in varying types of literature. Bruno Bettelheim's well-known analysis of fairy tale makes use of precisely this quality, in his insistence on fairy tale's importance for the psychological development of children. Again, this application depends on structure:

> A child needs to understand what is going on within his conscious self so that he can also cope with that which goes on in his unconscious. . . . It is here that fairy tales have unequalled value, because they offer new dimensions to the child's imagination which would be impossible for him to discover as truly on his own. Even more important, the form and structure of fairy tales suggest images to the child by which he can structure his daydreams and with them give better direction to his life. (7)

While many critics find Bettelheim's approach somewhat extreme (see Sale, 39ff., for the argument that Bettelheim is "distorting the [fairy tale] and partially rewriting it," and Zipes's more sweeping indictment, *Magic Spell* 179ff.), nonetheless his arguments are persuasive for the fairy tale as a particularly structured version of human experience. It is this structuredness which makes the tale easily accessible for the reader's identification with the processes depicted. It is also this structure which, as Zipes argues in *Fairy Tale as Myth*, becomes the carrier of ideology, codifying social power relations and, through the comforting familiarity which fairy-tale structures offer, institutionalizing them.

Various critics have sought to reduce the recurring structure or pattern of fairy tale to one core pattern, which is that of the quest. Both Eliade and Bettelheim, with their concept of fairy tale as rite of passage, touch on the importance of the classic quest motif as a psychological or social journey of discovery, but other critics find a more fundamental pattern at play here. Propp identifies an element of "basic harm," which he says "usually serves as the start of the plot" in fairy tale ("Fairy Tale Transformations" 111); Max Lüthi summarizes Propp's approach as one which finds "a lack (or a villainy which causes a lack) and its liquidation" as "the basic structural pattern of the fairy tale" (54), but refines this to insist that fairy tale represents "the general human pattern Need/Fulfilment of need. This Lack/Remedy is in fact the basic pattern of the fairy tale" (55). This provides a "slim, goal-oriented plotline" (56) which contributes materially to fairy tale's characteristic texture and feel as well as to its sense of pattern. Linearity of plot characterizes fairy tale; diversions and jumps in time (such as the retrospective tale embedded in Grimms' "The Glass Coffin") are rare. At the same time, structuredness works together with other

Chapter 1

elements to increase accessibility; namely, the tale's simplicity and its employment of symbol.

THE MARVELOUS AND THE UNREAL: SIMPLICITY, SYMBOL, MAGIC

In its calm acceptance of the marvelous, both in magical elements and in stripped-down logic and causation, fairy tale offers a distinctive and highly recognizable world which is characterized, as I have suggested above, by its deliberate removal from the real. Propp comments that "Obviously, the fairy tale is born out of life; however, the fairy tale reflects reality only weakly" ("Fairy Tale Transformations" 96). Thus, while its basic principles—life, death, love, hate, quest, challenge, reward, punishment—are those of human existence, the world in which such principles are enacted is significantly different from the real, so that normal expectations are completely transcended. "Once upon a time" signals a transition to a different reality from our own. Rosemary Jackson has suggested that not only is the world of the marvelous intrinsically different from our own, but it is also necessarily removed from it: "This secondary, duplicated cosmos, is relatively autonomous, relating to the 'real' only through metaphorical reflection and never, or rarely, intruding into or interrogating it" (42). The process of "metaphorical reflection" Jackson identifies is, in fact, a function of this distance, which leads to fairy tale's self-awareness, its presentation of itself as story rather than mimesis, as artifact rather than reality. More than this, fairy tale shows an awareness and encoding of itself *as text*, the classic opening "Once upon a time" signaling a precise relationship with reality which makes no pretense at reality, but which is continually aware of its own status *as story*, as ritualized narrative enactment. Tolkien identifies this as "the enchanted state: Secondary Belief"; significantly, "the moment disbelief arises, the spell is broken; the magic, *or rather art*, has failed" (36, emphasis mine). Participation in the marvelous universe of fairy tale—the enjoyment of the wonder fairy tale can evoke—depends entirely on recognition of the artificiality of that universe, the fact that it is a work of art. The shared author/reader awareness of how the genre works is based on a mutual recognition of the text as a created object, rather than any attempt to reconstruct reality. The strong underlying structures and textures of fairy tale are instrumental in creating this awareness.

A major contributing factor to its artificiality is in the characteristic simplicity of fairy tale, the extent to which it resists detail. It is sufficient to know that a man has three sons; whether he is a farmer or a merchant may not even be important. Bettelheim has noted how "the fairy-tale simplifies all situations, its figures are clearly drawn, and details, unless very important, are eliminated" (8). Lüthi also observes that "the fairy tale delights not just in the line as such, but above all in the simple, clearly drawn line" (40). The effect of this simplification, which contributes very materially to the fairy tale's characteristic texture, is one also of intensified significance. Where such details are given—the mirror and comb carried by the girl as she flees Baba Yaga's hut, for example—they attain a precise, heightened and powerful symbolic force. Tolkien insists that "fairy stories deal largely . . . with simple or fundamental things . . . made luminous by their setting" (59). Lüthi discusses this in terms of the characteristic symbolic clarity and polarized value of fairy tale: "the tendency to the extreme, which is at work in every nook and cranny of the fairy tale, not just in the contrastive juxtapositions of beautiful and ugly, contributes to this clarity and sharpness: great riches, half a kingdom, the hand of a princess . . . death" (43). While fairy tale may deal with simple objects and people, the setting of fairy tale allows such motifs to become resonant, holding a marvelous meaning above and beyond their basic shapes, and this increased resonance is one of its most recognizable features.

Lack of physical or circumstantial detail in the fairy tale thus goes hand in hand with a more profound effect, the simplification of morals and principles to the point where any conflict is dealt with in terms of absolutes—the hero, heroine, magical helper opposed to the villain, monster, or competing hero. Again, the effect is to heighten the significance of the issues, so that a fairy tale becomes the arena in which unequivocally defined forces confront one another before proceeding to an unambiguous resolution, an artificial and often perfect closure. The Disneyfication of fairy tale in the twentieth century has perhaps clouded the issue a little, in that a modern readership may expect such a closure to be the vaunted "fairy-tale happy ending." This is not necessarily the case; while many fairy tales do end in marriage or reconciliation, others offer retribution (the fisherman and his wife restored to their pigsty by the magical fish) or simply the definitive closing of an episode (the Three Fools sitting in their cellar with the ale running onto the floor, while the visitor leaves in disgust). The point is that closure is offered, an artificial oversimplification imposed on events so that they have a neatness and self-containment rather different from the messy, ongoing matters of real life. This is, after all, one of the major differences between narrative and reality: the imposition of a simple, recognizable shape.

Simplification extends to the protagonists of the tale; unlike other forms of prose narrative, the fairy tale has no real interest in human subjectivity or psychological characterization of the individual. Like the events of fairy-tale narrative, characters are rendered down [to] essentials, described in terms of one or two defining characteristics—foolish, brave, courteous, discourteous, good, evil. Bettelh[eim] notes that in fairy tale, "All characters are typical rather than unique" (8). Or, in Walter Benjamin's rather lovely phrasing, "Nothing commends a story to memory more effectively than that chaste compactness which precludes psychological analysis" (90). Lüthi extends this to encompass an element of *isolation:* "figures are also isolated, they wander individually out into the world. Their psychological processes are not illuminated: only their line of progress is in focus, only that which is relevant to the action" (42). Fairy tale is concerned not so much with personality as with the fact of the quest, and, with it, the illustration of moral absolutes. Ursula Le Guin's discussion of Jungian archetype in fantasy is particularly interesting here; she argues that "in the fairy tale . . . there is no 'right' and 'wrong,' there is a different standard, which is perhaps best called 'appropriateness' . . . Under the conditions of fairy tale, in the language of archetypes, we can say with perfect conviction that it may be *appropriate* to [push an old lady into an oven]" (56). This is perhaps one reason why fairy tale has survived over time and through a wide variety of cultures; it carries within it its own structures of right and wrong, satisfying and coherent in themselves because they are clear-cut and obvious.

At the same time, however, fairy tale, while structured with clear-cut relationships, cannot be read symbolically—it is marvelous narrative, not allegory. Motifs have resonance rather than meaning; the bread thrown to the dragon is a simple object resonant with all the attributes of home, hearth, life, creation, kindness, the ritual act of providing food to a dependant creature. It does not "stand for" anything. Le Guin, writing on myth and archetype in science fiction, puts this particularly well:

> In many college English courses the words "myth" and "symbol" are given a tremendous charge of significance. You just ain't no good unless you can see a symbol hiding, like a scared gerbil, under every page. . . . What does this Mean? What does that Symbolize? What is the Underlying Mythos? . . . a symbol is not a sign of something known, but an indicator of something not known and not expressible other than symbolically. [Students] mistake symbol (living meaning) for allegory (dead equivalences). (63)

In this, Le Guin echoes the writing of George Macdonald, a century earlier: "A fairy tale is not an allegory. There may be allegory in it, but it is not an allegory. He must be an artist indeed who can, in any mode, produce a strict allegory that is not a weariness to the spirit" ("The Fantastic Imagination" 14). It could be argued that allegory is an impoverished form when compared to fairy tale, in that its strict one-on-one equivalences deny the complex working of symbol; Macdonald's characterization in particular emphasizes the importance of multivalent meaning in a true work of art (64). This is perhaps an outdated view of allegory, what Gay Clifford calls "the legacy of much Romantic and post-Romantic criticism, in which the didacticism and intellectuality of allegory are seen as crude and wilful limitations upon emotional and archetypal significance" (3–4); however, in comparison with fairy tale I believe the distinctions made by Macdonald are valid. While allegory is a far more sophisticated form than Macdonald gives it credit for, it still operates in a manner rather different from fairy tale in my definition; most importantly, it is a literature which seeks to address ideas before story, or to subordinate story to ideas. In Clifford's words, "the allegorist wants to communicate certain generalized formulations about the nature of human experience . . . and shapes his narrative so as to reveal these" (7). Thus the similarities between the clean geometry and symbolic motifs of fairy tale and allegory are deceptive; despite the simplicity of its lines, fairy tale is told for its own sake, its meaning is contained *within* the narrative, so that the narrative does not "stand for" anything outside the tale. Fairytale symbols function resonantly rather than illustratively to suggest multiple meanings rather than to illustrate one aspect of reality.

As an adjunct to the structural simplicity of the narrative and its lack of real-world referents, an illusion of decontextualization or lack of historicity is integral to the effect of fairy tale and helps to create its characteristic universality; again, this operates as a metafictional technique which self-consciously distances the fairy tale from mimesis. "Once upon a time," "long ago and far away," deny the relevance of historical time and place. Fairy tale has no history—a king rules, not a particular king. The countries of fairyland require no maps; its protagonists simply follow the road, or walk through the forests. The *Star Wars* films use this distancing technique, so that "A long time ago, in a galaxy far, far away . . ." is a precise and evocative use of the fairy-tale convention. Lüthi suggests that the "Once upon a time" formula "immediately sets the beginning narrative off from the present, from the everyday world of teller and listener (or reader). . . . They create distance from the present and, with it, from reality, and offer an invitation to enter another world, a world past, thus one that does not exist" (49). Likewise, the "happily ever after" or other formulaic closure is the evocation by which "the narrator conducts himself and the listeners back into the real world" (50). Thus, for the duration of the tale, the reader or listener is effectively removed from the everyday world. As Tolkien says, fairy tales "open a door on Other Time, and if we pass through, though only for a moment, we stand outside our own time, outside Time itself, maybe" (32). Such encoded unreality requires a particular kind of response from the receiver of the tale. In order to properly enjoy and understand a fairy tale, it is necessary to accept the illusion it presents: to refrain from attempting to connect the fairy-tale realm with a particular historical reality, despite the instrumentality of that reality in the tale's construction. This is the "trick" that Bacchilega defines in the operation of fairy tale; her argument is interesting because it simultaneously identifies the complex ideological purposes which dictate fairy tale's historical development, and locates that struggle as somehow concealed or disguised by fairy tale's seduction of the reader, its presentation of itself in apparently unambiguous and universal terms which deny the intrinsic relationship between fairy tale and its historical context. Zipes argues for a similar pattern in his comparison between fairy tale and myth, suggesting that fairy tales blur with myth, offering a universalized mythic function apparently "invested with an extraordinary mystical power so that we collapse the distinctions" (*Fairy Tale as Myth* 3). As well as being related to myth, fairy tale mythologizes its own function to present a falsely universalized sense of its own structures.

The unreality of nonhistoricism, together with the reception of story as text rather than mimesis, is closely related to a different kind of unreality, namely the physical and scientific unreality of magic. Not all fairy tales contain magical motifs, but most assume the existence of some aspect of the marvelous: enchanters, witches or fairies, items with specific powers (the knapsack, the sack and the horn, or the ever-full pot or purse), or characters able to use mundane items in a magical fashion (the nuts which break open to reveal beautiful dresses, the mortar and pestle in which Baba Yaga flies). In this sense, fairy tale is structurally similar to the functioning of romance, a genre with which it overlaps in many ways, not only in its use of formula but also in its provision of a marvelous realm consciously removed from the real world. Northrop Frye's characterization of the marvelous in romance could equally be a characterization of fairy tale: "The hero of romance moves in a world in which the ordinary laws of nature are slightly suspended: prodigies of courage and endurance, unnatural to us, are natural to him, and enchanted weapons, talking animals, terrifying ogres and witches, and talismans of miraculous power violate no rules of probability once the postulates of romance have been established" (*Anatomy of Criticism* 33).

In fact, in *The Secular Scripture* he usefully defines actual fairy tale or folktale as "naïve romance" (3). His discussion of romance in *The Secular Scripture* is particularly interesting in that he identifies in romance, and in the related forms of myth and folklore, precisely the kind of religious thinking which Eliade discovers in fairy tale. Where Eliade is interested in rites of passage, however, Frye sees the vast body of "secular literature"—including myth, folklore, and romance—as providing a "mythological universe" which functions similarly to the biblical universe as a "vision of reality" rather than reality itself. He states, "Romance is the structural core of all fiction: being directly descended from folk tale, it brings us closer than any other aspect of literature to the sense of fiction . . . as the epic of the creature, man's vision of his own life as a quest" (15). Unlike other forms of literature, romance and fairy tale are thus *essentially* nonmimetic.

If the circumstantial elements of ahistoricity and unreality are central to fairy tale, they go hand in hand with the response they demand to such unreality. Fairy tale, as a form of magical narrative, shares with other genres its element of the fantastical or marvelous, but it requires an unquestioning acceptance of such marvels which is alien to most other magical narratives. Fantasy romance, for example, attempts to rationalize its magical element within some kind of logical framework and requires consistent rules within that framework. Macdonald insists that "to be able to live for a moment in an imagined world, we must see the laws of its existence obeyed. Those broken, we fall out of it" ("Fantastic Imagination" 15). Likewise, the fantastic and the uncanny (in the definitions of Todorov and Jackson) allow unrealistic manifestations to cause a clash of discourses, and hence disruption and disquiet. Jackson argues that, in fantastic narratives, "The narrator is no clearer than the protagonist about what is going on . . . the status of what is being seen and recorded as 'real' is constantly in question. This instability of narrative is at the centre of the fantastic as a mode" (34). This is a sharp contrast to fairy tale, which presents a stable and unquestioned narrative whose correct mode of reception is accepting wonder. Jackson elsewhere notes that fairy tale is necessarily "neutral, impersonalised, set apart from the reader. The reader becomes a passive receiver of events, there is no demand that (s)he participate in their interpretation" (154). This, of course, is a direct result of fairy tale's self-consciousness about its own fictive status; the narrative can be taken for granted, unquestioningly, because it does not require the reader or listener to relate the narrative to reality; it is a self-contained artifact. Fairy tale, then, is characterized by its lack of question; Todorov suggests that in narratives of the marvelous, "supernatural elements provoke no particular

reaction either in the characters or in the implicit reader . . . the supernatural events in fairy tales provoke no surprise; neither a hundred
years' sleep, nor a talking wolf, nor the magical gifts of the fairies"
("Fairy-Tale Transformations" 54). "Once upon a time" is a flat and
authoritative statement of event. This typical feature of fairy tale is exploited notably in tales by Donald Barthelme ("The Glass Mountain")
and Robert Coover ("The Gingerbread House"). Both of these tales
employ a textual device of listing the events of the tale in a series of
numbered paragraphs, effectively highlighting the flat, factual aspect
of the fairy-tale voice.

The marvels described by the factual register of fairy tale require
wonder as a response because they move the reader or listener into a
different world. At the same time, the abdication of critical response
is an integral part of the pleasure of the fairy-tale narrative, on which
rests its ability to satisfy desire. Tolkien comments that fairy tales are
"plainly not primarily concerned with possibility, but with desirability. If they awakened *desire*, satisfying it while often whetting it un-
bearably, they succeeded" (40). This is desire for the marvelous, the
pleasure of the narrative illusion, shared between teller/writer and
listener/reader, that brings the magical into being, to be celebrated
without question. Not only the creation of the marvelous causes pleasure, however; the repetition of familiar patterns and structures is itself pleasurable, Lüthi suggests, "That which has some technical purpose can, in the sense of an esthetics of the functional, be pleasing at
the same time. Formulas are memory props and transition aids for the
narrator. They are useful to him and comfortable, but they are addi-
tionally agreeable to him—just as the hearer is also delighted—when
they turn up time and again, because he feels the organising effect
they have" (44).

The pleasure of accepting wonder in experiencing the fairy tale is
thus complex, based both in the enjoyment of the marvelous and in
the geometric pleasures of pattern. But, if fairy tale's authority must
simply be accepted for enjoyment of the form, much of the authority
of fairy tale rests in the status of the narrator. "Once upon a time"
may only function as a flat statement of fact if the authority of the
narrator is not problematized. Fairy tale's narrator is omniscient and
far less present than the oral voice of the folkloric narrator, but the
structures and patterns of fairy tale dictate that the reader can never
quite forget that behind this unrealistic artifact must be an artist.
Robert Scholes comments that "the structure, by its very shapeliness,
asserts the authority of the shaper, the fabulator behind the fable" (2).
Thus the enjoyment of fairy tale's marvelous structures requires not
only unquestioning enjoyment of its marvelous world and unrealistic

structures but also the power of the tale-teller whose words make possible the fairy tale itself.

METAFICTIONAL GAMES: FAIRY TALE AND POSTMODERNISM

A principal activity of postmodernist critics . . . consists in disagreeing about what postmodernism is or ought to be, and thus about who should be admitted to the club—or clubbed into admission. —JOHN BARTH, 172

Recently, at a three-day-long symposium on narrative, I learned that it's unsafe to say anything much about narrative, because if a poststructuralist doesn't get you a deconstructionist will. —URSULA LE GUIN, *Dancing* 37

lol

Given the kind of proto-metafictionality I have argued exits in any fairy tale—its self-conscious problematization of mimesis—it becomes clear why fairy tale recurs so often in the modern texts whose more extensive deconstructive techniques are carried out in the context of postmodernism. Metafiction is a favored technique of the postmodernist writer, and fairy tale will lend itself particularly well to metafiction owing to its basic structure and assumptions—not only its problematical relationship with reality but also its apparently simple surface under which seethes complex historical and ideological layering which begs to be dissected and revealed. In this, the proto-metafictional awareness in classic fairy tale speaks directly to postmodern writing's extreme self-consciousness about the act of writing and the ongoing fascination with the resulting structure. Scholes's work *Fabulation and Metafiction* deals with a number of postmodern narratives in terms of the same interests in structure and unreality that are shown by fairy tale. His examples include works by John Fowles, Jorge Luis Borges, and John Barth, and he notes that they have in common ". . . an extraordinary delight in design . . . A sense of pleasure in form is one characteristic of fabulation" (2). Postmodern writers such as Roland Barthes, Calvino, Barthelme, and Coover make explicit this convergence of interests by playing specifically with fairy-tale forms in their writing. The interest in structure is underlined by other postmodern games with genre, such as Umberto Eco's equally self-aware play with the structures of detective fiction in *The Name of the Rose*. Fairy tale's inherent structuredness makes it ideally suited to postmodern play, which, as Patricia Waugh notes, "is facilitated by rules and roles. . . . The most important feature shared by fiction and play is the construction of an alternative reality by manipulating the relation between a set of signs . . . as 'message' and the context or frame of that message" (35). Awareness of the essential nonreality of fairy tale, together with its existence as a particularly coherent "set of signs," allows it to be playfully manipulated within the context of writer and reader's shared awareness of the form as both structure and fiction. At the same time, play with form—ringing the changes on fairy tale— works particularly well because the form is familiar and highly recognizable to the reader. (Angela Carter is a good example in this context; her feminist rewrites are shocking and effective precisely because we all know what to expect, and are consequently surprised when it fails to materialize.) The continual and ongoing presence of feminist rewriting in modern fairy tale underlines this particular awareness; political reassessment of structure depends primarily on the existence and shared understanding of such structures. Fairy tale becomes a fertile ground for feminist restructuring because its terms, particularly when their reception in Western culture is filtered through the influential works of Charles Perrault and the Brothers Grimm, are inherently patriarchal. Patriarchy becomes entrenched not only in content but also in the recurring utopian closure of the structure, which lends itself particularly well to rigid gender roles.

In arguing that the use of fairy tale by postmodern writers simply exploits tendencies inherent within the form itself, I offer a slightly different proposition to those many other critics of fairy tale who have exhaustively explored the notion of postmodernism in modern fairy tale without necessarily linking such self-conscious rewriting to any inherent aspect of the form. Stephen Benson's recent *Cycles of Influence* perhaps has the most in common with my approach, admirably demonstrating the importance of folktale to narrative theory. He surveys a range of theorists from Propp and Aarne to Lévi-Strauss, Barthes, and Algirdas Julius Greimas, and provides a strong semiotic framework for the analysis of fairy tale. He argues not only for the centrality of folkloric structures to modern literature and theory but also for "the possible role of the folktale" in the late twentieth century's "self-conscious reassessment of narrative" (13). Benson's investigation has some parallels with mine in its exploration of narratives which "share a common interest in tale-telling; in compact narratives that eschew . . . the descriptive fabric of the classic realist text . . . in narratives that relegate the question of realism in favour of a self-contained, overly fictional environment; and in the story-teller as self-confessed fabricator" (17). All these issues, he argues, are expressed through the defining and shaping lens of theoretical assumption which is rooted in the formalist readings of Propp and others. My approach is somewhat different, however. Choosing to start from the notion of self-consciousness in modern fairy tale, I shall apply such aspects of the broad and contentious body of postmodern theory that appear to be most relevant and illuminating to my investigation.

A more specific account of some aspects of postmodern narrative function in fairy tale is given by Cristina Bacchilega, who rejects stylistic aspects of postmodernism to focus instead on its ideological awareness, problematizing of subjectivity, and "[play] with multiplicity and performance in narrative" (19). Postmodern fairy tale, in her view, simply offers various different strategies for reinterpretation of fairy tale, "thereby generating unexploited or forgotten possibilities from its repetition," which "explodes its coherence as well-made artifice" (22–23). This process of definition is well suited to her exploration of gender in fairy tale, and supported appropriately by use of Linda Hutcheon's notion of postmodernism as a process of dialogue, both with the structures of text and those of history. However, while such an awareness is integral to the kind of analysis I am undertaking, this approach tends to treat fairy tale as simply another kind of text, subject to postmodernism's searching gaze in the same way as any other textual example upon which the roving eye of the postmodern writer chooses to settle. Instead, following to some extent Benson's argument for the centrality of folktale to narrative exploration, I would argue for a particularly close fit between the base structures of fairy tale and the self-conscious games of postmodern awareness. Part of this resides in fairy tale's specific relationship with notions of the real—not only the historical, in Hutcheon's sense, but also the concrete, the world *outside* as well as within the text.

Magical narratives unavoidably raise, although in slightly different ways, the notions of reality and the representational with which metafiction is concerned. Jackson suggests: "By offering a problematic re-presentation of an empirically 'real' world, the fantastic raises questions of the nature of the real and unreal, foregrounding the relation between them as its central concern" (37). Jackson declines to define fairy tale as a fantastic form, preferring to define it as a separate genre, the marvelous (42), which she describes as being characterized by certainty rather than hesitation. While I have argued that the marvelous is centrally concerned with confidence rather than doubt, and generally provides no such clash of reality and unreality as do the uncanny or fantastic modes, nonetheless there is space within the marvelous for a rather different awareness of unreality and reality. Within the functioning of the fairy-tale form can be found the same foregrounding of the relationship between real and unreal which Jackson attributes to the fantastic, in fairy tale's deliberate construction of itself as nonreality. This is a nonreality even further removed than the usual conceptual gap between the world of the reader and the created world of the text. Where realist fiction plays the textual game which requires the reader's complicity in a constructed reality, fairy tale denies its own realism from the start—as I have suggested, the classic opening "Once upon a time" signals unreality in unequivocal terms. More than this, any fairy tale—classic or modern—positions itself intertextually within a complete discourse of fairy tale as cultural artifact, so that any tale becomes a necessary dialogue between its own specific instance, and the (unreal) textual expectations of fairy tales in general. Modern fairy tale exaggerates this effect through the kind of awareness explored by Bacchilega. Harries argues that "complex" fairy tales are self-conscious, intertextual and multivoiced, and characteristically "insist that their audiences constantly keep . . . 'classic' versions in mind . . . reflecting on the differences between them" (16). It is not simply the "classic" versions being recalled, but the notion of fairy tale itself as a text within a textual tradition.

Waugh's definition of metafiction is useful in this context: "Metafiction is a term given to fictional writing which self-consciously and systematically draws attention to its status as an artefact in order to pose questions about the relationship between fiction and reality" (2). In its insistence on fictionality, fairy tale certainly "self-consciously and systematically draws attention to its status as an artefact"; the carryover of the oral voice of folktale constructs the tale as *tale*, as a created text rather than any attempt at reproducing reality. The unashamed presentation of the marvelous, as well as the unrealistic use of pattern and repetition in describing events, similarly draws attention to a nonrealist form of representation—to the tale as crafted object, artifact. In this sense, then, fairy tale has some inherently metafictional elements. While such deliberate nonrealism draws attention to the gap between reality and the constructed world, however, fairy tale by my definition specifically refuses to fulfill Waugh's criteria of "posing questions" about the unreal world it represents. Although the fictional nature of the fairy tale world is highlighted, we are not encouraged to question it at all; rather than an unstable relationship, we are presented with one whose terms of interaction between reality and fiction are a fait accompli. This is a powerful technique in the process Bacchilega identifies as the "trick" by which the form conceals its own ideological functioning.

The postmodern use of fairy-tale narrative is interesting in that the form actually appears to resist some potential effects of postmodern writing. Waugh notes how some varieties of postmodern text approach breakdown of structure: "contexts shift so continuously and unsystematically that the metalingual commentary is not adequate to 'place' or to interpret such shifts. The reader is *deliberately* disoriented" (37). She cites the work of William Burroughs as an example of this extreme effect, which can be seen as a result of the characteristic postmodern impulse to disrupt and reveal the codes of language, taken to its logical extreme. The invocation of fairy tale as a motif in postmodern play to some extent resists such an extreme process, since the nature and effect of fairy tale are inherent more in its form than in its content. Hutcheon's definitions are useful here; she comments on the nature of postmodernism's ironic invocations as "contradictory: it works within the very structures it attempts to subvert" (6). This tendency explains the ability of postmodern writers of fairy tale to question and redefine the nature of fairy tale without, in fact, necessarily destroying the structures which allow it to function, namely its calm acceptance of a particular notion of the real and unreal. Thus, while structure offers writers fertile ground on which to rewrite, rework, invert, investigate, and play with the fairy-tale form, the final dissolution of the narrative is denied them. If that ultimate structure dissolves, what they are writing is no longer recognizable as fairy tale at all, and there is not much point in invoking it. In this particular sense the fairy tale works flatly against Jean Baudrillard's concept of the simulacra in modern culture, which he defines as creating "a hyperreal henceforth sheltered from the imaginary, and from any distinction between the real and the imaginary, leaving room only for the orbital recurrence of models and the simulated generation of difference" (167). Far from having an existence divorced from any original form, postmodern fairy tale invokes the original form which it is reflecting, however distorted the reflection—one sense, in fact, in which the functioning of fairy-tale narrative bears out Propp's assertion that fairy tale resists other genres. Likewise, in its own strong sense of its status as imaginary, as fictional artifact, it avoids the failure of distinction between the real and the imaginary which Baudrillard posits. Thus fairy tale functions in postmodern writing simultaneously to enable and to limit the operations of postmodern writers upon the form; while structured, its narrative certainty in some ways resists breakdown under the postmodern gaze. At the same time, its inherent self-consciousness enables particularly complex metafictional play.

On a completely different level, postmodernism's interest in the collapse of boundaries between low and high art, most famously articulated by Fredric Jameson, is significant for fairy tale. Fairy tale represents a folk form appropriated into a literary mode, and is thus the site of a discernable process of cultural shifts, clashes, and appropriations, the breakdown of boundaries between forms. I shall deal with this in more detail when considering fairy tale forms within the specific context of popular literature and film in subsequent chapters.

MODERN FAIRY TALE: SURVEYING THE CROWDED FIELD

Metafictional fairy tale in the last hundred years has a wide tradition from which to draw for its play with structure and the marvelous, not only the well-known folkloric forms but also the adaptation of such forms into written literature over a long period of time. The geometry of the written tale is not simply that of folklore, but is a more literary awareness that incorporates aspects of the oral voice, building upon them to complex and sophisticated effect. Most interestingly, the specific trends of literary fairy tale at various times in its history have in the twentieth and twenty-first centuries given way to a particularly wide range of contexts and media for adaptation. Where the seventeenth and eighteenth centuries saw aristocratic and theatrical versions, and the nineteenth focused on children's literature and the nationalistic collection of folklore, the twentieth century was the site of a proliferation of forms. While the scope of this study is broadly comparative, some kind of selection is necessary, as I could not hope to give a comprehensive account of modern fairy tale in all its manifestations. This becomes in some ways problematic; notions of structure, metafiction, and self-conscious play in some ways represent a specific approach to modern fairy tale, but in other terms they are somewhat imprecise. Unlike fairy-tale studies focusing on feminist reinterpretations, or the socialization of children, or any of the myriad approaches of recent scholarship, an approach interested in self-conscious formal play runs the risk of encompassing almost all possible expressions of the genre in the last century. Given this, there is a definite danger that my selection of specific texts for analysis might be essentially random, skewed toward such texts as most clearly support or demonstrate my thesis. However, while it is true that I could subject almost any modern fairy tale to the kind of structural analysis I have outlined above, generally my choice of texts, even encompassing as it does the broad spectrum from the literary and postmodern to the popular and the cinematic, does represent a specific set of criteria for choice.

While noting the complexity of fairy-tale texture, the focus of my discussion is more on the structural than on the linguistic aspects of texture, although, obviously, the two are often related. I have tended to select texts which largely preserve the overall and clearly evident structure of fairy tale, rather than those which embed motifs or ideas from fairy tale within a more literary overall structure. This follows the kind of distinction made by Frank de Caro and Rosan Augusta Jordan, who identify the use of folkloric materials in literature as either the "exoskeleton" or the "endoskeleton" of the work. Folklore used as an exoskeleton effectively offers an "imitation of form . . . a *formal* or *stylistic* framework, using a *generic structure* as a model" (7). This usefully characterizes those writers or producers of modern fairy tale who set out, in my estimation, to actually produce fairy tale itself—to retell, reshape or reinterpret its marvelous geometry in a self-conscious fashion while producing a text identifiable as "fairy tale" before any other kind of categorization. This differs from texts described by de Caro and Jordan's formulation which use folklore as an endoskeleton—that is, whose outer structure conforms to "a literary rather than a folkloric genre" (7) in which folklore is used only "to allude to contexts, ideas, and values; to provide ironic reference; to expand thematic understandings" (8). In other words, for my purposes these writers are not actually producing fairy-tale narrative; they are producing some other kind of narrative which uses fairy-tale themes.

The necessity of this kind of distinction becomes clear when considering the focus of this study, which is on fairy tale as a self-consciously *structured* narrative form; de Caro and Jordan's description of exoskeletal fairy tale invokes precisely the concepts of form, framework, and structure which are central to my discussion. While endoskeletal uses of folklore may very well play with structural ideas, since in my formulation these are inextricable from fairy-tale function in general, these references are less evident or clear than they are in more explicitly fairy-tale texts whose play with form is on their surface rather than by implication. Margaret Atwood's "Bluebeard's Egg" is a good example here; it operates as a modern short story investigating identity and interaction within a marriage, using the Bluebeard tale tangentially and suggestively to add depth to that exploration, in precisely the endoskeletal terms de Caro and Jordan define. The story refers to fairy tale, and looks to fairy-tale structures for some elements of shape, but it is not in itself *a* fairy tale—it functions as a short story with a fairy-tale theme. Sheri S. Tepper's popular fairy-tale novel *Beauty* manages to fall, narrowly, within my parameters; the novel's wholesale mixing of science fiction, folklore, magical realism, and Christian mythology almost outweighs the fairy-tale elements, but the heroine *is* the Sleeping Beauty, and Tepper uses fairy-tale structures to impose shape and expectation on the story's historical and psychological elements, dragging them inexorably back to a sparser narrative. Terry Pratchett's *Witches Abroad* is also successful in retaining its identity, probably because the Discworld already has a certain fairy-tale quality in its use of archetype, and fairy-tale characters can be introduced as happily coexistent with Discworld characters without jarring. A. S. Byatt's "Cold" and "The Story of the Eldest Princess" are perhaps the most strongly marked examples of the true modern fairy tale in my selection, possibly because her narrative style is naturally sparse and she has a strong sense of pattern and motif. Carter, while using the familiar forms with a suitably vague sense of historical setting, in some cases is close to writing what I would identify as short stories with fairy-tale elements and themes, mostly as a result of her excesses of language, which operate directly against fairy tale's characteristic sparseness. ("The Erl-King" and "The Lady of the House of Love" are good examples here.) Nonetheless, her strongly marked use of symbol and the marvelous tend, in my view, to prevail over the denser texture.

A secondary aspect of this choice is integral to my discussion of fairy tale as a form which essentially relies on the marvelous for some aspects of its self-conscious function. Almost without exception I have chosen to explore texts which deliberately and unquestioningly accept both the marvelous as a mimetic framework and the classic fairy-tale flatly textured sparsity of tone. Such texts thus most clearly demonstrate the contribution of these qualities to metafictional awareness. Coover and Barthelme provide particularly good examples of texts that exemplify a kind of transformation fairy tale undergoes in the hands of the more radical kinds of postmodern writing, in which the problematization of reality becomes a textual rather than an inherent property. Texts such as Barthelme's "The Glass Mountain" or Coover's *Pricksongs and Descants* or *Briar Rose* offer a deliberate dissolution of fairy tale's authoritative narrative voice, and their more general interest in issues of language and narrative in some ways overshadow their interest in *tale*. In Bacchilega's terms such narratives too radically disrupt and expose fairy tale's "trick" instead of self-consciously exploring it. While they deconstruct notions of reality, these tales are not actually about magic or the marvelous; they deny realist representation on the level of narrative rather than the level of action. This is in itself a fascinating strategy, but it represents a line of discussion I have chosen not to pursue. My approach here forms an interesting contrast to Benson's *Cycles of Influence*, which demonstrates precisely the kind of leaning I have tried to avoid, focusing on authors such as Calvino, Barthelme, and Coover for semiotic rather than structural analysis. While undoubtedly such approaches and texts have useful insights to offer, I would argue that their strong and self-conscious theoretical underpinnings in some ways obscure, as much as illuminate, the structural notions with which I am concerned. This is possibly because of their deconstructive focus on detail, the exploration of a particular aspect of a tale's structure, perhaps gender, or subjectivity, on a microtextual level. This is somewhat antithetical to what I am attempting to do here, where, theoretically speaking, I am generally interested more in broader comparisons across texts than in detailed analysis within them.

This difference between the formal rewriting of fairy tale and thematic allusion also accounts for the fact that I have not dealt at any length with poetry, which necessarily refracts and fragments fairy tale in its highly compressed images. Conversely, I have not dealt with fairy-tale adaptations such as those of Emma Donoghue. Her stories in *Kissing the Witch* retain a strong fairy-tale shape and characteristic sparseness, but their primary interest is in psychology and the reclamation of fairy-tale sexuality for lesbian consciousness, and thus tend to excise the magical. While, on the one hand, Donoghue's embedding of fairy-tale motifs as image or metaphor constitutes a fascinating self-conscious play in itself, this conforms to some extent with de Caro and Jordan's endoskeletal use of folklore. On the other hand, I have included the film *Ever After* in my analysis despite its similar refusal to entertain the existence of magic in its version of "Cinderella" because it in other ways leaves the tale intact and strongly framed as self-conscious fairy-tale narrative.

Among the literary texts I have chosen to investigate, only those by James Thurber are American; all other authors are British. In the film chapter, American films predominate, but Britain and Europe are well represented in the works of Neil Jordan and Jean Cocteau. While I did not make a conscious decision to favor British authors when planning this analysis, nonetheless I do not think the predominance of British texts is arbitrary or accidental. The strong tradition of children's fairy tale in Britain in the Victorian age is possibly the reason for the slightly skewed representation of authors in this investigation, generally producing a stronger adherence to the classic texture of fairy tale than in American works. American magical narrative in the nineteenth century is most strongly characterized by the works of romance writers such as Nathaniel Hawthorne and Edgar Allan Poe, and lacks the influence from the self-conscious writers of fairy tale common in England and Europe. The result seems to have been a tendency for British works to correspond more closely to my requirements of fairy-tale texture, to the purpose of actually writing fairy tale, rather than writing experimental texts which use fairy-tale motifs. Thus, while I am generalizing in discerning such tendencies, I believe the Victorian writers played an important role in determining the shape and direction of metafictional fairy tale in the twentieth and twenty-first centuries.

Within the boundaries I have imposed in terms of texture, by selecting texts that *are* fairy tale rather than *using* it, I have had to omit twentieth-century forms such as fairy-tale poetry, women's romance, experimental postmodern narratives, advertising, the television series, and a large number of Hollywood films. However, even with these restrictions I am able to explore not only literary versions in both short story and novel form but also popular stories and novels within the science fiction and fantasy frameworks, as well as a wide range of film adaptations, both live action and animated. The following chapters set out to develop and explore the theoretical points made above by investigation of particular instances of the modern fairy tale: Thurber, Carter, Byatt, popular fantasy, and film. The choices I have made aim to compare the more commonly investigated authors such as Byatt and Carter with less canonical texts. In looking at the fairy tales of James Thurber I hope to uncover the considerable sophistication and self-awareness underlying texts which have tended to be considered as children's works. Thurber's characteristic cynicism finds fascinating contrasts and transformations with the utopian structures of fairy tale, but at the same time his stories betray an ongoing insecurity about those structures, an awareness of slippage and doubt, and the problematizing of meaning, reflected on the linguistic level as well as the structural. Angela Carter is a recurring subject for this kind of analysis; in focusing on her structural projects, her intertextuality and strong awareness of fairy-tale symbol, I wish to avoid a repetition of the usual feminist reading. At the same time, her *structural* awareness of feminism as a discourse provides another form of intertextuality, another pattern to intersect with those of fairy tale. This feminist awareness is shared by A. S. Byatt, whose stories are perhaps those that exemplify most clearly the self-consciousness about narrative with which I am concerned. Her metafictional sense is particularly clear because of the sparseness of her narratives, her commitment to the textural qualities of fairy tale. Byatt's sense of tale as artifact, through the image of the geometric pattern enshrined in a glass paperweight, has in some ways informed this entire study.

In discussing popular fantasy and science fictional versions of fairy tale, I have offered some kind of survey of the genre, as well as focusing on three specific authors. The purely intellectual investigation of narrative within the science fiction ghetto is somewhat affected by its status as a popular and commercial form, but its strong generic markings allow for interesting intersections with fairy tale which Tanith Lee, Terry Pratchett, and Sheri S. Tepper fully exploit. Lee's concerns are also feminist, expressed through the structures of horror and the erotic as well as fairy tale, often with deliberate flamboyance; Pratchett shares with Byatt a strongly stated self-consciousness about narrative, contextualized within the Discworld's humanist framework. Tepper's more complex novel uses fairy tale as a framework which supports and sustains her radical play with other genres. In the case of film, fairy tale has moved into an entirely new medium whose realist representation tends to run counter to fairy tale's interest in the marvelous and unrealistic. In live-action film this is alleviated by film's use of visual symbol and a strong fairy-tale flavor in costume and setting, as well as its ability to recreate some aspects of the oral voice. I have investigated both popular and high-art films, contrasting Jean Cocteau and Neil Jordan to Hollywood romances and Disney, as well as exploring the implications of live action versus animated formats. In the case of animation, the convention itself problematizes representation by its lack of realism, which accounts for the long-term association between fairy-tale film and the animated format. Disney's sense of fairy tale as artifact, however, is in many ways subordinated to their need to present tale as commodity within the Disney consumer culture. Finally, using as a case study the recent fairy-tale films *Shrek* and its sequels, as well as parodic versions such as *Enchanted, Happily N'Ever After,* and *Hoodwinked,* I have dealt with a particularly prevalent movement of fairy tale in the twenty-first century into what is effectively fairy-tale parody, an extreme and heightened form of self-conscious play. This continues the form's function as adaptable folk narrative which self-consciously and affectionately reflects generic structures and assumptions as well as those of contemporary culture. In our time, of all in its history, fairy tale perhaps most powerfully expresses the tensions over ownership and ideological content which have always affected it. Nonetheless, I argue that fairy tale has found a significant space in contemporary culture, where it is alive and well.

The large range of texts I am exploring is, overall, grounded in the notion of self-awareness, the deliberate and conscious invocation of genre and form in a way which highlights notions of structure. Obviously, this awareness is woven in and out of the other issues explored by these very diverse texts, and at times structural play is effectively hijacked by competing concerns, most notably feminism, consumerism, humor, and linguistic play. The beauty and strength of the fairy-tale form, however, is in its resilience, its identity as a strong and shining artifact which enables expression while resisting absolute appropriation. Whatever their purposes in employing the marvelous geometry of fairy tale, these writers and filmmakers offer, ultimately, a celebration of structure, a self-conscious employment, and thus appreciation, of craft.

2

NICE AND NEAT AND FORMAL: JAMES THURBER

The record and report of maidens changed to deer and back again, all nice and neat and normal, all nice and neat and formal. —*White Deer* 39

It seems a little strange to identify in James Thurber, *New Yorker* humorist, essayist, and cartoonist, a fairy-tale writer with a cogent and particularly self-conscious awareness of the genre. Thurber is very much an American institution, best known for his vast body of essays, short stories, fables, plays, cartoons, and illustrated poetry produced between 1920 and his death in 1961. He is less celebrated for his two short fairy-tale novels, written ostensibly for children—*The White Deer* (1945) and *The Thirteen Clocks* (1950). A third, *The Wonderful O* (1957) is not strictly a fairy tale within my definition, and I will not deal with it in detail here, but it shows similar structural and generic play. Other fairy tales are shorter pieces aimed at younger readers, including "The Great Quillow" (1944) and the illustrated children's book, *Many Moons* (1943), written in the same decade as the two children's novels. In addition to these pure versions of the form, many of his essays, fables, and short stories shade into play with fairy tale at some point or another.

If fairy tales are always to be read as intertext to their own traditions, Thurber's work represents yet another level of intertextuality in

Parts of this chapter originally appeared as "Nice and Neat and Formal: Entrapment, Transformation, and Narrative Convention in Thurber's Fairy Tales," *Fissions and Fusions: Proceedings of the First Conference of the Cape American Studies Association.* Ed. Lesley Marx, Loes Nas, and Lara Dunwell. Cape Town: University of the Western Cape, 1997. 124–30.

that his fairy tales, and particularly their sense of narrative form, are informed and illuminated by their relationship with his other, more well-known writings, as much as by the assumptions of the form. As an often-cynical humorist Thurber seems an unlikely producer of fairy tale, and in fact the closure and happy ending of the fairy-tale form in many ways operate directly against his trademark tendency toward a kind of melancholy chaos. Nevertheless, in the magical narrative of fairy tale Thurber most strongly expresses his manifesto for the power of the imagination and fantasy against an increasingly mundane and bewildering world. Here he is more akin to popular rather than literary revisions of fairy tale, mining the form's essential utopianism to impose the classic "happy ending" on messy reality; part of this, perhaps, is due to the texts' ostensible identity as children's literature, with its attendant requirement for innocence and naive acceptance of unreality. At the same time, his self-conscious pursuit of utopian closure, particularly in contrast to the more cynical realism of his other writing, underlines his essentially metafictional approach to marvelous narrative, his validation of its magical and unrealistic space. His fairy tales also have in common with his other writings a continuing interest in linguistic structure, play, and nonsense, which are dependent upon his awareness of the essentially arbitrary rules and structures of language itself. From here, it is a short step to the play with structure on the level of genre and form. Thus, while he predates the postmodernist movement, his interests and awareness are in many ways akin to those of more modern writers.

Fairy tale is a genre not usually associated with comedy. If fairy tale represents, as Mircea Eliade insists, an "infinitely serious and responsible adventure" (201), then its basic gravity might be expected to cause a conflict of structure and expectation when mixed with the comic: laughter is not a response entirely compatible with wonder. While comic versions of fairy tale do exist they tend to be satirical in nature, possibly because it is easy to parody the distinctive structuredness of the narrative for comic purposes. Tolkien admits the perfect compatibility of fairy tale and satire, commenting that "there is satire, sustained or intermittent, in undoubted fairy stories" (12). The modern pantomime is perhaps the best example of satirical fairy tale, but other examples can be found in British writers contemporary to Thurber— in Osbert Sitwell's *Fee, Fi, Fo, Fum*, Anthony Armstrong's *The Naughty Princess*, or Carol Brahms and S. J. Simon's savvy Disney-and-ballet-conscious satire, *Titania Has a Mother*. All these works to some extent update fairy tale to contemporary settings, gaining their humor from the resulting clash of discourses, a tendency which reaches a climax in James Finn Garner's more recent *Politically Correct Bedtime Stories* and *Once Upon a More Enlightened Time.* In this process, however, some of the essential texture and feel of the fairy tale is lost; the tale becomes jaded, cynical, and knowing rather than reflecting the innocence and wonder which seems intrinsic to the pure form. Terry Pratchett's Discworld versions of fairy tale (*Witches Abroad* and *The Amazing Maurice and His Educated Rodents*) are perhaps the most successful of recent comic versions, betraying a profound respect for the form which sustains the reworkings even through the updating in realism and social comment to which they are subjected. While he is fully capable of satire, Thurber's fairy-tale awareness is closer to that of Pratchett than to parodic contemporaries, showing a similar affection for fairy-tale wonder.

A certain cynicism is true of large parts of Thurber's work, in his essays, stories, and most notably his fables, which demonstrate, as Catherine McGehee Kenney suggests, an "angry insistence upon correcting life rather than accepting it" (6). This comment is interesting in that it denotes a specific structural and metafictional interest—an attempt to impose artificial and utopian structure on the formlessness of reality. Thurber's writing is marked by a striving against the inherent chaos of modern life and human relationships in a search for coherence and benevolent order which strongly marks the literary against the real; given this, it is not surprising that he is drawn to the structured and self-consciously unreal resolutions offered by the fairy-tale form. His affinity with fairy tale resonates well with the "little man" protagonist common to his tales and cartoons, the middle-class individual, bewildered by existence, and continually dominated, terrorized, and humiliated by the world around him. Fairy tale tends to deal with disempowered and marginalized figures—the youngest son or daughter, the idiot, the deformed or half-animal individual, who in the perfect structures of fairy tale is usually triumphant, conforming to fairy-tale's utopian impulse toward empowering the underdog. In the fairy tales, Thurber's confused "little man" attains, more strongly than anywhere else in Thurber's writing, a measure of serenity and achievement, but the contrasts between the fairy tales and Thurber's more realistic writing points definitively toward his awareness of utopian closure as a fictional construct.

Thurber generally avoids cynicism and satire in his fairy tales; their comedy is a gentler, more innocent kind that celebrates rather than parodying the form. E. B. White underlines this element of unstudied play in Thurber's writing in noting that "During his happiest years, Thurber did not write the way a surgeon operates, he wrote the way a child skips rope, the way a mouse waltzes" ("James Thurber" 172). In this playfulness Thurber prefigures some of the self-consciousness of the postmodernist writer, the ability to recognize and ring changes on structure and expectation. In the use of the fairy-tale form, Thurber's dynamic sense of structure and its breakdown is most strongly expressed. His relish for the extreme and illogical situations best exemplified by essays such as "The Night the Bed Fell" (*My Life*), becomes a chaotic deconstruction which acts against the framework of the tale to provide both comedy and a whimsical delight in the unexpected. He is thus a fully metafictional writer, conscious at all times of tale as crafted structure, a geometrical order toward which his characters continually strive.

While there are comic elements in many of these tales—the Golux and his nonsense rhymes, the buffoonery of King Clode and his eldest sons—and frequent attacks on the institutionalized stupidity of modern society, fairy tale works in his hands because his comedy always has an underlying seriousness. Comic elements are mostly peripheral to the stories, while the most basic of fairy-tale values are central— love, hope, valor, honor, freedom, and, as Thurber says in the dedication to *The Wonderful O*, "other good O words." Kenney identifies precisely this "figure of seriousness in the carpet of Thurber's humor," and concludes that "he is usually funny for the same reasons that he is a serious artist: because he probes the foibles and failures of human experience with delicacy and insight" (3). As a form which deals with the most basic and earthy aspects of human experience, fairy tale is revealed as having the potential to be both comic and deeply meaningful. In Thurber's fairy tales his tragicomic despair is constrained to find its potential salvation through the demands of the form, producing a comic awareness which is both gentler and more real.

Despite its celebratory aspects, Thurber's use of the marvelous is allied with a strong awareness of fantasy as potentially escapist, an inevitable awareness given his ongoing cognizance of the artificiality of the utopian structures he celebrates. I have argued earlier for fairy tale's inherent structural self-consciousness about its own unreality: Thurber's highly self-aware sense of meaning and structure is continually used to highlight and exacerbate the relationship between real and unreal. Here, his fairy tales exist in intertextual dialogue with the more realist chaos of his essays and other stories, to particularly illuminating effect. "The Secret Life of Walter Mitty" (*My World*) offers dream-escapes undermined by a realistic framing tale which renders Mitty's romancing illegitimate in terms of his dysfunctional life. Robert Morsberger cites numerous instances to support his point that "Thurber recognized the dangers of carrying the imagination to extremes. . . . For all of his fantasy, Thurber satirized those who mistook illusion for reality" (56); his comments underline the inevitability of metafictional awareness in Thurber's writing. Stephen Black makes the same point, discussing particularly the parable of escape provided in "A Box to Hide In" (96–97). Yet Thurber's fairy tales lack the realistic frame and function essentially on their own terms, in a fantastic space legitimized both by the nod to the children's market and by fairy tale's status as magical narrative rather than reality. Like Mitty, Thurber is able to escape from an oppressive reality into the construction of a narrative with its own rules and expectations, where the place of the hero is assured. At the same time, the fairy tales simply underline Thurber's recurring point: the imagination is valid and necessary, and fantasy is an important ideal. This validation is perhaps seen most strongly in the fable "The Unicorn in the Garden," which celebrates the power of gentle acceptance over aggression and manipulation, and which ultimately stands for the triumph of fantasy over reality, or of imaginative beauty and wonder over the mundane. This simply reiterates Tolkien's sense of the necessity of the magical, and the powerful effects of *eucatastrophe* as a response to human desire (see chapter 5).

It also, of course, exemplifies the triumph of male over female, one of the few in Thurber's work. The notion of a problematized heterosexual relationship is central to Thurber's writing, and finds its natural antithesis in the utopianism of fairy-tale structure. E. B. White has characterized Thurber's art as being partly concerned with "the melancholy of sex" (*Is Sex Necessary?* 135); he is also on record as saying that "James had it in for women" (in Maddocks 599). In the investigations into the melancholy and comic chaos of modern life, Thurber is interested, above all, in the failure of human relationships, and particularly the relationships between men and women. His cartoons and stories continually depict the little man cowed or devoured by woman; occasionally, as in "The Catbird Seat" (*Thurber Carnival*) or "The Unicorn in the Garden" (*Fables for Our Time*), the little man triumphs over womankind. We are seldom or never shown any happy sense of togetherness, or any positive depictions of women. Thurber's first published work, the collaboration with E. B. White called *Is Sex Necessary?* pillories the popular Freudian psychology of its time, insisting instead on human relationships which function on misunderstanding, illogic, and confusion, all made particularly surreal by Thurber's formless illustrations. Thurber's subsequent cartoons also offer images of woman as devouring and monstrous ("House and Woman" [*Men, Women, and Dogs* 118] shows the "little man" as very small indeed by comparison), and of bitter, accusatory relationships ("Well, who *made* the magic go our of our marriage—you or me?" [*Men, Women, and Dogs* 103]). Thurber's denial of the possibility of the couple in these images to insist instead on isolation, results in a rather bizarre quality as the "little man" is forced to endure a confusing and alienating world without support, as exemplified in the woman's thunderous expression in "Darling, I seem to have this rabbit" (*Men, Women, and Dogs* 64). Ultimately, mutual understanding is denied to the point where human interaction becomes downright threatening, as in the pistol-wielding wife of "Have you seen my pistol, honey-bun?" (*Men, Women, and Dogs* 79).

Dissonant heterosexual relationships thus tend to be used to savagely comic effect in Thurber's writing, and his fairy tales are possibly the only legitimate space he finds in which to establish a utopian sense of closure which celebrates the happy heterosexual couple. The tendency toward reconciliation and closure in fairy tale offers Thurber the potential not only for the triumph of innocence over cynicism (seen most notably in his two children's tales, "The Great Quillow" and *Many Moons*) but also for the eventual unity of the male/female couple which more realistic settings deny him. Romantic union, to the point of white horses and sunsets, concludes Thurber's three novel-length fairy tales—*The Wonderful O, The Thirteen Clocks,* and *The White Deer.* This use of the form's structural predisposition foreshadows, in a completely oppositional sense, the feminist explorations of later writers such as Carter and Byatt. Like Carter, Thurber recognizes in fairy-tale structure an inevitable heterosexual utopianism which he claims and celebrates rather than, like Carter, exploring and deconstructing.

At the same time, the fairy tale seems to offer Thurber a symbolic space in which to present female characters who are not only attractive and powerful but also actively idealized. Rosanore in *The White Deer* is a dreamy, disconnected presence, but Saralinda in *The Thirteen Clocks* has a warmth and beauty that are integral to the solution of the puzzle, while Andrea in *The Wonderful O* is a locus of wisdom and insight. Here, the idealized woman becomes legitimate and desirable, retaining practicality while still providing inspiration and a site for the stereotypically "feminine" virtues such as love and wisdom. (Angela Carter would mutter "consolatory nonsense" [*Sadeian Woman* 5], and it is true that Thurber here resorts to the "pedestalism" he deplores in *Is Sex Necessary, but* it is somewhat beside the point of this analysis to offer stringent feminist analysis of Thurber's rather problematical female figures, although they largely operate within the traditional patriarchal parameters of fairy-tale archetype). In both *The White Deer* and *The Thirteen Clocks* Thurber permits himself idealism, structuring the tales with deliberate artificiality to invoke both fairy-tale conventions and the high-flown romanticism of the courtly love tradition.

Thus, Thurber's intrinsically structural fairy tale finds considerable consolation in that structure's ability to impose heterosexual reconciliation: the writer driven to a happy ending almost in spite of himself.

Not a Mere Device: Language, Structure, and Meaning

A minor but significant part of Thurber's writing involves short, highly defined forms that allow him to playfully unwrap and invert their structural functioning; his best-known short story, "The Secret Life of Walter Mitty" (*My World*), is an acute play with genre as much as an investigation into the nature of fantasy and escape. A similar impulse can be traced in the minimalism of his cartoons, which employ a sparse, concise drawing style which invokes structures and relationships only in as much detail as is needed for recognition of the absurd inversions involved. The drawings themselves mirror a kind of structural breakdown in their radical oversimplification and reductionism, what Dorothy Parker has identified as "the outer resemblance of unbaked cookies" (57); they invoke structure by overturning it. Thurber's reliance on form in certain of his stories is something of a contrast to the essay-style pieces he wrote for the *New Yorker* and other periodicals over a long period, which, while operating in the equally confined space of the nonfiction article, tend more toward indeterminate narrative. The frustration and fragmentation his essays depict, however comically, are at the opposite extreme to the order-affirming structures of fairy tale, in which heroism is ultimately reasserted and the form's mechanisms of closure and reconciliation are celebrated.

Somewhere between the two extremes lie the fables, whose cynicism relies on sustained parody of Aesop's traditional moral narrative, and whose play with structure serves rather to reinforce their cynical message. In this process, narrative convention is utilized in cynical fabulation rather than in nostalgic celebration. "The little girl and the wolf" is a particularly good example, self-consciously contrasting the paradigms of fairy tale and those of fable. In this rather modernized retelling of Little Red Riding Hood, the girl, mistrusting the wolf who "even in a nightcap" looks "no more like your grandmother than the Metro-Goldwyn lion looks like Calvin Coolidge," takes an automatic out of her basket and shoots the wolf dead (*Fables for Our Time* 5). Thurber's moral is that "it is not as easy to fool little girls nowadays as it used to be." The fable cuts through the willing suspension of disbelief required by the Red Riding Hood original to point out its essentially sentimental and idealized failure of realism. (I am reminded irresistibly of Terry Pratchett's tough-minded child in the Red Riding

Hood sequence in *Witches Abroad,* and in Pratchett's own impatience with the woolly-headed idealism of the fairy tale form. Tellingly, both Thurber and Pratchett are comic writers with a profound sense of literature as social or psychological comment.) Instead, the fable pulls into place a rather different structure of moral certainty, that of a cynical modern awareness which insists on loss of innocence. A similar example informs "The Princess and the Tin Box" (*The Beast in Me*), in which the classic pattern of choice between valuable and worthless gifts is resolved with the Princess's practical choice of wealth. The moral states, "All those who thought the princess was going to select the tin box filled with worthless stones instead of one of the other gifts, will kindly stay after class and write one hundred times on the blackboard 'I would rather have a hunk of aluminium silicate than a diamond necklace'" (43). Clearly, in the context of the fables the obvious and well-worn paths of fairy-tale structure are somewhat inadequate in the real world, in sharp contrast to the celebration of tradition found in the fairy tales themselves. This, again, throws into relief the metafictional willingness of the fairy tales, assisted as they are by their marvelous format, to accept the unrealistic instead of feeling bound to point out its inadequacies.

The fables highlight the constructedness of narrative in their provision of a moral, reducing the story to the status of conscious exemplar; however, even outside the concrete boundaries of fairy tale or fable Thurber's work is characterized by extreme self-awareness as a writer. His *New Yorker* essays, in particular, play necessarily with a self-conscious authorial voice and the reshaping of reality as text through wordplay and fanciful analysis of language. Such linguistic self-awareness is also illustrated in the fairy tales, which use techniques such as alliteration, repetition, and rhyme to draw attention to the artificiality and constructedness of language. Thurber is thus always aware of structure on the microlevel of language as well as on the macrolevel of form, but his linguistic self-consciousness allows him to develop metafictional awareness to new levels: if language and story are both artificial constructs, then ultimately what is constructed is meaning itself. This circles straight back to Waugh's definitions of metafiction, in which "the simple notion that language passively reflects a coherent, meaningful and 'objective' world is no longer tenable" (3); language does not describe, it actively creates both textual reality and actual reality. This is perhaps at the heart of Thurber's drive to investigate the underlying structures which make sense of our lives. In many of the essays and short stories linguistic structures fail, slide, and are lost, as Thurber's protagonists—particularly the 'little men'—simply cannot find sense or meaning in their interactions; even in the fairy tale, narrative slippage continually threatens the characters and is reconciled only in the denouement.

In common with many postmodern writers, Thurber finds both amelioration and the perfect dramatization of this slippage of meaning in the notion of narrative structure. In his hands, however, structure tends ultimately toward the upbeat closure of popular narrative and classic fairy tale rather than to the deconstructed indeterminacy of the postmodernists. Meaning can be found, or perhaps imposed, through fantasy conceived of in terms of strong, harmonious structures. Thus Walter Mitty engages in the self-conscious construction of meaning through introverted tale-telling; the heroic outcomes of his fantasies provide a meaning that is more important than the cynical truth of real life and the failure of his relationship with his wife. Charles Holmes notes that "Mitty's daydreams are the veriest claptrap, made up of the clichés of popular fiction and movies" (*Clocks of Columbus* 218)—the submarine commander, the great surgeon, the flying ace. These popular narratives are particularly highly structured, and ultimately consolatory; they enable Mitty to use random and arbitrary details of his life to transcend the ordinary and access a kind of imaginative meaning which offers him both self-worth and escape. Their clichéd, even puerile, encodings of meaning are those of romance, constructing a hero whose abilities are those identified by Northrop Frye—above the level of the normal human. Holmes traces this generic influence in "Mitty" to Thurber's childhood fondness for the "popular melodramas of the time"—westerns, Sherlock Holmes, dime novels, and the stories of O. Henry (*Clocks of Columbus* 13). Surviving Thurber *juvenalia* include westerns and one piece of science fiction, "interesting only because they show the extent to which his imagination was shaped by the clichés of the popular adventure story" (17). While this influence is obviously lost in the essays and most of the short stories, it surfaces in "Walter Mitty," in the series of essays on soap opera which demonstrate Thurber's interest in this essentially formulaic genre (*Beast in Me*), and, most strongly, in the fairy tales. In all these cases, the generic coding looks toward a kind of lost innocence, a naïveté which is perhaps the result of Thurber's associations of popular genre with childhood.

The imposition of genre structures on meaning signals meaning as essentially an artificial construct and, despite the embracing structures of genre, Thurber is continually aware of the way in which meaning is created from moment to moment, in ways that may be entirely arbitrary. The most exaggerated illustration of the arbitrary development of meaning is probably in Thurber's drawings, which, as Dorothy Parker has noted, "deal solely in culminations. . . . You may figure for yourself, and good luck to you, what under heaven could have gone before" (66). This construction apparently denies logic, or insists on the diverse and possibly random nature of causation. The process recalls the theorizing of Elizabeth Sewell on the Victorian genre of nonsense writing, as exemplified in the works of Edward Lear and Lewis Carroll; interestingly, in his use of falsely naive drawings in interaction with text, Thurber is very much akin to Lear's illustrated limericks. Sewell argues that nonsense writing is concerned with the breakdown and rearrangements of "certain sets of mental relationships" (3), offering the reader a "subtle and insubstantial pleasure" (4). Dorothy Parker's response to Thurber's cartoons suggests that this is, indeed, the case: the pleasure of the process is in trying to come up with the possible logical sequence which could cause this particular moment. Most tellingly for Thurber, and particularly for his fairy tales, however, Sewell insists that the play of nonsense is above all self-consciously linguistic—"this world of Nonsense is not a universe of things but of words and ways of using them, plus a certain amount of pictorial illustration. . . . In Nonsense all the world is paper and all the seas are ink" (17). In fact, the removal of meaning from the realm of the concrete to that of the abstract allows a new freedom, where ideas can be juxtaposed without reference to the realistic limitations on such ideas being brought together. This is *precisely* what Thurber achieves with the cartoons captioned "Have it your way, you heard a seal bark" (*Beast in Me* 68: a seal on the headboard of a marital bed) and, in fact "That's my first wife up there" (*Men, Women, and Dogs* 129: the husband pointing up to a woman, ambiguously crouched and possibly stuffed, on the top of a bookcase). The unrealistic elements of his drawing style, plus the abstract conventions of cartoon itself, allow us to bring more easily into contact ideas which in reality could not be juxtaposed. Once again, this awareness is the essence of metafiction, the ongoing awareness that writing is artifact, words on a page, and that its relationship to actual reality is, at best, tenuous.

While the cartoons offer a vivid pictorial illustration of Thurber's nonsense relationships, in fact it is in his writing that his most self-conscious and complex rearrangements occur. Numerous Thurber essays play in different ways with the confusion and rich suggestiveness of language. One technique is the play with meaning in substituting arbitrary structures (sound, collections of letters, alliteration) for normal linguistic meaning, notably in the word games of "Here Come the Tigers" (*Beast in Me*), "The Tyranny of Trivia" (*Lanterns and Lances*), and "Do You Want to Make Something Out of It?" (*Thurber Country*). Another is the breakdown of sense, and the fantastic realms conjured by the resulting nonsense, when mispronunciation and misuse of words are allowed to run rampant: the language of Delia in "What Do You Mean It Was Brillig" and the hired man Barney in "The Black Magic of Barney Haller" (*Thurber Carnival*) are good examples. The satirical treatment of linguistic breakdown and the failure of meaning is also seen in "A Final Note on Chandra Bell" (*Thurber Country*), in which the presentation of nonsense as sense is ridiculed, incidentally parodying certain of the more incomprehensible flights of the modernists. This kind of linguistic play is completely central to Thurber's fairy tales, and in part gives them their distinctive charm. Indeed, the central premise of *The Wonderful O* is linguistic, the loss of a letter becoming the central quest motif for the tale as well as an exploration of arbitrary meaning and the power of assonance.

In many ways Thurber's linguistic disruption relies heavily on the use of sound, which may well have something to do with his increasing blindness in his later years—his brother accidentally shot out one of Thurber's eyes with an arrow when he was a child, and he wore a glass eye for the rest of his life, during which his sight gradually deteriorated (Holmes, *Clocks of Columbus*). Holmes notes Malcom Cowley's comment that Thurber's blindness intensified sound effects in his prose, "as if one sense had been developed at the cost of another" to produce "a completely verbalised universe" (*Clocks of Columbus* 12). Breakdown may inhere in the disruption of words to change their sound, through mispronunciation or loss of meaning such as that which occurs through the loss of a letter in *The Wonderful O*. Alternatively, new meanings may be constructed by constructing words which are meaningless in normal English but highly significant in the tales. Good examples are Jorn, Thag and Gallow, Quillow and his use of "woddly," the Golux, and the Todal. While many of these new coinages are names, and thus purport to convey a straightforward relationship between the word and the individual so named, at the same time the words hover suggestively on the brink of meaning simply through the sound of the word itself. In linguistic terms these inventions provide a fascinating exploration of the process of Saussurian signification, in which the orderly relationship of signifier with signified becomes disrupted. Ferdinand de Saussure posits that "the linguistic sign unites, not a thing and a name, but a concept and a sound-image. . . . The two elements are intimately united and each recalls the other" (66). Thurber's word games rely heavily on the sound of a word, the notion of the word as an abstract rather than a concrete thing, in a way which highlights Saussure's original notion of signifier as both "sound-image" and "acoustic image," "the psychological imprint of the sound, the impression that it makes on our senses" (66). At the same time, the abstract signifier is divorced from its signified in precisely the way that Sewell requires for the free play of nonsense.

Most significantly for Thurber, Saussure points out that "the bond between the signifier and the signified is arbitrary" (67), and it is this arbitrary relationship that Thurber's word games most cogently explore. New words are coded and used as signifiers, sound images which purport to convey meaning; however, such meaning must be entirely arbitrary since the reader has no knowledge of the system which contains them. At the same time, the reader's familiarity with the understood processes of normal linguistic signification leads to an ongoing attempt to fit these words into familiar structures. This is successful, in that meaning is generated, but such meanings are far from definitive and endlessly ramify. In this process, meaning comes to inhere in the signifier itself, in the sound of the word and the associations it invokes. Thus Thurber's heroes are Prince Jorn and Prince Zorn of Zorna; in the absence of more concrete meaning, their names evoke the rhymes born (birthright), torn, thorn, lovelorn (the romantic suffering of the youngest son or the disguised hero), horn (as in the horns of Elfland), or forlorn (as in fairy lands forlorn). Thag, Gallow, and Jorn are an endlessly suggestive triumvirate: Thag is a thug, Gallow is both callow and worthy of being hanged, but the three names also sound spoonerized, encouraging the reader to rearrange them in an attempt to restore normal signification. No rearrangement is definitively meaningful, all are suggestive, and meaning tends to accrete rather than replace any interpretation with one more appropriate. This powerful metafictional technique forces the reader to question the structures of language and their relationship with the world they create.

In the fairy tales the linguistic play with order and chaos becomes most complex, since the imaginative space of fairy-tale structure, its denial of realistic causation, allows for a creativity that is at times magical in its effects. At the same time Thurber is able to break down and reassemble meaning not only on the linguistic level but also on the level of form itself. Like language, fairy tale offers a clearly defined and recognizable system whose boundaries are perfectly understood by the reader, supplying the necessary basis for play and allowing signification to be disrupted on a narrative as well as a linguistic level. Throughout Thurber's fairy tales, the harmonious structures of the form continually fail to mean what we believe they should mean. As in his linguistic play, meaning slides and shifts: the princess is not a princess, the jewels are not jewels, the quest is not a quest. The interesting aspect of the breakdown of signification on this metalevel is that fairy-tale narrative employs symbolic meaning, and a symbol is not the same as a signifier. Saussure insists that "one characteristic of the symbol is that it is never wholly arbitrary; it is not empty, for there is the rudiment of a natural bond between the signifier and the signified" (68). Thurber's treatment of fairy tale, however, allows for precisely the same breakdown in the relationship between symbol and meaning as in the breakdown of signification. It is not only fairy-tale symbols that function as signifiers: patterns of narrative become detached from their proper relationship with the whole, and their significance undergoes radical change. Participants in the fairy story grope for the shape of the story, which continually eludes them, fragmenting and reassembling around them. Thus the deer-princess cannot complete her narrative once she is restored, nor can Zorn of Zorna be granted the nine and ninety days necessary to complete his quest. However, unlike the ongoing suggestiveness of the linguistic play, order is eventually reasserted in the fairy tales: the one clear signifier that Thurber declines to deconstruct is the happy ending. More importantly, this suggests that while he may play with meaning in fairy-tale structure, he also reaffirms that such structure *has* meaning and value. I shall attempt to unwrap his various plays with structure in analyzing the different fairy tales, below.

Wiser Than Your Wise Men: "The Great Quillow" and *Many Moons*

Many Moons (1943) and "The Great Quillow" (1944) could be seen as the start of Thurber's real play with fairy-tale forms. *Many Moons* is a child's picture book in which Princess Lenore, ill from "a surfeit of raspberry tarts," asks for the moon, prompting her father and his advisors to construct progressively more panicked and futile responses. The problem is eventually solved by the King's Jester, through consultation with Lenore herself. "The Great Quillow" chronicles the depredations of the giant Hunder on a small village; the hero is the toymaker Quillow, whose manipulations of language persuade the giant he is mad and drive him out. Both stories are aimed at children, being shorter and less sophisticated than *The White Deer* or *The Thirteen Clocks*, and it could be argued that in them Thurber was simply gearing up for his real effort. The writing of apparently frivolous children's stories as a sideline to a more serious literary career could also be seen as a feature of the time; parallels can be found in E. B. White's *Charlotte's Web* (1952) and T. S. Eliot's *Old Possum's Book of Practical Cats* (1939). Like Thurber's fairy tales, these represent a relaxation into a simpler and more innocent form, without in any way detracting from the writers' seriousness of purpose: while ostensibly aimed at children, all these works actually offer considerable depth, complexity, and thoughtfulness. At the same time, the focus on writing for children underlines, for White and Eliot as much as Thurber, the author's interest in a lost naïveté which serves as an antidote to the cynicism of modern life.

Both *Many Moons* and "The Great Quillow" are interesting in that they find space within the classic symbols of fairy tale for the autobiographical presence of the author. In the persona of the humorist, the classic archetype of the Wise Fool, Thurber projects himself into both tales, as the Jester in "Many Moons," and as the figure of Quillow, a "droll and gentle fellow," whose toy-making is considered by the town worthies to be "a rather pretty waste of time" (204). Thurber's revenge for the low status of the comic writer is to situate in both comic figures the wisdom and thoughtfulness which enable the solution of the classic fairy-tale quest or problem. This obvious identification with the underdog figure of the fairy-tale hero is significant in the chronological context of Thurber's fairy tales. By the time he comes to write *The Thirteen Clocks* in 1950, there is a rather more cynical inclusion of the author in the Duke of Coffin Castle, since it is the villain rather than the hero who shares Thurber's lack of an eye. While later fairy tales retain the value placed on innocence and wholeness, it is possible to see a development across the tales which parallels a gradual darkening in Thurber's work as a whole. Holmes notes the development from the comic "little man" of Thurber's early work into a bleaker and angrier vision of man "given over to folly and self-destruction" ("Art of Fantasy" 18). While *Many Moons* and "The Great Quillow" contain a certain amount of gentle satire, particularly of bureaucracy and mindless system, they almost entirely lack the later uncertainty and bleakness of vision which has started to creep into *The Thirteen Clocks* in an effective counterpoint to its eventual comedic resolution.

As a simple fairy tale *Many Moons* makes clever use of the ritualistic repetition inherent in the fairy-tale structure, in the King's request to three different ministers for a solution to the princess's illness, and in the ministers' ceremonial listing of their achievements—"ivory, apes and peacocks, rubies, opals, and emeralds, black orchids, pink elephants, and blue poodles, gold bugs, scarabs, and flies in amber." Such repetition is both celebrated and gently satirized—the lists of achievements are exaggerated to the point of being ridiculous, and are neatly undercut by the minister's accidental addition of his wife's shopping list, and by the king's doubt—"I don't remember any blue poodles." This comic exaggeration serves to underline the tale's moral lesson or, more accurately, like many tales, its lesson in simple wisdom, in rendering redundant the so-called wisdom and achievements of the ministers. As in Victorian tales such as George Macdonald's "The Light Princess" or E. Nesbit's "Deliverers of Their Country," the overlay of a modern bureaucratic system onto fairy-tale structure is used self-consciously to effect a comic clash of discourses. This is also very similar to A. S. Byatt's parody of government in "The Story of the Eldest Princess," which, interestingly, also trivializes the actual purpose of quest itself—a surfeit of raspberry tarts has the same arbitrary element as the sky turning green. The point is the process, not the object, of the quest. More importantly, the element of arbitrariness highlights the difference between meaningful structure (the ritual repetition and quest resolution of the fairy tale) and that which is meaningless. In their endless lists and provision of absurd solutions to the princess's illness, the ministers take on the mantle of the ill-mannered and arrogant elder sons of fairy tale, while the Jester becomes the despised but ultimately triumphant youngest-son figure. Thus the basic structures of fairy tale are affirmed, while structure for its own sake—that is, adherence to meaningless systems of precedent—is satirized.

Many Moons is akin to most of Thurber's fairy-tale writing in its concern with meaning, and with the disconcerting slippage meaning undergoes. The tale uses the standard fairy-tale format—a king, a palace, a princess, a problem and the quest for its resolution—but the structures are playfully undercut. The king is an impotent figure, obviously concerned but curiously inept; the quest is trivialized, the princess's illness the result of overeating. In true Thurber fashion, the quest is based on wordplay, here the concrete realization of idiom—Princess Lenore is quite literally crying for the moon, but her desire is treated as reality rather than idiom. The interesting aspect of this tale is the status of truth, the way in which reality shifts with true metafictional indeterminacy to conform to whatever narrative is currently being asserted. The King's dissatisfaction with the cloak of invisibility procured for him by the Royal Wizard is a microcosmic illustration of this process; while it definitely made him invisible, the King complains that he "kept bumping into things, the same as ever." Evidently the signifier "invisible cloak" is, for him, attached to a different signified from that of the Royal Wizard.

In the central concern with the nature and accessibility of the moon, the narrative conflicts are even stronger. The Lord High Chamberlain insists that the moon is "35,000 miles away and it is bigger than the room the Princess lies in. Furthermore, it is made of molten copper." The Royal Wizard states categorically that it is "150,000 miles away, and it is made of green cheese, and it is twice as big as this palace"; the Royal Mathematician believes it to be 300,000 miles away, "round and flat like a coin . . . made of asbestos . . . and pasted on the sky." The assertions of each apparently wise man are alike in that they insist on the impossibility of the quest, while simultaneously attempting to aggrandize the speaker, his authoritative knowledge, and his particular skills. It requires the gentle intervention of the Jester to supply the metanarrative that will make sense of these conflicting narratives by removing the whole issue from the realm of fact, into which each man is trying to pin it by spurious detail, and into its proper realm of myth. In mythic terms—that is, through the translating of the issue into a system of symbolic belief rather than a system of fact, and thus the recognition of its nature as artifact, its metafictional ability to shape as well as reflect reality— each narrative is perfectly valid at the moment of its assertion. The Jester, who is quite happy to accept the three ministers as "wise men," reasons, "If they are all right, then the moon must be just as large and far away as each person thinks it is. The thing to do is find out how big the Princess Lenore thinks it is, and how far away." The fairy-tale quest thus becomes one for personal meaning; the literal moon is shown to be inextricable in meaning from the symbolic moon Lenore can wear as a piece of jewelry.

The Jester's coherent metanarrative is one point of wisdom in the tale, offering an interpretative approach which shows considerable sensitivity to individual myth structures. The Princess becomes the other point of validated wisdom largely because she is a child. Her assertions about the moon are as absolute as those of the ministers, if less grandiose—it is "a little smaller than my thumbnail" and "not as high as the big tree outside my window." Unlike the ministers, however, she can offer some reasoning behind her statements—the moon must be smaller than her thumbnail since "when I hold my thumbnail up to the moon, it just covers it"; likewise, it must be lower than the tree "for sometimes it gets caught in the top branches." The reasoning is childlike, but realistic within a child's belief structures; she certainly offers a more meaningful and supported concept of the moon than do the spurious details of the ministers. The Jester may accept the three ministers as "wise men," but only Lenore's reasoning is completely valid since she is a child, her acceptance and wonder strongly affirmed by the tale while the absolutist or materialist statements of the ministers are shown to be meaningless. Part of this failure of meaning is in the ministers' inability to recognize true narrative structures. Their elaborate ideas to prevent Lenore seeing the moon—dark glasses, tents of black silk, and all-night fireworks—are absurd not only because they seek to disguise the truth rather than redefining it, but because they *are* elaborate. In this tale, the defining feature of genuine narrative is its childlike simplicity, which is that of the true tale, stripped of unnecessary realism. Thus the tale inverts itself; despite the mad rushing around of the king and ministers, and even the intervention of the Jester to have the symbolic moon constructed, the person who eventually solves the fairy-tale dilemma of the princess's illness is the princess herself.

"The Great Quillow" is a tale similarly based on narrative and the recognition of narrative; again, repetitive formula establishes the tale's identity even while repetition is undercut and used to show the dangers of adherence to inadequate systems of thought. The story sets up the endearing figure of Quillow, the toymaker who takes in good part his colleagues' ridicule, and who plays along with their game of pretending to wind him up like a clockwork toy. Where the other characters in the tale are defined by their profession—tailor, butcher, blacksmith—Quillow is the only one who has a name, signaling individuality instead of adherence to a symbolic system. His name works similarly to other Thurber constructs in the associations it evokes—pillow, quill, mallow, willow, all concepts with qualities of gentleness or softness, in the same way that the giant's name, Hunder, evokes thunder, blunder, plunder, or hunger. Quillow has a childlike and innocent simplicity and is associated strongly with children throughout, qualities which are set up against the bureaucratic impotence of the town councilors. As in *Many Moons,* repetition and formula signal lack of achievement, here the repetition of the giant's demands—the daily provision of "three sheep, a pie made out of a thousand apples, and a chocolate as high and wide as a spinning wheel" (203). The ritualized and repetitive complaints of the councilors, forced to create the items demanded by the giant, illustrate the danger of becoming trapped into a system. As long as the giant's demands have the quality of ritual, and hence narrative's ability to shape reality, it is impossible not to supply them, and the town is effectively enslaved.

In many ways the tale signifies the clash of competing narratives. Hunder attempts to impose on the town his personal narrative of conquest and ritualized robbery, repeating in village after village the same pattern of "I, Hunder, must have . . ." (206). His demands have the power of inevitability; he is not commanding goods to be provided so much as stating what will inevitably happen, preordained by narrative precedent. Against this is set Quillow's narrative of the apocryphal giant whose malady, with its strange symptoms (hearing only the word "woddly," seeing the town chimneys turn black, and being surrounded by blue men, all of which conditions are carefully reproduced by the wily Quillow and the villagers) is alleviated only by bathing in "the yellow waters in the middle of the sea" (213). This narrative is equally patterned and repetitive and has the same metafictional quality of shaping rather than simply describing reality. Quillow's cunning lies in his appropriation of precisely the narrative tactics employed by the giant; as long as the villagers do as other villagers have done, they are trapped in the tale's pattern and must serve the giant. As soon as the giant does as the previous giant has done, he, too, is doomed. The fact that the word "woddly," the black chimneys, and the little blue men are all faked does not in any way restrict their symbolic power in the story. Quillow thus recognizes and appropriates a central power of fairy-tale narrative, that of inevitability through pattern; the tale equally recognizes the entrapping qualities of structure and celebrates the empowering potential of structure in the hands of a self-aware storyteller. The reader's attention is drawn to this in the middle of the story, when the other artisans ridicule Quillow's tale, suggesting that his work cannot be as hard as theirs, "hammering out your tale . . . twisting it . . . levelling it . . . rolling it out . . . stitching it up . . . fitting it together . . ." (212). They are ironically unaware that his craft entails precisely this—it is equally as constructed, as creative as their own, and ultimately far more powerful. Again, this points to metafictional awareness of tale as artifact which, in Waugh's terms, "explicitly and overtly lays bare its condition of artifice" (4).

"The Great Quillow" marks, in its subtle elements of wordplay, the start of the linguistic games which are most fully realized in *The White Deer* and *The Thirteen Clocks*. The central theme here is characteristic Thurber—the breakdown of meaning on a verbal level which mirrors and draws attention to the breakdown of narrative as the giant's imposition of story is disrupted. We are given clues to the centrality of this process at various points in the tale: the blacksmith's horses are called Lobo, Bolo, Olob, and Obol, and Quillow's second day's tale involves characters named by incomprehensible strings of syllables such as Anderblusdaferan and Ufrabrodoborobe. The tale Quillow has neglected to invent is in fact about a king and his three sons who are riding through a magical forest—that is, apart from the ridiculous names it is the tale of *The White Deer*, interrupted by "woddly"s only to be told later, in full, by Thurber himself, the writer thus projected into the tale as tale-teller. The circular repetition of the horse's names, and the meaningless names of the tale's protagonists, are simply heralding the far more important breakdown in the giant's inability to hear anything except the word "woddly"—"All words were one word to him. All words were 'woddly'" (214). This is once again a clear exploration of the process of signification: for the giant all signifiers are suddenly one, despite the clear proliferation of signifieds which surround him, and that signifier, all at once compelled to mean everything, of course ends up meaning nothing. More importantly, this breakdown is essentially a breakdown of *narrative,* since Quillow has omitted to invent a story to tell the giant, and has simply filled in the time with meaningless rubbish. The breakdown signals the moment at which the giant's narrative starts to break down, as he is too afraid to eat and thus disrupts the process of his demands on the village. At the same time, Thurber employs the same subtle process of metanarrative he used in the Jester's explanations in *Many Moons,* and will use again in *The White Deer.* Breakdown is terrifying and anxiety-provoking, but in fact the shifting narratives are safely held within a larger metanarrative which ultimately explains and structures them—here, the false symptoms carefully created in the service of Quillow's plot to deceive the giant and chase him away. In the same way that I have argued postmodern writers retreat into fairy tale as a bastion against meaninglessness, Thurber's narrative is never deconstructed so far that its ultimate sense and purpose cannot be eventually reasserted.

Thurber's complex linguistic and narrative purposes in this story are neatly concealed behind a deceptively simple and childlike surface. The tale abounds in detail which appropriates the traditionally singsong, repetitive voice of the oral story—the orderly comments of the village artisans, the neat triads of superstition with which Quillow purports to explain the giant's malady, the ritualistic repetition of the malady's symptoms, the blue men popping up from behind every part of the landscape. The domestic nature of the story, its emphasis on eating and drinking and children's toys, and the enjoyably subversive nature of Quillow's tricks, conspire with the language to admirably fit the tale for children's consumption. The same is true of *Many Moons,* whose more simplistic language belies the tale's textual complexities. Both stories mine the clash between the domestic and the fantastic for a gentle, whimsical comedy deepened by the more complex language of the "The Great Quillow." Appropriately, given that he is writing largely for children, Thurber here omits the romantic outcome of fairy tale—narrative closure is affirmed, but it is only in later tales that the happy heterosexual couple is established. At the same time the narrative games in both these stories are sophisticated and entertaining at a level beyond the grasp of a child reader—a tendency recognized in many of the contemporary reviews of the two tales (Toombs, 122–26). In both *The White Deer* and *The Thirteen Clocks* Thurber repeats the concealing layer of naive whimsy, so that the fairy tales are always entertaining for children; however, in future tales the adult message is both more complex and considerably darker.

MARVELOUS, MORTIFYING, AND MEANINGLESS: *The White Deer*

Sorceries . . . run in cycles . . . spells are set in sets and systems. What's true of one peculiar case is true of all peculiar cases of the same peculiar sort. —*The White Deer*, 42

Written the year after "The Great Quillow," *The White Deer* is Thurber's first foray into book-length fairy tale, and, while approvingly received by critics, is noted in several reviews as being more suitable for adults than for children (Toombs, 132–34). This is a recognition of its linguistic and narrative complexity, despite the apparent simplicity of the story, which would still remain accessible to children. The plot makes full use of classic fairy-tale patterns—three brothers hunt a white deer who turns into a beautiful princess when cornered, forcing each brother to undertake a separate quest to win her and restore her lost memory. The contest is naturally won by the youngest, Prince Jorn. The emblem of the princess enchanted into the form of a deer is recursive, since King Clode, the father of the three brothers, also won his wife after hunting her deer-form in the forest. While the story self-consciously reiterates fairy tale as fairy tale, however, it also deconstructs and destabilizes the tale. The second-generation enchanted princess is less straightforwardly susceptible to resolution, being unable to remember her name or identity, and thus resists heterosexual union until the three princes have proved themselves worthy of her and restored her memory. The breakdown of familiar narrative and consequent slippage of fairy-tale meaning is, however, ultimately revealed to be part of a metanarrative which enacts the revenge of a witch on the nameless princess's father; dissolution eventually becomes resolution, and the power of structure is reasserted. As in the two shorter fairy tales, the efforts of authority figures—here King Clode and his various ministers, including the Royal Recorder, the Royal Physician, and the rather clueless Royal Wizard—are comic and futile, and only the efforts of the marginal younger son, despised by his elder brothers, actually succeed.

Numerous reviewers note *The White Deer*'s beautiful and poetic prose (Toombs, 132–33), which clearly separates the novel from the earlier children's stories. Stephen Black suggests that "in *The White Deer* Thurber employs a style which is at once elevated, poetic and comic, to suggest the 'medieval' world of the story" (108). The medieval feel, or otherwise, of the story does not seem to be the issue, however. Most strikingly, Thurber's language in the novel employs wordplay, rhyme, repetition, alliteration, and assonance to strongly highlight not only the function of storytelling as self-conscious craft but also the notion of language itself—as the constructor of fairy tale, and hence as constructed, but also as the difficult medium in which the characters must enact their fairy-tale narratives. Language in the novel comes to reflect and to stand for magic, the power of the marvelous or numinous to affect the lives of the characters, often despite their resistance to it. Language both enables and makes inevitable; in its inevitability, it is entrapping. In metafictional terms, it creates by describing, so that magic stands for language at the same time that language stands for magic.

The conflation between language and magic is signaled from the start of the tale, with the gentle, faraway tone of the narrator:

> If you should walk and wind and wander far enough on one of those afternoons in April when smoke goes down instead of up, and nearby things sound far away and far things near, you are more than likely to come at last to the enchanted forest that lies between the Moonstone Mines and Centaurs Mountain. . . . If you pluck one of the ten thousand toadstools that grow in the emerald grass at the edge of the wonderful woods, it will feel as heavy as a hammer in your hand, but if you let it go it will sail away over the trees like a tiny parachute, trailing black and purple stars. (*White Deer*, 3–4)

Aside from numerous examples of Thurber's ongoing love affair with alliteration, the passage is constructed in terms of contradictions, opposites, and paradoxes, a recurring feature of the story—up, down, far, near, heavy, light. The indeterminacy of these images reinforces the "if you should wander" opening, which performs the classic "long ago and far away" function of fairy tale as well as reinforcing the artificiality of a reality constructed in these terms. In this construction the magical space of fairy tale is not geographical, but mental—it is a mood, a tone, which the reader must accept before the magic of the tale can work, a recognition of a marvelous, unreal space whose rules will be different from those of reality, but equally compelling. At the same time the linguistic paradox signals and encodes the similar patterns of contradiction and tension which will characterize the shape of the tale. Things, the narrator warns, will not be as you expect; nonetheless, prepare simply to accept them with wonder, as is proper to the tale.

Language separates out characters in this novel; far more than the perilous tasks set before the princes, it is a testing ground which selects for worth in terms of imagination and verbal ability, and thus ultimately for self-consciousness about the fairy-tale project itself. The two elder sons, Thag and Gallow, are nonverbal, physical in nature, their only interest the chase and a certain kind of rough, physical bullying such as tossing the dwarf Quondo. While their names suggest some kind of orality, via the processes of almost-signification discussed above, it is the orality of eating (gag, swallow). In contrast, Jorn is associated firmly with the verbal, a manipulator of language who sings and tells stories "of a faraway Princess who would one day set a perilous labor for each of the Princes to perform" (5). In thus accurately foreshadowing the structure of the tale, he takes the position of narrator, enabling him to shape the tale in the same way that the Jester provides metanarration to the conflicting narratives of the ministers, or Quillow overcomes the giant's narrative with his own. To be a narrator is to have power, not only to engage in wordplay but also to impose one's own narrative on others; this is metafiction, and the power that Thurber celebrates is his own.

In *The White Deer*, wordplay is the symbol of narrative power. King Clode's bluff, hearty manner attempts to reject convoluted language, to have events "without a lot of this tarradiddle and tiraddle" (36). As his encounter with the woods wizard proves, resistance is futile; his own utterances slide between the plain and the playful throughout the tale, dropping continually into alliteration. With his words twisted by the woods wizard, he acquires momentarily the "great dignity" appropriate to a king, negating his buffoonery elsewhere: "Try twice that trick on Tlode . . . my mousy man of magic, and we will wid these wids of woozards" (16). This verges on nonsense, but the wordplay, allies him with the wizard and with Jorn, and reminds us that, in his day, when as a young man he rode after a deer who became a princess, Clode was the youngest son who fulfilled his quest and won her hand. He is also himself a tale-teller: his story of the quest which won him his wife operates as the first authoritative narrative within the story, reinforcing Jorn's idealized desire for a quest with a pattern to which the story could be expected to conform.

The opening scenario of the story, with Clode and his three sons in search of the white deer despite their misgivings about the magic of the Enchanted Forest, is a fairly straightforward fairy-tale narrative. Clode's dislike of the forest's magic—and its language—is overcome by an unambiguous appeal to his physical courage, which realigns him with his oafish older sons. From the moment the deer appears, however, an uncomplicated physical outcome is impossible: the deer runs through a forest of alliteration, "through a fiery fen and over a misty moor . . . climbed a ruby ridge, flung across a valley of violets, and sped along the pearly path leading to the myriad mazes of the Moonstone Mines" (18–19). The moment of transformation when deer becomes princess is inevitable, dictated not only by the precedent of Clode's tale and by Jorn's romancing but also by the magical language which has defined the deer. Clode's attempt to reduce her transformation to known parameters—his own experience, and his mundane hope that "her father has a decent taste in wines" (20)—is thwarted as the narrative begins to go seriously off track, denying easy resolution: she cannot remember her name. The clear narrative progression from transformation to heroic quests in competition to the marriage resolution experienced by Clode, is disrupted, despite Clode's attempts to reassert it later on by forcing her to set quests for his sons.

The namelessness of the princess is a central trope in the story, anchoring Thurber's interest in narrative symbol and its implications for identity as well as his playful deconstruction of the expectation engendered by fairy-tale narrative. As the structures of the tale slip away from expectation, so too do the identities of the characters involved. The princess's lack of name means that she is defined only by the magically conflated categories "princess" and "deer," and unanchored by any more definitively constructed signification. Her namelessness already begins to eject her from the simple narrative supplied by Clode, Jorn, or the precedents found by the Royal Recorder, "maidens changed to deer and back again, all nice and neat and normal, all nice and neat and formal" (43). Since she is nameless, she cannot lay claim to an absolute category of "princess," which should be supported by kingdom and family in addition to fairy-tale narrative expectation. Tocko's tale, of the ordinary deer given the power to assume the form of a princess, provides a competing narrative that inverts and denies her identity, providing an equally plausible signifier ("deer") that insists that the clear meanings of Clode's and Jorn's tales are simply wrong. The princess is not alone in this slippage; the uncertainties of her identity are mirrored in the dual personalities of the Royal Physician, both doctor and patient, and in the struggle for identity of the three princes on their quests.

The quests of the three princes are bedeviled by a similar quality of chaotic narrative insecurity, through the slippages of which the princes must fight to identify themselves as heroes rather than the victims of elaborate jests. Thag's "perilous labour" struggles to define itself as hero-quest (prince kills boar) against the confusing, dreamy world of the Valley of Euphoria, where "a sticky thickish liquid dripped and oozed and gave or rather lent the air a heavy sweetish fragrance" (50). This is the language of wordplay and thus of magic, its strange strings of signifiers suggesting meaning without actually defining it: "a lozy moon globbers in the pipe trees. . . . High up in a tree, a chock climbed slowly" (51–52). For Thag, this almost-signification is the language of seduction, attempting to lure him from his simple, physical investment in the quest into the confusing world of linguistic slippage. Thurber's dense, alliterative and involuted prose not only affects Thag ("I distrust this stickish thicky stuff . . . Hag's thad enough" [50]) but also circles back to infect the narratorial voice with the same breakdown ("thaggravated Had"). The round man in the tree is merely an agent of the same process of dissolution, wantonly playing with language to confuse and delay Thag, and to prevent the imposition of the expected narrative structure. In true heroic style, however, the thug-prince declines to be seduced: "he closed his mouth and held his breath and shut his eyes and galloped on" (53). Against the willpower required to resist the blandishments of wordplay, the actual fight with the Blue Boar is an anticlimax, laughably simple, and predetermined utterly by the expectations of fairy-tale narrative.

Gallow experiences a similar process of redefinition; however, where peril for Thag signifies the seductions of language, for Gallow it is a process of trivialization rather than beguilement. In Gallow's quest Thurber once more revisits his ongoing satirization of the meaningless structures of a bureaucratic system in the little men who demand pointless parchments from Gallow at every turn. A kind of commercialized corruption of the system also prevails, as the common symbols of fairy tale—dragons, giants, sleeping beauties—are here redefined as commercial opportunity: "Lost Babes Found . . . Giants Killed While You Wait . . . 7 League Boots Now 6.98" (63). Rather than the loss of meaning experienced by Thag, Gallow must face a slippage of meaning, a series of signs whose construction is completely alien and whose meaning obviously ramifies beyond that which he knows; his quest is, in his particular terms of reference, meaningless. The transactions with the little men signal the breakdown of familiar narratives, denying the meaning Gallow has hitherto found. His ultimate quest, facing the Seven-Headed Dragon of Dragore, is a corrupt carnival sideshow, "meaningless but marvelous" (71), as is his whole journey. The mechanical process of throwing balls into the open mouths of the dragon replicates the mechanical process of his quest, and of the narrative. The process underlines the lack of value in Gallow, the absence of some kind of essential love of romance or awareness of correct narrative which defines the hero, and which only Jorn has. The unfolding of the tale suggests that Thag and Gallow experience bankrupt narratives not only because they are doomed to failure by the metanarrative (both the three-sons structure of fairy tale, and the Wizard Ro's manipulations) but also because they are shallow thugs who lack the necessary metafictional awareness of story.

Despite his status as the younger son and the narrator/word-user who is destined to succeed, Jorn's quest suffers from a similar failure of meaning to that of his two brothers. Ironically, his fairy-tale predestination as the youngest son actually disrupts the signification of his quest; because the princess favors him, she sends him on an errand which is less dangerous and testing than Thag's or Gallow's. While the signifiers in the quest seem meaningful—a monster to vanquish, an object to bring back—the meaning they hold is almost immediately redefined as something very different, the monster a scarecrow and the object hence valueless. Despite his reluctance to undertake a rigged contest, Jorn is held to the quest by the tale's structure—and by the precedent of his father, who similarly fought a "clay and boxwood" creature (9)—and departs as his brothers do. In this case, absolute signification, the structure which insists Jorn's success is the ultimate signifier in the fairy-tale plot, causes breakdown in meaning, as if to suggest that only the chaos of disrupted signification is generative.

In fact, the quest narrative Jorn experiences suffers from particularly complex narrative conflicts, with his personal, heroic vision struggling against the witch's attempt to derail him, and the Wizard Ro's virtuoso metanarrative which ultimately makes sense of the conflict. Meaning shifts continually and bewilderingly throughout these structures. Jorn's dissatisfaction with his paltry quest renders the clay and sandalwood Mok-Mok and the cherry orchard meaningless in terms of his heroic structures, which the Mok-Mok literally mocks, and he desires instead "a difficult riddle to do, a terrible task to undergo, a valiant knight to overthrow" (77). The witch's intervention seems momentarily to restore meaning, but that meaning is deconstructed in its turn. The riddle is difficult only in the sense that it is difficult for the Sphinx to say without moving its jaws, the terrible task is merely lengthy and terribly tedious, and the Black Knight is an aged and unworthy opponent. By the time Jorn has collected his chalice full of cherries, the symbol acts as signifier to a complex layer of self-conscious narrative meanings—the princess's romantic hopes, Jorn's aspirations to heroism, the witch's revenge, and Ro's manipulations.

As with "The Great Quillow" and *Many Moons,* the tale relies on the development of the metanarrative to make sense of the confusing conflicts. While the metanarrative is not precisely the tale envisaged by Clode or Jorn, its essential structure (princess rescued from her deer form to marry the worthiest prince) remains the same, with the addition of elements from Tocko's tale despite the fact that his deer-into-woman scenario is basically irrelevant. The metanarrative hinges, as does Tocko's tale, on the concept of love; both Rosanore and the nameless deer are doomed if love fails them. The central aspect of the tale's resolution is thus not, in fact, the quests, which are revealed as so much heroic posturing, but the moment of declaration when Jorn professes his love for the princess. This highlights the failure of meaning at the heart of Clode's deer tale, which imposes hetero-sexual union without love, revealed by Clode's characterization of his far-from-romantic relationship with his wife. Here Thurber is both invoking and critiquing structure: unthinking structure for its own sense is rejected; self-aware structure is validated. Their marriage dis-plays the essential failure of empathy which is present in so many of Thurber's other depictions of heterosexual relationships: Clode speaks of his wife as "a pretty enough gray-eyed minx . . . with no stomach for the chase, and a way of fluttering up behind a man before he knew it, moving like a cat on velvet" (8). *The White Deer* comes to rewrite Clode's tale and improve upon it, replacing the mechanical structure of fairy-tale marriage with one that insists on love as an essential part of the utopian fairy-tale closure.

Thurber's sense of closure and reconciliation is thus completely bound up in the concept of love, a romantic development of the het-erosexual couple common to so many fairy tales. The motivation for the whole story is the failure of love (the thwarted passion of Nagrom Yaf), and her vengeance is played out, not on King Thorg who spurned her love, but on the result of Thorg's union with a princess he, presumably, loved—their children, Tel and Rosanore. Denied a place in the happy heterosexual union of the fairy tale, Nagrom Yaf (a far more sinister-sounding reversal of Morgan [le] Fay), chooses to avenge herself by similarly denying that place to Rosanore. The witch's spell condemns Rosanore to namelessness and loss of iden-tity; as in Nagrom Yaf's own experience, the possibility of roman-tic union breaks down and satisfying structure is withheld. Denied love, Nagrom Yaf presumably expects it to be equally denied to Rosanore by the three princes convinced she is a deer. The involuted structures of the tale thus work continually on narrative precedent and repetition, but the central theme they repeat is that of love. This reverses the bitterness and lack of mutuality inherent in many of the relationships Thurber depicts in his other writings; while there is bitterness here, in Nagrom Yaf's disappointment and revenge, it is condemned and punished. Rosanore and Jorn are slightly two-dimensional characters, the stereotypical fairy-tale lovers, and it is the tale's structuring rather than their actual interactions that insists their love is nonetheless real.

The ultimate narrative manipulator of this tale is, unlike earlier tales, an unseen presence rather than a central character. The woods-wizard Ro is obviously an inheritor of the linguistic play and genuine magic associated with the enchanted forest, the power of the marvelous expressed as narrative. He exists in opposition not only to the fake magic of the Royal Wizard but also to the purveyors of powerless narrative: Tocko with his vagueness and the Royal Recorder's overly legal fondness for forcing reality to conform to precedent, the ultimate denial of metafictional play. The final revelation of Ro's presence behind the scenes gives coherence and unity to the plot, explaining a large number of enigmatic figures who emerge, in true fairy-tale fashion, to mysteriously advise Prince Jorn. The tale's apparent proliferation of characters and confusing multiplicity of potential meanings is thus neatly resolved into the coherent and satisfying happy ending, including the destruction of Nagrom Yaf in an epilogue that plays gently with the tale's interest in authoritative narrative. In many ways, the complexities of Thurber's narrative games simply serve to reinforce the pleasure of fairy-tale closure, allowing the reader to emerge from the enchanted forests of language into a simpler, plainer country, but refreshed and satisfied by the quest.

Very Like a Witch's Spell: *The Thirteen Clocks*

> What manner of prince is this you speak of, and what manner of maiden does he love, to use a word that makes no sense and has no point? —*The Thirteen Clocks* 38

The Thirteen Clocks has a comparatively sparse linguistic texture when compared with *The White Deer,* and the tale is simpler, its narratives interlocking and largely cooperative, in contrast to the convoluted competing narratives of *The White Deer.* The evil Duke of Coffin Castle is ward to the captured Princess Saralinda, setting impossible tasks to the princes who desire her, and rejoicing in their downfall. His frozen, sadistic existence is finally ended by Zorn of Zorna, assisted by his enigmatic helper the Golux, when the prince finds a thousand jewels through sleight-of-quest, eventually robbing the Duke of both princess and jewels. In its treatment of fairy-tale elements and its comic inventiveness *The Thirteen Clocks,* while somewhat darker than any of Thurber's other tales, remains fresh and innovative. Like *The White Deer,* the story is concerned with the classic fairy-tale pattern of the prince sent to undertake a quest to earn the hand of the princess; like *The White Deer,* the meaning and structure of that quest shifts in signification, its meaning continually under question. The narrative games Thurber plays are less complex here, but the underlying message of value is more thoughtful, and he seems as concerned with the idea of evil as with the idea of love. Significantly, and rather paradoxically given the darker tone, the tale adds laughter to its central value structure, which parallels Thurber's belief in the power of humor expressed elsewhere in his writings, and which is thrown into strong relief by the tale's qualities of darkness. Perhaps partially as a result of this darker tone, *The Thirteen Clocks* is generally more restrained in its linguistic play, and Thurber slips only occasionally into the dense alliteration, assonance, and rhyme he uses in *The White Deer*. The end of chapter III, with its "ticking thicket of bickering crickets" where "bonged the gongs of a throng of frogs" (73), is a striking example of wordplay which stands out precisely because it is generally lacking in the rest of the narrative.

While the prince's quest is quintessentially that of fairy tale, some of the darkness of the tale's vision can be attributed to its equal reliance on the symbols and structures of a rather different formulaic genre, that of the Gothic. The brooding castle on the hill, the melodramatically gloved and cold-blooded villain, signal the Gothic as clearly and self-consciously as the wandering minstrel-prince signals the fairy tale, and the conditions of the quest—forests, storms, darkness—are common to both, allowing the journey to switch between genres or to invoke them simultaneously. Thurber's interest in Gothic literature is a marginal presence in his other writing, but it conforms to his interest in formulaic and popular forms. Burton R. Pollin has noted in exhaustive detail Edgar Allan Poe's influence on Thurber, and explores the tension between Thurber's purposes as a writer of comedy, and those of Poe as the ultimate "melancholic" (139). Melancholy acts as an integral aspect of Thurber's humor, and certainly in *The Thirteen Clocks* the melancholic Gothic vision coexists surprisingly peaceably with both fairy tale and comedy. However, the Gothic genre influences do account for the underlying darkness of vision in the tale, the sense (ultimately denied) that the quest is doomed and the characters struggle against impossible odds. The Jack-o'-lent the Golux and the Prince encounter sums this up precisely: "The way is dark and getting darker. The hut is high and even higher. I wish you luck. There is none" (73).

Gothic melodrama in the story serves to underline fairy tale's aspects of stereotype and archetype; not only the prince and princess, but the villain himself, are absolutely correct and necessary for the purposes they fulfill in the narrative. The Duke of Coffin Castle takes center stage in a way denied to Nagrom Yaf, and I have suggested above that he partially represents Thurber himself, linked by the loss of one eye. He is a wonderful villain, "six foot four, and forty-six, and even colder than he thought he was" (17), in many ways more colorful and more central to the story than either Zorn of Zorna or Saralinda. Both prince and princess are, like Jorn and Rosanore, ideal figures rather lacking in character, as is necessary and perfectly appropriate to fairy tale. The development of the Duke, whose viewpoint we are given on an equal footing to Zorn's in all his interactions with Hark and Listen, is perhaps what adds depth and complexity to Thurber's inventive use of the structure. After all, as Thurber reminds us, it is right and narratively necessary that evildoers *should* do evil, since their evil is what provides the challenge of the quest. He underlines this with the invention of the Todal, a marvelous monster whose purpose is "to punish evil-doers for having done less evil than they should" (51). This recognition of structural and symbolic purpose allows the Duke to spill over the boundaries of his villain character, to become an attractive figure in his melodramatic excesses, limping, cackling, tinkering with the clocks, and devising impossible tasks for suitors. He is attractive precisely for his wholeheartedness, his level of commitment to his role, and hence to the engine of the story, summed up nicely in his unashamed claim that "we all have flaws . . . and mine is being wicked" (114).

While the Duke is the fairy-tale challenge rounded out into Gothic villain, his power lies partially in the fact that, like Quillow or Jorn, he is a manipulator of narrative, using language and story as dexterously as Thurber does himself to enmesh the suitors for Saralinda's hand. They are instructed to "cut a slice of moon, or change the ocean into wine. They [are] set to finding things that never were, and building things that could not be" (22). The Duke's impossible narratives construct a reality which is powerfully imposed on the suitors, and which work in the service of his metanarrative to fulfill the terms of the witch's spell and keep Saralinda for himself. As a user of narrative, he also recognizes it at work, and the Golux knows that "the Duke has awe of witch's spells" (36), which in the context of the story are precisely no more or no less than narrative itself. Witch's spells state, with neatness and inevitability, the shape and detail of what will happen: where wordplay is magic in *The White Deer*, here magic is narrative. The shape of the witch's spell which hedges about the Duke's abduction of Saralinda, sets out precisely the shape of the tale—the suitors, the quests, the loophole by which the villain may be thwarted. The Duke's respect for witch's spells marks his recognition that they inevitably entrap him in the expected downfall of the villain. As the story progresses, the Duke displays increasing rage as Zorn of Zorna reveals more and more of the characteristics of the hero. The more Zorn is the hero, the more the Duke is inevitably the villain, and doomed to defeat. "Never tell me what I always am!" he snarls at Hark (93). In addition, the Duke also recognizes the specifics of the particular narrative which entraps him—the prince whose name begins with X and doesn't, the nameless champion who defeated the Duke's strongest man, the discovery that the Golux is his invisible spy. The Duke echoes this structuredness in the quest he sets out for Zorn, the object which must be obtained within a certain time and under certain conditions: a demanding structure which confirms the Duke's status as a powerful narrator. It also underlines the novel's interest in paradox, impossibility, the arbitrary—all central aspects of the chaotic breakdown of meaning with which Thurber is always concerned. The status of the Duke as villain allows play with meaning which centers on the arbitrary, not only in his impossible quests but also in his eccentric villainies—suitors are slain for "trampling the Duke's camellias, failing to praise his wines, staring too long at his gloves, gazing too long at his niece" (22). It is as if, by constructing meaningless narratives and illogical causal links, the Duke seeks to evade the rigorous logic of the spell or narrative which will signal his downfall.

For a tale so hedged about with inevitable witches' spells and inflexible outcomes, *The Thirteen Clocks* has an unlikely interest in the indeterminate—perhaps, in another expression of Thurber's ambiguous relationship with order and chaos, *because* of that inflexibility. The Duke's downfall is in paradox, a prince whose "name begins with X, and doesn't" (102), and his castle is repeatedly the site of the indescribable, most notably in the inhabitants of the dungeon and the "something very much like nothing anyone had seen before" (96) which trots across the room. The Duke's final nemesis, the Todal, is likewise curiously indeterminate, described by characteristics which somehow fail to define it at all clearly—it is a "blob of glup" that "makes a sound like rabbits screaming, and smells of old, unopened rooms" (50). (Parallels can be drawn with Lewis Carroll's Snark, defined by flavor and habits but not by any concrete attribute.) For the Duke, the indeterminate is threatening, undermining the rigid grip he has on his identity as villain, and hence on the narrative itself. He may well be worried; indeterminacy, jewels that are not tears but "slish" and "thlup" (123), prove his downfall, and his fate is the indescribable blob of the Todal. This is an exploration of fairy tale's unambiguous structure in negative—a metafictional insecurity about narrative which chronicles its breakdown only to ultimately affirm its power.

The figure of the Golux is at the core of this interest in uncertainty and failure of definition, operating not only as the natural opposite to the Duke and his iron grip on narrative but also as a manipulator of story no less powerful for being uncertain. Where the Duke is defined completely by his place in the narrative, the Golux resists definition and description, an indeterminacy signaled most strongly by his "indescribable hat" (31). He has no clear fairy-tale precedent other than the enigmatic helper who often appears to assist the hero of fairy tale, but like the Duke he spills out of that definition to establish himself as a compelling character in his own right. Like the Duke, too, he is associated with a breakdown in meaning, but an inversion rather than an absence ("I came upon a firefly burning in a spider's web. I saved the victim's life . . . The spider's. The blinking arsonist had set the web on fire" [34]); he insists that "I am a man of logic, in my way" (84). Again, this recalls Sewell's theories of nonsense as being a rearrangement of ideas into new relationships, a different kind of meaning rather than an absence. His quasi-logical games certainly work to save the quest, in his recognition of how Saralinda can restart the clocks. While being associated throughout with uncertainty and lack of definition, he is nonetheless a powerful catalyst to narrative behind the scenes, a metanarrator in opposition to the Duke. His power over the Duke is signaled by a complex symbolic network centering on notions of visibility—where the Duke cannot see properly, lacking an eye, the Golux cannot be seen. The Duke, half-blind, cannot recognize the Golux's structures until it is too late; the Golux, invisible, can conceal his structures until he is revealed as the "Golux ex machina" the Duke fears (116). His invisibility and his function as one of the Duke's invisible spies place his identity in further uncertainty, but one which remains flexible and generative, thus defeating the locked narrative identity of the Duke.

As an aspect, and perhaps a symbol, of its interest in narrative, *The Thirteen Clocks* centers on the idea of time, a concept whose importance is signaled by the thirteen clocks of the title. This is a recurring theme for Thurber, who deals with it elsewhere in his fable "The Last Clock" (*Lanterns and Lances*), where time becomes equated with meaning. Time, of course, is central to narrative, which after all is simply the orderly description of the progression of events. In slaying Time, as he believes, the Duke has controlled narrative and also doomed himself to inhumanity and stasis; however, the stoppage of time stops the inexorable advance of the *tale*, the structures of which will ultimately thwart the villain. The Duke's fascination with clocks is in fact a fascination with the active place in the tale he has relinquished in favor of the metafictional thwarting of narrative. Time is also central to fairy tale, as Zorn recognizes: "in spells and labors a certain time is always set" (46), and the Duke's quest set for Zorn, by deliberately allowing him insufficient time, dooms him to failure. However, the mechanical view of time is revealed as being inadequate in the tale's value structures—the Golux insists that "time is for dragonflies and angels" (46), and that the Duke's imposition of mechanical limits on the quest is meaningless. This is demonstrated by the success of the quest, which sets up mechanical time as something associated with the Duke: cold, hateful, and rigid, and trapped in a lifeless stasis. Against this is placed the "clockwork in a maiden's heart, that strikes the hours of youth and love, and knows the southward swan from winter snow, and summer afternoons from tulip time" (110). Time, in the Duke's sense of it, is revealed as being akin to the meaningless structures Thurber pillories in his writing—the fact that the Duke's clocks have stopped is irrelevant, since real time, human time, continues regardless.

The same interest in time is seen in the encounter with Hagga, the magical helper who ultimately provides them with the necessary thousand jewels, and who is introduced by the Golux's failure to accurately remember her age: "The Golux had missed her age by fifty years, as old men often do" (78). Hagga, however, while standing for a similar inhuman removal from time to that of the Duke, is the unlikely point in the tale for Thurber's introduction of the theme of laughter and its importance. Hagga represents the standard fairy-tale element of the girl who is rewarded for her virtue and courtesy by being given the power to weep jewels. However, her story is given added dimension and reality by Thurber's investigation of what this actually means to her—she has simply become the victim of tragic tales inflicted on her by the greedy. While the meaning of the gift slides away from the normal value assigned to it, the most important inversion is that of weeping to laughter: tears, as a signifier, can have more than one meaning, and Thurber insists on the validity of interpreting them as laughter rather than sorrow. The jewels produced by laughter are ephemeral, which rescues the gift from the same overuse to which her weeping was subject and gives them an essentially comic meaning in the structure of the quest as a whole. Zorn fulfils the Duke's requirement, but in the eventual dissolution of the jewels, the joke is on the Duke; their meaning changes to reflect his failure and downfall rather than his greedy acquisitiveness. Hagga's laughter gives Thurber some excuse for wordplay, in the Golux's insane, linguistically self-aware limericks, but it is also interestingly free from causal logic, happening "without a rhyme or reason, out of time and out of season" (86). This reintroduces the theme of indeterminate time which has been associated with her, underlining the sadness of her timeless existence despite her laughter. However, her laughter, as the Golux and prince leave, also signals the happy ending of the tale, the affirmation of Zorn and Saralinda's successful love even if such human happiness is denied to Hagga.

Thurber's essay "The Case for Comedy" (*Lanterns and Lances*) is a manifesto for the power of laughter, which is, he insists, quoting Lord Boothby, "the only solvent of terror and tension" (119). Interestingly, he also suggests that "form . . . is the heart of humour and the salvation of comedy" (123); true humor is structured, working on recognition and the satisfaction of closure. Thus the presence of an explicit call for humor is not out of place in the fairy-tale structures of *The Thirteen Clocks,* which has its fair share of terror and tension, resolved by Hagga's laughter as much as the happy ending for the lovers and the downfall of the Duke. Thurber writes, "The true balance of life and art, the saving of the human mind . . . lies in what has long been known as tragicomedy, for humour and pathos, tears and laughter are, in the highest expression of human character and achievement, inseparable" (120). The Golux's invocation to Zorn and Saralinda is, "Remember laughter. You'll need it even in the blessed isles of Ever After" (120). For Thurber, fairy-tale closure does not promise an inhuman freedom from sorrow; however, he embraces the form for its power to provide both the structure and the inherent sense of value on which his comic vision depends.

3

THE BLOODIED TEXT:
ANGELA CARTER

Angela Carter has made the metafictional arena of fairy tale and folktale very much her own; while only *The Bloody Chamber,* her 1979 collection of short stories, offers sustained and explicit fairy-tale reworking, she has also translated and edited collections of fairy tales, in the two Virago volumes and in her own translation of Charles Perrault. An essentially postmodern awareness of tales and folklore also weaves through most of her quirky, individualistic output, as fragments of tales in her novels, and in the folkloric roots of many of her short stories. This denotes her powerfully self-conscious investigation of old forms in new contexts; in the words of Stephen Benson, "her relationship with the fairy tale lies at the core of her contemporaneity" ("Literary *Märchen*" 31). While fairy-tale presences may at times be tangential in her work, her concern with magical and symbolic narrative gives much of it a more generally antirealist trend, which in works such as *Nights at the Circus* verges on magical realism. Like many postmodern writers she is also fascinated with genre and structure, exemplified most strongly in her self-conscious and at times critical exploration of romance, Gothic, and horror conventions. Most importantly, however, as a feminist reviser of fairy tales her awareness of structure is absolutely ideological, and she characteristically deconstructs and assaults, innovatively and often explosively, the system of assumptions about gender and sexuality which marks our cultural narratives, and the traditional, complacently heterosexual utopia of the fairy-tale ending.

While play with structure and expectation is a central technique, another important feature of Carter's fairy tale is her writing style, which is lush, expressive, self-indulgent, and at times pyrotechnic. She invokes textuality through language as much as form, since there is no chance for the reader, continually jolted by linguistic excess, to immerse him- or herself in the absorbing reality created by prose. Language thus becomes a metafictional technique which operates forcefully within her disruption of fairy tale's illusion of structural neutrality. Her idiosyncratic meld of structure and language can be overly energetic; as Salmon Rushdie has noted in his introduction to Carter's *Burning Your Boats* (x), she is possibly stronger as a writer of short stories and tales than as a novelist, since the limitations of the short tale in some ways serve to control and contain the fireworks of her narrative style, which in longer works can become exhausting. Carter herself comments, "The limited trajectory of the short narrative concentrates its meaning. Sign and sense can fuse to an extent impossible to achieve among the multiplying ambiguities of an extended narrative" (Afterword to *Fireworks*, reprinted in *Burning Your Boats*). Here she effectively underlines her awareness of the short form as structurally defined and in some ways essentialist, but nonetheless it is sometimes difficult to reconcile her vivid, abundant prose with the characteristic sparseness of the traditional fairy-tale narrative. Her writing is almost anti–fairy tale in texture, yet her tales paradoxically retain their fairy-tale identity despite linguistic profusion and its associated invocation of other genres, perhaps because her sense of structure, while critical, is so strong. The mutability and possibility of fairy tale in Carter's hands also relies heavily on the notion of fairy tale as originally an oral voice—the self-consciousness of the act of tale-telling as craft highlights the possibilities inherent in the notion of *re*-telling. More importantly, this play with voice necessarily invokes ideological investigation; as Mary Kaiser has noted, the notion of oral retelling emphasizes the importance of specifically cultural intertext as "the politics, economics, fashions, and prejudices of a sophisticated culture [replace] the values of rural culture that form the context of oral folklore" (30).

Carter's interest in structure is always employed in the service of feminism. Her exploration of female sexuality, and of the position of women in the structures of classic fairy tale and other genres, particularly pornography, has made her work happy hunting grounds for legions of feminists with attitudes varying from adoration to outrage. To engage with Carter on almost any level is effectively to engage with her feminist critics. Many of the more vocal of these, particularly those rooted in the radical feminism of the 1970s and exemplified by antiporn and anti-fairy-tale critics such as Andrea Dworkin, take issue with Carter's unabashed exploration of heterosexual sexuality within the structures of patriarchy. In particular, critics such as Robert Clark and Patricia Duncker have to some extent misread her subversive interest in structural predestination and underestimate those aspects of her writing that are parodic, deliberately excessive, and gleefully disruptive. Carter is at her most extreme in *The Sadeian Woman,* her polemical work written in the same year as *The Bloody Chamber,* and which operates as a powerful intertext to her fairy-tale revisions. *Sadeian Woman* explores the difficult ground of pornography and attempts to theorize it in the service of women, a project which offers, in its discussion of the rigid structural and symbolic expectations of pornography, surprising parallels with fairy-tale heterosexual utopianism. Carter suggests structural similarities between the familiar tropes and patterns of the two genres in the sense that both offer a reductionist and symbolic expression of heterosexual interaction, in structural terms which present themselves as natural and inevitable. More recent criticism acknowledges the importance of the performative in her work, her concern with spectacle and theatricality which explores structure using strategies of parody and excess and which consequently meshes well with my interest in the self-conscious and metafictional.

In the light of this, the major difficulty in undertaking any analysis of Carter seems to be the impossibility of actually saying anything *new* about her. Intertextuality becomes inevitable, not only because of her own interest in genre and text but also because there is simply so much written about her. Stephen Benson's review essay on Carter criticism describes "the Carter effect" in postgraduate studies, where she is the subject of innumerable dissertations (Benson, "Literary *Märchen*" 30), and provides a thoughtful and comprehensive survey of critical responses to *The Bloody Chamber.* A similar, useful summary of key feminist debates is found in Robin Ann Sheets's "Pornography, Fairy Tales, and Feminism." The huge body of feminist Carter criticism covers a multiplicity of approaches, many of which deal with the importance of fairy-tale narrative in her writing. Fairy tale itself is the focus of Danielle Roemer and Cristina Bacchilega's recent *Angela Carter and the Fairy Tale,* originally a *Marvels and Tales* special edition, which neatly fills in any existing folkloric gap in the body of critical work. I shall attempt to find a space in which to examine Carter by focusing on the ways in which her explorations of fairy tale and feminism hinge on her use of self-aware narrative technique, not only her deliberate assaults on structure in general but more particularly her use of language, intertextuality, and the redeployment of symbol in innovative ways which resist compilation into the familiar systems and symbolic order of myth.

Part of this disruptive effect is a result of the concept most central to Carter's writing—certainly to her narrative rewritings—which is that of *play*. She insists on deconstructing structure without replacing it with any definitive structure of her own: as Anny Crunelle-Vanrigh comments, Carter "takes her reader along the paths of indeterminacy, revelling in a state of never-ending metamorphosis" (129). Elaine Jordan has also noted that in the collection "each project is tactical and specific within a general feminist and materialist strategy—you cannot lay a grid across her work and read off meanings from it, according to a law of the same" (122). This partially explains the contradictory insights of critics, but it also contributes to the metafictional quality of her writing, since the notion of structure, as constructed, crafted, recrafted, and essentially nonrealist, is effectively highlighted by her characteristically playful disruptions. The shifting and often mischievous nature of Carter's writing allows her to explore possibilities, declining to give a definitive text so that her works are always capable of multiple readings. Nicole Ward Jouve notes that "if the word [postmodernism] hadn't been around, someone would have had to invent it for Angela Carter" (149). *The Bloody Chamber* is a striking example of this, each tale in the collection offering a different possible response to the difficulties of patriarchy encoded within fairy-tale structures. Carter explores various approaches to female sexual subjectivity through fairy-tale symbol and expectation, but the dissolution of structure, despite the urgency of the ideological project, is not replaced by any definitive answer. She comments that in *Bloody Chamber* "it turned out to be easier to deal with the shifting structure of reality and sexuality by using sets of shifting structures derived from orally transmitted traditional tales" ("Notes" 71). It is not difficult to see why the feminist movement, collectively possessed of the conviction of its own seriousness and a need for a definitive political stance, has difficulty with her open-ended writing. At the same time she is often a deliberately provocative writer; in her introduction to *Expletives Deleted,* a collection of her essays, she admits that there is "a strong irascibility factor in some of these pieces. A day without an argument is like an egg without salt" (4). However, there is more than a simple desire to be contrary in her fiction, which in its complex nonrealist vigor cannot be dismissed simply as combative. This playful lack of absolutes exemplifies precisely the aspect of postmodernism discussed by Linda Hutcheon, its necessarily contradictory expressions as it works *within* the systems it subverts (6). Carter's narratives become magical in intent as well as content: she deals not in the simple one-to-one transformations of allegory, but in the complex invocations of the master magician, simultaneously enacting, celebrating, and reworking the stuff of the imagination.

The Geometry of Gender: Carter and the Feminists

> What she saw found its way into all her fictions, imaginatively deflected into structural metaphors that often baffled her critics. . . . She was . . . a true witness of her times . . . —Robert Coover, "Passionate Remembrance" 10

Carter mines the structures of classic fairy tale with the specific purpose of exploring their implications for female subjectivity and sexuality, but critical debates are somewhat more complicated than this might suggest. Feminist analysis of *The Bloody Chamber* tends toward an inevitable contextualization of Carter's erotic fairy-tale rewrites within the debates on pornography invoked by *The Sadeian Woman,* and thus within major issues in the feminist thought of the time. In the huge bulk of feminist responses to Carter's writing it is possible to discern a historical development which separates itself into two main strands. Earlier feminist responses, mostly in the 1980s, rely on the radical feminisms of the 1970s, in particular the fairy-tale rereadings of Andrea Dworkin and Gilbert and Gubar, and the intersections of feminist literary criticism with the pitfalls and possibilities of pornography. Writers such as Patricia Duncker, Robert Clark, Susanne Kappeler, and Avis Lewallen take issue with Carter's provocative treatment of female sexuality and argue that the reactionary power of either fairy tale or pornography is sufficient to warp and flaw any real attempt at establishing female subjectivity or empowerment within its structures. Later critics such as Elaine Jordan, Robert Rawdon Wilson, Mary Kaiser, and Robin Ann Sheets, however, gradually deconstruct the feminist critiques with their stronger sense of Carter's essentially postmodern techniques, and their recognition of the functioning of her ideological explorations firmly within the strategies of structural play. Most recently, critics develop this awareness of her deconstructive qualities to include the work of Judith Butler on the performativity of gender; among them, Gregory J. Rubinson, Sarah M. Henstra, Cristina Bacchilega, and Joanne Trevenna offer readings of Carter which rely to some extent on the recognition of gender as artifice, as do several of the contributors to the volume edited by Joseph Bristow and Trev Lynn Broughton. This latter critical tendency is particularly interesting for my purposes, representing as it does a kind of metafictional awareness of ideology as well as of text, and a useful tool for unwrapping Carter's self-conscious play with the structures of literature and culture. Unlike earlier accounts, it also creates a space for an awareness of the complex multivalence of Carter's explorations.

The structural power of fairy tale, in the sense which parallels the uncritical awareness of universalized form characteristic of structuralist theory, is very much at the heart of early feminist criticisms of Carter. This kind of feminist attitude is summarized pithily by Patricia Duncker, perhaps one of the most influential of Carter's detractors: "The infernal trap inherent in the fairy tale, which fits the form to its purpose, to be the carrier of ideology, proves too complex and pervasive to avoid. Carter is rewriting the tales within the straitjacket of their original structures" (6). Duncker quotes Dworkin extensively in support of a definition of fairy tale solely in terms of its reactionary heterosexual utopianism: active men and passive women, with marriage as the ultimate goal. She represents a school of feminist criticism which argues that it is effectively *impossible* to rewrite fairy tale from a feminist viewpoint; that its structures, not only its themes and motifs, are inherently patriarchal and will prevail regardless of the author's intentions. In this, of course, they are effectively seduced into believing fairy tale's construction of itself in structuralist terms, a magical artifact universalized and free of ideological struggle, the "trick" noted by Bacchilega as integral to its function (7). A similar point is made by Lucie Armitt, whose analysis of structural framing in *The Bloody Chamber* notes that "by firmly situating these texts within a predetermined formulaic inheritance it is actually Duncker, rather than Carter, who is ensnared" (89). Robert Clark's attack is particularly ironic in this context: he argues for the need to ". . . break the structuralist silence on the question of social origin and mediation. . . . Carter, however, works within a more a-historical and structuralist understanding of myth . . . in assuming an ideology that is so universally powerful she also seems to anticipate her writing's subjection to it" (156). This is an extremely surface and rather insensitive reading of Carter, one that succumbs to fairy tale's structuralist illusion in a way Carter herself does not. Clark thus altogether misses her fiercely critical approach to structure, her invocation of system only in order to break it down, as well as the rootedness of her writing in a powerful awareness of historicity and its implication in structures of meaning.

This sense of fairy tale as universalized and essentialist seems particularly oversimplified when one considers that fairy tale, however smoothly it presents a unified surface, has always been the site of gender struggle. Jack Zipes has commented on the origins of Perrault's tales in "the conversation and games developed by highly educated aristocratic women in the salons . . . Their goal was to gain more independence for women of their class and to be treated more seriously as intellectuals" (*Beauties, Beasts* 2). This parallels the kind of "old wives" origin noted by critics such as Maria Tatar, Marina Warner, and Elizabeth Wanning Harries, the notion of tale-telling as originally the business of women, moving into the patriarchal realm only with Perrault's successful domination of the written versions in the late seventeenth century. Roemer and Bacchilega note that "by the mid-1800s the French women's work had been overlooked in the developing fairy-tale canon in favour of the more acceptable male author Charles Perrault" (11). Certainly the French fairy tale pioneers the figure of the Fairy Godmother, the powerful, knowing female figure who stands completely apart from the expectations of normal patriarchal society. Most importantly, the fairy tale had offered a disguised but powerful medium for women "to critique social conditions of the day, particularly the social institution of forced marriage and the general lot of women in a predominantly male-controlled world" (Roemer and Bacchilega 11). Benson points out the impossibility of claiming fairy tale as a truly or unambiguously female narrative ("Literary *Märchen*" 47) but also acknowledges Carter's awareness of this problem; in her introduction to *The Virago Book of Fairy Tales* Carter speaks of her wish to demonstrate, through her selection of folktales, "the richness and diversity with which femininity . . . is represented in 'unofficial' culture: its strategies, its plots, its hard work" (xiv). The patriarchalized versions we take for granted today are thus less stable and absolute than Duncker and her ilk would have us believe, and offer a historical rebuke to those feminist writers who deny the possibility of feminist critique within the margins and interstices of fairy tale—who are thus, in purely structural terms, complicit with fairy-tale's ideological illusions.

Carter's versions of fairy tale set out to explode precisely this unthinking structuralist determinism; in both *The Bloody Chamber* and *Sadeian Woman* she is absolutely aware, often critically, of the more radical schools of feminist thought as an intertext. Given the shifting significances of the *Bloody Chamber* narratives, it is interesting to note that Carter is perfectly capable of a more straightforward, less multivalent feminist investigation of the traditional fairy-tale narrative. Her three-part tale "Ashputtle *or* The Mother's Ghost" (*American Ghosts and Old World Wonders, in Burning Your Boats*) offers a fairly unambiguous feminist document which, very much in the Dworkin mode, deconstructs the complicity of women themselves in the processes of patriarchy via a self-conscious rewrite of the Grimms' "Cinderella." In its three versions of the story, "Ashputtle" investigates the competition between women for male attention, "the drama between two female families in opposition to one another because of their rivalry over men" (390). The tale's discursive, analytic narrative voice offers precisely what *The Bloody Chamber* refuses to provide: an explicit and authoritative feminist interpretation of the traditional tale. This is metafiction in yet another guise, tale as political artifact self-consciously explored. Carter seems to abandon the richer possibilities of *The Bloody Chamber*'s complex symbols in this tale, offering instead the kind of radical feminist rewrite which echoes the anti-fairy-tale rhetoric of Dworkin—"fairy tale mothers . . . [have] one real function . . . characterised by overwhelming malice, devouring greed, uncontainable avarice" (41). It is tempting to see the change in style between *The Bloody Chamber* and "Ashputtle" not only as a reflection of a more mature, less exuberant or radical writer fifteen years later, but as a response to the kind of acrimonious critical attack the earlier work engendered.

While "Ashputtle" seems to explore feminist intertext with a less judgmental eye, in *The Bloody Chamber* an intertextual and critical awareness of feminist debates is integral to some of her retellings. The opening tale, "The Bloody Chamber," is the best example of Carter's ironic invocation of stereotypical feminist expectation, both in the tale's symbolic punishment of the protagonist's desire with a literal brand of shame, and in its denouement. The bride's "eagle-featured, indomitable mother," riding to the rescue wielding her revolver (7), is a feminist cliché, the strong woman appropriating phallic power; she is contrasted with the castrated and powerless male figure of the blind piano tuner, who playfully invokes the feminist issues around the male gaze. (Jordan's analysis of this story [121–22] offers a particularly cogent debunking of too straight a reading of this feminist cliché.) The complete discomfiture of the Count—"the puppet master, open-mouthed, wide-eyed, impotent at the last" (39)—is another parody of vindictive feminist revenge. Invoked as a flawed and inadequate intertext, this kind of feminist inversion achieves very little in terms of Carter's interests, since it rescues the heroine without touching her subjectivity or agency. Like the original "Bluebeard," the tale continues to offer the phallic rescue ("a single, irreproachable bullet" [40]) of the passive heroine, who makes only the faintest attempts to develop beyond that passivity. Duncker's approval of this story (11–12) thus seems a little insensitive, since she entirely misses the ironic tone. She reflects with satisfaction that "the hand of vengeance against Bluebeard is the woman's hand, the mother's hand bearing the father's weapon. Only the women have suffered, only the women can be avenged" (12). In direct rebuttal of this, Jouve, analyzing the dislike of mother figures in Carter's work, concludes that "no other writer I can think of has so repeatedly and passionately jousted against what feminists call 'biological essentialism'" (156); perhaps the best example of this is the ironic, parodic versions of motherhood Carter unleashes in *The Passion of New Eve*.

In fact, essentialism perhaps functions as the central target for Carter's attack; she spurns equally the notion of the predetermined selves offered by patriarchy and by feminism. A logical progression from this rejected notion of fixed identity is found in the element of the theatrical in so much of Carter's writing. Marina Warner's discussion in Lorna Sage's *Flesh and the Mirror* collection notes the prevalence of images of drag and the bottle blonde attached to Carter's heroines, who thus "produce themselves as 'women' . . . Carter's treatment of travesty moves from pleasure, in its dissembling wickedness and disruptiveness of convention, to exploring its function as a means of survival—and a specifically proletarian strategy of advancing, through the construction of self in image and language" ("Angela Carter" 248). For this reason the recent critical applications of Judith Butler's theories to Carter's work are more fruitful, not only because Carter's sense of gender is, indeed, performative but also because this notion of a constructed identity, reified through repetition, is mirrored in her sense of fairy-tale structure itself. Joanne Trevenna notes how the applicability of Butler's theories to Carter's writing has effectively *reclaimed* Carter as a feminist writer in that it has "provided a new feminist focus for reading Carter's fiction and has thereby reinforced her status as a major feminist literary icon" (268). Interestingly, the bulk of the performative-gender criticism—in the Bristow and Broughton volume alone, five of the articles deal with performativity to some extent—tends to be applied to Carter's novels, with comparatively few direct critiques of her fairy tales in these terms. Nonetheless, the analysis extends itself naturally to systems of genre as well as gender identity, as it does in Bacchilega's analysis. Trevenna points out the extent to which performative gender is "thoroughly naturalised as 'a construction that regularly conceals its genesis'" (quoting Butler, 269), a quality it shares with the fairy-tale 'trick' described by Bacchilega. In *The Bloody Chamber* the 'trick' of both gender and structure is recognized and examined by female characters who reflect on their artificially structured entrapment within the roles set out for them by fairy-tale traditions, and the limitations placed on their sexual identity by those roles and predetermined narrative outcomes. The often-experimental performance of roles embedded in fairy tale becomes a performance of structure, one which, through irony, exaggeration, and parody, insists on the artificiality of the system.

Bacchilega's discussion of Judith Butler in the context of fairy tale emphasizes the metafictional implications of performative repetition as a generic tool: "postmodern fairy tales reactivate the wonder tale's 'magic' or mythopoeic qualities by providing new readings of it, thereby generating unexploited or forgotten possibilities from its repetition . . ." (22). She also points out how unavoidably ideological this becomes, as the self-conscious process of investigation in postmodern fairy tales leads inevitably to "awareness of how the folktale . . . almost vindictively patterns our unconscious" (22). Metafiction and ideological reinvestigation become inevitably entwined: "repetition functions as reassurance within the tale, but this very same compulsion to repeat the tale explodes its coherence as well-made artifice" (23). Genre and gender thus become conflated in their presentation in metafictional terms—structures whose spurious authority is both enacted and undermined. Lucie Armitt's analysis extends this notion of self-consciousness to insist, along with Warner, on the importance of *excess* to this reiteration of artifice, since the boundaries of the artificial are effectively highlighted only when they are interrogated and transgressed, creating "the precarious relationship between narrative overspill and narrative containment" which characterizes the collection (91). Playful exaggeration creates parodic fairy-tale moments such as Bluebeard as Sadeian pornographer or Beauty wagered by her father at cards, but perhaps the most powerful symbolic exploration of this in the tales is in "The Tiger's Bride," which returns continually to images of constructed identity. "Tiger's Bride" is something of a paean to excess, flaunting the condition of its own nonrealist textuality in flamboyant images of the marvelous—a mirror which has "magic fits" (61), tears which become jewels, a maid who is a clockwork doll, a valet who is a monkey, a sable fur that is a pack of rats. The tale trembles on the brink of a dozen fairy tale texts, invoking and then abandoning each to give a sense of intense but fractured significance to each moment, and to underline the artifice of narrative and identity. This includes both masculine and feminine genderedness: the Beast is performing his own role, "a carnival figure made of papier-mâché and crêpe hair" (53), his face an "artificial masterpiece" (58). He is counterpointed by the Hoffmanesque clockwork girl who attends the protagonist in a parody of mechanically performed identity.

Problematically for a Butlerian reading, however, against this notion of construction is placed an ideal of identity apart from culture and construction, expressed in the "Tiger's Bride" narrative as the nakedness of both girl and beast. This illustrates the point made by Joanne Trevenna, who points out that Carter's view of identity construction is not entirely similar to Butler's: "While Butler claims that gender is thoroughly naturalised and therefore ultimately unlike the process of an actor taking a role, Carter theatrically presents the process of gender acquisition as being like that of an actor playing a role and thereby suggests a subject position prior to gender acquisition and maintains a sex/gender division which is also rejected by Butler" (269).

Trevenna's argument suggests that Carter's sense of gender construction relies more on the theories of earlier feminists such as Simone de Beauvoir; perhaps as a result of her interest in heterosexuality and its ultimately biological imperatives, Carter assumes a basic sexual identity upon which the strata of performative identities are constructed. A similar essentialism is found in "Wolf-Alice," in the child's development of identity through the physical imperatives of menstruation. Despite Trevenna's suggestions, however, the ultimate fate of the heroine of "The Tiger's Bride" suggests that Carter's dislike of essentialism is as strong as ever; while the girl's naked body serves as an icon of stripped-away acculturation, it is deconstructed by the tiger's tongue. The newly exposed "beautiful fur," the "nascent patina of shining hairs" (67) is apparently revealed beneath the objectified father's daughter, but in fact it is a hard-won identity the girl has created through her interaction with the tiger, as much a construct as any other self she displays in the story. In keeping with Butler's theories, Carter offers bodily, sexual identity as simply one more of the constructions of self. This postmodern sense of embodiment is in keeping with the tendency in Carter's writing for "nature" and the "natural" never to be a simple or idealized alternative to the problematical but fascinating layering of culture. "The Erl-King" is particularly interesting in this context precisely because of its rhapsodical evocation of natural beauty, an impulse at odds with Carter's more characteristic interest in the artifacts of culture. The tale makes powerful points about the way in which the real or natural, here the forest as a direct parallel to the trope of nakedness in "Tiger's Bride," *becomes* a construct under culture. Nicole Ward Jouve has commented on Carter's firm rootedness within the acculturated community rather than any idealized natural space—"Carter is city through and through. No time for twilights, identifying birds or plants by name . . ." (146). In the context of Carter's overall concerns in The Bloody Chamber, the linguistic and descriptive excesses of the autumnal landscape in "Erl-King" are thus immediately suspicious; like the naked body of the tiger's bride, their apparent naturalism is deceptive.

DESIRE AND LOATHING: SEXUALITY IN FAIRY TALE

The notion of ideological structure in fairy tale is interestingly paralleled by Carter's theoretical discussion of Sade and sexuality in *The Sadeian Woman*. She finds structural parallels between pornography and fairy tale in that pornography, like fairy tale, "involves an abstraction of human intercourse in which the self is reduced to its formal elements" (4). In many ways her claim of kinship with Sade relies on his identity as *structural* writer, one who lays bare the cultural systems of his own time. Rubinson comments that Carter most values in Sade "his uncompromising irreverence towards so many of the institutions, virtues, ideals, and taboos of a theistic, androcentric world" (719). Tellingly, Carter insists that pornography relies on "the process of false universalising. Its excesses belong to the timeless, locationless area outside history, outside geography, where fascist art is born" (12). This is exactly the apparently ahistorical and universalizing space in which fairy tale operates, and the identification of this as a potentially fascist process is essential in understanding Carter's reworking of the "consolatory myths" provided by mythic versions of women in fairy tale (*Sadeian Woman* 5–6). Both fairy tale and pornography represent methods of communication in which meaning inheres entirely in the structural relationship of symbols. In fairy tale this is a wide variety of motifs and patterns, while in pornography, symbolism reduces to "the probe and the fringed hole . . . a universal pictorial language of lust" (4). Thus Carter's investigation of sexuality in *The Bloody Chamber* shares a basic metafictional awareness with her investigation of fairy tale itself—both are structures whose form and meaning are related to reality, but do not mirror it directly. Like fairy tale, pornography offers a set of symbols whose crafted arrangement must be decoded and consciously linked to reality, particularly since both forms present themselves as universalized truths.

At the same time, Carter's exploration of pornography makes the vital point that structure is a vehicle of false universalizing; the reductionism of symbol in both fairy tale and pornography conceals the essential fact that such symbols are absolutely the product of the social relations of their place and time. This is a view of fairy-tale origins most powerfully represented by Jack Zipes, whose influence on Carter's writing is acknowledged by Warner ("Angela Carter" 245–46). Zipes argues strongly for any fairy tale as "variable depending on the natural condition or social situation which was its reference" (*Art of*

Subversion 7). Thus, while the structure of a fairy tale tends to reflect historical sexism, it also holds out the promise of adaptation to reflect its retelling under a different historical scenario, a retelling not defined by patriarchy. Zipes later reinforces this by distinguishing between the "duplication" and the "revision" of a fairy tale; duplication reproduces the inherent ideologies in a tale, whereas revision "incorporates the critical and creative thinking of the producer and corresponds to changed demands and tastes of audiences" (*Fairy Tale as Myth* 9). This is exactly what Carter argues for pornography, in positing the existence of a "moral pornographer" who "might use pornography as a critique of current relations between the sexes" (*Sadeian Woman* 19), rather than providing an absolute and unthinking reflection of those relations. Thus the disapproving feminist response to Carter's tales is problematical in that it confuses critique with replication, and responds in alarmist terms to the presentation of heterosexual desire without giving sufficient credit to the self-conscious exploration present in that representation.

In both pornography and classic fairy tale the abstracted symbols which make up the system are skewed toward active male/ passive female dichotomies, in a way which leaves very little space for the expression of a specifically female subjectivity or desire; it is this problem which Carter most urgently addresses. One could read her technique here as a re-energizing of fairy tale with its more primitive, oral roots, restoring the heady dangers of sex, rape, and bestiality which were eradicated from the tales in the nineteenth century, and thus rendering explicit its conflicts. The classically passive female of the familiar Western fairy tale is reactivated to find a far more active role in the tales' inevitable heterosexual union. "The Courtship of Mr. Lyon" is an important document in this process, its tones of white and pastel effectively dramatizing the flavorless, colorless upshot of the eradication of desire. Carter explicitly rejects contemporary feminist views which suggest that heterosexual desire is somehow shameful. Instead, with particular power in tales such as "The Bloody Chamber" and "The Erl-King," the rich language of Carter's retellings pulls the reader into the perverse desire of the protagonist—the female reader, in particular, must acknowledge her own complicity as much as the protagonist's in the uncritical utopianism of both fairy tale and the erotic. Carter acknowledges the powerful symbolism of the "happy ever after" as an image of sexual reciprocity, flawed by the social circumstances of patriarchy, but nonetheless a compelling ideal. Marina Warner confirms the presence and importance of this utopian impulse in Carter's "quest for eros" in the fairy-tale form, specifically its concern with "beastly metamorphoses . . . improbable encounters, magical rediscoveries and happy endings" (*Beast to Blonde* 243). Carter refuses any simplistic rejection of female desire even in the context of patriarchal structures, but seeks instead to explore it, and to find its equal, balanced expression together with male desire; she thus re-energizes the happy ending of fairy-tale cliché with its ideological implications.

In the determined contextualization to which she subjects essentialist abstractions of sexuality, Carter's awareness of the economic aspects of culture is particularly strong. In *Sadeian Woman* she comments that "no bed . . . is free from the de-universalising facts of real life . . . we still drag there with us the cultural impedimenta of our social class, our parents' lives, our bank balances" (9). These are realities over which the abstracted idealism of fairy tale tends to gloss, eliding the social and economic dependencies suggested by the prince's classic acquisition of a lower-class bride. Early in *The Bloody Chamber* Carter works hard to detach sexual desire from its overshadowing economic trappings: "Bloody Chamber," "Mr. Lyon," "Tiger's Bride," and "Puss-in-Boots" are rooted in the sharp contrasts between poverty and wealth, and the entrapment of the female protagonist within those structures. This necessarily invokes Carter's polemic in *The Sadeian Woman*—"relationships between the sexes are determined by history and by the historical fact of the economic dependence of women upon men" (6–7). One is struck by the extent to which the early tales in this collection move in an arc which represents the self-conscious and highly dramatized struggle of their protagonists to free themselves from the seductions of wealth, quite as much as the seductions of sexual desire. The language, in its vivid awareness of luxury, mires the reader in a process which perfectly parallels the extent to which the development of female sexuality is entangled in economic necessity and unequal economic power. "Tiger's Bride" delivers its message neatly encapsulated in the punchy opening sentence: "My father lost me to The Beast at cards" (51); "Puss-in-Boots" uses comic opera structures to reinforce the economic underpinnings to fairy-tale marriage, with the girl's self-serving sexual desire mirrored exactly in her desire for her husband's wealth. This makes explicit the extent to which economic structures are, of course, central to Perrault's original story, which opens with the division of "worldly goods" (Zipes, *Beauties, Beasts* 21) and ends with a moral emphasizing "prosperity" (24).

In Carter's world, these complex interactions of sexuality and society are too pervasive and powerful to be easily solved, and her use of playful repetition effectively offers different alternatives to the structural problems of heterosexual desire; several of those alternatives are flawed and incomplete. While different responses to female sexual subjectivity are explored, sequence is integral to meaning across the tales in *The Bloody Chamber;* the responses represent a development or progression in the exploration of the theme. Within this trajectory, some natural groupings occur, linked more to Carter's political ends than to the rather hodgepodge occurrence of specific fairy-tale originals. "The Bloody Chamber" stands alone as a response to certain kinds of feminism, but the following two "Beauty and the Beast" variants are a natural pair, using beast-symbol to explore women's sexuality at the two extremes of repressed purity and regressive physicality. "Puss in Boots" continues that theme of animalistic sexuality in a more acculturated setting. The next three tales, "Erl-King," "Snow-Child," and "Lady of the House of Love" all seem to me to offer variations on the theme of the devouring female, and explore the unavoidable entrapments of patriarchal versions of the powerful woman. The three final tales are alike both in their wolf themes and in their representation of a more active and developed female subjectivity. This view of the text as sequence echoes critics such as Jordan who emphasize the importance of development across the tales; at the same time, their development of female subjectivity is echoed by similar sequential unwrapping on the level of text and genre.

LEGENDARY HABITATIONS: GENRE AND INTERTEXT

Unlike many other contemporary fairy-tale revisionists, in *The Bloody Chamber* Carter is responding largely to the specific fairy-tale versions of Charles Perrault, whose works she had translated in 1977, two years before publishing *The Bloody Chamber*. The identity of Perrault as a French, male writer of fairy tale perhaps dictates some of the choices she makes in terms not only of the elements within the tales she investigates but also in the other generic intertexts she employs to juxtapose to such structures. Although tales such as the "Beauty and the Beast" variants and "Erl-King" have slightly different antecedents (respectively, female eighteenth-century writers, and the Brothers Grimm), it is Perrault's distinctive storytelling voice to which these versions largely react. This voice is both interrogated and highlighted by Carter's proliferating intertextualities, re-energizing both the classic fairy-tale forms and Perrault's particular versions of them, by complex cross-pollination with other literary traditions. At different points *The Bloody Chamber*'s tales invoke Gothic, women's romance, Sade, erotica, opera, comedy, and a deliberately oral, folkloric voice. Most interestingly, these genres all reflect in powerful terms Perrault's status as a male writer producing a particularly patriarchal mythology of women's identity and destiny. Thus the somewhat misogynist views in Perrault's versions of classic tales find reflection and exaggeration in the powerless and rigidly defined women of love stories (passive partner or object of rescue), Gothic (demonic feminine or victim), pornography (objectified body), or Romantic icon (unrealistic object of the strictly male poet); gender is thus inextricable from genre, and both are exposed as falsely universalized structures. This allows *The Bloody Chamber* to function with what Benson has identified as "a deliberately excessive strategy that serves both to heighten the implicit constructedness of the fairy tale as a literary genre and to draw attention to the particularity of each retelling as requiring inspection on its own terms" ("Literary *Märchen*" 45); as Carter's feminist detractors have discovered, there are no easy answers here.

The specific Perrault intertext aside, Carter's interest in fairy-tale *narrative,* particularly, has a great deal to do with the nature of language itself. I have discussed earlier the tendency of fairy-tale narrative to exhibit a characteristic textual sparseness, where detail is minimal and there is no attempt to build atmosphere. Carter's strength as a fairy-tale writer is her ability to disrupt this without compromising the essentially fairy-tale nature of her tales. This is a powerful metafictional strategy: the reader's attention is perpetually drawn to the nature of writing as artifact because of the elaboration and excesses of the writing style. The tales highlight their own constructedness through their refusal to elide the writing in any realist illusion. Carter thus achieves a back-door route to the inherent metafictionality signaled by fairy tale's "Once upon a time," dexterously juggling the difficult tensions between metafictional excess of style and the necessary timelessness and lack of detail fairy tale requires. Such stylistic elements, so alien to Perrault and fairy tale generally, are achieved by borrowing largely from the structural intertexts of the other genres with which Carter chooses to explore and energize her fairy-tale forms; thus, the decadent, high-society descriptive detail of "Bloody Chamber," or the deliberately overstated Gothic atmosphere of "Lady of the House of Love"—all shadows and destiny.

The invocation of other genres and literary styles is by no means random. Sequence is integral to Carter's development of female subjectivity across the collection, but I also find that the development of the female protagonist across the tales inversely parallels the gradual weakening of intertextual—and particularly *literary*—reference throughout the collection, highlighting Carter's ideological interest in the spurious structures of culture and providing a particular kind of metafictional awareness in each tale's relationship with the whole. "The Bloody Chamber" offers specifically literary intertexts in the identity of Bluebeard, linked by his title and his book collection to the Marquis de Sade and sadistic pornography, but the heavily erotic and romance structures of the earlier tales have given way by the end of the collection to far broader cultural intertexts: Freud and Sade in "The Snow Child," Lacan and folkloric beast-child narratives in "Wolf-Alice." This is not an absolute progression; indeed, "Lady of the House of Love" provides a powerful resurgence of intertext after the sparseness of "Snow Child"; however, the difference between the multiple literary genres invoked by "Bloody Chamber" and the cultural intertexts of the last three stories is marked. In addition, invocations of later intertexts are also more delicate, tending toward the symbolic rather than the linguistic—the Countess's boots, the rose, the mirror, are the points of intertext which sustain the tale, rather than any aggressively stylistic qualities. The process across the collection points to the inadequacy of literary artifice, the imposition of culture as false construction; the interactions between fairy tale and other literary genres are used to expose the failure of such genres. Carter's choice of generic intertext in the first part of the collection is logical, tending toward the structured and ritualistic: women's romance and the erotic ("The Bloody Chamber," "The Courtship of Mr. Lyon," "The Tiger's Bride"), comic opera ("Puss-in-Boots"), Romantic poetry ("The Erl-King"), Gothic horror ("The Lady of the House of Love"). Such genres are highly structured, working within rigid conventions, but they are also signaled by particularly excessive linguistic qualities with which Carter plays. Such linguistic excess effectively highlights fairy-tale sparseness; toward the middle of the collection, "The Snow Child" underlines this process by virtue of its comparative simplicity, throwing into sharp relief the excesses of Romantic nature which precedes it and the heavy Gothic detail which follows.

The first tale, "The Bloody Chamber," offers a particularly strong set of generic markers, a somewhat excessive mix of women's romance and the erotic, the standard wedding-night peepshow, focusing on the virgin bride. The poor and virgin bride marrying into wealth and nobility is a motif familiar not only from fairy tale but also from its derivatives: the Barbara Cartland romance, the Gothic plot, or the society comedy of Colette, a specific intertext Carter acknowledged, and one which offers "the heightened diction of the novelette, to half-seduce the reader into this wicked, glamorous, fatal world" (Jordan, "Dangerous Edge" 197). The linguistic coding—"delicious ecstasy of excitement," "great pistons ceaselessly thrusting," the nightdress that "teasingly caressed me . . . nudging between my thighs" (*Bloody Chamber* 7–8)—signals the titillation of the straightforwardly erotic. Fairy-tale motifs are recognizable throughout the story, but are likewise over-dramatized: the castle is from the first the "sea-girt, pinnacled domain" of fairy tale, "that magic place, the fairy castle whose walls were made of foam, that legendary habitation . . ." (8). A parallel process occurs in the somewhat pastel second tale, "The Courtship of Mr. Lyon," whose literary intertext is similarly that of romance, but one more Victorian, polite, restrained: the genteel drawing-room marriage plot. The French fairy tale's social context is a strong metafictional undercurrent to this tale, its embroidery-and-pretty-gowns terminology subtly exaggerated to underline their essential inauthenticity as substitutes for female desire. Similarly, "Puss-in-Boots" invokes the operatic only to brandish its artifice ("once you know how, Rococo's no problem" [69]), playing with the comic artificialities of operetta and theatrical bedroom farce, the situation comedy of the cuckolded older man. The cat's name, Figaro, most obviously underlines the operatic and sexual subtext. The tale plays entertainingly with the trickster archetype, recasting the original fairy tale's social climbing as equally opportunistic sexual philandering.

The interactions between generic structures in these tales are endlessly fascinating and complex. Details and tone shift continually, jolting or drifting the reader from one literary awareness to another, as fairy tale and other genres jostle for position. It is a testament to the power and familiarity of the fairy-tale form that, despite the considerable distractions of language, these tales retain their fairy-tale identity; as Vladimir Propp has commented, the fairy tale resists other genres, they shatter against it ("Fairy Tale Transformations" 107). Of course, the drift between structures is cannily used by Carter to underline her ideological lessons, most frequently in terms of the shifting identities of the female protagonists. "The Bloody Chamber" is perhaps the most interesting example here, as erotic seduction of the virgin bride slowly becomes, more and more sinisterly, the immolation of the victim of pornographic sadomasochism, and the inevitable death of Bluebeard's wife. Blinded by her own desire, her participation in the seduction of luxury and sexual initiation, the bride fails to realize the fairy-tale plot until it has closed around her like a trap. Bacchilega's analysis of this tale notes the same effect: "The narrator's sensual style both uses and exposes seduction as a trap" (*Postmodern Fairy Tales* 121). It is not an avoidable trap: her fall in all three structures—the fairy tale, the erotic, the sadistic—is completely predetermined. In the pornographic narrative, the existence of innocence presupposes corruption in exactly the same way that the prohibitions of fairy tale presuppose transgression, or the identification of the victim as Bluebeard's wife presupposes her death. The tale's power is in the slippage between the structures; the reader cannot avoid awareness of the girl's entrapment when it is so insistently reiterated.

The complex intertextual functioning of "The Erl-King" entails a similar, if more formless shifting between tale structures on an ongoing basis, but here it finds its effect in indeterminacy rather than predestination. This heightens Carter's metafictional effect; the reader is forced to read the tale as a continual textual process, given the lack of any central structure by which it can be safely identified. Carter adopts the symbology of Goethe's original in conflating desire and sexuality with a fairy, otherworldly figure whose power is expressed through and inheres in the natural landscape; however, in "Erl-King" this nature-spirit figure is revealed to be a spurious and entrapping construct of Romantic (and hence patriarchal) culture. "The Erl-King" is, as Harriet Kramer Linkin has suggested, a sustained play with the Romantic investment in an idealized notion of nature. Romantic clichés of the individual's investment in the environment abound: "The two notes of the song of a bird rose on the still air, as if my girlish and delicious loneliness had been made into a sound" ("Erl-King" 85). Carter's invocation of Romantic tropes requires that we read the tale *as text* in particularly inescapable terms which rely on Romanticism's self-consciousness about its own poetic and cultural project. At the same time, the beauties of the forest are decaying rather than vital— "withered blackberries" like "dour spooks," "the russet slime of dead bracken," "a sickroom hush" (84). While the tale immerses itself in nature, nature is coded, through its reconstruction in literary terms, as a threat whose construction directly opposes the "natural beauty" so dear to the Romantics. Carter also invokes, but inverts the gender roles of, the Grimm tale "Jorinda and Joringel," in which the tale's denouement allows the rescue of the caged and transformed Jorinda by her lover, rather than permitting avoidance of the usual maiden's fate through the woman's own recognition and intervention. In yet another set of intertexts, the tale's notions of death ultimately rely on the motif of strangling hair. In the Romantic framework, as Linkin notes, this recalls the similar winter landscape and isolated cottage setting of Browning's "Porphyria's Lover," in which a male speaker strangles his female lover in order to keep her pure and eternally his (308). The inversion of the circumstances in Carter's version refigures the tale as a reworking of Samson and Delilah, in which hair stands for masculine power which is stolen or appropriated by a castrating female figure.

This self-conscious textuality is emphasized by Carter's flexible use of voice, which changes confusingly between first, second, and third person—"A young girl would go" . . . "It is easy to lose yourself" . . . "I thought nobody was in the wood but me" (85). While mirroring the struggle for subjectivity, this grammatical drift allows the use of a second-person form which signals an almost proverbial universal, an enactment of inevitability through cultural repetition—"Erl-King will do you grievous harm" (85). However, the proverbial voice slides continually out from narrative certainty as it is replaced by the changing and uncertain voice of the protagonist. Even in her triumph at the end of the tale, we are unsure whether the denouement is planned, present, or past as tenses drift: "When I realised what the Erl-King meant to do to me ... Sometimes he lays his head on my lap ... She will carve off his great mane" (90–91). Linkin argues that this change in voice, the drift between description, anticipation, and retelling, functions as a re-enactment of the tale's various possibilities (316–17). This culminates in a version in which she entraps the Erl-King in her own net of language, a "pastiche of nineteenth century poetry and poetics ... In her struggle for control ... she turns him into an image of nature, encasing him in her language just as she believes he would have entrapped her" (317). Certainly the reader emerges from the end of the tale claustrophobic and stifled, shaking off language as the Erl-King shakes leaves from his hair.

A similar effect is seen in "Lady of the House of Love," where the female vampire likewise oscillates helplessly between herself as devouring feminine, and herself as Sleeping Beauty. Carter's use of language and motif to invoke specific textual patterns is striking, a self-conscious exercise in atmosphere and cliché. Interestingly, Carter uses exactly the same tense-shifts in "Lady of the House of Love," and to similar purposes; like "Erl-King," the tale enacts several possible structures through its drifting tenses before settling, slightly more obviously than does "Erl-King," on a single denouement. The tale's insistence on shadows, "a sense of unease" (93), the cat arching and spitting, marks the presence of the supernatural, but it is a supernatural of "disintegration," "Rot and fungus everywhere" (93). In contrast to the accepted textualities of romance in earlier tales, here structured textual detail deconstructs itself, the clichés revealed as spurious, artistic sham, disintegrating even as they are developed. The tale's metafictional element is thus particularly strong, approaching the self-awareness of Byatt in its depiction of narrative as both constructed and entrapping. The tale's language signals repetition—"sonorities," "reverberations," "echoes," "a system of repetitions," "destiny" (93–95). Interestingly, and in an inversion of the dominance of the Bluebeard tale in "Bloody Chamber," here the vampire narrative predominates over the fairy tale. The fairy-tale Sleeping Beauty structures are inherent mostly in the enchanted suspension of the Lady, underlined mostly by details such as the roses, and obvious only when the prince arrives and the Countess pricks her finger. The tale's narrator is particularly evident in the story, a dispassionate and knowing presence whose fairy-tale authority is somewhat under-mined by Carter's use of tense. As in several other tales in the col-lection, tense signals both narrative self-awareness and the breaking of structures, since the Countess's timeless present tense—ongoing, eternal, inescapable—is disrupted and moves into normal fairy-tale narrative past tense with the intrusion of the young British cyclist.

The cyclist functions as the pivot of the narrative, his rational-ism making obvious the problematic nature of both vampire and fairy-tale structures. Carter's relatively precise historical identifica-tion—"the pubescent years of the present century . . . a young officer in the British army" (97)—would normally serve to deconstruct the ahistoricity of more traditional fairy tale; in Carter's hands it tends to emphasize it by contrast. From the moment he enters the village, and despite his characterization both in heroic motif and active, mas-culine past tense, the cyclist's historical nature is subsumed into the unreal space of fairy tale and the Gothic. Carter's investment in this clash is, as usual, gleeful and perfectly self-conscious; she defines explicitly, with obvious enjoyment, the narrative discord where, "This being, rooted in change and time, is about to collide with the timeless Gothic eternity of the vampire" (97). Fairy-tale ahistoricity is thus perfectly emphasized in this tale, in its melodramatic exaggeration via the Gothic framework, and in its disruption by a hero whose mo-dernity is exaggerated to the point of being ridiculous. More power-fully, the fairy-tale potential for death inherent in the various narra-tives is continually held up against the grim reality of death in the trenches, problematizing the symbolic deaths of fairy tale's unreal space by comparison with history.

Anyone Will Tell You That: Folktale as Intertext

If Carter plays, as I suggest, with both the literary and the symbolic, it is in the folkloric that she finds, perhaps, her most important and ef-fective metafictional play. Benson has identified Carter's characteris-tic provision of a multiplicity of potential meaning as itself a folkloric strategy ("Literary *Märchen*" 45); his analysis points out the extent to which Carter's multiplicity of generic intertexts and her refusal to offer a definitive narrative moment are likewise folkloric in their recogni-tion of "narrative as an ongoing process" (46). The shifting authorial voice also represents, in Sage's view, a "nostalgia for anonymity, for the archaic powers of the narrator whose authority rests precisely on *disclaiming* individual authority" (2), and which thus has considerable ideological power to defuse the inherently patriarchal authority of the singular narrative voice.

The final three stories of *The Bloody Chamber,* sparser and infinitely less literary than preceding tales, are particularly strong sites for
play with the folkloric voice, and provide as much of a conclusion to
the project as Carter is ever going to give us. The primary intertext for
all three is "Little Red Riding Hood," probably Perrault's best-known
tale, and Carter energizes its girl/wolf motif to ruthlessly highlight
both Perrault's essential misogyny and his underlying eroticism.
Bacchilega has suggested that the tales represent Carter's "dialogue
with the folkloric traditions and social history of 'Red Riding Hood'"
(59); her version exposes the original by weaving it, not with literary intertexts, but with the folkloric traditions which provide stories
about wolves and werewolves. This oral voice and fragmented folkloric element is recognized and explored with particular power in Neil
Jordan's film *The Company of Wolves,* which combines elements from
all three stories. The comparative lack of intertexts, certainly in contrast to literary pastiches such as "Bloody Chamber" or "Erl-King,"
suggests that she has worked through different textualities and now
returns to a more basic, stripped-down version. Revisions here are
often disconcerting, probably because the voice tends toward that of
peasant folktale, which is altogether cruder and less polite than the literary posturings of the more familiar fairy tales. Details are far from
glamorous—severed paws, menstrual blood, and lice are a far cry
from the oppressive opulence of "Bloody Chamber" or even the vampire lady's fastidious animalism. Folktale weaves in and out of both
"The Werewolf" and "The Company of Wolves," in the voice of folk
wisdom and superstition, restrained, angry, and harsh: "Anyone will
tell you that" (108); "There was a hunter once, near here" (111); "They
say there's an ointment the Devil gives you" (113). The narratives are
densely packed with tale-vignettes, each contributing thematically to
the whole, but each told starkly. Carter's use of tense signals the presence of both a universal, proverbial present and the more familiar past
tense of ordinary storytelling, so that action is framed and contextualized by the proverbial, a process explored in more detail in Donald P.
Haase's discussion of the film *The Company of Wolves.* At the same
time, the language tends to recede from notice, rather than obtruding
itself; the point here is the tale-shape, not the style.

Significantly, it is women who are largely victimized by the embedded folk narratives. A witch is simply "some old woman whose cheeses
ripen when her neighbours' do not, another old woman whose black
cat, oh, sinister! *follows her about all the time*" (108). Marina Warner
has noted the association of fairy tale with old wives' tales, the power of
women as holders of narrative (*Beast to the Blonde* 16ff.), but here the
reverse is true—no one in particular seems to hold these narratives,

and powerful women are effectively demonized by their representations. Here, Granny-Werewolf as the demonic woman passes wisdom on to the next generation, but involuntarily; this is no comforting version of female solidarity, and the lessons of power carry within them their own destruction. The tale, focusing on the girl and her grandmother, displays a curious absence of men, but they are present in minor but telling detail—the girl is "armed with her father's hunting knife" (109), so that any power she has is phallic, on loan. Likewise, the narrative power by which she destroys her grandmother—she "cried out so loud the neighbours heard her and came rushing in," to recognize and stone the witch (109–10)—is that of patriarchal culture. The tale thus sets out to problematize folk narrative, like fairy tale itself, as a constructed, artificial thing that imposes an illegitimate shape on reality. However, its artificiality allows it to be both recognized and used; ironically, the narratives which forbid women power can be turned against themselves to allow their user to seize power despite the prohibitions. Thus the curiously self-possessed and rather worrying girl-child can calmly destroy the old woman and then take on her mantle—"the child lived in her grandmother's house; she prospered" (110). The suggestion is that the demonic, inherently female power is inherited through violence and usurpation, and ultimately through a rather cold-blooded appropriation and use of encoded and superstitious cultural narrative. Unlike the protagonist of "Erl-King" or the virgin bride of "Bloody Chamber," the child transcends her own identity as Red Riding Hood to stand outside narrative, using it for her own purposes. This is fairly terrifying stuff, but becomes even more so as the tale takes on a curiously circular resonance: the child may triumph, appropriating her grandmother's power, but in that act she also appropriates her grandmother's fate. Comparisons with Tanith Lee's "Wolfland" are inevitable here; the tale makes precisely the same equivalence between grandmother and wolf, although Lee's investigation of female power is infinitely less subtle. To an extent unavailable to Lee's more obvious narrative, Carter is simply exploring the limited power in the demonic female archetype; if embraced, it is indeed empowering, but because of the cultural narratives encoding that power, it will eventually be destroyed on the same terms on which it was created.

Apart from the folkloric invocations, the most powerful intertext to both "The Company of Wolves" and "Wolf-Alice" is probably modern psychology, a nod to the trend in psychological criticism of fairy tale, but here given Carter's own particular spin. "The Company of Wolves" is rife with psychological detail, an almost medical awareness of the girl's adolescent ripeness, and a sociological figuration of the symbolic power of the wolf. Structure and symbol become pointedly resonant, the tales providing a vehicle for exposition in a manner far more straightforward than the generic games of earlier stories, and one which nods to folkloric narrative as a vital, primitive encoding of subconscious processes. The process reaches its apotheosis in "Wolf-Alice," which takes psychological intertext to its logical conclusion, that of attacking instead of simply analyzing the tale. "Wolf-Alice" undermines and denies its own magical narrative; we are never permitted to be sure if the Duke's werewolf ghoulishness is an actual transformation, or mere insanity. Metaphorical and literal language become confused: "Nothing can hurt him since he ceased to cast an image in the mirror" (120); he leaves "paw-prints," but ignores garlic, the cross and holy water (121), but at the same time he wears a "fictive pelt" (125). The reader is left to thread the confusing maze in which the patterns of the marvelous, perfectly literal in earlier tales, are problematized by the presence of the metaphorical: animalism as social marginalization, mirrors as metaphors of identity, the ghoul as madman. Textuality is breaking down almost completely, leaving only fragmentary invocations of narratives which fail to provide any underlying structure to the tale. This is familiar territory for Carter; a characteristic refusal to engage in any reductionist process that denies the complexity either of heterosexuality under culture, or of fairy tale itself. Even the invocation of Lewis Carroll's *Alice through the Looking Glass*, which is suggested by the combination of the girl's name and the mirror motif, is not explored in any detail. Rather, it operates as a pointer toward the tale's interests, the maturation and empowerment of the female child through the symbol of the mirror, and through exploration of a culture which is presented as inverted and alienating.

Within the range of narratives across the collection, "Wolf-Alice" is the most realistic story, in that it is the least introvertedly intertextual; it also explores most profoundly the problem of the sexual alienation of man as well as woman in the culture of patriarchy. Wolf-Alice may originate outside the accepted bounds of culture, but even the Duke "came shrieking into the world with all his teeth, to bite his mother's nipple off and weep" (122). Acculturation means tragedy, the imposition of impossible structures of relationship for both men and women. Existing outside those structures, the Duke and Wolf-Alice are given the chance to discover their actual identities through interaction with each other. This is a functional reversal of the tendency of earlier tales, which is toward the abandonment of culture by those who have experienced and rejected its constructions of sexuality (most notably in "Tiger's Bride"). The games of language, symbol, and structure Carter plays in earlier tales are here seen at their most effective in that they do not overwhelm the essential rite of passage, the basic motif of folklore, with which the tale is concerned.

DEMONS, BEASTS, AND OTHERS: CARTER AND FAIRY-TALE SYMBOL

If, as Armitt suggests, Carter mounts an assault on "narrative containment" in fairy-tale forms in *The Bloody Chamber* (91), it is only a facet of her more comprehensive dislike of the constraining structures of myth in general, the essentialist structuralism of the symbolic. This receives its most direct and irascible expression in *The Sadeian Woman,* in which Carter comments that "All the mythic versions of women . . . are consolatory nonsenses; and consolatory nonsense seems to me a fair definition of myth, anyway. Mother goddesses are just as silly a notion as father gods" (5). Elsewhere she states, tellingly, her belief that "all myths are products of the human mind and reflect only aspects of material human practice. I'm in the demythologising business" ("Front Line" 71). This is metafiction on the grand scale, a self-conscious, profoundly iconoclastic, and, above all, ideological awareness of artifice. Brought to the familiar motifs and symbols of fairy tale, this gives Carter's rewrites an ironic, multivalent flavor; she offers tantalizingly apparent symbols which fail to compile as expected, resisting formulation into fairy tale's characteristically authoritarian structures. Nicole Ward Jouve's analysis of the mother figure in Carter points to precisely this kind of iconoclastic rejection of the popular Freudian and body-centered symbols of certain feminist discourses; she points out that in Carter "one word does not lead to another. One word can move without the other. Plot is continuously being invented. It does not proceed out of an internal necessity. Images do not grow out of their own momentum. Symbols (caves or colours) are not allowed to signify, except ironically . . ." (164). Symbols in *The Bloody Chamber* are powerful but shifting, refusing to be locked into the expected cultural categories, and, in their endless ramification, precluded from forming any sort of symbolic order.

Part of this assault on symbolic system is carried by Carter's somewhat offhand approach to the timelessness of fairy tale; the tales in *The Bloody Chamber* often rework and update the textual motifs of the classic tales to offer a postmodern jolt as the fairy-tale world is rendered into contemporary terms. Many of Carter's settings in the collection are far more modern than the timeless medieval of fairy tale, and the tales are laced with detail—railways, bicycles, telephones, opera, nineteenth-century erotica, a car breaking down—which appear to work directly against fairy-tale codes. Surprisingly, she pulls this off, maintaining the delicate balance where modern motifs are allowed to operate *as symbol*, evocative but separate from a rigid order, in a way which transcends their nature as realistic detail and does not materially attack the timelessness and traditional functioning of the tale. This conforms to what Leopold Schmidt, discussing the updating of symbol in modern oral retelling, has defined as "prop shift": the modernizing of a motif without disrupting its narrative function (in Lüthi 69). The modern details are treated as symbol, achieving a resonance which transcends their more mundane functionality. Thus the train in "Bloody Chamber" becomes an explicitly sexual evocation which echoes the undertones of sexuality in the classic girl/beast relationship; the telephone fulfills the function as messenger, taking the place of Sister Anne in summoning or heralding a rescue, or serving, through its failure, to entrap the bride completely in an essentially fairy-tale imprisonment. The effect of this is intrinsically metafictional, eliding the usual gap between reality and fairy tale, so that the mundane becomes marvelous and the marvelous, mundane. "Puss-in-Boots" is a good example of this kind of symbolic play: the cat Figaro emphasizes the marvelous, paradoxically, in glossing over it. His boots fit his master one moment and himself the next, and his cat-identity shifts continually into the human and back again—the old woman "doesn't see the doctor's apprentice is most colourfully and completely furred and whiskered" (82). This exposes and exaggerates the attitude of wondering acceptance classic fairy tale requires in its reader, and embodies the symbol of the cat as self-conscious construction, irreverently alert to its own symbolic function and the play between reality and the marvelous.

While *The Bloody Chamber* offers an ongoing investigation into the functioning of symbol, Carter's early tale "The Loves of Lady Purple" (in *Fireworks: Nine Profane Pieces*) provides an interesting context to the process since the tale explores the power of narrative symbol to confer identity, its framework refiguring as horror the notion of absolute and undisrupted symbolic correspondence. The legend of Lady Purple, nymphomaniac and devouring feminine, achieves in its ritualistic repetition the ability to bring to horrible, vampiric life the wooden doll who enacts the myth. *The Bloody Chamber* likewise investigates fairy tale as a set of symbols which confine and at the same time create both men and women through the systematically symbolic roles set out in the tales. In many tales Carter effectively appropriates the animal figures of fairy tale, displacing them from their accepted narrative roles to recreate them as alternative icons of sexuality. It might be easy to see some of Carter's symbolic revisions as simply inversionary: sleeping princess as vampire, grandmother as werewolf, girl-to-tiger rather than beast-to-prince. To do so, however, obscures the remarkable sophistication of her metafictional project; the symbolic inversions are profoundly intertextual, in that much of their meaning is created by their conscious relationship with Perrault's version in the mind of the reader, but the disruptions created are shifting, complex, and multivalent. Beasts of various kinds are probably Carter's most potent symbols, the space in which she can most powerfully explore the notion of sexuality as an animal urge quite apart from its constructions through culture. Fairy-tale animals encapsulate, even in their most classic forms, the beguiling combination of the animalistic and the civilized; they are at once powerful and urbane, figures of transgressive eroticism redeemed by the trappings of intellect (speech) and the excuse of magical transformation. It is no accident that magical beasts are the focus of the repeated tales in Carter's collection: two versions of "Beauty and the Beast" and three wolf-tales, in addition to the joyous appropriation of the philandering trickster feline in "Puss-in-Boots."

In a very deliberate inversion, however, the opening shot in Carter's campaign with sexualized beast-symbols, "The Courtship of Mr. Lyon," indicates the direction the collection will take by defining the negative, rather than the positive, of the theme: the animal here is very tame indeed. The "Beauty and the Beast" story can be seen, in its French versions, as a socializing tool which attempts to reconcile aristocratic women to the terrifying otherness of an unknown partner in a marriage of convenience. Certainly this subtext is at the forefront of Carter's awareness in this tale, even if the underlying sexuality of the beast motif is deliberately denied. Reconstruction of the tale's symbolism ensures that sexuality is eradicated so that archetypes are all domestic—daughter, nurse, Mrs. Lyon; even at her most willful the protagonist has only "the invincible prettiness that characterises certain pampered, exquisite, expensive cats" (49). At any point where animal sexuality is hinted at, Beauty resists and reclassifies it: the lion-figure seems to her haloed like "the great beast of the Apocalypse . . . with his paw upon the Gospel" (46). The classic threatening demand of the Beast—the sacrifice of a daughter in the father's place—becomes the banal injunction "bring her to dinner" (45). The Beast is tamed, not only by his smoking jacket but also by the innocence and beauty of the girl, in the classically patriarchal, very Victorian process that idealizes virginal girlhood as a sort of talisman against unbridled masculine lust. (Interestingly, this is exactly the process adopted by Disney in their animated *Beauty and the Beast,* which rather underlines Carter's point: safe, desexualized beasts and Daddy's girls are for children.) Whether Daddy's girl or the Beast's, Beauty is Miss Lamb, a virginal innocent, constructed entirely in terms of purity—"you would have thought she, too, was made all of snow . . . white and unmarked as a spilled bolt of bridal satin," her selected gift the white rose (41). Carter's return to the traditional third-person voice of fairy tale signals very clearly the lack of subjectivity of the protagonist, the inadequacy of this pale vision which is so trapped within the symbolic system of virtue, and which so dramatically de-fangs the erotic potential of the beast-symbol.

This tale offers a sharp contrast to "The Tiger's Bride," which restores and celebrates the physicality the previous tale denies. The tiger's physical presence is one of the most compelling in Carter's collection—"a great, feline, tawny shape whose pelt was barred with a savage geometry of bars the colour of burned wood. . . . How subtle the muscles, how profound the tread. . . . I felt my breast ripped apart as if I suffered a marvellous wound" (64). He is a figure of sexual—and masculine—power, against which the virginal girl is a "frail little article of human upholstery" (64). The symbolic beast here appropriates meaning, however, to reach a point where the tale's conclusion denies human culture in order to celebrate the power of the symbol. Only the bestial is real in this universe, necessitating the pact toward which the tale moves—"a peaceable kingdom in which his appetite need not be my extinction" (67). The moment of transformation, beautifully inverted, achieves equality by legitimating female desire rather than civilizing and denying male sexuality, and necessitates the complete loss of acculturation, and hence humanity—"his tongue ripped off . . . all the skins of a life in the world, and left behind a nascent patina of shining hairs. My earrings turned back to water and trickled down my shoulders" (67). The tale thus triumphantly denies the patriarchal solution (virginal self-sacrifice tames male sexuality) of the French original, *and* the denial of female heterosexual desire which has plagued the two preceding tales. In celebrating the animal, however, it robs of real-life force its potential solution to the problem of unequal power within culture articulated by the tale's original. Against the celebration of tiger-sexuality in "Tiger's Bride," "Puss-in-Boots" stands out as a deliberately irreverent and gleeful undercutting of bestial power; Carter here domesticates animal sexuality while still insisting on its irrepressible and hedonistic expression. The first-person oral voice nods wickedly to the urban characterization of the tomcat as a symbol of unbridled sexuality, but one which functions on a reduced and harmless level; this is Figaro's naughty all-male smoking-room story told to a complicitly prurient audience. Thus the classic figure of Puss-in-Boots, booted and bowing, a feather in his hat, represents Carter's lack of reverence for her own symbolic refigurations, her ability to delight in play; the artificialities of culture are here adopted cheerfully, rather than producing the angst of "Tiger's Bride." The tensions between animalism and culture are here comic rather than tragic.

The three concluding tales of the collection offer differing approaches to the same notion of animal sexuality as "Tiger's Bride" and "Mr. Lyon," although abandoning the feline for the lupine. "The Werewolf," "The Company of Wolves" and "Wolf-Alice" place the wolf symbol within a peasant agricultural context, harnessing the mystique of the beast as an icon of fear, power, and terrible attraction. "The Werewolf" is a disconcerting revision of the Red Riding Hood formula, its compressed narrative producing disorienting shifts in pattern and symbol; the conflation of grandmother and wolf is hardly more shocking than Red Riding Hood's self-serving pragmatism. "Company of Wolves" provides a more self-consciously Gothic and rather rhapsodic celebration of the wolf's power and control over its own world, seeming to offer a sense partially of envy for the wolf-symbol. That symbolic place in the world, self-contained, terrible, and desirable, is a chimeric and seductive possibility for women; its appeal is noted even while the absolutism of the parallel is denied. The wolves have beauty and power, their eyes "luminous, terrible sequins stitched suddenly on the black thickets" (110), but also sadness, their howl a "mourning for their own, irremediable appetites" (112). Wolves are trapped in folkloric narrative that defines them just as firmly as women, and, like women, they are feared and reviled for their potentially predatory power. At the same time, "Company of Wolves" explores the notions of fear and desire conflated within the figure of the wolf; being devoured becomes metaphor for sexual initiation, at once terrifying, annihilating, and attractive.

If wolves are a sexual symbol in these tales, this makes a strange equivalence between desire and predestination, a kind of punishment inherent in a sexuality exposed as being by nature both powerful and transgressive. The celebratory edge to Carter's description of the wolves seems to point toward some kind of desire for freedom from acculturation, but the tale refuses such simplistic readings by rendering Red Riding Hood's beast more complex, a werewolf rather than simply a beast. By characterizing the wolf-seducer as the highly cultured hunter, a "fine fellow" who is entirely the opposite of rustic (114), Carter offers culture as veneer, a seductive surface of city clothes which hide the beast beneath—"He strips off his trousers and she can see how hairy his legs are. His genitals, huge" (116)—a process which parallels the tiger's stripping of his bride in the earlier story, but without the misleading neatness of the utopian conclusion. Urbane or not, the hunter provides access to an untamed version of sexuality the tale's natural imagery—wolves, winter—ultimately celebrates. At the same time, however, his sophistication echoes that of Puss, paradoxically both the denial of desire and the potential for its fulfillment; the power of the magical beast is that animal lust is coupled with the ability to reflect upon it, encapsulating passion and intellect in one self-conscious symbol. It is easy to see why Carter chooses the werewolf rather than the wolf as the best vehicle for her symbolic exploration of the interactions between culture and desire.

"The Company of Wolves" revolves around the motif of being devoured as sexual initiation through the image of man as wolf, and offers a careful and sensual deconstruction of the erotic potential in the tale's traditional strip tease—"What shall I do with my blouse? Throw it on the fire, dear one. You won't need it again" (117). Unlike Jordan's film, the tale's closing image offers the almost biblical reconciliation of child and beast, rather than the perfect unity of transformation the film—and "The Tiger's Bride"—celebrate. The symbol has developed from "Tiger's Bride"; sexuality does not need perfect and unbridled expression, free from culture, but reconciliation within cultural confines. Likewise, the image is not of bestial sexuality tamed, as in "Mr. Lyon," but of a wild and natural sexuality which is embraced and understood. Self-conscious to the last, the tale's closure provides a kind of perfect structural stillness in which the conflicting demands of society, culture, body, and nature have been balanced and reconciled into a potent symbol which offers a poetic and celebratory calm.

> The blizzard will die down . . .
> Snowlight, moonlight, a confusion of paw-prints.
> All silent, all still.
> Midnight; and the clock strikes. It is Christmas Day, the were-wolves' birthday, the door of the solstice stands wide open; let them all sink through.
> See! sweet and sound she sleeps in granny's bed, between the paws of the tender wolf. (118)

Among their powerful invocations of symbol, Carter's tales necessarily explore and refigure the classic symbol of patriarchy, the devouring feminine, since its imposition is a natural consequence of the empowerment of women the collection pursues. These symbols dramatize Carter's statement, in *Sadeian Woman*, that "a free woman in an unfree society will be a monster" (27). The protagonist of "Erl-King," strangling the entrapper with her own hair, the dominatrix Countess of "Snow Child," and the vampiric sleeping beauty of "Lady of the House of Love" exemplify the symbolic restructuring of sexually powerful woman into monstrous feminine. This is a dramatization of the kind of response to fairy tale by radical critics such as Dworkin: "[women] know that not to be passive, innocent and helpless is to be actively evil" (35). Carter, however, while perfectly aware of the patriarchal textualizing of the powerful woman, employs various other intertexts to problematize and complicate the female symbols in these tales. The recurring use of the rose as symbol, realized effectively in Jordan's film version of "The Company of Wolves," becomes a more subtle emblem of this demonic feminine, vaginal, desirable, and thorned.

The title of "The Snow Child" is misleading, since the tale's most memorable figure is not the virginal snow-maiden, but the dominatrix Countess and her "high, black shining boots with scarlet heels and spurs" (91). Through this image the tale evokes, more explicitly than does any other in the collection, the structures and symbols of the Sadeian erotic. Like Carter's "Ashputtle," although with a more dreadful economy, the tale explores the notion of female sexual power through recognition and legitimization by the male. Kaiser notes that it also makes explicit the Freudian subtext of "Snow White," "reducing the tale to its skeletal outlines as a fable of incest" (33). However, as Duncker has commented, the Countess's boots "[reveal] the Mother as a sister to Sade's Juliette, the sexual terrorist" (7), and it is this mechanistic view of female sexuality, echoing Carter's exploration of it in *The Sadeian Woman*, which centrally informs the tale. Carter's view of Juliette is as "rationality personified . . . Her mind functions like a computer programmed to produce two results for herself: financial profit and libidinal gratification" (79). In "The Snow Child," sexual gratification, power as sexual adjunct, and economic power are entwined and explicitly encoded as symbol. Furs, boots, and jewels externalize in economic terms the power of the Countess, conflating the "financial profit and libidinal gratification" (this last suggested by the Count's "virile member" [92]) sought by Juliette. As well as the female sexual jealousy of "Snow White," the tale makes use of the Slavic tale of the Snow Maiden, which invokes the motif of the melting snow-child created as a response to desire. In the Slavic version (Léger 143), this is the innocent desire of an old man and woman for a child, whom they craft out of snow and who subsequently comes to life. The echo of this version in Carter's tale underlines the incest motif (the Count desires both daughter and sexual partner), as well as externalizing sexuality as inherently destructive—heat melts snow. The contrast of virginity with desire is underlined by the tale's opening ("Midwinter—invincible, immaculate" [91])" and by the intrusion of the familiar folkloric motif of "Snow White" and "Sleeping Beauty" that of the woman pricking her finger. Loss of virginity is death, specifically the death of desirability. With the accomplished sexual figure of the Countess beside him, the only value in the snow-maiden for the Count is, in fact, her virginity, and the symbolic rape by the rose—and the Countess—debars him from enjoyment of that. Thus, while he has her, "weeping," this transitory possession does not prevent her from fading into nonexistence, leaving the Countess triumphant in her sexual maturity. The symbolic transfer of sexual experience from the Countess to the snow-girl via the rose is a compact and resonant motif, confirming both the predatory power of the sexually confident woman and the central theme of female jealousy which underpins the "Snow White" tale. Above all, it is self-conscious use of symbol; the intertext of Freudian psychology insists that the symbols are actually *read*, rather than simply being received.

The same motif of virginal blood, the symbolic deflowering in the pricked finger, also provides the moment of fairy-tale recognition in "The Lady of the House of Love," in which Carter rewrites the devouring feminine as tragic figure. The Sleeping Beauty narrative gains considerable symbolic and stylistic force from Carter's intersection of the tale with the clichés and tropes of the classic nineteenth-century vampire story. At the same time, the Sleeping Beauty's thorn-surrounded castle is reinterpreted in a less concrete fashion, a cultural and patriarchal entrapment which dooms the Lady to an unfulfilling existence. Exaggeration functions partially as a form of comic undercutting in this tale, which is consequently rescued from the heaviness of the Gothic setting and, like much of Carter's writing, ultimately refuses to take itself too seriously. The tragic Gothic intensity of the heroine is undermined by her association with the animal—"Delicious crunch of the fragile bones of rabbits and small, furry things she pursues with fleet, four-footed speed" (95)—but also with another fairy-tale association, the ogre of "Jack and the Beanstalk"—"I smell the blood of an Englishman" (96). The cutting of threat with comedy has been extensively treated by Marina Warner in her work *No Go the Bogeyman: Scaring, Lulling, and Making Mock,* whose title suggests precisely this need to dispel unease with laughter in representing the devouring other. Warner suggests that "mockery perhaps defends against the painful potential [of the medieval grotesque]," which, "though [it] does not claim to represent the reality of phantasms at a deep level, continues lightfootedly, capriciously, safely contained in the abstract realm of representations" (247). Carter rewrites the romantic female vampire as a somewhat different symbol, that of the ogre, somehow clumsy, pathetic, and comic as well as terrifying. The transformation is perhaps best exemplified by the crone attendant, who will "tidy the remains into a neat pile and wrap it in its own discarded clothes," which she then "discreetly buries in the garden" (96). Warner's comments also serve to explain Carter's play with the bicycle motif and the supremely rationalist cyclist set against a Gothic grotesque, as an antidote to the aspect of "the grotesque's fancifulness [which] strikes observers as horrible: it indulges in inconsequential whimsy but its very detachment from logic and biology can take a disturbing turn" (247). We may find the bicycle amusing as a symbol, but it provides a rational sanctuary from the disturbing illogic of the vampire at the same time that its comic exaggeration offers relief from the unease of the grotesque.

Of course, part of this unease is inherent in that cliché of Gothic eroticism, the female vampire herself. On the most obvious level, the re-energizing of the Sleeping Beauty as vampire negates and reverses the patriarchal construction of the symbol—the ultimate passive woman, asleep and awaiting the kiss of the prince, becomes a powerful devouring feminine. The effectiveness of Carter's use of this conflation rests in its ability to expose the devouring feminine as yet another entrapping patriarchal technique. Part of the unease of "Lady of the House of Love" picks up on the erotic anxiety expressed in the figure of the female vampire, whose possession of fangs appropriates in particularly obvious symbolic terms the phallic authority of the male. She is highly disturbing in that those fangs empower her with the ability to make any victim—male or female—into a female symbol. This is not simply in the emasculation of the male through his helpless seduction by the beautiful vampire, but in the vampire's physical power to literally create the female symbolic—the hole, the wound, the absence filled by the phallic instrument of the vampire— in the victim. Any vampire figure becomes the site of erotic anxiety in patriarchal discourse precisely because of its power to appropriate the phallic identity of the male victim, which is perhaps why so much Victorian Gothic insists on the virginal female as prey. In Carter's hands, erotic anxiety is redoubled and emphasized by the disturbing image of a Sleeping Beauty whose apparent passivity is a delusion and a snare. Moreover, it is a particularly erotic entrapment, a quality emphasized by Carter's play with the trappings of what she defines quite explicitly as the perverse bordello where, "amidst all the perfumes of the embalming parlour, the customer took his necrophiliac pleasure of a pretended corpse" (105). Above all else, the tale's emphasis on tawdry trappings reveals all its symbolism of the Gothic narrative as a male erotic construct, spurious and invalid, and underlines the entrapment of the Countess within it.

The tale is notable in the collection for its wholesale rejection of narrative structures, none of which are admitted as valid—in the clash of narratives, Gothic, fairy tale, and historical/rational, all narratives fail. Despite obvious sleep/death parallels, the Sleeping Beauty's finger-prick operates as a symbolic reversal in which the Countess wakes up into reality rather than being cast into sleep; the symbolic deflowering marks an initiation into real world rather than constructed, although it is one in which her only option is death. The fragments of her dark glasses, on which she wounds herself, signal a restoration of vision, but they also deny the possibility of reflection and thus of identity in the same way as does the vampire's traditional lack of a mirror image. Carter will pick up on this idea of reflection later in the mirror of "Wolf-Alice," but for now the devouring feminine rebounds primarily on itself—the price of escape from a destructive symbol is destruction.

However, the tale's historical grounding works interestingly here, in that it insists that death is inevitable in any narrative—the boy escapes the doomed patterns dictated by his identity as the vampire's victim, but he will nonetheless die in the trenches. The shared death of the Countess and the soldier suggests a strange kind of mutuality, an enactment of the familiar motif of orgasm as death which is reinforced by the symbol of the rose, the traditional metaphor for the female sexual organ. Denial of narrative becomes both an escape and a kind of fulfillment. His denial of the Gothic narrative makes it possible for her, too, to reject it, and that rejection makes possible a symbolic inversion of the Sleeping Beauty's fate, despite the boy's too-ready desire to serve as prince to her sleeping maiden. Certain feminist responses to this outcome are, of course, annoyed: Duncker argues that "what the Countess longs for is the *grande finale* of all 'snuff' movies in which the woman is sexually used and ritually killed, the oldest cliché of them all, sex and death" (9). Certainly this impulse is present in the tale, but, as usual, Carter's self-conscious use of these and other narrative tropes is far more complex than Duncker's comments would suggest. Like any other tale in this collection, "Lady of the House of Love" investigates a situation rather than enacting a solution; here, the power of the various patriarchal narratives is such that the only possible escape is death. In many ways, the exaggerated, rationally irresistible sun-god figure of the young soldier playfully underlines this, and one cannot help but feel that there is a certain justice in Carter's vindictive enjoyment as she consigns him to the same fate as her doomed, vampiric Sleeping Beauty.

Vampires and roses are traditionally powerful symbols, but Carter's treatment exposes their flawed operation as patriarchal constructs. It is only really in the last story of the collection, "Wolf-Alice," in which a symbol is found which succeeds in addressing and transcending the problem of female sexuality under patriarchy. The mirror in "Wolf-Alice" for the first time supplies the notion of identity which is not necessarily linked inextricably to the sexual; while menstrual blood comes to symbolize time, the mirror is a neutral construct, lacking the gender implications of other symbols. Wolf-Alice's process of maturation is a vivid and poignant illustration of the theories of Jacques Lacan in its reliance on the mirror as symbol for the process of development whereby the individual recognizes the self as object. Rosemary Jackson's useful summary of the psychoanalytic in fantasy identifies Lacan's mirror phase as "a shift . . . to the ideal of a whole body with a unified (constructed) subjectivity" as well as a theory reliant on an "understanding of the ego as a *cultural construction*" (89). Thus, while Wolf-Alice's sense of time is accessed via her awareness of her own menstrual flow, it is her discovery of the "friend" in the mirror that leads to the moment of discovery of herself; "her relation with the mirror was now far more intimate since she knew she saw herself within it" (124). While she vaguely associates the mirror-Alice with her own menstrual flow, this recognition is not inherently sexualized. Heterosexual desire is formulated only later, when she recognizes the Duke as an object of pity and, in his mirror image, as a being akin to herself. Her process of constructing an identity for herself is only complete when she finds a place within the structures of culture, in interaction with another of her own kind. More importantly, it is the girl who comes to an awareness of her own identity in isolation, and who then restores the man to his humanity, not the pattern of sexual initiation we have seen in earlier tales.

While a highly individualistic narrative, "Wolf-Alice" is thus ultimately not out of place in a collection based on Perrault. Neither fairy tale nor really folkloric in its roots, it nonetheless follows fairy-tale patterns in its presentation of a profound human scenario, stripped down to archetypal participants and symbolic challenges. Critics such as Mircea Eliade have noted the importance of fairy tale as offering an essentially initiatory scenario, "passing, by way of a symbolic death and resurrection, from ignorance and immaturity to the spiritual age of the adult" (201). In its presentation of a profoundly satisfying symbolic resolution, "Wolf-Alice" partakes of an essential aspect of fairy-tale narrative which remains unobscured by psychoanalytic complexities of characterization (Lacan's theories are expressed in symbolic terms, and thus do not break fairy tale's rules) or by Carter's excessive language. In this, it achieves, more fully than any other tale in the collection, the resolution toward which every tale is groping: how women may exist fully and as heterosexually sexualized individuals under the structures of our culture. In its comparatively sparse texture, it also signals the departure from literary—or literarized—fairy tale to a rediscovery of older forms. The collection's conclusion thus finds a balance lacking in earlier tales, whose intertexts and linguistic games become part of the cultural problem. Here, while other texts are evoked in order to add complexity and subtlety, they are very much a subtext, perfectly controlled at last. Paradoxically, in rewriting fairy tale Carter finally finds the structural space she requires; having demonstrated her mastery of language, symbol, and patterning, in the end she must move through the classic tales of Perrault and others into a less culturally determined space. "Wolf-Alice" is not strictly a fairy tale, but perhaps it is a perfectly self-conscious expression of what fairy tale could and should be.

4

CAUGHT IN A STORY:
A. S. BYATT

Everybody knows it's fiction, but then everybody knows the whole thing is fiction. —A. S. BYATT in Wachtel, 88

The award of the Booker Prize to A. S. Byatt's novel *Possession: A Romance* in 1990 cemented Byatt's position as a literary figure and sparked the steady stream of academic attention which has greeted both *Possession* and Byatt's other works. An intensely intellectual and literary writer, Byatt betrays in all her works an interest in the presence and repercussions of literature. Her recurring attention to fairy-tale and folk forms is thus subsidiary to her far larger interest in form, writing, and narrative tradition as a whole. This literariness is perhaps due in part to her identity as an academic and critic as well as a writer of fiction; her academic career has included postgraduate study at Oxford and in America, and teaching at London University, with published criticism on Iris Murdoch and the Victorian poets, among other texts (Todd, *Writers* x–xi). Much of her work is highly self-aware and self-reflexive, her protagonists tending to reflect her own identity as academic, writer, or narratologist. This gives her writing an intelligence James Wood has identified as "Byatt's greatest problem as a writer"; he argues that "while part of her imagination yearns for a visual immediacy, the other part constantly peels away into analogy, allegory, metaphor, and relations with other texts" (121–22). As a result, she continuously explores and deconstructs the nature and workings of her narratives, and the

Part of this chapter originally appeared as "Ice, Glass, Snow: Fairy Tale as Art and Metafiction in the Writing of A. S. Byatt." *Marvels and Tales* 20.1 (2006): 47–66.

problematical relationship between narrative and reality. Her essay "Old Tales, New Forms" makes this explicit in admitting her fascination with the European Prize entries which were "threaded through with brilliant and knotty reflections on the relations of myth, story, language and reality" (123).

Byatt is thus a recurrently and integrally metafictional writer, whose self-consciousness is linked to narrative in her awareness of the novel and short-story forms. She discusses the relationship between mimesis and metafiction in her essay " 'Sugar'/'Le Sucre,' " recounting her delight in the discovery of Proust and the possibility for a text to be realist and "at the same time to think about form, its own form, its own formation, about perceiving and inventing the world" (22–23). Throughout her texts, realist as well as fairy tale, art and literature both reflect and create the world. Reality in her texts is very much a construct of art: of literature, as in *Possession* or *The Biographer's Tale,* or of storytelling, as in her fairy tales. This is extended to include painting, seen in her interest in Van Gogh, whose works pervade *Still Life* and, to some extent, *The Shadow of the Sun,* and in the artistic focus to *The Matisse Stories* and many of the tales in *Elementals.* Her keen sympathy for the aesthetic and creative value of art is rendered complex by its reflective and refractive capacities in her novels, and by the relationship between the structures of art (visual or literary) and her ongoing interest in realist depiction. Julian Gitzen notes the tendency for Byatt's characters to "remain tirelessly alive to both the bond and the gap between words and their referents and between art and its subject. Her fiction persistently dramatises this distinction by making it either a significant feature of the narrative or the very focus of action" (84). Thus the lives of the protagonists in *Possession* are reflected in, and come to reflect, their literary productions—Christabel's fairy tales, Ash's poetry, or the Freudian criticism of Roland or Maud. Reality, or rather the fictional representation of reality, becomes structured in literary or fairy-tale terms, emphasizing Byatt's interest in fairy tale as simply the most extreme example of literature's ability to refigure reality in terms of structured text. This is particularly striking in the case of Byatt's realist tales which slide into classic fairy-tale forms—the middle-aged narratologist given three wishes by a genie, the artist in France whose swimming pool becomes inhabited by a potential fairy bride in "A Lamia in the Cévennes." The story shape and the realist setting are coequal, mutually influential, inextricably involved.

Byatt's recurring interest in realist narratives such as history and biography, or even science, is more difficult to integrate with her self-aware explorations of narrative. However, historical and biographical writing encapsulates in itself precisely the intersection between reality and narrative with which she is most concerned; both deal with narrative versions of reality in the strongest possible form: events which actually happened. The presence of etymological science in "Morpho Eugenia" (*Angels and Insects*) is another example of this tendency, offering the most realistic scientific explorations couched as allegorical fairy tale. In Byatt's stories, historical or scientific detail is embedded in the lives of the protagonists at the same time that the lives of the characters are articulated via such detail. Examples include the Victorian context of *Possession* and *The Biographer's Tale*, the history of Nîmes in "Crocodile Tears," and the lives of moths in "Morpho Eugenia." These stories set out to self-consciously transform reality *into* narrative, not only the narrative experienced by the characters but also the narrative created by them in the unfolding of their experiences. A similar process is at work in *The Virgin in the Garden,* where the life of Elizabeth I resonates with the coronation of Elizabeth II and with Frederica herself, creating modern events as historical narrative at the same time that historical event is recreated as modern narrative. Fairy tale becomes simply one strand in Byatt's storytelling, another example of the same impulse that underlies her use of history, biography, or any other genre—an exploration of the processes used by humanity in reflecting its experience as narrative, reflected over again in Byatt's own narratives in an act of ongoing creation. History and biography are exposed as artifact, story, the artificial creation which mimics reality in much the same way as does Byatt's creation of fictional reality through her fiercely physical and detailed prose. The process recalls Waugh's definition of metafiction, in the tendency of metafictional texts to "explore the possible fictionality of the world outside the literary fictional text" (2).

Byatt's interest in this relationship between reality and storytelling accounts for her characteristic use of embedded tale, most explicitly in *Possession* and "The Djinn in the Nightingale's Eye," although turning up even in short stories such as "Crocodile Tears." Embedded narratives are the perfect site for the interaction of reality and art; the realist frame text highlights the constructedness of the embedded tale, while meaning is able to resonate continually and richly between story and frame narrative. Embedded stories signal themselves unavoidably as tale rather than mimesis and highlight their own structured narrative voice through the existence of the narrator as a character in the frame narrative. It becomes easy to see why Byatt's fascination with folktale and fairy tale becomes partially subordinate to her writing of novels and novellas. Actual stand-alone fairy tales are rare in her literary output; most of her tales are called into service to develop thematic and structural aspects of longer texts. Even the tales in *The Djinn in the Nightingale's Eye* include two of the embedded stories from *Possession;* in terms of individual fairy tales Byatt has produced only "The Story of the Eldest Princess" and "Cold," unless you wish to count her translation of Madame D'Aulnoy's "The Great Green Worm" from the French.

If Byatt's fairy tales are often embedded, the texts in which they are embedded also tend toward explicit structure, invoking and exploring genre narratives such as romance in a way similar to some of Thurber's non-fairy-tale writing. Toward the end of *Possession* Roland observes that "coherence and closure are deep human desires that are presently unfashionable. But they are always both frightening and enchantingly desirable" (422). Later, he muses that "the expectations of Romance control almost everyone in the Western world, for better or worse, at some point or another" (425). Coherence and closure are very much the characteristics of fairy tale and romance but also have interesting implications for biography; even history offers a finite and coherent narrative of reality, defined by date and place, in the same way that biography defines reality by the life of one individual. In an interview with Eleanor Wachtel, Byatt admits the "intense pleasure" with which she uses the narrative definition offered by a romance or Shakespearean comedy plot: "I love those Victorian novels in which, when you come to the end, you're told the whole history of every character . . . it makes me very happy" (88). Far more so than history or biography, romance offers one of the strongest examples of coherence, its patterns and symbols both recognizable and predictable. Byatt's interest in romance is ongoing from her first novel, *The Game,* which uses Arthurian and medieval elements to explore the relationship between the two sisters. *Possession* obviously offers her most overt use of romance; André Brink comments that "the peculiar shape [*Possession*] assumes is inspired by the way in which it inserts itself, as a Postmodernist novel, into a tradition of romance" (288). Parts of the Frederica series play with romance in their references to Tolkien-style narrative (*Babel Tower*) and in some of the heterosexual relationships explored symbolically throughout the series. Byatt's interest in romance forms is also expressed in her empathic and approving essay on the historical romances of Georgette Heyer, in which she argues for Heyer's novels as "an honourable escape" which "provide[s] simple release from strain—the story with simple streamlined rules of conduct and a guaranteed happy ending" (*Passions* 258). Romance, however, is not the only form in which Byatt explores coherence and closure; *Babel Tower*'s embedded narrative is pornographic, invoking a genre whose symbolic narrative I have earlier compared to fairy tale (see chapter 2). "Jael" and "Christ in the House of Martha and Mary" are also interesting in their use of the Bible as intertext; the realist story is infused with the symbolic force of biblical narrative, itself a highly defined form offering familiar symbolic relationships and moral closure.

The danger of Byatt's intricate intertwining of reality with narrative, particularly with embedded tales, is that the embedded tales may come to have too immediate and obvious a relationship with the fictional reality to which they relate. Fairy tale, while a symbolic form, is not allegory, as I have suggested; too strict a reading of symbol as equivalence impoverishes the possibilities of the narrative. Recent criticism on *Possession* suggests there is a problem in too rigorous a reading of Christabel's fairy tales, for example, as allegorical representations of her relationship with Ash and Blanche. Monica Flegel spends some time analyzing "fairy tale references" associated with various characters (416ff.), and Victoria Sanchez also works to establish allegorical elements in the tales (42ff.). This is a valid response to Byatt's complex use of intertext, but at the same time it risks losing the integrity of the tale itself in favor of focusing on what it "means." The point of a fairy tale is never to "stand for" anything but itself. To be fair, most of Byatt's critics offer complex readings of embedded tales, only at times approaching the dangerous ground that Byatt warns against in *Possession:* to read a tale only as Freudian analogy, historical event, or feminist manifesto is false. Leonora exemplifies this when she realizes that "LaMotte has always been cited as a lesbian-feminist poet. Which she was, but not exclusively, it appears" (485).

Byatt began a doctoral dissertation on religious allegory in seventeenth-century texts, but, interestingly, justifies the choice of "the allegory bit of it . . . because I wanted to write novels, and was interested in narrative" (*Passions* 3). In her view, allegory, like fairy tale, exemplifies the mechanics of narrative in particularly strong and obvious forms. Many of Byatt's tales have allegorical elements, most notably Matty's scientific parable in "Morpho Eugenia" and the war fable "Dragon's Breath," but to see them exclusively in terms of message is problematical. Richard Todd's insistence on the term "wonder tales" for Byatt's stories highlights precisely this issue, and he argues that "the true wonder tale must somehow manage to hover suspensefully between "message" and "thickening mystery" (*Writers* 43)—polarities which are defined in a discussion of Matty's fairy tale in "Morpho Eugenia." Todd's definition of Byatt's tales as "wonder tales" focuses on the relationship with meaning, where the essence of the fairy tale is the sense of wonder, and explanation or overt intention are unnecessary to the tale's function—if too much is explained, the power of the tale is lost. Byatt's critical writing insists on this when she identifies fairy tale as a "form in which stories are not about *inner* psychological subtleties, and truths are not connected immediately to contemporary circumstances" (*Histories* 124). This is partially problematical, because "Dragon's Breath" and Matty's tale *are* allegorical and their truths *are* connected directly to contemporary reality (Sarajevo and science, respectively). At the same time, however, the use of symbol in Matty's tale, and the paradoxical uncertainty around the identity of the dragons, renders the effect of the tale complex beyond the simple allegorical relationship. This slippage toward allegory is perhaps another manifestation of the "problem of intelligence" Todd identifies in Byatt (see above).

Byatt's dislike of strongly polemical or allegorical writing is seen in her attitude to feminism. While she undoubtedly has feminist purposes in much of her writing, these are much simpler to investigate than in the writing of someone like Carter. Byatt, on the one hand, explores her feminist interests through her narrative investigations and subordinates political concerns to those of narrative. Carter, on the other hand, uses narrative techniques to enable political concerns; her use of narrative is self-aware and complex, but the exploration of female sexuality is the focus, not the exploration of narrative for its own sake. Todd defines Byatt's feminist impulse as one which "operates as *an augmentation of a total discourse,* rather than as a simplistic replacement of what has been traditionally privileged by what has been traditionally marginalised" ("Unheard Voices" 99). Byatt supports this: "I am much less happy about a great many resolute feminist rewritings of fairy tales, making wilful changes to plots and forms to show messages of female power (often written under the enthusiastic misapprehension that fairy tales in general show powerless females)" (*Histories* 143). Tales by and about women pervade Byatt's stories; she explores not only the female archetypes of storytelling—Melusina, Patient Griselda, the Eldest Princess—but also the patterns of story which predetermine female roles. In Byatt's terms, female empowerment is the result of narrative empowerment: narratives can equally entrap women into limited roles, warn them about such potential entrapments, or allow them to seize control of the narrative and write themselves into a position of control. I shall deal with the feminist aspects of Byatt's tales in discussing narrative entrapment, below.

While structure and intertext are essential to Byatt's use of fairy-tale forms, it is also interesting to note the affinities between her writing style and the stylistic tendencies of fairy-tale and folk forms. The sparseness of Byatt's writing, with its controlled lucidity and misleading simplicity, is very close to the language of fairy tale. She shares with fairy-tale writing the quality pointed out by Max Lüthi, "the beauty of the clear, the definite, the orderly—the beauty of precision" (40). Byatt writes:

> By the time I wrote *Possession* . . . I felt a need to *feel* and *analyse* less, to tell more flatly, which is sometimes more mysteriously. The real interest of this to a writer is partly in the intricacies of the choice of words from line to line. I found myself crossing out psychological descriptions, or invitations to the reader to enter the characters' thought-processes. I found myself using stories within stories, rather than shape-shifting recurrent metaphors, to make the meanings. (*Histories* 131)

This is precisely how fairy tale works; its complexity and subtlety comes from the interaction of symbols and the expectations of narrative, rather than from psychological or emotional detail. Interestingly, Byatt manages to sustain this apparently flat effect in her writing despite her commitment to realistic description. Her tales provide infinite depth of physical detail (the effects of the green sky in "Eldest Princess," the crystal cave in "Cold") without losing the effect of fairy tale's integrally stripped-down texture.

Given the consistency of Byatt's interests across the various texts relevant to my analysis, it has proved more useful to structure this chapter thematically rather than by looking at the texts individually. In discussing issues of narrative, narrative entrapment, narrative embedding, and the folkloric voice, I shall focus largely on the tales in *The Djinn in the Nightingale's Eye* and *Possession,* in addition to the story "Cold" from the collection *Elementals.* While fairy-tale fragments occur in the Frederica series (*The Virgin in the Garden, Still Life, Babel Tower,* and *The Whistling Woman*), these are minor and seem to function largely as metaphor; I will not address them here. Likewise, comparatively few of Byatt's short stories employ fairy-tale elements. Tales in *The Matisse Stories,* despite intertexts such as Andersen's "The Snow Queen" in "The Chinese Lobster," tend to use painting rather than fairy tale as intertext, and stories in *Sugar* seem to have an almost biographical function. *Elementals* comes closest to folklore in its interest in the magical creatures of the title, and, in addition to "Cold," several (notably "Crocodile Tears" and "A Lamia in the Cévennes") have strong folkloric or embedded fairy-tale elements I shall examine in passing. Likewise, her more recent

Little Black Book of Stories embeds folkloric elements in its otherwise realist tales; in particular, "The Thing in the Forest" and "A Stone Woman" employ magical motifs in the service of poignant psychological explorations.

A PATTERN I KNOW: STRUCTURE AND INTERTEXT

The awareness of fairy-tale structure is present in Byatt's work in two main forms. More rarely, she undertakes direct intertextual retelling of actual folk or fairy tales such as the Fairy Melusina or Grimms' "The Glass Coffin," but mostly her tales are original variations on fairy-tale themes and offer a sustained and investigative sense of the recurring patterns and expectations of classic fairy tales. Reworked tales will characteristically be infused with awareness of a far broader range of texts: "The Threshold," for example, invokes Shakespeare's *The Merchant of Venice,* and "Gode's Tale" contains echoes of Andersen in addition to a more generalized play with folkloric elements. This focus on known exempla of pattern and structure is integral to Byatt's self-consciousness as a writer; not only the writer and reader but also Byatt's characters need to be wholly aware of the fact that they are "caught in a story" (the title of the anthology for which "The Story of the Eldest Princess" was written), which is, above all, familiar. The Eldest Princess exemplifies both structure and realization when she says, "I am in a pattern I know, and I suspect I have no power to break it" (*Djinn,* 48).

"The Glass Coffin" is perhaps the best example of Byatt's playful investigation of the potential in a postmodern reworking that is held up continually against the original from which it derives. The story is a reasonably faithful adaptation of the Grimm version, achieving individuality as much through insertions of new detail and the conceptual weighting created by Byatt's language as from the resonance of the tale with the frame narrative of *Possession.* The effect of reading Byatt's "Glass Coffin" even as a stand-alone tale is one of increased richness in comparison to the original, a proliferation of narrative possibility despite the tale's familiar shape. The tailor encounters not only the little man but also his animals, and his quest is guided, not by a mysterious voice, but by a careful delineation of the narrative potentials and the requirement for him to make a conscious choice. The presence of the dog, the cockerel and his wife, and the cat, goat, and cow, invoke the familiar test of courtesy common in fairy tale, but they also recall the beast-fable style of folklore, the odd assortment of domestic animals closest, perhaps, to those of "The Musicians of Bremen." Thus, while Byatt's version deviates structurally and in detail from the original, the new elements remain instantly recognizable. Another addition is the element of choice added to the narrative; arising from his successful negotiation of the test, the tailor is offered a choice between three items, a purse, a pot, and a key. While each item is essentially simple and mundane, in the manner of fairy tales it is also highly symbolic; each object encapsulates and recalls a familiar fairy-tale narrative in itself. The tailor reflects, "I know about such gifts . . . it may be that the first is a purse which is never empty, and the second a pot which provides a wholesome meal whenever you demand it . . . I have heard of such things . . ." (*Djinn* 6). In his choice of the third item, the glass key, the narrative is less obviously defined, since "he did not have any idea about what it was or might do" (7). The key is an interesting addition to the tale, providing a more direct sense of the narrative potential which needs to be unlocked by the tailor's actions. In the original, the glass coffin needs no unlocking, but opens at the tailor's touch. The emblem of the key perhaps signals, as much as anything else, the intellectual demands of Byatt's reworked version, the layering of meaning the reader must unlock. The key is a fascinating symbol in itself: another Grimm tale, "The Golden Key," is a strange fragment which peters out suggestively, and the young lad who finds the key is abandoned by the tale before he has finished turning it in the lock. The tale concludes, "and now we must wait until he has quite unlocked it and opened the lid, and then we shall learn what wonderful things were lying in that box." George Macdonald's story of the same title similarly refuses to apportion definite meaning to the key, rather using it in a diffuse fashion to suggest the unlocking of understanding of the self. If Byatt's appropriation of the key as a symbol of narrative meaning is curiously indefinite, it is in good company.

A similar density characterizes Byatt's use of the Melusina legend in *Possession*. While this story is folkloric in its treatment within *Possession* (it is retold orally by Fergus in addition to its adaptation into Christabel LaMotte's poem), its actual literary intertexts are firmly signaled. Fergus's characteristic reference to Rabelais' *Gargantua and Pantagruel* (33) serves to configure and mock Melusina's monstrous tail as female appropriation of the Freudian emblem, a sausage as well as a snake. Similar Freudian intertexts are applied to folklore and fairy tale throughout *Possession*, complicating fairy tale's symbolic functioning by reference to a whole new system of symbol. Aside from Freud, the details of the tale in the novel seem to derive from the medieval French version of Jean D'Arras, with its mythology of the Lusignan ruling family. More strongly, however, Christabel LaMotte's name signals a different intertext, that of Friedrich de la

Motte's nineteenth-century prose romance "Undine," another tale of a female water-creature betrayed by her husband. The lack of direct reference to Jean D'Arras in the novel suggests that the thematic concerns of LaMotte's "Undine" (jealousy, love betrayed) are more central to Byatt's purposes than the fairly straightforward fairy bride betrayal of the Melusina tale. While fragmentary in terms of actual narrative, the Melusina tale in *Possession* exemplifies the complex layering of Byatt's intertextuality and the importance of the tale's investigation as *tale;* its literary antecedents are central to the construction of meaning in the novel.

Recognizable patterns and shape, rather than narrative voice, thus define Byatt's sense of the fairy tale, a tendency seen even more strongly in "The Story of the Eldest Princess," which, while not actually retelling a known tale, works around the classic pattern of three siblings. Vladimir Propp has noted how the fairy tale adheres to rules of structural similarity: "the actors in the fairy tale perform essentially the same actions as the tale progresses, no matter how different from one another in shape, size, sex and occupation, in nomenclature and other static attributes. . . . The functions of the actors are a constant; everything else is a variable" ("Fairy Tale Transformations" 94). Thus, Byatt's Eldest Princess sets out to attempt the quest which will save her country, only to realize that she is doomed to failure. In fairy tales, the eldest two siblings always set out, only to be "turned to stone, or imprisoned in vaults, or cast into magic sleep, until rescued by the third royal person, who did everything well, restored the first and the second, and fulfilled the quest" (47). In that moment of essentially postmodern realization, the Eldest Princess becomes aware of her place in a narrative which imposes pattern and thus predictability on her actions. It is interesting to note the frequent recurrence of words such as *fate* and *destiny* in Byatt's tales, offering a sense not only of the magical predestinations of fairy tale but also of their ability to illustrate the equally powerful predestinations of narrative.

In terms of Byatt's metafictional project, this awareness of pattern is central to the awareness of narrative as story, artifact, construction. Fairy tale offers a narrative stripped down to an essence of representation—once upon a time, three princes, a magical horse, a princess in a tower, three wishes—and which thus exposes the artifice and constructedness of narrative. Gillian Perholt comments, of her paperweights, "I like the geometrically patterned flowers best. . . . More than the ones that aim at realism, at looking real . . ." (275). Fairy tale conventions problematize their own relationship with reality as much by the artificialities of pattern and repetition as anything else. "The Glass Coffin" underlines this aspect of narrative in its recurring insistence on craftsmanship, the little tailor as "a fine craftsman" whose pie is "decorated . . . with beautifully formed pastry leaves and flowers, for he was a craftsman, even if he could not exercise his own craft" (3–5). Likewise, his eventual choice of the glass key is because he is himself an artisan "and could see that it had taken masterly skill to blow all these delicate wards and barrels" (7). Similar issues of artistry inform the glass sculptures of "Cold," which are very much akin to Gillian's paperweights.

Central to this structuredness of narrative shape is the notion of narrative closure, which twentieth- and twenty-first-century readers have come to associate unavoidably with fairy tale, despite the more ambiguous shape of some folkloric narratives. Byatt's strong awareness of this relates once again to her sense of the two-way transformations of reality into narrative and narrative into reality. Roland's thoughts on closure as a "deep human desire," discussed above, reflect the human need to impose shape onto our experience of reality. Byatt comments, "I stumbled . . . across the idea that stories and tales, unlike novels, were intimately to do with death. . . . Whether we like it or not, our lives have beginnings, middles and ends. We narrate ourselves to each other in bars and beds" (*Histories* 132). This tendency to experience reality as narratively shaped is, however, ambiguous, not least because of the postmodern context in which Byatt is writing. While admitting the existence of a "genuine narrative hunger" in readers, Byatt suggests that such an interest is only valid "as a technical experiment" (in Wachtel 88). More importantly, as Jane L. Campbell notes, narrative structure and coherence gives rise to a problem of overcontrol: "[Byatt] is especially concerned with the life-denying consequences of attempting to control another's life by becoming its author, and explores this subject in an early novel, *The Game*" (106). The omniscient narrator of realist fiction cannot be allowed to impose absolute structure on the tale, precisely because its author is interested in metafiction, and metafiction, in Waugh's terms, relies on the instability of the text. Any novel has dialogic aspects, a "conflict of language and voices" which realistic fiction resolves "through their subordination to the dominant 'voice' of the omniscient, godlike author . . . Metafiction *displays* and *rejoices in* the impossibility of such a resolution" (6).

The effect of this in Byatt's writing is a paradoxical awareness of fairy-tale structure and a tendency to examine and hence disrupt that structure, denying the authority of its narrator or narrators. Byatt's narratives largely refuse fairy-tale closure, remaining open-ended. In "The Djinn in the Nightingale's Eye," the djinn comments to Gillian that her tales are "strange, glancing things. They peter out, they have no shape" (242). The delays and refusals of closure in "The Djinn in the Nightingale's Eye" are thematically interesting in that they serve to explore and reflect the issues confronting Gillian—old age, a decaying body, and ultimately, her own, inevitable death. As the narrative delays closure, so is Gillian's death delayed indefinitely by the wish granted by the genie. Even "The Glass Coffin," which faithfully reproduces the Grimm fairy-tale ending (marriage and happiness), tries to disrupt it with the tailor's offer to allow the rescued princess her freedom (21). The tailor's failure to escape narrative predestination could perhaps be attributed to the tale's place in *Possession,* as a tale told by Christabel LaMotte, and thus part of a Victorian realist narrative tradition which renders her capable of accepting closure more easily than her twentieth- and twenty-first-century descendants. The more postmodern Eldest Princess, having resisted and rejected the narrative closure of her fairy-tale identity, arrives at the end of her story without achieving any closure at all. Instead, she finds a place where she can be both free and content, telling stories in the forest with the old woman and her creatures: it is "a good place to go to sleep, and stop telling stories until the morning, which will bring its own changes" (72). Her youngest sister is left with a thread of narrative (another parallel to George Macdonald's writing, here *The Princess and the Goblin*) which leads into an undefined—because untold—future. Likewise, Gillian Perholt, having released the djinn, continues uneventfully with her life, the tale ending with the djinn's return to see her, briefly, and with the possibility of future visits left ambiguously open-ended. Byatt thus tries to escape the closure and hence the intrinsic entrapment of narrative in an essentially postmodern reinterpretation of the structure of fairy tale. This awareness of the potential for entrapment in the shape of narrative is integral to her writing and provides one of its strongest recurring themes.

Glass, Ice, and Narrative Entrapment

Images of glass and ice pervade A. S. Byatt's fairy tales—Gillian Perholt's glass paperweights, the glass bottle in which the djinn is imprisoned, the glass key and box in her retelling of the Grimm Brothers' "The Glass Coffin," the ice of "Cold," the glass case in "The Chinese Lobster." The most sustained example of this is perhaps Gillian Perholt's glass paperweights in "The Djinn in the Nightingale's Eye":

> Gillian collected glass paperweights: she liked glass in general, for its paradoxical nature, translucent as water, heavy as stone, invisible as air, solid as earth. Blown with human breath in a furnace of fire. As a child she had loved to read of glass

balls containing castles and snowstorms, though in reality she had always found these disappointing and had transferred her magical attachment to the weights in which coloured forms and carpets of geometric flowers shone perpetually and could be made to expand and contract as the sphere of glass turned in her fingers in the light. (182)

Glass and ice similarly illustrate an essential aspect of Byatt's narratives, which, like Gillian's paperweights, have a "paradoxical nature"; like a glass bottle, they both enclose and reveal, they are simultaneously transparent and containing, invisible yet entrapping. Like the djinn's bottle or the glass paperweight, these substances appear to be solid, to hold meanings which seem to offer themselves transparently to our view; yet, like Gillian's paperweight, they shift and change as they are tilted, to offer multiplicity of meaning within their apparently simple stasis. Both ice and glass are thus images of art, of artifact and the creation of artifacts. In her essay "Ice, Snow, Glass" Byatt notes that ice and glass stories all "have images of art. The queen in Snow White is entranced by a black frame round a window . . . Snow White . . . becomes an object of aesthetic perception, framed in her glass coffin" (*Histories* 156). Later, she comments on her enjoyment of the Grimms' tale "The Glass Coffin": "A fabricated world in a glass case gives a delight an ordinary castle doesn't" (157). Glass and ice are often structured in her works: geometrically patterned paperweights, or the snowflakes and the plethora of shaped glass creations of "Snow." As in "The Glass Coffin," the glassworks of "Cold" often enclose miniature realities—the glass castle, the glass beehive full of bees (*Elementals* 141–44). In this enclosure or entrapment glass and ice operate not only like art but also like narrative. Meaning is thus captured in stasis within the work of art—another aspect of fairy tale's particularly transparent structure which perhaps accounts for Byatt's tendency toward allegory, and for her ongoing awareness of entrapment within allegory, or narrative, or art.

The glass metaphor continues to be appropriate to the sense in which meaning shifts, is opaque, even in something as transparent as a fairy tale, but is ultimately subordinate to form, to the nature of the tale as tale rather than embedded message. The fairy tale is a form of narrative which is complete in itself, independent of message, and in which message is always subordinate to form. The glass key in "The Glass Coffin" operates as a powerful metaphorical motif in this context. In the paradoxical manner of glass, the meaning the key offers is at once obvious and hidden; while transparent, it also contains nothing, so that its clearly offered meaning is actually invisible. Like fairy tale, the key is transparent, apparently empty, its meaning contained entirely in its shape rather than its content. Both pot and purse are, like bottles and paperweights, containers; the key is just a key, an object that presupposes a container to be unlocked, but which will unlock rather than contain, and offers release rather than enclosure. Like a glass paperweight, the tale's function is simply to exist as an artifact, a construct complete and legitimate in and of itself. As in Gillian's description of glass, the fairy tale ". . . is not possible, it is only a solid metaphor, a medium for seeing and a thing seen at once. It is what art is . . ." (274).

It is easy to see how Byatt finds fairy tale a particularly powerful medium for exploration in this context, since, as Zipes comments, fairy-tale form and content are effectively the same thing—form is meaning, meaning is integral to structure: "it is through the structure or composition of the tale that we can gain an understanding of its meaning or enunciation, what it is trying to communicate" (*Art of Subversion* 5). Here, the expectations and ritualized repetitions of the fairy-tale form are central. Recognizable and recurring patterns entrap the protagonists of the tale into making choices which are dictated by the conventions of the tale. Certainly many of the tales in *Possession* repeat the entrapment images: the choice made by the Childe in "The Threshold," for example, when the protagonist, faced with the choice between gold, silver, and lead, knows the correct choice is always lead, despite his personal preferences—or, indeed, the preferences of the writer. Likewise, the tailor in "The Glass Coffin" is entrapped by the narrative which comes into play at the moment of his choice of the glass key, which leads him into an adventure described and thus predestined by the little gray man. It is easy to account for Byatt's interest in this particular tale, which repeats many of the elements of the original story in the Brothers Grimm. The young woman in her glass coffin, and the miniature castle under its glass dome, contain and enclose not only the woman and the place but also the narratives which explain them, and which are released when the glass is broken and the woman tells her story.

Within the narrative of "The Djinn in the Nightingale's Eye," the predicament of the djinn illustrates most powerfully this process of entrapment. Imprisoned in his bottle by the actions of a jealous King Solomon, the djinn is doomed to allow three wishes to any person who releases him. The whole mechanism of the *Arabian Nights* tales thus sets up the expectation of the djinn as servant to the bottle, as obliged to grant the wishes of the bottle's owner, thus neatly conflating elements of "The Fisherman and the Jinni" with the lamp-genie of "Aladdin." At the same time, since the djinn reveals his history in the form of narratives told to Gillian Perholt, the effect is that of the djinn imprisoned in his own narratives, in the history he relates. These narratives are constructed in the manner of fairy tales; each story is framed by the opening of the bottle, and the exhausting of the three wishes, and thus achieves a ritualized and repetitive effect. Gillian's encounter with the djinn invokes the series of narratives which entrap him neatly in the fate of his bottle curse, and which appear to predestine him to another cycle of release, three wishes, and return to imprisonment.

However, this process of tale-telling finally frees him, in that his stories reveal and endear him to Gillian, and, in revealing his imprisonment, lead her to desire his freedom. Gillian's comment on this is interesting: "The emotion we feel in fairy tales in which the characters are granted their wishes is a strange one. We feel the possible leap of freedom—I can have what I want—and the perverse certainty that this will change nothing; that Fate is fixed" (259). This brings us, then, to the opposite aspect of narrative in Byatt's work; paradoxically, like the glass of a paperweight, narrative encloses and empowers, its patterns entrap at the same time as they offer the potential for release. Above all, narrative empowers when careful choice is employed; while containing, enclosing, and defining through its inherent structure and nature, it also offers, through that structure and nature, the potential for release, freedom, and choice. Perhaps this is one of the issues articulated by Byatt's tale "Cold," which remains consistently aware of the paradox at the heart of glass—cold and transparent, like ice, but created by fire.

Again, we are brought to the essential paradoxes of narrative, the need for tale-telling to enclose and define at the same time that it must, in Byatt's view, liberate and empower. But the paradox is really several paradoxes—narrative entraps and frees, but narrative is also paradoxical in its search for meaning, the way in which it relates to reality—like glass, it must mirror and reveal, it is at once reflective and transparent. One of Gillian's papers in "The Djinn in the Nightingale's Eye" refers to the manner of tale-telling in Turkey, where stories are introduced "perhaps it happened, perhaps it didn't, and have paradox as their inception" (259). Meaning and reality, like the protagonists in the tales, are both enclosed and released through the structure of narrative. Ultimately, power lies in the act of telling tales, of taking control of the narrative. Gillian shies away from telling her own story, the story of her life thus far, to the djinn, refusing to enshrine in narrative the disempowerment she suffered while married to her faithless husband. The stories of her life she does tell him—her experience at a friend's wedding, for example—directly motivate and inform her subsequent use of her wishes. Similarly, the Djinn's tales of entrapment, together with his story of the diminishing wishing-ape, motivate Gillian to release him. Narrative thus, above all, empowers choice.

One of the main mechanisms by which narrative empowers is that of recognition. Byatt's Eldest Princess recognizes the fact that she is caught in a story because "she was by nature a reading, not a travelling princess . . . she had read a great many stories in her spare time, including several stories about princes and princesses who set out on Quests" (47). This familiarity enables her to identify the pattern in which she is participating—as Propp's definition suggests, her identity as the eldest, rather than the youngest princess, predetermines her function in the story. Similarly, Gillian Perholt's narratologist background allows her to use her three wishes intelligently; she immediately identifies the aspect of pattern and structure to the wishes ("Are there limits to what I may wish for?" [195]), and her reactions are circumscribed by her knowledge of the Grimms' fairy tale about three wishes, in which the old man ends up wasting his wishes in attaching a sausage to his wife's nose. This essentially cautionary tale motivates her careful exactitude and forethought in choosing her wishes—"I have three wishes. . . . I do not want to expend one of them on the possession of a tennis-player" (197).

At the same time, the numerous subnarratives embedded in the framing tale offer their own form of caution which is strongly linked to Byatt's feminist awareness. Narrative empowers, she seems to suggest, but it particularly empowers women. I have noted, above, Marina Warner's comments on the origins of fairy tale as a form of women's narrative, the tradition of the "old wives' tale" presupposing a female storyteller (*Beast to Blonde* 14). Thus the tales told in critical papers—Gillian on Chaucer's "Patient Griselda," Orhan on the *Arabian Nights*—offer versions of women's disempowerment or empowerment through their varying degrees of ownership and manipulation of the tale. As Gillian comments, the unease of Patient Griselda's tale lies in the part played by her husband: "The story is terrible because Walter has assumed too many positions in the narration; he is hero, villain, destiny, God and narrator" (120). The frame tale for the whole *Arabian Nights* deals with misogyny, the belief in women's essentially carnal nature, which leads to the need for Scheherazade to preserve her life through the manipulation of narrative. These tales link with Gillian's life as a divorced woman whose husband has left her for a younger woman, and whose ability to identify that loss with release and empowerment stands in sharp contrast to the powerless Patient Griselda. She can also be linked with Scheherazade's ability to free herself from male domination through tale-telling—much of Gillian's freedom and self-reliance is centered on her identity as a successful and independent critic, a narratologist and teller of tales. This mirrors Byatt's identity and purposes as a writer, providing a metalevel to the notion of control of narrative and its importance for women. However, this is simply the most obvious level on which Byatt's investigation of narrative, particularly fairy-tale narrative, operates in the service of a gendered awareness of power.

Glass, Ice, Intellectualism, and Passion

Christien Franken's critical volume on Byatt makes some interesting claims for Byatt's problematical status as a feminist writer, noting her ambivalence toward the popular poststructuralist tools of modern feminist criticism (4). Franken's tone is disapproving, as she cites Byatt's influence by Leavisite criticism and artistic notions of quality in writing: "As a consequence of her identification of female identity with limitation, the critic A. S. Byatt is unable to understand why young feminist writers and feminist literary theorists would want to hold on to the concept" (29). The satirically drawn figure of Leonora Stern in *Possession* exemplifies the problem Byatt has with exclusivist feminist viewpoints: "The truth is I can't bear Leonora's style because she reduces everything to sex and gender as though there is nothing else in the world" (in Franken 90). The problem for Byatt in the eyes of modern feminism, however, is not that she lacks a feminist sense of literature; it is that her sense of feminism is entirely subordinate to her sense of literature as art. She finds herself "returning to Virginia Woolf's elegant dictum 'it is fatal for anyone who writes to think about their sex' . . . I think myself, if you're interested in art rather than propaganda, this is a crucial thing to remember" (in Franken 29). Byatt's use of fairy-tale narrative, in particular, is thus largely free of the particular kinds of radical sexual and gender exploration common to writers such as Angela Carter, or even Tanith Lee. However, I think Franken's tone of slightly pained reproach at Byatt's lack of wholesale feminist commitment in the popular mold badly undervalues the depth and complexity of female identity, and particularly the identity of the female *artist,* in Byatt's writing.

While images of ice and glass illumine Byatt's interest in narrative entrapment and empowerment, there is a sense in which they are also symbolic in a particularly gendered sense, one Byatt highlighted in her essay "Ice, Snow, Glass" (*Histories*). Here, she discusses her sense of ". . . the conflict between a female destiny, the kiss, the marriage, the child-bearing, the death, and the frightening loneliness of cleverness, the cold distance of seeing the world through art, of putting a frame round things" (156). Ice and glass become a metaphor for art, "putting a frame round things," and for intellectual distance. Both of these are held up in contrast to the demands on women made by marriage and childbearing, and to the warmer, more emotional qualities of sexuality. Byatt addresses this in an interview with Nicholas Tredell, in which she articulates the desire to be "both at once, a passionate woman and a passionate intellectual" (in Franken 28). Franken later refers to Byatt's "use of the word 'lamination' to explain her desire to keep these layers of identity—the passionate woman and the intellectual—apart" (28). Intellectualism and sexuality are thus, to Byatt, separate rather than integrated, in sharp contrast to the Leonora Stern school of sex-in-everything; they thus translate rather well to the symbolic and metafictional exploration in which Byatt engages.

The symbolic potential in ice or glass is exemplified most strongly in the story "Cold," which uses warmth and cold to polarize male and female in a way curiously similar to the light/dark imagery of George Macdonald's story "The Day Boy and the Night Girl." Where Macdonald's Victorian sensibilities lead to a simplistic rendering of sexual difference, however, Byatt's apparently obvious allegory is complex and, ultimately, paradoxical and compromising. In "Cold," cold and heat (ice and desert) are contrasted to illustrate female coolness and intellectualism threatened by the male through emotional warmth and sexual love. Fiammarosa, the icewoman princess, is both an artist and an intellectual in her cold solitude—"She studied snow-crystals and ice formations under a magnifying glass" and "produced shimmering, intricate tapestries that were much more than 'good enough'" (134). In love with her desert prince, she loses something of that hard, self-contained identity, becoming aware that "inside her a little melted pool of water slopped and swayed where she had been solid and shining" (157). At the same time, however, the point of intersection between herself and Prince Sasan is glass, which brings together the hard, transparent beauty of ice, but also the sand and heat of Sasan's desert kingdom. Fiammarosa's icewoman nature is likewise two-edged, and Byatt resists the oversimplified equation of physical cold with sexual coolness: Fiammarosa's experience of cold is intensely sexual, a "paradoxical burn" that "pricked and hummed and brought her, intensely, to life" (126). Her feelings are strong enough that she chooses to marry Sasan and live in his desert kingdom although the climate threatens her with dissolution and death. Byatt thus seems to be making a fairly straightforward feminist point about the subordination of women to marriage, and the loss of female identity created by the overwhelming feelings of sexual love. It is, after all, Fiammarosa who makes the sacrifices, in keeping with her own cynical realization that princesses are "gifts and rewards, handed over by their loving fathers . . . princesses are commodities" (135). The symbolic poles of the tale are in this sense similar to more obviously feminist rewrites such as those of Angela Carter; although infused with Byatt's intellectualism, her feeling that there is "something secretly good, illicitly desirable, about ice-hills and glass barriers . . . something which was lost with human love, with the descent to be kissed and given away" (*Histories* 155).

"Cold" is rescued from feminist allegory by its complexity and compromise, the fact that what saves this apparently doomed union is, in fact, art. If glass and ice are akin in texture despite their very opposed origins in heat and cold, they are also alike in that Byatt associates both mediums throughout with artistry, creativity, and artifact. Ice is the stuff of snowflakes and Fiammarosa's geometric tapestries; glass enables Sasan to create marvelous images and the incredible glass caverns which eventually provide Fiammarosa with a home in which she can survive. Art thus not only bonds the polar oppositions of gender but also, more importantly, creates the medium in which sexual love can exist and be expressed. As with any Byatt work, this functions at yet another level of meaning: the love story is made possible not only by art/glass but also through and within the artistic creation of narrative, particularly the highly structured and patterned narrative of fairy tale. Recurring elements of patterning and structure relate back to fairy tale, its structure of repetition and expectation paralleled in the geometric precision of the snowflake or the lovingly crafted, fantastic worlds of Sasan's glass sculptures. In a sense, Fiammarosa and Sasan exist only because of story itself, because fairy-tale narrative supposes the existence of princes and princesses, and provides such strong symbols in which to encapsulate and enshrine their lives. Ultimately, this is yet another manifestation of Byatt's interest in romance, the structured and self-consciously unrealistic narrative which insists on the artifact of the happy heterosexual resolution. However, both romance and feminist exploration are transcended, characteristically for Byatt, by the affirmation of fairy tale as metafiction, the validity of art.

The woman as artist becomes a recurring figure in these symbolic representations of sexual difference, and is seen again, very strongly, in the Melusina figure of *Possession*. Here, the recurring glass/ice images of Byatt's writing are figured slightly differently, in the related images of water—the watery Melusina but also her fountain in LaMotte's poem, the physical watery landscapes of Yorkshire, and, rather more mundanely, bathrooms. Bathrooms seem to recur in Byatt's fiction generally—not only the numerous and idiosyncratic spaces of *Possession* but also as the site of epiphany in *The Shadow of the Sun*, or a moment of enjoyment for Gillian in "The Djinn in the Nightingale's Eye." (A rather tongue-in-cheek, but nonetheless entertaining and literate account of bathrooms in *Possession* is given by Patrick Wynn in an article written for the Tolkien fan journal *Butterbur's Woodshed*, which identifies Melusina as "a Bathroom Myth, pure and simple . . . this story is just another example of that age-old question posed by every man who has ever been forced to pace for hours outside a locked bathroom door, namely 'What the hell is she doing in there?!'") Gender issues aside, bathrooms are watery places, and water has similar properties to glass—both are marvelous and ambiguous liquids, reflective, transparent, malleable. Bathrooms are also places of shining tile, mirrors, semitransparent shower curtains, and panes of glass, not to mention extremes of hot and cold. In *Possession* bathrooms not only refigure the discovery scene of the Melusine story (in the perfect folkloric moment of Roland caught peering through the keyhole at Maud in her dragon dressing gown) but also literally reflect the personalities of their owners.

In Maud's bathroom, "a chill green glass place" with "glass tiles into whose brief and illusory depths one might peer, a shimmering shower curtain like a glass waterfall" (56), one finds not only a marvelous, fairy-tale realm but also the perfect symbolic expression of Byatt's desire for cool, clean, intellectual dispassion. In an interview with Eleanor Wachtel, she identifies this desire (also articulated by the academics in *Possession*) for "being able to be alone in a white room, with a white bed, and just think things out" (86). The same impulse is seen in "The Threshold," where the cool, watery silver lady offers "a closed casement in a high turret, and a private curtained bed where he would be most himself" (*Possession* 154). As well as being watery and glassy, bathrooms are intensely *private* spaces. This withdrawn privacy is integral to Byatt's sense of the female artist figure, and the folkloric Melusina is constructed in precisely these terms, as a builder of castles and cities as well as someone who must ritually retire to her private space. Franken argues for LaMotte's obvious fascination with "a concept of autonomy and creativity and a relationship between the two. The fact that Melusina owns her own space on Saturdays in which she is left alone and the fact that she creates madly and is applauded for it is attractive to LaMotte" (100). The perverse feminine is thus marginalized in favor of a redefinition of the folkloric motif in essentially artistic terms: Melusina is not only a "tragic portrait of motherhood," echoing LaMotte's own experience (97), but also a threatened artist, as LaMotte is, and as Byatt, presumably, fears to be herself. Images of water are thus integral to art, but the stereotyped feminist interpretation of water as feminine, sexual, and generative, as in Leonora's analysis of "hidden holes and openings through which life-giving waters bubble and enter reciprocally" (*Possession* 244), are invoked only to be undercut by the novel's gentle ridicule of Leonora. Byatt's actual interest in water is not in its sexually creative symbolism, but in its relationship to glass and its more abstract ability to mirror and reflect the demands of art.

Ultimately, the strongest intersection of the woman as artist with the motif of glass comes with the invocation of yet another folkloric, or perhaps romance, pattern, that of the Lady of Shalott. Byatt's writing continually betrays, both explicitly and implicitly, her affection for the Victorian romances of Tennyson and pre-Raphaelite art, which provide familiar patterns of narrative in a way very similar to fairy tale. The cracked mirror of the Lady is yet another incarnation of the glass surface, expressing most strongly the betrayal of female artistry at the heart of LaMotte's story, the perfect, creative solitude destroyed violently by the intrusion of a male figure and sexual passion. Byatt writes:

> The Lady has things in common with the frozen death-in-life states of Snow White and of the lady and her castle in the glass coffins. She is enclosed in her tower, and sees the world not even through the window, but in a mirror, which reflects the outside life, which she, the artist, then weaves into "a magic web with colours gay" . . . Preserving solitude and distance, staying cold and frozen, may, for women as well as artists, be a way of preserving life. (*Histories* 157–58)

In some ways the complexity of glass and water in Byatt's work attempts to redeem and rethink the too-perfect structures of the Lady's doom, to refigure the relationship between men, women, and art in more ambiguous terms that allow the possibility of freedom rather than insisting on the certainty of destruction.

GENIES IN BOTTLES, JEWELS IN TOAD'S HEADS:
NARRATIVE EMBEDDING

Perhaps one of the most notable aspects of Byatt's exploration of fairy tale is her tendency to embed her fairy tales in longer, often realist narratives. This is significantly different from the practice of most other contemporary fairy-tale writers, who, like Angela Carter, tend to publish collections of stand-alone tales, as Byatt herself does in *The Djinn in the Nightingale's Eye*. Even that, however, is misleading in Byatt's case, since two of the five tales in the volume were previously embedded in *Possession*, and "The Djinn in the Nightingale's Eye," the longest tale in the collection, makes sustained use of embedded narrative. It is as though Byatt's hyperawareness of the constructed nature of fairy-tale narrative, and hence of its intrinsic need for a narrator, cannot conceive of such narratives as separate from the frame which gives the narrator concrete identity. Even "The Story of the Eldest Princess," which, with "Cold," is Byatt's closest approach to the stand-alone fairy-tale narrative, embeds multiple mininarratives within its relatively simple fairy-tale frame, as does "The Glass Coffin," providing another reason for Byatt's interest in this particular tale from Grimm. Embedding, of course, is about fictionality; it is central to Byatt's metafictional project. Italo Calvino's essay "Levels of Reality in Literature" discusses the extent to which *any* form of literature embeds levels of narrative within the text, using the *Decameron* and the *Arabian Nights* as examples of explicit embedding. Either way, his conclusion is that "literature does not recognise Reality as such, but only *levels*. Whether there is such a thing as Reality, of which the various levels are only partial aspects, or whether there are only the levels, is something that literature cannot decide. Literature recognizes *the reality of the levels*" (*Literature Machine* 120–21). Embedded texts problematize reality and thus signal fiction as metafiction, reality as constructed artifact.

The embedding process works to emphasize Byatt's notions of reality and narrative, creating in effect two levels of operation in which the artificial (the marvelous, patterned and familiar form of the fairy tale) highlights the "real" of the frame narrative. This is similar to the effect Calvino notes in Boccaccio's *Decameron:* "between the tales and the framework there is a clean stylistic split that highlights the distance between the two planes" (117). In Byatt's work, the effect is particularly obvious in the novel form of *Possession,* which contrasts the omniscient narrator's modern account of Roland and Maud with the very distinctive voice and texture of LaMotte's fairy tales, both entire and fragmentary, included within the narrative. A similar but more complex effect can be seen in the detailed contemporary setting of "The Djinn in the Nightingale's Eye," which is textured largely as realist novella despite the obvious fairy-tale nature of its djinn and three wishes. A fascinating process of overlap occurs, however; the frame tale in both these texts slides between marvelous and realist, as slippage from the embedded tales infects the frame narrative. The mock-fantastic opening of "The Djinn in the Nightingale's Eye" characterizes our own time as one when "men and women hurtled through the air on metal wings . . . when pearly-fleshed and jewelled apparitions of Texan herdsmen and houris shimmered in the dusk on Nicaraguan hillsides" (95); this renders the mundane vividly magical while simultaneously denying the possibility of the marvelous. The playful antirealism alerts the reader to the forthcoming embedded tales as well as to the frame narrative's ultimately fairy-tale shape.

In its detail and complexity, the frame narrative's account of Gillian's life lacks the recognizable sparseness of fairy-tale texture: its psychological insights and meticulously described mundane settings at least partially contradict the narrative's fantastic structure. The familiar fairy-tale texture which would legitimate the marvelous and which is obviously lacking in the frame narrative is restored in the tales Gillian and her colleagues explore in critical retellings and in the oral tales told by the Djinn. In *Possession,* slippage from the embedded tales affects Roland and Maud, whose life begins to resemble the romances of LaMotte in its sexual inevitability and in the lost-descendant revelations which conclude the novel. The interactions of frame narrative with embedded tale act to elide and overwrite the contrast in textures: resonating structures simply highlight the fact that the frame tale is fairy tale as much as the embedded narratives. The realist illusion of the frame narrative is thus disrupted in true metafictional fashion, once again highlighting constructedness, artifice, and the fiction of realism. Embedding, and the resulting contrast and slippage between fairy tale and realist frame, permits Byatt to explicitly brandish the self-conscious artifice of the tale in a way a stand-alone tale can do only implicitly.

The same self-consciousness is true even when the frame tale is far from realist, an effect seen most strongly in "The Story of the Eldest Princess" and "The Glass Coffin," which effectively offer fairy tales embedded in fairy tales. In "Princess," the fairy-tale frame is host to a series of oral, folk-style narratives (the stories of the Scorpion, the Toad, and the Cockroach), which invoke popular folk beliefs and also provide cautionary exempla to the Princess. It also includes brief fairy tales embedded as literary fragments rather than represented orally, as the old woman tells the Princess the tales of her two sisters. "Princess" is particularly effective in that its embedded narratives are the only sites of closure in the tale, whose open-ended conclusion proposes to continue indefinitely with the process of embedding stories in the frame. The old woman actually claims the process of embedding as liberation from the need for the frame tale to accede to the demands of story: "We collect stories and spin stories and mend what we can and investigate what we can't, and live quietly without striving to change the world. We have no story of our own here, we are free, as old women are free, who don't have to worry about princes or kingdoms, but dance alone and take an interest in the creatures (*Djinn* 66).

Embedding, then, allows the ultimate demonstration of narrative power, which rests, not in the tales themselves, but in those who tell them and are thus free of them and in control. Similarly, "The Glass Coffin" conflates embedding with issues of power; the old man's narration of what the tailor will experience functions as an embedded narrative with strong predictive power, since things simply *will* happen as the old man describes. The lady's embedded story works in the opposite direction, to give the history of her entrapment; paradoxically, the telling of the narrative both recreates that entrapment and signals her freedom from it. The embedded tales play with the flow of time in the story, allowing jumps forward and back in a way very different from the usual placid flow of fairy tale. However, through this process Byatt is able to reaffirm the identity of the tale as a whole, created object which can be accessed at any point without disrupting its integrity.

Whether fairy tale within fairy tale, or fairy tale within realist frame, perhaps the most important result of the recurring presence of embedded narratives in Byatt's work is the way in which they encourage the reader to draw parallels between the frame tale and the embedded narratives. Mieke Bal points out the extent to which the embedding of obviously discrete texts in a frame text allows texts to partake of the characteristics of discrete and subordinate discourses—to function with two identities simultaneously. The result of this is increased signification: "An embedded unit is by definition subordinate to the unit which embeds it; but it can acquire relative independence. This is the case when it can be defined as a specimen of a more or less well-delimited genre. It then has more or less complete signification. This is enriched, set off, even radically transformed by its relation with the embedding unit, but it has absolutely no need of it to be coherent" (48).

In remaining separate yet related, embedded texts endow meaning and signification with added depth and complexity; fairy tale is perhaps the most extreme example of Bal's "well-delimited" genre, and hence contributes particularly strong forms of signification to the frame narrative. This, more than textural contrast, is perhaps the greatest implication for Byatt's practice of embedding. Byatt writes, "I have myself become increasingly interested in quickness and lightness of narrative—in small discrete stories rather than pervasive and metamorphic metaphors as a way of thinking out a text" (*Histories* 130).

Embedded tales are able to function as warning, and thus empowerment to potentially entrapped characters, because they are simultaneously independent of and involved with the frame narrative; they retain their shape even while their events resonate across to the frame narrative. In "The Djinn in the Nightingale's Eye," the folkloric and fairy-tale traditions invoked are largely those of the East rather than the Western tradition from which Byatt most often draws. The

Djinn's tale swapping with Gillian, and particularly his status as an entrapped individual within the bottle curse, identifies him as well as Gillian with the figure of Scheherazade, the strategic tale-teller from the frame narrative of the *Arabian Nights*. In the tradition of Scheherazade, the tales told gain additional importance and urgency because of their implications for the frame narrative. At the most obvious level Scheherazade will survive another night and the Djinn may persuade his owner to free him. In addition, however, "The Djinn in the Nightingale's Eye" parallels the way in which the actual *content* of the *Arabian Nights* tales tends to invoke and revisit the theme of the frame narrative—feminine infidelity, the justice of Sultans, the survival of fairy-tale protagonists against all odds. At one point the Djinn tells Gillian, "in harems the study of apparently uneventful personal histories is a matter of extreme personal importance" (206), thus firmly placing the tale within a tradition of tales whose telling is strategic as well as simply pleasurable. Other peoples' tales are important because the patterns of narrative they offer function as warnings, and thus potentially as empowerment, to the characters of the frame narrative; they are also expressions of power on the part of the teller. The tales of Patient Griselda and the wishing-monkey, as well as the Djinn's stories of harem life, codify and display the knowledge Gillian needs to make sense of her wishes.

At times this causes Byatt's use of fairy-tale form to approach the moral pointedness of the fable. A striking example occurs in "Crocodile Tears," from the *Elementals* collection, where the story of the Companion, a classic fairy tale of the magical helper to the fairy-tale hero, provides an emotional warning to the tale's protagonist. This, again, is in the image of ice, but here ice and death, the undesirable extreme of the process of withdrawal from the world Byatt sees as necessary to the artist. Resonating with the frame tale, the story of the Companion allows Patricia, the protagonist, to re-evaluate death as both closure and obligation, and to re-enter the world she has left. Its presentation, orally retold in a partially fragmentary fashion, allows focus on those elements of the tale most appropriate to the frame narrative, while nonetheless retaining a sense of the tale's overall structure and coherence.

In terms of the functioning of the fairy tales, their embedding in various texts naturally changes their meaning and implication; it is no longer possible to sink into the comforting mimesis of narrative, the illusionary world created by the tale's omniscient narrator. Instead, the reader is forced to confront the tale's structured status, and to acknowledge the reciprocal influences of frame narrative and embedded artifact. Richard Todd points out that " 'The Glass Coffin' and 'Gode's

Story' are absolutely transformed by their existence within the narrative matrix of *Possession,* even though the wording of the tales may be identical outside that context in *The Djinn in the Nightingale's Eye"* (*Writers* 43). The resonance of LaMotte's "The Glass Coffin" and the oral Breton narrative of "Gode's Tale" with the life of LaMotte adds new layers of meaning to the apparently bland surface of the tales' incarnation in *The Djinn in the Nightingale's Eye.* "The Glass Coffin" becomes, in addition to its emphasis on art and entrapment, a parable for the happy, sequestered coexistence of Christabel and Blanche, disrupted by the "black artist" (*Possession* 66) who stands for Ash. The tale's gender distributions are interesting; the apparently sexless sibling relationship of the lady and her brother recaptures the intensity of Christabel's life with Blanche and also hints at a transgressively sexual partnership in the regendering of one of them, presumably standing for Blanche against Christabel's lady-behind-glass. At the same time, the tale could be reread with Blanche as "black artist" (she is a painter), attempting to deny Christabel the happy heterosexual union offered by the tailor (Ash). The tale is hence rescued from parable or allegory by the wide possibilities offered by its symbols in play with the frame narrative, so that the reader must engage in continual reinterpretation as tale and novel unfold.

"Gode's Tale" is an even stronger example of this process. My experiences teaching *The Djinn in the Nightingale's Eye* at third-year level suggest that the story is, in fact, almost completely opaque when extracted from the frame of *Possession.* Students were unable to account for the "little dancing feet" of the story, or the moment of "an owl cry, or a cat miawl" in the barn, and "blood on the straw" (*Djinn* 31), until learning of the frame circumstances of Christabel's illicit pregnancy and the ambiguity around the possible death of her child. Alone, "Gode's Tale" provides a particularly folkloric and emotionally compelling ghost story which operates with a great deal of the "thickening mystery" attributed to Matty's tale. Within the frame of *Possession* it contributes materially to the unraveling of Christabel's story, providing slanting references to pregnancy and transgression which resonate particularly strongly with the later significance of the séance in the Victorian narrative.

Another consequence of Byatt's use of frame narrative is seen in her ability to embed what are no more than fairy-tale fragments in the wider narrative. This results in a process almost of invocation rather than reproduction; it is unnecessary to complete the partial tale since we know the shape and can extrapolate the whole structure from the suggestive fragments. In this process, the fragmentary tales are ultimately given coherence and completion through their resonance with frame events. This is seen strikingly in "The Threshold," which forms the threshold of *Possession* itself, signaling the moment of revelation and choice of future path experienced by Roland and Maud as well as the Childe within the tale. The three ladies, gold, silver, and dark, need no explanation; they exemplify fairy-tale choice in familiar, classic symbols whose outcome, as Byatt notes, is inevitable: "he must always choose this last, and the leaden casket, for wisdom in all tales tells us this, and the last sister is always the true choice" (*Possession* 155). At the same time, however, the embedding of the fragment in the frame tale of *Possession* means that the tale only becomes fully meaningful when we realize its implications for the choice made by Christabel LaMotte. In choosing the dark lady, LaMotte has rejected sexual passion (gold and sunlight) and artistic seclusion (silver, associated with cool and water, and hence intellect in Byatt's system); what she is left with is neither, but a kind of abdication, the "Herb of Rest" (154). Other fragments of *Tales for Innocents* are equally recognizable tale openings (51–52), but their meaning is only decodable with reference to LaMotte and other frame characters; they variously signal artistic longing (the queen who desires the silent bird) or rejection of Victorian domesticity (the clumsy third daughter). Perhaps the most extreme example of this fragmented embedding is in the frequent references to Christabel as a princess in a tower; together with images of Maud's long blonde hair, these fragmentary evocations implicitly construct an embedded Rapunzel tale despite the fact that such a tale is never actually retold.

Fragments of fairy tale in *Possession* share with retold tales in "The Djinn in the Nightingale's Eye" a meaning peculiar to the frame tale's circumstances. Such fragments are rendered meaningful not only in their resonance with events of the frame but also through their analysis by characters in the frame tale. Thus the feminist import of Gillian and Orhan's various stories is deconstructed for us by the academic characters of the frame narrative, rounding out the fragmentary nature of their retelling. The effect is one of increased richness of texture while the flow of the frame narrative is only momentarily disrupted, rather than the full switching of reading mode required by a fully recounted tale. Once again, the range of effects possible in the use of fairy-tale forms is materially increased by the fact of their embedding, and Byatt's considerable sophistication and layering is both enabled and emphasized.

Byatt's focus in general is literary in the extreme, referring continually to books and the process of writing. However, her use of embedding, in particular, provides a logical and fruitful site for play with the oral voice; as I have noted above, embedded oral narratives have the potential to embody the narrator in the frame narrative. While this is obviously an artificial emulation of the oral tale, the frame tale's apparent mimesis enables the illusion of spoken tale rather than the literary, written retelling it is in fact. Neil Jordan's film *The Company of Wolves* creates a similar effect, although he is working with the considerable advantages of film, already an aural and visual medium, and the immediacy of actors retelling tales in voice-over, rather than the flatness of words on a page. A literary recreation of an oral tale can only gain strength and legitimacy from its insistence on the reality of the narrator, whose character not only infuses the tale with personality absent from the flatter surface of a literary tale but also who is present in person in the frame narrative. The oral illusion also places emphasis on the metafictional nature of the tale as artificial, a told construct within the larger context whose assumption of reality highlights the lack of reality in fairy tale. In keeping with the resonance of frame tale with embedded tale, the site and circumstances of the retelling become vital for the tale's meaning. "The Djinn in the Nightingale's Eye" provides ample evidence of this, in the sharp contrasts between tales retold as conference papers, or tales told in more vital and immediate surroundings—the museum guide's retelling of the Gilgamesh tale, or the Djinn's stories given erotic and immediate circumstance by his presence on Gillian's hotel bed. "Gode's Story," too, offers a village folktale whose immediacy rests largely in the character of Gode, repository of folk wisdom; her distinctive voice and status as perceptive wise woman lend authority to the tale's moral symbolism. Likewise, the setting of the Breton coast during the mythic setting of Toussaint, the midwinter storytelling festival, legitimates the ghosts and hauntings within the story.

GEOMETRICALLY PATTERNED FLOWERS: LITERATURE AS STRUCTURE

> The pleasure of writing . . . was in handling the old, worn counters of the characterless persons, the Fate of the consecutive events, including the helpless commentary of the writer on the unavoidable grip of the story, and a sense that I was myself partaking in the continuity of the tales by retelling them in a new context in a way old and new. —BYATT, *Histories* 131

In some ways it is perhaps misleading to analyze Byatt entirely as a writer of fairy tale. Like Thurber and Carter—or, indeed, like many other modern fairy-tale writers—she employs fairy tale as one aspect of her varied literary output. Unlike Carter or Thurber, her interest in fairy tale is not, in fact, for its own sake; fairy-tale and folkloric techniques are simply one item in the formidable toolbox with which she approaches the mechanisms of literature as a whole. What she is interested in is, as she says above, "the grip of the story" and "the continuity of the tales." In some ways, she perhaps best exemplifies the particular awareness for which I argue in my introductory chapter: that of fairy tale as the most inherently self-conscious literary form, one whose strong patterning is ideally suited not only to the deconstruction of its own conventions but also those of literature. Like Carter, Byatt provides a particularly complex and playful response to the essentially symbolic aspects of fairy tale, the "old, worn counters of the characterless persons," but her dense systems of symbol are absolutely unlike Carter's feminist symbolism in that they are endlessly recursive. The apparent resonance of glass or ice, heat or cold, enclosure and entrapment in Byatt's work is only peripherally a feminist project, or any other sort of project at all. What her fairy-tale symbols do is to reflect, not ideas, but themselves—the nature of fairy tale, and hence the nature of narrative, literature, and art. Such an awareness of art is, however, unavoidably linked to the awareness of reality, unable to exist except in a relationship with reality. She concludes that " 'happy every after' is, as Nooteboom said, a lie, a look in a mirror. Ordinary happiness is to be outside a story, full of curiosity, looking before and after" (*Histories* 150). Exploring the "happy ever after" of fairy tale is to be aware of it as tale, to be able to explore and expose, with happy curiosity, the artifice of the literary.

5

STRUCTURED SWORD AND SORCERY: THE POPULAR FAIRY TALES OF LEE, PRATCHETT, AND TEPPER

Fairy tale has traditionally found easy and successful expression in modern popular contexts—it is a simple, recognizable, and symbolically powerful form of narrative easily adaptable to a range of texts from advertising and romance novels to the Hollywood film. In particular, any approach to fairy tale in terms of its self-aware structural games must necessarily carry over into the realm of popular expressions, not only because of the formulaic nature of many popular texts but also because of the extent to which popular literature offers a fascinating echo of the community expressions and basic human concerns entrenched in folkloric structures. This, however, is a far from uncontested development; the twentieth and twenty-first centuries are characterized by the rising power of corporate ownership of popular forms, in a process in many ways diametrically opposed to the communal production of folklore despite the mass appeal of the resulting artifacts. In the formulation of many critics the intervention of technology is seen as a process whereby folk culture becomes mass culture, a process mirroring, but far more pervasive than, the shift from oral to literary forms. The concomitant ideological problems arising from this commercial appropriation of popular forms have been variously chronicled by critics from Theodor Adorno and Max Horkheimer to Stuart Hall and Jack Zipes, as have the notions of popular culture as potentially individualistic and subversive, as argued by theorists such as John Fiske. Despite these issues, fairy tale in the modern popular media remains a site of broad cultural

Some of the material in this chapter first appeared as a conference paper given to the University of Cape Town's postgraduate conference; "All the World's a Pizza: Postmodernism, Popular Culture, and Pshakespeare in Terry Pratchett's Discworld," *Inter Action* 5 (1997): 194–202.

investment, its accessibility in intellectual and practical terms making it in many ways a far closer echo of its folkloric roots, despite its mass-market aspects, than are the more literary productions with which I have until now been concerned.

Central to the common workings of fairy tale and popular narrative is the encoding of genre as formula, the complex process of structural familiarity and recognition, combined with elements of peripheral novelty in each repetition; John Cawelti has most famously articulated this notion of popular structures. Thus fairy-tale elements tend to simply reinforce the already-powerful workings of generic structure in popular texts. The iterations of this combined generic awareness are endless, and the sheer bulk of available texts somewhat boggling. My focus on essentially narrative concerns means that I have not chosen to explore the incredibly rich and various invocations of fairy tale in such media as advertising, or its echoes in more realist genres such as women's romance; likewise, the powerful and important operations of fairy tale in cinematic narrative have merited their own chapter. My interest here is in written popular narrative, either the modern fairy-tale short stories, which most closely reproduce the resonant brevity of the folkloric tale, or the retelling of fairy tale in full-length popular novels.

The novel form provides a somewhat problematical landscape for fairy-tale explorations; in its length, detail, historicity, and demand for psychological depth, it runs the risk of compromising the essential texture of fairy tale—to inhibit, in fact, fairy tale's contrived simplicity and hence its illusion of a universalized truth. Significantly, the texts I have previously dealt with have not included actual novels; Carter and Byatt both chose to pursue their literary retellings within shorter forms more faithful to the folkloric originals, and Thurber's works are not only textured with fairy-tale simplicity but also avoid true novelistic length and texture through the format aimed at children. Despite this apparent incompatibility of format, however, the endless adaptability of fairy-tale narrative finds new power in the more realist texture and detail of the novel, replacing the unquestioning wonder of fairy-tale simplicity with the authority of novelistic world-building. In particular, popular fairy-tale novels have found a significant and successful niche, as well as a natural compatibility, within those subgenres of the contemporary novel which paradoxically use the novel's convincing detail to depict unreal or magical worlds. The important common feature of the marvelous means that many of these alternative popular formulae are found within the specific generic codes of fantasy, science fiction, and horror. Because of the nonrealist encodings of these genres fairy-tale elements are able to operate relatively undisrupted, their familiar narrative techniques echoed, supported, and explored through intersection with novelistic codes as well as through the popular market's reliance on recognizable formulae. Despite this mass-market framing, however, the intersection of fairy tale with popular genres also provides a fertile ground for self-conscious genre play which is necessarily based in structural awareness.

THE COMMUNITY VOICE: FAIRY TALE AND POPULAR CULTURE

There is an underground connection between fairy tales and modern fiction—between one of the oldest forms of literature and one of the most recent. More often than we realise, the stock situations and stock characters ... of the classic fairy tale reappear in the novel we read today. —ALISON LURIE, 29

The invocation of the notion of the "popular" in the context of fairy tale must immediately invoke the "folk" definitions attached to its oral form, and thus create the possibility that there may be modern incarnations of "folk" culture even within a technologized age of mass culture. Like fairy tale, modern mass-market texts could be seen to reflect and perpetuate the concerns and dreams of the "folk," in the sense of a culture's population at large; at the same time, issues of production and ownership suggest that this is a highly contested arena of culture. Walter Benjamin most clearly articulates this concern about the place of the genuine folk voice in a technological age, describing not only a loss of authenticity as soon as the oral story is written down in a book, with the resulting isolation of both the novelist and the reader, but ultimately the replacement of storytelling with mere information ("Storyteller" 87–88, 99). Zipes likewise acknowledges that "there would seem to be something totalitarian about the manner in which the voice of the early oral fairy tales was stolen from real, live 'people' ... and used by corporations seeking to profit from our fantasies and longing for happiness." Nonetheless, the development of technology has not merely usurped folk texts, it has also developed new forms of text, in many ways actually increasing access and communication. As Zipes comments, a view of mass culture as simply destructive of community is "facile and one-dimensional, emanating from a mechanical and deterministic view of human nature and history ... it is more important to grasp the diverse ways in which the fairy tale as a genre has been used" (*Happily Ever After* 6).

The notion of "popular culture" is thus another theoretical mine-field, encompassing a bewildering variety of approaches, definitions, and foci. Dominic Strinati neatly summarizes the main debates, which circle around the origin of popular material—does it "rise up from the people 'below' or does it sink down from elites 'on high'?"; its purpose, whether designed for sale and profit or as an artistic expression in its own right; and its ideological function—does it represent the indoctrinatory values of the elite, or the resistance and subversion of the underclass? (3). His balanced account of various historical approaches to popular culture ultimately locates it as a site of ongoing tension and contestation. This is interesting in that it parallels the conflicts in structuralist and postmodernist approaches to narrative. The sense of mass culture as the outcome of a monolithic, top-down process, with the means of production owned and defined by a corporate elite, as exemplified in the theories of the Frankfurt School, is curiously similar to structuralism's sense of universal, overarching definitions. (Indeed, as Strinati points out, Umberto Eco's analysis of the James Bond novels combines precisely these two theoretical strands [93]). As with the interaction between structuralism and postmodernism, rigid ideas of cultural structures are both assaulted and subsumed by more agile and multivalent theories which insist on the constructed nature of the apparent monolith and allow for competing discourses in its construction. Stuart Hall's "Notes on Deconstructing the Popular" is an influential articulation of this sense of popular culture as a site of struggle, providing the historical perspective lacking from more structuralist accounts and demonstrating his debt to Antonio Gramsci's sense of culture as a complex process of negotiation between dominant and subordinate groups.

Once more, broader cultural issues are reflected on the level of text and narrative. The prevalence of postmodern modes of expression in contemporary mass culture, encompassing pastiche, multiplicity, collage, and the failure of master narratives, clearly embodies the suggestion that, as with postmodern exposures of fairy tale's structuralist "trick," monolithic notions of popular culture are susceptible to assault and breakdown, demonstrating the illusion of their apparently totalitarian control. These are, of course, the narrative tricks and assaults already seen in the "literary" productions of Byatt and Carter, demonstrating yet another category of opposition in contemporary culture. Here the structuralist/monolithic notions of mass-cultural influence enable the construction of "popular" as a pejorative label, associating literature with a purely commercial process, texts written to sell rather than to offer any original or intellectual investigation of ideas. Cawelti explicitly links the childhood experience of the familiar story at bedtime to adult formula literature: both are concerned with "highly predictable structures that guarantee the fulfilment of conventional expectations" and are associated with "relaxation, entertainment and escape" (1). Such texts thus come to exist in a notional relationship with an opposing category of "canon" or "literary" production—high versus low culture, "real" literature versus mere entertainment. Once again, however, this universalized idea of value becomes problematical under the assault of the contemporary. Within the texts of popular fairy tale in the late twentieth- and early twenty-first-centuries can be discerned a self-conscious play with textuality and parody which shadows the more intellectual impulses of "literary" fairy tale, and whose processes are closely allied even while they are different. This exemplifies the process of cultural slippage associated with most forms of postmodernism: in Fredric Jameson's terms, "the effacement in them of the older (essentially high-modernist) frontier between high culture and so-called mass or commercial culture" (2). The result of this is not only, as Jameson points out, the acquisition and incorporation by "high" culture of low-status genres such as romance and science fiction, it also leads to the slippage of postmodernism's intellectual stance of irony, fragmentation, and self-consciousness into certain areas of low cultural status.

The issues raised by considering fairy tale in the context of popular culture are thus both complex and fruitful, requiring negotiation of notions of orality, historicity, structure, and technology on many levels. Despite this, however, structural parallels between folkloric and popular forms are often clear cut. Fairy tale shares, and at times influences, some features of popular literary and film genres such as the women's romance exemplified by Harlequin or Mills and Boon, the detective thriller, sword-and-sorcery fantasy, and the Hollywood love story: predictability, simplicity of narrative, use of archetypal motifs, and a notion of closure which imposes specific pattern on the narrative. This follows the process seen in Walter Ong's discussion of the oral roots of formula. While he is concerned largely with post-technological orality, he ultimately concludes that the formula is intrinsic to most modern popular forms: "formulary devices . . . have their place in secondary oral culture, too, and in particular in our popular arts, including literature" (*Rhetoric, Romance, and Technology* 285). Most interestingly for my purposes, in this formulaic intersection popular fiction shares with fairy tale the dual characteristics of extremely patterned and easily recognizable structures, and a sense of narrative as utopian, tending toward satisfying closure. In this the predetermined forms of fairy tale are strongly akin to the functioning of popular formulae.

At the heart of these characteristics is the concept of escapism, the idea that this kind of narrative is oversimplified and unrealistic, offering a kind of reading pleasure based on wish fulfillment and ease of consumption rather than any intellectual challenge or adequate mirroring of the real world. Zipes notes how popular narratives such as those of Hollywood rely on "true and tested stories to continue framing and narrating the wish-fulfilment of all classes of people to give them hope—and, of course, to make some money in the process" (*Happily Ever After* 2). The notion of the upbeat ending recurs across many (although not all) popular genres; in the women's romance the happy heterosexual couple is the inevitable ending; in detective fiction, the crime will be solved and the criminal punished. It could be argued that the "fairy-tale happy ending" is an intrinsic part of these genres, fulfilling an important narrative and psychological function in the construction of reading pleasure. This is seen in approaches such as that of Bruno Bettelheim, who argues that the satisfying outcome of fairy tale persuades child readers that anxieties about separation and death in the real world can be overcome: "this rekindles hope, which without such fantasy would be extinguished by harsh reality" (133). Perhaps the best account of this function is by Tolkien, in his important essay on fantasy, in which he explores the importance of "eucatastrophe . . . a sudden and miraculous grace . . . giving a poignant glimpse of Joy, Joy beyond the walls of the world, poignant as grief" (68). He defends the fantasy genre against charges of escapism, arguing that escape is not necessarily wrong, that a process of recovery and consolation is necessary to preserve a notion of the ideal in the human psyche. More than this, his argument suggests that the archaic tale structures reflect a transcendent ideal of beauty, "beyond the walls of the world," and an integration of humanity with that beauty, which we have lost and wish to regain, if only imaginatively. Unrelieved realism, in his view, presents present-day ugliness as inevitable, precluding the concept of something better. His argument pertains specifically to fantasy, but a similar conclusion could be drawn with other genres: the arrest of the criminal in detective fiction preserves an ideal of morality and justice, in the same way that women's romance insists on the utopian potential in love and sexuality. Similarly, such genres tend toward the archetypal rather than the psychologically real, and motifs such as the hero and heroine of the romantic paperback, or the lonely detective battling crime, have a strong symbolic function underlining their provision of some kind of ideal.

The conclusion must be drawn, then, that the structure of fairy tales, and of those parallel modern forms which offer the similar qualities of simplicity, predictability, and utopianism, are fulfilling a very specific function for their readership. It is not a stretch to link this to the far older forms of "popular culture" which have given rise to the fairy tale as we know it, and to suggest that the oral folktales of peasant life are in some ways structurally and psychologically akin to modern popular genres. In their *Re-Situating Folklore*, Frank De Caro and Rosan Augusta Jordan note the tendency for folklore to be "viewed as limited to context removed from those of the intellectual elites who looked at folkloric communication from an outsider perspective—limited to . . . such groups as the peasantry, 'primitives,' the working class, or simply 'the common people'" (16). Their argument follows theorists such as Alan Dundes in acknowledging the limitations and flaws in this assumption and the problematical ideological and social forces behind identification of "the folk," but nonetheless supports the notion that there is a natural linkage of ideas between folklore and "popular" culture. As we understand it, in its earliest, oral form fairy tale was an expression of a communal folk culture, offering a removed and symbolic version of peasant experience as well as an escape into fantasy and wish fulfillment. Not only are the motifs of many fairy tales agricultural and domestic, but the classic pattern of the miller's undervalued youngest son who rises to marry a princess also encodes typically underclass longings after wealth and class status. At the same time, folkloric motifs are also about the most basic of human needs—food, survival, sexuality, death. Critics such as Maria Tatar have detailed the process of adaptation from folklore to literary versions, pointing out that both sexual innuendo and graphic violence were found in traditional folktales. Walter Ong comments that all oral discourse is "involved purposefully in the real life world, where men, women and children live and eat and grow, and talk about existential concerns, and come to practical decisions" ("Mimesis to Irony" 5). Again, parallels can be drawn with modern genres; women's romance is about sexuality, the detective novel about death. Even the classic adventure patterns of the western, thriller, sword-and-sorcery epic, or pulp science fiction tale encode, in their basic violence, notions of survival at a fairly primitive level. Popular reading seems to sketch, in this removed and symbolic form, fundamental human survival impulses similar to those of folklore, and which suggest that, in the main, popular reading pleasure is about reassurance and the celebration of structure and closure in the basic patterns of life.

There are interesting implications, however, for this notion of fairy tale as inherently akin to the popular in its address to fundamental patterns of human life. The literary fairy tale has become the most common medium through which the modern audience experiences the form; however, it retains a self-conscious connection with its less mannered folkloric roots. Zipes recognizes the ability of literary fairy tales to "[appropriate] oral folk tales and [create] new ones to reflect upon rituals, customs, habits, and ethics and simultaneously to serve as a civilizing agent" (*Happily Ever After* 3–4). To me, much of the interest in fairy tale is the way in which its literary expressions invoke their oral roots and depend upon an awareness of what I choose to identify as a "folkloric voice": a self-aware invocation of oral tradition in the tone and phrasing of the tale. Ong argues for precisely this concept of oral remnants which underpin and permeate the literary word, "the background of the spoken word, in which literature has its pristine and its permanent roots" ("Mimesis to Irony" 1). Ong's approach echoes the assumption of much literary fairy tale in that it tends to self-consciously invoke oral transmission as a utopian mode from an idyllic pastoral past, a form of communication whose presence in a literary work thus implies greater authenticity and relevance to its culture. This is, of course, problematical, as Eric L. Montenyohl points out: in fact, the relationship is far from historically linear, and the presence of any notion of oral performance, far from being a superseded cultural expression characteristic only of preliterate people, is "a complex issue, one rooted in the relationships of orality and literacy *within* a particular culture" (245). Like its assumption of totalitarian structuredness as a generic given, literary fairy tale nonetheless appropriates some aspects of oral authority in constructing and presenting its apparently seamless surface. Walter Benjamin argues strongly for the importance of oral storytelling as a direct transmission of the wisdom of experience, and suggests that "among those who have written down the tales, it is the great ones whose written version differs least from speech of the many nameless storytellers" ("Storyteller" 84). His claims are borne out by the extent to which modern literary fairy-tale writers slip into an imitation of oral address—Carter's second-person proverbial tone in "The Company of Wolves," Byatt's play with the Breton narrator in "Gode's Tale." At the other end of the textual spectrum, Disney's films traditionally exploit the notion in their opening voice-overs, invoking the reassuring oral voice of the trusted storyteller. This is very much part of fairy tale's inherently metafictional project, one of the techniques through which it signals itself as artifact, told tale rather than real life.

Quite apart from the spurious identification of orality with preliterate authority, this folkloric voice—the cozy intimacy and once-upon-a-time wisdom of the teller—is conceptually problematical in other ways. The path of fairy tale from the earliest oral forms to the most sophisticated of literary expressions is a contested development, both in the adaptation of folk forms through history, and in the definition of such forms by critics. The literary fairy tale explicitly invokes a peasant, pre-literate past—the antithesis of metafictional literary games—and does so only to obliterate it. Elizabeth Harries points out that even the earliest written versions were "following written models" rather than oral ones; she comments, "The history of fairy tale is not primarily a history of oral transmission but rather a history of print" (4). Bacchilega's discussion chooses to define fairy tale as a " 'borderline' or transitional genre," which "bears the traces of orality, folkloric tradition, and socio-cultural performance, even when it is . . . marketed with little respect for its history and materiality" (3). More importantly, the notion of historical narrative, in this usage, becomes an artificial and spurious construction; true historicity is overwritten and destroyed by the literate modes which ape it. As Bacchilega states, "the fairy tale also magically grants writers/tellers and readers/listeners access to the collective, if *fictionalised* past of social communing" (5, emphasis mine). Thus, the inherent metafictionality of literary fairy tale is partially constructed by this awareness of "folk" roots, such roots being, not in any historical reality, but in an idealized notion of peasant identity, a concept of being "in touch" with a communal expression about which the modern literary fairy-tale writer can, in fact, know nothing. This leads to the increasing distance about which Benjamin is so concerned: "the storyteller . . . has already become something remote from us and something that is getting even more distant" (83).

In this notion of a dialogue with an artificial notion of oral historicity, modern literary and postliterate fairy tale necessarily invokes, yet again, the concerns of postmodern literature. Linda Hutcheon has commented on the historicity of postmodernism, its process of dialogue with the past, as well as its tendency to reject the kind of cultural humanism encoded by historical values. In the re-creation of a fictitious oral or communal voice, literary fairy tale deals in nostalgia, a desire to recapture a lost, edenic past. This impulse has been definitively explored by Jean Baudrillard, who argues in "Simulacra and Simulation" that the contemporary notions of primitive societies and their importance for our culture, are simply false, a simulacrum which attempts to restore a nonexistent past to our current media-dominated and postindustrial culture. He states: "When the real is no longer what it used to be, nostalgia assumes its full meaning. There is a proliferation of myths of origin and signs of reality; of second-hand truth, objectivity and authenticity . . . We need a visible past, a visible continuum, a visible myth of origin to reassure us as to our ends, since ultimately we have never believed in them . . ." (171). In the hyperreal of media images, fairy tale seems one last link with a simpler, more human past; since we cannot actually reclaim that past, because we have destroyed it, it is necessary to artificially recreate it. Thus it is possible to see the proliferation of fairy tales in the last two hundred years as something linked inescapably with industrialization. From the Victorians onward, we have sought to compensate ourselves for the lost (always unrealistic) ideal of the feudal and agricultural existence which was destroyed by mechanization.

If fairy tale's self-conscious project relies on the invocation of an idyllic communal past, this becomes even more problematical in the context of a media- and consumer-driven age. The communal expressions of oral folklore are revised and erased in the more fixed writer/reader relationship of literary tale; even more so, the relationship is appropriated and exploited in the expressions of popular culture which are transmitted by mass cultural means. Critics such as Benjamin and Ong stress the importance of oral folklore as an unmediated experience of shared culture; Ong insists that "the oral performance is precisely not distanced from either performer or audience" (2), and that "the oral performer typically is speaking for everyone to everyone about what every adult already knows" (5). Literature, with its more personal written codes, already distances the narrative; a mass text, with its accompanying issues of ownership, commercial purpose, and fixed but pervasive form, appropriates some of the cultural spaces of the oral, but absolutely transforms the way in which they are used. De Caro and Jordan comment on the technical demands of folkloric narrative, which, "in contrast to the 'mass media', requires little, often virtually nothing, in the way of . . . equipment, technicians, editors or sales personnel for communication to occur" (2). The mass media is produced via a complex and expensive mechanism which alienates the receiver from the actual means of production of the text, and is absolutely removed from the simple teller/listener relationship of oral folklore. Yet many of these new technologies, among them film, television, and the Internet, have the ability to mimic oral transmission in various ways: an aural and visual rather than written format, a certain informality of address, a common and shared culture among a broad section of the population. In some ways these technologies have over time opened a new space for genuine folkloric communication—home video, fan narratives, the Internet as a new forum for the spread of urban legend. Nonetheless, in an ironic echo of fairy tale's deceptively authoritative surface, the "popular" aspects of mass culture also mimic and subsume the authenticity of actual folkloric interaction, replacing its purpose of reflecting communal experience with a more complex project which, while necessarily entailing both an artistic purpose and a reflection of their viewers' lives, needs, and desires, frequently subsume these elements to commercial intent. This commercial aspect is hardly new to fairy tale; in the nineteenth century, the Brothers Grimm produced multiple editions of their Nursery and Household tales, editing later editions with an eye to the market, and removing elements of sexuality which might offend a bourgeois readership. Maria Tatar reports a letter from Jacob to Wilhelm on the new 1815 edition: "I do not think we can print it as it was; there is much to be improved and added—something that will also prove favourable for sales . . ." (in Tatar 12). Fairy tale is thus identified with a process of revision toward commercial rather than artistic ends, long before twentieth-century consumerism; nonetheless, consumerism has expanded and exaggerated this process.

Regardless of the potential inauthenticities of fairy tale's claim to folkloric authority, I think it can be argued that the oral, folkloric elements within fairy tale help to situate it, under certain circumstances, firmly within the realm of the popular. The genre's continual groping toward a lost "folk" status underlines the extent to which, historically, fairy tale has been appropriated by the processes of written narrative, removing the genre from the realm of the common folk into the elite world of the educated, and the restoration of even a spurious orality attempts to reverse the process. Under these circumstances, the notion of inherent metafictionality, and the self-reflexive play with structure, undergoes certain changes. The process of recognition and mutual understanding of narrative conventions remains unchanged, since fairy tale, in itself a popular narrative in the sense that it is common to a wide audience, is very much a given of Western culture. At the same time, the reflexive and self-conscious nature of some popular fairy-tale narratives seems to go directly against some formulations of popular culture, particularly mass culture. Clement Greenberg's analysis of mass art condemns it as kitsch, as the antithesis of reflexiveness: "Avant-garde art is introverted—it is about itself (it is about its medium). Kitsch is extroverted; it is about the world" (in Noël Carroll 33). My identification of fairy tale as inherently metafictional, and my choice of several kinds of popular narrative which employ fairy-tale motifs self-reflexively, follows Carroll in tending to deny Greenberg's characterization. Nonetheless, in analyzing the structural games played by popular fairy-tale texts, an awareness of a shifting balance is necessary; self-conscious play, artistic choice, and ideological investigation are often present, but the moderating effect of commercial necessity should never be forgotten.

PULP PRINCES: FAIRY TALE IN THE SF GHETTO

In the popular context, explicit fairy tale retellings are most frequently found within the genre I shall define as "fantasy romance":

the mass market novels, most often multivolume, that have flooded a post-Tolkien market with sword-and-sorcery epics unashamedly in the Middle-Earth mold, allowing hundreds of heroes to complete epic quests with the aid of swords, dragons, magic, beautiful women, talking animals, nonhuman races, and the like. The structural parameters of fantasy romance, following the definitions of Northrop Frye and others, are very similar to those of fairy tale. Like fairy tale, science fiction and fantasy have a particularly strong generic marking which identifies the formula for marketing purposes and, as Jacques Derrida has noted, dictates how the text is to be read: "The generic mark . . . is a mark always outside the text, not a part of it—such as the designations 'science fiction' or 'fantasy' on the book spine or cover—a mark that codifies the text on bookstore shelf or under hand, calling into play the codes and reading protocols by which the texts become readable" (65). Within the context of science fiction and fantasy, that generic mark operates to create what Ursula Le Guin has identified as "the SF ghetto," characterized by ". . . brush-offs from literary snobs, and . . . blasts of praise and condemnation from jealous, loyal, in-group devotees" (*Language of the Night* 176–77). Within popular literature, the cult following of sf and fantasy removes it one step further from the literary on the scale of value—it is perceived by the mainstream not only as popular entertainment but also as popular entertainment read only by aficionados who form a recognizable and low-status subculture. This is, to some extent, justifiable; like many popular forms, the fantasy ghetto is particularly market driven, and hence tends at times to the formulaic, a tendency that often subverts its genuinely exploratory and imaginative potential. Bruce Sterling's comment on the pressures of commercialism is characteristically colorful: ". . . as Robert E. Howard spins in his grave, the Chryslers of publishing attach rotors to his head and feet and use him to power the presses" (1). For my purposes, then, there appears to be some tension around the notion of deliberate, self-conscious play within popular texts, given the extent to which such texts are habitually perceived as being explicitly antiliterary. This is, however, a simplistic characterization, one subverted by a number of factors: the social, ideological, and exploratory potential within the sf/fantasy forms themselves; the particular ideological and intellectual projects of individual writers; and the extent to which self-conscious narrative play can itself be a strategy exploitable for commercial purposes.

Given the strength, complexity and widely understood rules of generic function, popular works which manage to transcend their market-driven formulae are often particularly intelligent and self-aware, in another category entirely to mass-market pulp; this is partially the inevitable result of self-aware writing which consciously takes on the problems of generic stereotyping. Such writers add to their self-consciousness an awareness of the constraints of their medium, and thus a certain identity crisis. Terri Windling is a good example of the articulation of such an awareness; as part of the online "Artists without Borders" project she identifies herself as one of a group of writers who "can be found in the area of 'adult fairy tale literature,' which is interstitial by its very nature—crossing, as it does, the boundaries between oral and written storytelling, between adult and children's fiction, and between the genres of fantasy, historical, and mainstream literature, with dollops of Jungian psychology and feminist poetry thrown in for good measure." Windling defends the collective's interest in such boundary crossing by suggesting they produce "crossbred works for the crossbred, multi-cultural society we live in today"; certainly, while the market for interstitial works is not as large as that for pulp fantasy in the mold of David Eddings or Robert Jordan, writers such as Windling are successful and highly regarded in the sf community, and underline the extent to which even such an accepted and strongly defined generic ghetto is in fact a complex and multivalent arena containing an extremely broad range of readers, writers, and texts.

The success of these hybrid forms is also a testament to the very real parallels between fairy tale and fantasy romance. To return to my initial definitions of fairy tale, many of the aspects I note there are reproduced, to a greater or lesser extent, in the modern fantasy novel. The central motif of pattern, carrying with it structures of inevitability and fatedness, is often present; one knows, in Tolkien's *Lord of the Rings,* that the hobbits, the equivalent of the miller's third son in being small, domestic heroes, will triumph; that the king will return to be united to his princess; and that the evil sorcerer will be destroyed, the heart of his power simultaneously the seed of his destruction, like the hidden heart of the giant. The otherworldly settings of the fantasy novel to some extent reproduce fairy tale's sense of a different landscape, far away if not necessarily long ago, and that necessary condition of unreality, or of a tangential relationship with reality. Like fairy tale, fantasy romance is about symbol, its significance in resonant stereotype rather than realistic psychological exploration. There is more space for character in fantasy romance than there is in fairy tale, but often characterization is superficial, and true development is enacted on the landscape and the quest itself.

The other recurring theme in fairy tale within the fantasy ghetto is its occasional intersection with the science fiction genre. While science fiction and fairy tale may seem, at first glance, unlikely bedfellows, Tolkien's discussion "On Fairy Stories" is notable in that it refers to one of the great early works of science fiction, H. G. Wells's *The Time Machine,* in the same breath as Macdonald's fantasies or the Edda (45). This is significant: it suggests that, despite the apparent differences in technological concept, quest, adventure, and wonder are elements common to both genres. Eric S. Rabkin's article, "Fairy Tales and Science Fiction," identifies the miraculous and the distancing of time, either past or future, as the common theme; he argues that "the coincidence of wish fulfilment and temporal domains in both science fictions and fairy tales is no accident" (80). He also isolates "the reliance on clarity, elemental colours and cleanliness" as a fairy-tale trait, quoting Max Lüthi's comment on fairy tale's "imperishable world . . . this explains its partiality for everything metallic and mineral, for gold and crystal" (82). The parallel is clear with the characteristically clean lines and artificial environments of much futuristic fiction, and certainly the examples I investigate below, Sheri S. Tepper's dystopian future explored through the eyes of a fairy-tale character, and Tanith Lee's more idealized far-future landscape, are poignant and powerful. Perhaps the most striking parallel, however, is that between fairy tale's repetitive patterns and the tendency in science fiction toward formulaic narrative. Fairy tale probably has the most in common with the early days of science fiction in the 1940s and 50s, when the genre tended to operate as a highly stereotypical folk narrative. In common with fairy tale, sf was often simplistic, offering no real characterization, and focusing on the completion of a quest in an environment of challenge and wonder. Parallels with fairy tale are obvious, as Rabkin comments: "Two of the most persistent stylistic traits of fairy tales are the propensity to externalise all inner states and to deal in extremes" (80). The success of George Lucas's *Star Wars* series of films, with their rescued princesses, heroes with swords, and talking animals, trade at least partially on the audience's recognition of and identification with folkloric elements; an aspect reflected in *Time* magazine's feature article on *Return of the Jedi,* which it identifies as "George Lucas'[s] marvellous rocket-propelled fairy tale" (Clarke 74).

While fantasy/sf and fairy tale are strongly linked genres, self-aware use of their intersections is far from inevitable. Folkloric retelling has a great deal to do with the pleasures of recognition, and numerous examples abound of tales retold and elaborated simply for the enjoyment of the romance form and the familiar narrative. As Zipes comments, classic forms are retained because, "We are safe with the familiar. We shun the new, the real innovations" (*Myth as Fairy Tale* 5). A good example of familiar retelling in modern fantasy is Robin McKinley, whose novel *Beauty* provides an attractive and essentially undisturbed version of "Beauty and the Beast." Her other collection, *The Door in the Hedge,* includes retellings of "The Frog Prince" and a rather charming "Twelve Dancing Princesses." While these stories are more richly textured than the classic originals, providing situational and psychological detail, they remain timeless and unrealistic, focusing on fairy tale's romance aspects of nostalgia, wonder, and utopian wish fulfillment; on a narrative level they elaborate on the classic tales without actually disrupting them. The exception here is *Deerskin,* her shockingly explicit exploration of the incest/rape motifs in the "Donkeyskin" tale. A useful analysis of *Deerskin* is provided in an article by Amelia S. Rutledge, who notes McKinley's unflinching treatment of the incest/rape plot, and the novel's genuine interest in the heroine's need to rebuild an identity shattered by her parents' narcissism. Here again, however, the more standard fantasy framework reasserts itself to consolatory effect. McKinley is becoming steadily more complex and mature as a writer, but even her more recent *Spindle's End,* while exploring the problems of narrative predestination, displaces rather than denies the princess's fate.

The same is largely true of Jane Yolen, another high-profile fairy-tale fantasist, whose tales, collected in works such as *Tales of Wonder,* are mostly original tales in fairy-tale form. While she uses stronger elements of sadness and loss than McKinley, Yolen's short stories are likewise romance-based rather than horror-based, and also tend to drift further from classic exemplars than McKinley's—*Tales of Wonder* includes several stories with science fiction frameworks, as well as some contemporary tales which embed loose fairy-tale references (Baba Yaga, the selkie, a magical ribbon given by a dead mother to her daughter, a brother and sister transformed to geese). Yolen's most interesting and ambitious work is probably *Briar Rose,* which reinvents the Sleeping Beauty story in the context of a Holocaust concentration camp, lending resonances of tragedy and horror to the entrapment motif of the story. At the other end of the fantasy/fairy tale scale, Patricia C. Wrede's rather entertaining Enchanted Forest series, *Dealing with Dragons, Searching for Dragons* et al. are straightforward comic parodies of fairy-tale form very much in the Pratchett mode, updating clichés and formulae with a certain down-to-earth practicality, although without Pratchett's biting social comment, and relying mostly on incongruity and obvious inversions for comic effect.

Both the popularity of the fantasy/fairy tale crossover and the self-aware and exploratory use of romance narratives in fantasy fairy tale is exemplified more strongly in Tor Fantasy's "Fairy Tale" novels. This ongoing series, edited by Terri Windling, shows a preference for fairy tales translated into specific historical contexts, from

Patricia C. Wrede's Elizabethan *Snow White and Rose Red* to Steven Brust's elliptical, challenging exploration of modern-day artists in *The Sun, the Moon, and the Stars*. Pamela Dean's *Tam Lin* and Charles de Lint's *Jack the Giant Killer* likewise use a fairy-tale framework for a contemporary setting, and in terms of texture are fairly far removed from the timeless simplicity of fairy tale. Like most of de Lint's work, *Jack the Giant Killer,* and its sequel *Drink Down the Moon,* are set in a contemporary Canada populated by a hidden faerie community that colonized America along with its human settlers. *Tam Lin* is effectively a tale of campus life in the 1970s, the faerie framework of the Tam Lin ballad realized slowly amid the contemporary detail; Dean's version of the Queen of Faerie entering the mortal world as the charismatic head of an academic department, with all the power plays, allegiances, entrapments, and seductions of faerie neatly overlaid on departmental politics, is compelling and satisfying as well as being amusingly irreverent. Both of these novels are interesting in that their so-called fairy-tale nature is more accurately that of folklore and ballad; both, like Ellen Kushner's successful fantasy novel *Thomas the Rhymer,* are more interested in the intersection of normal human life with what Tolkien has called the "perilous land" of faerie (3) than in any serious exploration of classic fairy-tale narrative. Likewise, Wrede's *Snow White and Rose Red* offers an explicit exploration of the fairy tale, but chooses to energize its Elizabethan historical framework with reference to the magical realm of faerie and some rather Shakespearean faerie court politics; a similar effect is seen in the nineteenth-century religious fanaticism of Gregory Frost's *Fitcher's Brides,* a retelling of the Bluebeard story. Lee's *White as Snow* operates more straightforwardly within an undefined fantasy kingdom, intersecting the Snow White story with the Persephone myth and allowing Snow White's dwarves to take her literally underground. This is somewhat less successful than Lee's shorter fairy tales; the novel's effect is overall uneasy, shapeless, scattered, and prone to the fantasy clichés of Christian/pagan conflicts and pagan eroticism. Generally, novels in this series tend to conform structurally to the traditional fantasy romance, with its emphasis on a removed and magical other world more than on fairy tale's set of simplistic relationships—perhaps an inevitable tendency given the novel's length and expectation of detail. Nonetheless, the fairy-tale elements remain easily recognizable, and in many cases provide satisfying depth and layering of meaning; above all, the continuing success of the series points to the ability of readers to decode and appreciate narrative reference and structural play despite the popular and mass-market nature of the works.

As a further example of the fantasy/sf ghetto's embrace of the fairy-tale form, numerous collections of modern fairy tale, or at least short stories with fairy-tale themes, exist. Lester Del Rey, a longtime and well-known writer and editorial figure in modern speculative fiction, has edited a collection called *Once Upon a Time,* which includes commissioned fairy tales by such fantasy and sf luminaries as Isaac Asimov, C. J. Cherryh, Katherine Kurtz, and Anne McCaffrey. Many of these tales, unfortunately, degenerate into sentimentality; few show any genuine respect for or interest in the form. (Isaac Asimov's satirical "Prince Delightful and the Flameless Dragon" perhaps comes closest.) Where *Once Upon a Time* conforms to the romance expectations of fairy tale—and of the readership of the fantasy and sf authors represented—Ellen Datlow's *Snow White, Blood Red* and its successors live up to the original's dedication to Angela Carter in providing a more thoughtful kind of tale and also one with a darker edge. Datlow, the fiction editor of *Omni* magazine for over a decade, is firmly in the fantasy/sf mainstream. In addition to introductions by both editors, *Snow White, Blood Red* supplies a five-page bibliography of modern fairy tales, including many dealt with in this book (Datlow and Windling 407ff.). The tales in the collection are, however, largely what I would define as short stories with fairy-tale themes, rather than actual fairy tales—few retain the characteristic texture, simplicity, and timelessness I have defined as being central to fairy tale in its pure form. Nonetheless, many of these tales are provocative, innovative, and self-aware, including motifs such as Rapunzel's witch as an embittered rape victim, a Red Riding Hood whose wolf is a womanizing stepfather with his eye on his new stepdaughter, an alien shape-changing Puss in Boots, and a Snow Queen effectively superimposed onto the emotional coldness of a fashionable city crowd.

The large subcategory of fantasy using fairy-tale motifs makes it particularly difficult to choose texts for detailed analysis. Throughout this subgenre, innovative play with structure tends to be subsumed into the popular format, so that familiarity is not disrupted too disturbingly; the characteristic complexity of message and refusal of absolute meaning offered by Carter and Byatt is largely absent. This in some ways reflects the fantasy romance's stereotype as "entertainment" rather than "literature," and the broader commercial success of predictable, unchallenging pulp versions of magical narrative. While many of the more interesting fantasy and sf writers resist this effect, few are entirely free from an awareness of market forces. The result is that texts in this section are somewhat thinner than elsewhere in my discussion, their use of fairy-tale motif inevitably curtailed by the popular formula within which they write. My final selection of works by Tanith Lee, Terry Pratchett, and Sheri S. Tepper represents a sampling of more complex popular texts, particularly interesting for my purposes in their self-conscious awareness of narrative; Lee's and Tepper's works bear comparison with Carter's feminist revisions, and Pratchett's awareness of narrative is in the same mold as Byatt's. At the same time, the use of fairy tale within the fantasy or sf framework means that more than one structural convention is present in these texts, which to an extent liberates these authors from the need to keep their structural encodings intact. In these texts the two generic codings, sf/fantasy and fairy tale, work off each other, allowing for a certain amount of genuinely innovative fairy-tale exploration, encased and cushioned within the known and undisturbed parameters of the popular formula. Lee's often-radical inversions of fairy-tale form are coupled with a straightforward and undisrupted use of popular erotic, horror, and fantasy narratives, whose familiar terms prevail over the often-shocking distortions of familiar fairy tales. Likewise, Pratchett's tongue-in-cheek invocation of the clichéd fantasy landscape, together with the powerful formulaic framework of the Discworld, allows him to site his mischievous disruptions of fairy-tale and generic expectation within a reassuringly familiar environment. Despite the effect of market forces which require a certain uniformity to Discworld texts, sophisticated structural play results. Tepper's *Beauty* is a more complex novel which interleaves the sf format with an almost magical-realist narrative; here, interestingly, she reverses the polarities I have found in other authors, in that the strong fairy-tale framework grounds and scaffolds a bewildering series of generic invocations, including sf dystopia, fairyland, time travel, magical dream worlds, and Hell. While the Sleeping Beauty tale acts as metanarrative to the complexities of her novel, its functioning is both interrogated and laid bare by the intersections of other narrative styles and shapes. All three writers are particularly interesting in that they are highly successful and prolific representatives of the sf/fantasy genre ghetto, but negotiate the expectations of their success delicately and cleverly in order to allow their intellectual and their popular agendas.

INVERSIONS: TANITH LEE

Tanith Lee's works place her firmly within the confines of fantasy/sf writing. A prolific and popular writer who has produced over forty novels since the 1970s, she has written fantasy and science fiction novels, adult and young adult fiction, and a wide range of short stories and collections. She has won the World Fantasy Award several times, and commands a cult following which possibly justifies the hyperbole of the *Village Voice* quotes reprinted on the cover of *Red as Blood*: "Princess Royal of Heroic Fantasy" and "Goddess-Empress of the Hot Read." Sarah Lefanu has commented that Tanith Lee "goes in for [sword and sorcery] in as full-blooded a way as any devotee of the literature could hope for" (123). Lee's work sits firmly and certainly profitably within the generic ghetto, covering various kinds of formulae —classic fantasy romance, or sword and sorcery; science fiction; and, most importantly for this discussion, fantasy which invokes both erotic and horror fiction. These genres rely on a very highly structured and encoded narrative formula—either titillation/release in the case of erotic fiction, or the threat/ fear/ revelation/ resolution tropes on which horror writing is built. Perhaps inevitably given the sheer volume of her writing, a lot of it is unashamedly pulp. Her several works using fairy-tale forms are among her most sophisticated, and this is true particularly of her 1983 collection *Red as Blood: Tales from the Sisters Grimmer,* with which I am here concerned. This retells a selection of fairy tales largely originating with the Brothers Grimm (with the exception of a version of the "Pied Piper of Hamelin" and a tale apparently based on Hoffman's "The Sandman"), but with various narrative inversions which play effectively with the reader's expectation of the original tale.

Fairy tale is intrinsically not too far distant from elements of horror and the erotic; as critics such as Tatar have pointed out, the original oral forms of fairy tale were a manifestation of peasant culture, rooted in an agricultural lifestyle, and dealing with the more primitive aspects of human life—sex, violence, death. Like Carter's tales, many of Lee's rewritings restore erotic elements which were expunged from the Grimms' fairy-tale collection when it was translated into English for a conventional Victorian readership, as well as aspects of graphic violence more modern retellings have tended to remove. Lee's use of the reader's recognition of fairy tale relies on the gap between the known, cleaned-up version of the tale, and the primitive horror elements in her rewrite. At the same time, while the inversions are often deliberately shocking, they are contained within the intersecting horror genre, whose formulaic basis and highly recognizable use of narrative motif—the vampire, the werewolf, the monster, black magic, death—allows for radical inversions of fairy tale while still retaining some motifs of familiarity. A slightly different but parallel process takes place in her final story of the anthology, "Beauty," which employs a similar intersection of inverted fairy-tale motifs with undisrupted and recognizable science fiction elements. Lee is thus able to develop genuinely innovative explorations of the fairy-tale genre, while remaining within the bounds of popular narrative, and neatly avoids the problem of alienating her readership—and thus reducing her sales—with too much novelty.

Lefanu notes that Lee "has a wit and a subtlety that is brought to bear on the modes within which she writes with a result that is subversive both of readers' expectations and traditionally narrative methods" (123). Inversions and revisions characterize Lee's retellings, together with a deft ability to see beyond the familiar motifs into their more uncomfortable implications. Bruce Sterling has commented approvingly on *Red as Blood* as "a very punk book—all red and black," and comments, "These stories are TWISTED—tales of bloodlust, sexual frustration, schoolgirl nastiness, world-devouring ennui, and a detailed obsession with Satanism that truly makes one wonder" (1). Lee's Cinderella version, "When the Clock Strikes," rewrites the Cinderella figure as a manipulative and vengeful witch, whose traditional fairy-tale ability to bewitch the prince in a few hours becomes considerably more sinister. Likewise, "Thorns" plays with the inherent horror in the idea of someone who has been asleep for a hundred years, the awakened princess and her court "sad, weird figures" who were "so old, and yet they had hardly lived at all" (48). Probably the most successful of Lee's tales, however, is her rewrite of the Snow White tale. Called "Red as Blood," Lee's version was a Nebula award nominee, and presents a subversive and severely inverted version of the familiar story.

It is possible to see "Red as Blood" as Lee's mischievous redefinition of the classic moment from "Snow White":

> Once upon a time, in the middle of winter, when snowflakes were falling like feathers from the sky, a queen was sitting and sewing at a window with a black ebony frame. And as she was sewing and looking out the window, she pricked her finger with the needle, and three drops of blood fell on the snow. The red looked so beautiful on the white snow that she thought to herself, if only I had a child as white as snow, as red as blood, and as black as the wood of the window frame! (Zipes, *Complete Grimm* 196)

In Lee's retelling, the Queen is considerably more sinister—she "smiled, and licked at her finger," and "She never came to the window before the dusk: she did not like the day" (27). The familiar moment is redefined in terms of horror, not fairy tale—white skin, black hair, red lips are clichés of the fairy tale, but they operate equally as clichés of the horror genre, where they define the accepted visual encoding of the vampire. Lee's story thus operates from that point of intersection between horror and fairy tale where the physical tropes are identical, and proceeds to use that intersection to invert the expectations of the tale—Bianca, the Snow White figure, is a vampire, a curse on the land like her mother before her. (The strangely compelling logic of this inversion is seen in the popularity of this motif—Neil Gaiman's much later story "Snow, Glass, Apples" is another instance of Snow White's inversion into vampire, although it avoids Lee's use of religious imagery and its erotic elements are considerably more explicit.) Lee's use of the magical mirror is a particularly clever intersection of vampire cliché with fairy-tale item—its power is to reflect all in the land, except, of course, Bianca, who, true to classical vampire mythology, shows no reflection in a mirror. The power of Lee's writing, rather than actually disrupting the well-known structures, is in forcing the reader to accept that they could hold a disturbingly different meaning from the one that has always been taken for granted.

In a similar inversion, the stepmother is the "beautiful Witch Queen" (26), golden-haired and wielding white magic associated with the Catholic Church—she invokes her mirror in religious Latin ("*Speculum, speculum . . . Dei gratia*" [26]), and tries to give her stepdaughter a crucifix. The introduction of Christian symbolism to the very different symbol structures of fairy tale can often jar, but Lee's use of religious imagery is effective. Catholicism is a strongly ritualized and symbolic practice which resonates well both with the fairy-tale setting and with the self-conscious Gothicism of its horror elements. The conclusion of the tale is particularly daring. Bianca, trapped in an ice coffin after being fed consecrated Host by her stepmother, is rescued by a Prince who is presented as a mythologized Christ-figure, and whose presence changes and redeems her:

> . . . she seemed to walk into a shadow, into a purple room; then into a crimson room whose emanations lanced her like knives. Next she walked into a yellow room where she heard the sound of crying which tore her ears. All her body seemed stripped away; she was a beating heart. The beats of her heart became two wings. She flew. She was a raven, then an owl. She flew into a sparkling pane. It scorched her white. Snow white. She was a dove. (35)

The Christ-figure is a fairly characteristic intrusion. Lee is not scared to invest her tales with figures who transcend the more normal domestic parameters of the tale. In her frequent use of gods ("Paid Piper" and "Red as Blood") and Satan ("When the Clock Strikes" and "The Golden Rope") she recalls the Grimms' fascination with Christian rather than pagan versions of the folktales (Tatar 10) but also jars the expectations of readers more accustomed to the secular resonances of the modern versions.

Despite the presence of the Christ-figure, the climax of "Red as Blood" offers a conclusion structured in essentially fairy-tale terms—transformation, a central trope of fairy tale, together with symbolic color, traditional fairy-tale repetition (three rooms, three birds), and the presence of animals. However, Lee is able to blend fairy-tale elements successfully with Christian symbols: the colors are those of the ecclesiastical year; the raven, owl, and dove are all biblical birds who enact Bianca's transformation from Old Testament evil to New Testament purity, and her experiences in the three rooms seem linked to the sufferings of Christ. The strong moral polarity of the horror narrative—vampires as demonic, un-Christian entities susceptible to holy water and the Host—provides a familiar generic basis for the tale's inversions, to some extent undercutting the unease both of the Christian/fairy-tale overlay, and of the deliberate attack on the reader's assumptions about the tale. The extreme nature of the Christian elements, however, could be seen to be necessary given the structural corner into which Lee has effectively painted herself. Having inverted Snow White into the vampiric villain, a particularly powerful anodyne is necessary for the tale to reach its correct structural conclusion, with the heroine united with her prince and evil vanquished.

Other tales in *Red as Blood* offer like inversions of fairy-tale expectation. "The Princess and Her Future" is similarly a clever and deliberately shocking inversion of the Frog Prince tale, employed for sheer chill effect. As with the identification of the "red as blood, black as ebony" cliché in the Snow White story, Lee here seizes on the disturbing element in the Frog Prince story: how pleasant could it possibly be to marry a man who was once something as cold, slimy, and unattractive as a frog? (Terry Pratchett picks up on the same unease in *Witches Abroad,* where the ex-frog Duc of Genua still has frog eyes and keeps a large pond and a supply of flies in his bedroom.) In Lee's version the rakshasha, a demon "which could take any form it chose: lovely, to entice; fearsome, to terrify" (97), squats at the bottom of its cistern infusing the whole story with a nicely judged sense of latent, inexorable threat. When the princess, Jarasmi, loses her golden ball in the pond, she reaches in to retrieve it and has her hand grabbed, in the classic horror mold, by something "cold and glutinous" (100). This dramatizes the unpleasant implications of the original tale's slimy rescuer, a dramatization made more effective by Lee's writing. As the demon arrives to claim its bride:

> A river of quiet was in the gardens, rolling toward the lighted palace. And as it came, the leaves grew still on the bushes, and the night-flying insects lay heavy as drops of moisture in the bowls of flowers. The fountains fell spent and did not rise again.
>
> Quite suddenly, the birds in the cages about the room stopped twittering. The musicians' hands slid from their instruments.
>
> Something smote upon the palace door. (101)

The entire landscape of the palace and gardens comes to reflect the threat the demon represents, and to increase the sense of inexorable power—and inexorable narrative momentum—with which it is identified. What this is actually doing is to exaggerate the strong structural implications of the original, its sense of fairy-tale obligation: having had her ball returned to her, the princess is bound by her promise and cannot escape. Here, although the princess makes no promise, she is equally trapped, an entrapment highlighted and made menacing by Lee's clever use of traditional horror elements. The potentially erotic appearance of the creature, transformed into a prince in the princess's chamber, is infused with the same menace, which Lee reinforces with similar touches of horror: "his touch was delightful, and all her strength seemed to flow away . . . he kissed her, and every lamp in the chamber died" (103). The disruption of the familiar boundaries of the tale is disturbing, but at the same time the flavor of erotic horror—the familiar clichés of sex with demons, titillating as well as horrifying—move the tale into another, equally recognizable realm. The tale's denouement, with Jarasmi and her new husband alone in their carriage, has a certain stark inevitability: "He assumes, very quickly, and with a degree of simple pleasure, his other form. . . . Jarasmi's frenzied shrieks are muffled and, in any case, do not continue long" (105). The ending recalls Perrault's version of Red Riding Hood, which ends with the wolf pouncing on the girl and eating her up.

In some ways, this also reflects Lee's recurring feminist interests, which at times have an overstated and rather simplistic quality—perhaps another expression of the popular nature of her writing. Her interest in the power, or powerlessness, of women is often dramatized in extreme form. In works other than her fairy-tale rewrites, among them *The Book of the Damned* and *The Book of the Beast, Heroine of the World, Heart-Beast, The Silver Metal Lover,* and numerous short stories from various collections, Lee's heroines frequently change gender, undergo rape, or experience sexual encounter with animals or robots, among other motifs related to gender identity and othering. In

"The Princess and Her Future," Jarasmi's fate highlights the patriarchal nature of fairy-tale structure, becoming a graphic metaphor for the fate of women in marriage: entrapped, helpless, and, ultimately, devoured. While dramatic, this is a simplistic characterization, and demonstrates another of the flaws in her depiction of women: they tend to be defined at the traditional fairy-tale extremes of complete passivity (Jarasmi, Jaspre, the girl in "Black as Ink"), or demonic power (Bianca, Ashella, the witch woman in "The Golden Rope," Anna). Again, however, these feminist concerns work within and outside of familiar frameworks; the unease engendered by a feminist awareness of women graphically demonstrated to be victims, is soothed by the equal incidence of familiar patriarchal and fairy-tale stereotypes—the witch, the glamorous temptress, the manipulative sorceress. Lee is ultimately limited in her feminist awareness by the commercial and structural demands of the kind of popular narrative she is writing; while popular fiction has not been untouched by the increasing feminist awareness of the last century, it tends to include such motifs in a superficial and equally stereotyped fashion.

"Wolfland," Lee's version of Red Riding Hood, is perhaps the best illustration of her use of fairy tale to explore notions of female power. The story has more in common with Angela Carter than any other in this collection, following Carter's pattern of mixing fairy-tale structure with the style and setting of another genre—here, nineteenth-century Gothic, specifically Bram Stoker's *Dracula*. Motifs in "Wolfland" are similar to those in Carter's "The Werewolf"; both authors investigate the possibilities in conflating the figures of the grandmother and the werewolf while exploring the growth to individual power of the Red Riding Hood figure. In Lee's case, however, the inversion of grandmother as werewolf is not as shocking, buffered as it is by nineteenth-century formality in setting and tone. "Wolfland" self-consciously uses fairy-tale motifs such as Lisel's opulent red velvet cloak and also the clichés of nineteenth-century Gothic—the journey is simultaneously Red Riding Hood's innocent foray into the primitive desires of the forest and Jonathan Harker's journey to the castle of the vampire. The story also explores implications inherent in Perrault's "Red Riding Hood"—the complicity of the child with the ravishment of the wolf. Rather than straying from the path, however, Lisel is complicit in her kinship with her terrifying grandmother.

The tale's political explorations tend to reduce to an unambiguous polarity of gender roles, which is a stark contrast to Carter's complex relationships. The figure of Anna, a powerful woman who represents triumph and vengeance over a patriarchal past, is offset by her granddaughter Lisel, a spoiled beauty in whom Anna's self-assuredness and strength are echoed only as a self-absorbed wilfullness. Again, Lee shows a tendency to degenerate into patriarchal and mythical stereotypes in her representation of female figures—the spoiled beauty is as much a cliché as the devouring feminine of Anna's werewolf and the wolf-woman goddess who gives Anna her werewolf powers. This comes perilously close to Angela Carter's robust statement that mythic figurations of women are "consolatory nonsense" (*Sadeian Woman* 5): idealized or brutal, myths of empowerment are ultimately only another kind of entrapment. "Wolfland" functions rather like "The Princess and Her Future" in offering a raw representation of the power or powerlessness of women, overstated in the enormous presence of the wolf-goddess and the brutal images which characterize Anna's stereotypical relationship with her husband—"he got his pleasure another way, and the poor lady's body gave evidence of how" (129). In keeping with Cawelti's framework of familiarity, this is a structure as perfectly recognizable and unambiguous as fairy tale itself; the disturbing inversion of the Red Riding Hood tale is softened by the reader's recognition of an undisrupted cultural trope (the abused woman) as much as by the equally undisrupted nineteenth-century Gothic setting. Lee's generic intersection of fairy tale and horror thus picks up another element, the genre of a kind of popular feminism whose relationships are as simply stated as those of any other popular formula. Thus, while Lee's affirmation of female power is strong and evocative, the combination of horror and fairy-tale structures within the popular context tends inevitably toward a simplistic and melodramatic overstatement of her obviously very real interest in issues of gender and otherness.

The final story in *Red as Blood*, the science fiction fable "Beauty," is perhaps Lee's most innovative adaptation of fairy-tale structure into a completely different setting, but it retains the texture and feel of the tale. While using the basic structures of the French "Beauty and the Beast" tales, the story plays with notions of wonder and the marvelous in its translocation into the far future rather than the far past. By overlaying the Beast motif with the equally familiar science fiction notion of the alien, it also explores the concept of the other. In keeping with Rabkin's claim of the basic structural similarities between science fiction and fairy tale, the generic mixing is surprisingly effective. Arthur C. Clarke's famous statement, that "any sufficiently advanced technology is indistinguishable from magic," has passed into science fiction folklore; Lee's tale creatively plays on this possibility. The magical aspects of Jeanne-Marie Leprince de Beaumont's or Gabrielle-Suzanne de Villeneuve's, tale are replaced with equally wonder-filled technology—extended life spans, obedient machines, a world of comfort and convenience whose agents, while mechanical, fill the same niche as the invisible servants of fairy tale. The story shows an acute awareness of the importance of wonder and the marvelous as intrinsic to fairy tale, while intensifying the French originals' sense of threatening otherness through the sf motif of the alien.

Lee's use of science fiction is not only technological but also imposes some rather different social circumstances on the familiar patterns of the tale. Where the "Beauty and the Beast" original places Beauty in a motherless family whose father is a failed merchant, and with elder sisters who are spiteful and jealous, Lee chooses to make use of science fiction's social aspect to develop a feminist angle to the tale. The classic fairy-tale absence of the mother becomes a celebration of technology's power to rewrite social circumstances: two of Levin's daughters are artificially conceived and produced, "his seed . . . mixed with the particles of unknown women in crystal tubes" (168). Estár is the daughter of a woman "from whom he had long since parted." The setting thus denies conventional fairy-tale notions of family structure, substituting instead a utopian ideal of sexual freedom which triumphantly overrides the missing maternal figure, affirming a family warmth and stability despite her absence. This futuristic insistence on alternative and un-fairy-tale family relations is continued in Estár's sisters: Joya is black and bisexual, pregnant with a child whose father is unknown and immaterial; Lyra's lover is Asian; and neither of them fulfill the fairy-tale role of husband. Both sisters are attractive individuals and affectionate to Estár, an aspect of Lee's feminist interests which removes fairy tale's traditional sexual jealousy between women to focus instead on the tale's central relationship, the girl and the beast.

In dealing with the original tale's structures of otherness, Lee has invoked and relied heavily on mythic versions of the narrative—Estár is "ill-named for a distant planet, meaning the same as the Greek word *psyche*" (168). The tale thus explicitly invokes Apuleius's tale of Cupid and Psyche, embedded within *The Golden Ass* (another tale of man conflated with beast), which employs the same patterns as the French tales—a beautiful young woman alone in the power of a terrifying and potentially monstrous male figure. Lee's use of the classical narrative structure allows her to emphasize certain aspects of the tale—the explicitly sexual aspect to the relationship (Cupid and Psyche are lovers), the dependence of the motif of monstrous otherness on an act of perception, and a pivotal point of realization and revelation rather than transformation. Significantly for Lee's purposes in this tale, Marina Warner has identified the power of the Cupid and Psyche tale to offer an essentialized view of heterosexual relations. She describes it as "a founding myth of sexual difference. . . . Such a divine erotic beast [is] a figure of masculine desire, and the plot in which he moves presents a blueprint for the channelling of erotic energy—both male and female—in society at any one time" (*Beast to Blonde* 274).

As in many of Lee's other tales, "Beauty" focuses on a point of inversion: rather than Beauty having to overcome her revulsion at the Beast's physical experience in order to agree to marry him, Estár has to overcome her feelings of inferiority. As in the classical version, the other is kept hidden from her because he is a god, not because he is monstrous. Lee's interest in sexual relationships perhaps impels this inversion—at one point Estár "wondered if one always loved, then, what was unlike, incompatible" (191). This motif sets out to examine the dichotomy at the heart of a heterosexual relationship—how to apprehend, comprehend, or connect with the other when the attraction is based on difference. Here, Lee's version comes to parallel exactly the intentions of de Beaumont's original tale, to provide a parable for young women terrified by marriage with an unknown man. Sadly for Lee's feminist purposes, the rewriting of the male as godlike other rather than the brutal or animalistic other explored by Carter, is even more disempowering to women. The alien is "compelling, radiant of intellect and intelligence . . . he was beautiful. Utterly and dreadfully beautiful. Coming to the Earth in the eras of its savagery, he would have been worshipped in terror as a god" (202). Estár's humiliation is that of the mortal woman loved by a god: "the lightning bolt, the solar flame . . . she had been scorched, humiliated and made nothing, and she had run away, ashamed to love him" (202). Warner suggests that "When women tell fairy tales, they . . . contest fear; they turn their eyes on the phantasm of the male Other and recognise it, either rendering it transparent and safe, the self reflected as good, or ridding themselves of it (him) by destruction or transformation" (*Beast to Blonde* 276). Lee has recognized and transformed the other, but in doing so she glamorizes it to the point where she badly disempowers Estár—the attempt to raise Estár to equality in the scientific explanation for her difference never overcomes that moment of lightning-bolt revelation.

Even worse, Lee's attempt to rationalize the instantaneous, helpless love that Estár feels for the alien, is to provide another quasi-scientific explanation—she and the alien are not paired randomly, but by design. He tells her that "You came to me, as all our kind return, to one with whom you would be entirely compatible" (207). While recognizing and using the structured fatedness of fairy tale, this creates a kind of Mills-and-Boon cliché of lovers who were "meant for each other." As the crowning problem, the point of the union is that of the standard, fairy-tale marriage—children. Estár is ultimately no more than a brood mare; the alien race is sterile, but its children implanted in human wombs can reproduce with the full aliens to produce alien offspring. Lee's innovative rejection of fairy-tale family structures in the first part of the tale is negated by the tale's ending; however much the futuristic setting allows for social innovation, really girls and boys are meant for each other, and for happy families, all along. The more liberal, less stereotyped structures of Levin and his daughters are those of inferior humans, after all, who simply fail to understand; Estár's relations with them in future will be distant and slightly patronizing of their helpless, human incomprehension. The reversal of poles of beauty in the original narrative simply replaces one form of disempowerment with another, even more extreme, form.

"Beauty" is frustrating because its effects are so diverse. On one hand, Lee's innovations are interesting and fruitful, and she manages to transform the tale into effective science fiction fairy tale. On the other hand, she succumbs to the problem critics like Patricia Duncker have found in writers such as Carter, the "infernal trap" (6) of structure too intrinsically tied to ideological implication. The romance structures of the fairy tale are in this case strong enough to wrench back into conventional shape Lee's attempt to update them. Bruce Sterling's review of *Red as Blood* gives a slightly different account of this failure, identifying Lee's "apparent awkwardness" as "the result of a refusal to compromise. It is the sign of an artist struggling to explain her visions in what amounts to a private dialect. Even the failures are a left-handed tribute to her integrity" (1). In Sterling's view, the unease in Lee's political expressions marks her faithfulness to her ideas even when the pressures of the popular form would seem to require a smoother, less jarring finish; she sacrifices popular gloss to her principles, but cannot entirely throw off the popular in order to fully explore her visions. Lee's inversion of the classic "Beauty and the Beast" is brave and striking, and her use of the tale to explore notions of otherness is impressive indeed. However, as with others of her tales, she ultimately fails to control the effects of the popular prototypes which provide comforting familiarity in the midst of her inversions.

DIVERSIONS: TERRY PRATCHETT

The Discworld novels invoke something slightly more than the usual sf/fantasy genre label. Terry Pratchett regularly makes the British best-seller lists with his novels about the Discworld, a world "as round and flat as a geological pizza, although without the anchovies" (*Equal Rites* 8), and which travels through space on a giant turtle. Across the over thrity novels in the series, the Discworld operates as an ongoing fantasy realm composed equally of self-conscious fantasy clichés and warped versions of motifs from contemporary culture; its wizards, for example, parody self-important fantasy archetypes equally with modern-day academia. The world's cheerful acceptance of wizards, witches, nonhuman races such as elves, dwarves, and trolls, the whole sprinkled liberally with gods and heroes, designates it as fantasy parody, but it is an essentially postmodern creation. Pratchett's awareness of genre allows him to invoke and explore an apparently disparate series of narrative traditions, held together firmly by the sword-and-sorcery rationalization. The Discworld's peculiar blend of tongue-in-cheek fantasy, cultural collage, parody, humanism, and incredibly bad puns is firmly situated in the consumer culture, and has far wider appeal than one would expect given the novels' roots in Tolkienesque fantasy. This is perhaps an index of their quality and intelligence, their very acute response to the multiplicity and complexity of modern consumer society and its attendant cultures. At the same time, they provide a particularly interesting example of the workings of familiarity as defined by Cawelti; within the Discworld's diverse map Pratchett is able in different novels to revisit particular groups of characters whose personalities and histories have developed over time to a high level of sophistication. The continuing and ever more detailed Discworld becomes a comfortable and highly recognizable arena for the Discworld's many readers, ensuring the continued popular success of the series despite the potential discomfort of Pratchett's often biting deconstruction of modern society.

Pratchett's use of parody, literary reference, and cultural iconography is the basis of the series' comedy; the presence of fairy tale in *Witches Abroad,* the novel on which I shall focus my analysis, is simply one example in a long list of generic and textual games. The Discworld operates obviously as a fantasy landscape, with the wizards, heroes, trolls, dwarves, elves, and witches of typical pulp fantasy, but its construction parodies and questions the fantasy basis. Pratchett comments that his adaptation of the "Tolkien-type imagery" involves a deliberate attempt "to treat it as if the characters are real," in defiance of the numerous "bad copies of Tolkien" which are saturating the popular market (Interview on *Loose Ends*). His dislike of the excessive nobility of Tolkien's creatures is indexed, not only in the cruelty and superficiality of the elves of *Lords and Ladies* but also in his antidote to Thorin Oakenshield—dwarves with names such as Timkin Rumbleguts and Cheery Littlebottom. The novels are interesting as popular culture because they are themselves popular, but simultaneously comment self-consciously on the popular genre of fantasy from a position *within* the generic ghetto defined by Ursula Le Guin. Pratchett situates himself self-consciously within the fantasy/science fiction framework: "It pisses me off that fantasy is unregarded as a literary form. When you think about it, fantasy is the oldest form of fiction. What were the storytellers of old doing when they talked about the beginnings of the world? They were weaving fantasies" (*January* magazine). Thus an awareness of the working of classic fantasy continually and ironically weaves throughout the Discworld, but as a facet of the author's awareness of the far older traditions of the marvelous. Tolkien is present very notably in *Witches Abroad* in the invisible runes on the door into the dwarf stronghold, and in the witches' encounter with a "small grey creature, vaguely froglike," on an underground river; it hisses "It'ssss my birthday." Nanny Ogg hits it on the head with a paddle (59), in a movement neatly encapsulating Pratchett's attitude to the pretentious unreality of much pulp fantasy. More importantly, this awareness points to metafictional aspects of Pratchett's obvious sense of genre, and of the problematical interface between the marvelous and the real.

Pratchett's literary comment is not confined to the texts of the sf ghetto; a wealth of reference energizes the novels, making the fantasy Discworld no more than a framework for Pratchett's often cynically acute comments on the modern consumer society whose buyers support the novels and associated merchandise. The Discworld is, after all, "a world and mirror of worlds" (*Reaper Man* 7). Pratchett's introduction to the official HarperCollins Web site admits, "the Discworld . . . started out as a parody of all the fantasy that was around in the big boom of the early '80s, then turned into a satire on just about everything, and even I don't know what it is now" ("From Terry"). In particular, it functions as an exercise in literary pastiche; as Elizabeth Young comments in *The Guardian*, "One of the pleasures of [Pratchett's] books is the way in which literary classics . . . float through them in a way that would be pounced on as inter-textual in another author" (45). In fact, Pratchett is receiving increasing critical attention, suggesting that academics are, indeed, pouncing on his intertextual qualities. As well as fairy tale, *Witches Abroad*'s passing references invoke, in a random sample, chaos theory, voodoo, the Goon Show, the stereotypical British tourist, Tolkien's dwarves, Victorian vampire Gothic, airline companies, the Pamplona bull festival, Mississippi riverboats, DEFCON, the film of *The Wizard of Oz*,

Cluedo, and Casanova.* The postmodern implication of such references is clear: the novel relies equally for its comic effect on the reader's recognition not only of classic texts, fairy tale among them, but
also on popular elements such as modern consumer culture and the
sword-and-sorcery framework of the world. The equation of canonical
and popular texts within the arena of reader familiarity exemplifies
postmodernism's classic erosion of boundaries between high and
low culture. In its exploration of textual and cultural multiplicity, the
Discworld comes to correspond to Jameson's description of "speech
through all the masks and voices stored up in the imaginary museum of a now global culture" (18).

Pratchett's narrative structures are ultimately neat, relying more
on the narrative conventions of romance and popular fiction and consistently delivering "a resolution which, if not your traditional happy
ending, at least has some kind of symmetry" ("A Glimpse Inside").
Significantly for his use of fairy tale, his insistence on a moral framework is strong, as Farah Mendlesohn's analysis consistently demonstrates; while often cynical, the Discworld operates on a principle of
basic human decency, or at worst, the predictability of basic human
nature. In this sense, the popular framing of the novels outweighs
their use of postmodern strategy; they reflect, comment on, and reproduce the multiplicity of modern culture in a way which offers
the judgment, resolution, and closure postmodern texts characteristically refuse. John Clute points out that this is intrinsic to the essentially circular nature of comedy, which books such as *Hogfather*
explicitly work to retain; thus, while Pratchett writes parody, it is "almost always benign, open-ended, without points of animus" (10). It
becomes clear that the use of fairy tale in his novels is inevitable; like
Byatt, he appears to be drawn to structured narrative which coun-
teracts the fragmentary nature of the modern culture he parodies.
To return to Cawelti's theories of formula narrative, the Discworld's
narrative structures—both in traditional form and in the consistent

---

*"chaos . . . made really good patterns that you could put on a T-shirt" (7); "She had called
upon Mister Safe Way, Lady Bon Anna, Hotaloga Andrews and Stride Wide Man" (10);
"You can't get the wood" (30); "The last thing we want is foreign parts up close" (39)
and throughout; "It's really expensive, getting proper invisible runes done" (50 and ff.);
"Vampires have risen from the dead, the grave and the crypt, but have never managed it
from the cat" (83); "Three Witches Airborne . . . Pan Air . . . We could call it Vir-" (87);
"the time of the Thing with the Bulls" (93); "the Vieux River . . . Old (Masculine) River"
(95); "Asking someone to repeat a phrase you'd not only heard very clearly but were also
exceedingly angry about was around Defcon II in the lexicon of squabble" (136); "You
know, Greebo, I don't think we're in Lancre" (140); "my name is Colonel Moutarde" (228);
"Casanunda . . . I'm reputed to be the world's greatest lover" (229).

and carefully built-up environment of the Discworld itself—provide the necessary element of familiarity which enables the popular audience comfortably to consume the disrupted view of modern culture the novels present.

As an intensely self-conscious writer, Pratchett offers an explicit and thoughtful awareness of the power of narrative—as he says in the opening pages of *Witches Abroad,* as well as the more recent *The Amazing Maurice and His Educated Rodents,* this is "a story about stories" (*Witches Abroad* 10, *Amazing Maurice* 9). A. S. Byatt gives Pratchett an approving nod from the literary establishment, calling him "one of the great modern storytellers" and identifying *Witches Abroad* as "one of the best stories I know about the dangerous aspect of the network of tales" (*Histories and Stories* 148–49). Likewise, the publication of a volume of Pratchett criticism including essays by such luminaries as John Clute suggests that the complexities and sophistication of Pratchett's writing are worth serious attention. As in Byatt, an awareness of narrative runs through all Pratchett's work, seen most explicitly as a recurring and somewhat satirical sense of the nature and importance of fairy tale. Reacting against the Disneyfication and general cuteness of fairy tale in the twentieth and twenty-first centuries, his awareness of narrative is folkloric, returning to a more earthy and brutal pattern which denies idealism in favor of a certain bloodiness. The Hogfather, the Discworld's version of Father Christmas, leaves a bag of bloody bones for bad children; Pratchett, alert to the artificial processes which have consigned fairy tale to the nursery, comments, "it's these little details which tell you it's a tale for the little folks" (69). Similarly, the "Grim Fairy Tales," which appear as a running gag in the Discworld series, are ironically glossed as "happy tales for little folk." As well as being "about wicked people dying in horrible ways," the Grim Fairy Tales provide the dangerous folkloric knowledge which enables the reconstruction of the glass clock in *Thief of Time* (106). *The Amazing Maurice* expands on this to specify the authors as Agoniza and Eviscera, the Sisters Grim, who are "not big on tinkling little people. They wrote . . . *real* fairy tales. Ones with lots of blood and bones and bats and rats in" (77). Pratchett shows a wry awareness of the intersections between fantasy's marvelous universe and the demands of real life, refiguring fairy tale as a vital and essential tradition whose patterns of human behavior encapsulate important knowledge; however, he is also aware how far such knowledge has been concealed by the trivial and overprettified thing fairy tale has become. The novel which precedes and leads into *Witches Abroad, Lords and Ladies,* explicitly deals with the dangerous utopianism of folklore in its depiction of Magrat, desperate and hopeful, challenging the Queen of the

Fairies for the possession of her lover; unlike the Child Ballad, things are never that easy.

Witches Abroad thus functions partially as an investigation of the particular wealth of shared cultural knowledge offered by fairy tales. As an integral part of this awareness, however, Pratchett is also investigating the extent to which such narratives hold the power to shape, rather than simply reflect, the lives of people.

> . . . their very existence overlays a faint but insistent pattern on the chaos that is history. Stories etch grooves deep enough for people to follow in the same way that water follows certain paths down a mountainside. And every time fresh actors tread the path of the story, the groove runs deeper.
>
> This is called the theory of narrative causality and it means that a story, once started, takes a shape. It picks up all the vibrations of all the other workings of that story that have ever been.
>
> This is why history keeps repeating all the time.
>
> So a thousand heroes have stolen fire from the gods. A thousand wolves have eaten grandmothers, a thousand princesses have been kissed. A million unknowing actors have moved, unknowing, through the pathways of story.
>
> It is now *impossible* for the third and youngest son of any king, if he should embark on a quest which has so far claimed his elder brothers, *not* to succeed. (8–9)

In his sense of the power of narrative, Pratchett comes remarkably close to the self-consciousness demonstrated by Byatt; however, where she focuses on the causal entrapment of the protagonist within fairy-tale narrative inevitability, Pratchett is more interested in the dehumanizing effect of narrative alienated from the reality of the characters. In his awareness, narrative is a political act, a powerful and dominant discourse, and its potential for entrapment is more than limiting on action, it is profoundly dehumanizing. Stories thus have a darker side, a sinister power which cannot be avoided simply by realizing that it is there: "Stories, great flapping ribbons of shaped space-time, have been blowing and uncoiling around the universe since the beginning of time. And they have evolved. The weakest have died and the strongest have survived and they have grown fat on the retelling . . . stories, twisting and blowing through the darkness" (8).

To see real life entirely through the structures of story is thus problematical, as is underlined by the character of Malicia Grim in *The Amazing Maurice;* her attempt to wrench her experience into the expectations and structures of fairy tale is dangerously unrealistic. The lesson she must learn is that "real life isn't a story. There isn't some kind of . . . magic that keeps you safe" (147). Pratchett's awareness of narrative is thus inherently metafictional, his writing infused with a clear sense of the *moral* imperative to keep narrative in its proper place, never to confuse the marvelous with mimesis. This is one of the functions of the Discworld, its insistence on restoring a lost logic and realism to fantasy's marvelous spaces—Ankh Morpork as a fantasy city with a sewer system, Rincewind as a wizard with a realistic attitude to adventure. Matthew Hills's fascinating article on narrative spaces in the Discworld presents a particularly good analysis of the ways in which the Discworld shades in and out of reality across the series and, more particularly, its maps. In *Witches Abroad* this process of awareness is materially assisted by the voices which guide the tale, those of the three witches. Granny Weatherwax, Nanny Ogg, and Magrat are a recurring character-group in the Discworld series, offering an ongoing deconstruction of the maiden/mother/crone trope so beloved of modern paganism; their strong-willed parochialism does not prevent them from offering a particularly clear-sighted critique of human folly.

An awareness of the real is thus integral to Pratchett's investigation of narrative; more specifically, it becomes a moral duty to recognize the difference between the fictional and the real, the story and the individual. Lilith de Tempscire, the mirror-wielding villainess of *Witches Abroad*, is powerful because of her recognition that "stories exist independently of their players. If you know that, the knowledge is power" (8). In her narrative manipulations she commits the greatest crime possible in the Discworld's moral structures, one which recurs time and again in Pratchett's novels—objectification. Granny Weatherwax tells Lilith, in their final confrontation, "You shouldn't treat people like they was *characters*, like they was *things*" (270). This idea is developed more fully and very dramatically in a later Discworld novel, *Carpe Jugulum*, in which a "modern" vampire arrangement with a subject village has the villagers lined up like cattle to be drained in a civilized fashion (223ff.). Granny's manifesto is explicitly stated: "There's no greys, only white that's got grubby . . . And sin . . . is when you treat people as things. Including yourself. That's what sin is" (210). Narrative and reality *must* be kept separate; all use of story must be metafictional, it cannot be conflated with, or allowed to spill over into, the real world. By focusing on the needs of the narrative rather than the needs of the individual, Lilith dehumanizes the people over whom the stories give her power. The novel sets up stories, particularly fairy-tale, as a potentially totalitarian discourse with a strongly self-justifying ideological framework. There are interesting parallels here with the kind of cultural process identified by Adorno and Horkheimer—the manipulation of a passive mass market by a kind of cultural monolith whose power lies in recognition, and manipulation, of the patterns within which people prefer to see the world. As Zipes has noted, the processes of capitalization are essentially dehumanizing (*Breaking the Magic Spell* 97), strengthening the parallels with Pratchett's view: "The power of the capitalist system to dominate and manipulate humanity and nature" is in itself a narrative as compelling as any fairy tale; in its victims, "both reason and imagination have atrophied" (97).

Granny Weatherwax, the most powerful of the three witches, is an interesting figure in this context. She functions very much as Lilith's opposing double, a twin sister whose allegiance to the cause of humanity rather than narrative makes her the theoretical "good" to Lilith's "evil." Pratchett, however, never resorts to unambiguous melodrama, and his depiction of the various shadings and temptations of the "good" in this novel, in itself functions as a powerful subversion of fairy-tale narrative's classically unambiguous polarities—and of the deus ex machina figure of the godmother, the ultimate totalitarian despot to the heroine's destiny. (The figure of Black Aliss, the witch who fulfills the gingerbread house/christening curse niche in the Discworld fairy tales, exemplifies this ambiguity; an ancestress of Granny herself, Aliss was "not *bad*, but so powerful it was sometimes hard to tell the difference" [114].) Granny Weatherwax is able to disrupt Lilith's tales for precisely the same reason that Lilith can manipulate them—she recognizes the power inherent in them. This means that, while exerting her abilities to combat Lilith, she must fight continually against *becoming* Lilith by interfering with people "for their own good." The novel thus doubly underlines the power of an accepted cultural discourse to dehumanize both the victim and the oppressor. In a telling point, Pratchett's wicked godmother bases her power in mirrors, her image multiplied endlessly and soullessly. As the novel comments, "mirrors and images . . . steal a bit of a person's soul and there's only so much of a person to go round . . . people who spend their lives appearing in images of one sort or another seem to develop a *thin* quality" (10). The implication, in an interesting extension of Adorno and Horkheimer's analysis, is that modern mass culture (endlessly multiplied images such as film and television) equally dehumanizes the producer and the consumer—narrative power applied powerfully but resulting in a loss of humanity all round. The apparently random inclusion of a form of voodoo magic in *Witches Abroad* is, in fact, a precise continuation of theme, its notions of the devotee's possession by voodoo gods paralleling exactly the notion of role and the power of role in fairy-tale narrative.

Lilith's grip on the "fairytale city" of Genua is another example of this process; similarly to the Disney view of fairy tale, her ideal is all cleanliness and sparkling colors, no room for anything shabby, ugly, or individual. "Genua was a fairytale city. People smiled and were joyful the livelong day. Especially if they wanted to see another livelong day" (74). The inhabitants of the city are savagely punished for what Lilith calls "crimes against narrative expectation" (75). Thus the toymaker is imprisoned because he fails to sing songs or whistle while he works, or tell stories to the children; his defense, "I just make toys . . . that's all I'm good at. I make good toys. I'm just a toymaker," is inadequate before Lilith's vision of the stereotypical toymaker of legend. Her sense of narrative deals only in cliché and has no room for individuality or humanity. More frighteningly, her understanding of the tales which employ such structures gives her the power to enforce them in a terrifyingly totalitarian fashion. This conforms to Adorno and Horkheimer's identification of "the determination of . . . executive authorities not to produce or sanction anything that in any way differs from their own rules, their own ideas about consumers, or above all themselves" (32). The difference between indoctrinated passive consumption and the complexities of actual human needs is neatly summed up in Granny Weatherwax's ballroom speech: although the three witches are godmother figures, they are "the kind that gives people what they know they really need, not what we think they ought to want" (260).

While the novel's overt concern is obviously with narrative, particularly fairy-tale narrative, on a wider cultural and moral level, Pratchett's use of more obvious fairy-tale structures and references recurs throughout *Witches Abroad*. By invoking and disrupting various fairy-tale forms, he uses reader recognition of traditional and contemporary narratives for comic effect as well as for the furtherance of his ideological agendas. On the broader level, the journey of the three witches to Genua is based on the Cinderella story: Emberella is destined by her one godmother, Lilith, to marry the Prince, but regards the idea with horror. The reason for this is the entwining of the Cinderella narrative with that of the Frog Prince story—the prince is, in fact, a frog, changed to man form by Lilith's enchantments, but needing the traditional marriage with a princess to make the change permanent. As does Lee in a very different retelling of the story, Pratchett picks up on the unease in the Frog Prince story—how attractive can a man be who was once a frog? As Emberella says, "He looks slimy. He makes my flesh crawl. . . . They say he's got funny eyes" (178). Where Lee seizes on the horror elements of the concept, however, Pratchett uses it almost entirely to comic effect, in a process which echoes the parameters of the Discworld—to inject a little down-to-earth reality into fantasy concepts, and to follow them to their logical—and often comical—conclusion. At the same time, the dehumanization implied by the process is chilling. He speaks of *Witches Abroad* as giving him "the opportunity for retelling the Cinderella myth as if it were real and as if real people were involved, because unfortunately the problem with Cinderella is that it's only delightful as a story if all the people involved are tailors' dummies with no emotional lives of their own. As soon as you start thinking about real people being involved in a fairy-tale context these are all horror stories" (Wignal).

Within the Cinderella/Frog Prince metatale are frequent passing references to other fairy tales, which offer a microcosm of the rewriting process the three witches exert on the main tales. The Sleeping Beauty sequence, which opens the series of fairy tales, is a particularly good example of the fairy-tale narrative's attempt to reassert control after the incursions of the three witches into its structures, and is incidentally a wonderfully comic piece of writing:

> There was never any noise in the sleeping castle. . . . It had been like this for ten years. There was no sound in the—
> "Open up there!"
> "Bony fide travellers seeking sucker!"
> —no sound in the—
> "Here, give us a leg up, Magrat. Right. Now . . ."
> There was a tinkle of broken glass.
> "You've broken their window!"
> —*not a sound* in the— (*Witches Abroad* 113)

The tale's desperate attempt to retain its atmosphere is comically juxtaposed to the earthy, hearty, and above all human voices of the witches as they disrupt Sleeping Beauty's enchanted castle. The moment echoes the well-judged comic sequence which plays with the film version of *The Wizard of Oz* and in which the hardness of Nanny Ogg's new, willow-reinforced witch's hat resists the descending farmhouse in a perfect symbolization of the extent to which the more metaphorically hardheaded witches resist the power of the tale. Granny's distaste for cliché ("'Ah. A chamber,' she said sourly. 'Could even be a bower'" [114]) is coupled with her first statement of her manifesto against the inhumanities of narrative manipulation: "Cutting your way through a bit of bramble is how you can tell he's going to be a good husband, is it? That's fairy godmotherly thinking, that is! Goin' around inflicting happy endings on people whether they wants them or not, eh?" (118). Her sense of the basic wrongness, in human terms, of the structures and patterns imposed by the fairy-tale stereotypes is reinforced even more strongly in the second fairy-tale encounter, that of Red Riding Hood. Here, Pratchett points out the inherent brutality of the child being sent to visit her grandmother when the wood is known to be wolf infested. Society's similar callousness to the old woman within the parameters of the tale is underlined by the witches' status as elderly women on the edge of society, although the identification of witches with victims is entirely ironic: "'I always hated that story,' said Nanny. 'No-one ever cares what happens to poor defenceless old women'" (122). Red Riding Hood, far from being a featureless, stereotyped child, has a particularly realistic childish bloody-mindedness: "Bet you a trillion dollars you can't turn that stump into a pumpkin" (121). Pratchett's children are always remarkably unsentimentalized little horrors.

It is, however, in the depiction of the wolf that Pratchett makes his most telling point about the dehumanizing effect of a totalitarian narrative. In the transformation of the wolf into something that can meet the requirements of the tale—"Real wolves don't walk on their hind legs and open doors" (127)—the novel deals intrinsically with concepts of identity which, in fact, transcend the human. Lilith requires the wolf to be able to think in order to perform as expected, but Pratchett has strong views on the imposition of human mental complexities on the animal—an ideology which works directly against the sentimental tendency to anthropomorphize animals in many fantasy and fairy-tale contexts. (This point is made equally strongly in *Amazing Maurice,* in which the chapter head-quotes from "Mr Bunnsy Has a Big Adventure" ruthlessly satirize the twee child's storybook creatures.) Lilith's interference with the wolf has left "cracked and crippled attempts at cognition peeling away from the sleek arrowhead of predatory intent. . . . No wonder it was going mad" (128). Far more than in the case of humans warped to the purposes of the tale, the warping of animals to fit human narrative patterns is presented as an unforgivable cruelty. The same logic is inherent in the passing reference to the Three Little Pigs—changed by Lilith to live in a house, they are "the only animals stupid enough to let the wolf get near them" (133), and are eaten by the wolf. Faint resonances in these tragically humanized animals offer a trenchantly realistic version of the sentimentalized animals of Disney animated fairy tale, a reference made pointedly explicit in Granny Weatherwax's angry comment: "It's all wishing on stars and fairy dust, is it?" (137). In fact, the Disney style of fairy tale is anathema to Pratchett not only because it is unrealistically idealized but also because it is *unthinking*.

Fantasy has always been the poor cousin in the speculative fiction ghetto: Bruce Sterling refers trenchantly to fantasy as sf's "small, squishy cousin," which "creeps gecko-like across the bookstands," taking advantage of sf's "reptilian torpor" (1). The tendency to cliché and formula in fantasy romance does, perhaps, prejudice its functioning when compared to sf's potential for genuine thought experiment. However, the achievements of writers such as Pratchett (and, to a lesser extent, Lee) demonstrate that awareness of the fantasy formula, and of the older fairy-tale structures underlying the fantasy genre, can be a strength rather than a weakness. Pratchett's use of fairy tale in *Witches Abroad* is highly sophisticated, the novel seamlessly integrating fairy-tale motifs, both traditional and modern, with those of the familiar Discworld setting. His understanding of the structures and power of narrative is assured. His complex exploration of narrative and his strong humanist polemic are evident, but his awareness of the clash between fairy-tale expectation and human nature never completely disrupts the functioning of the Discworld's popular form. This is a careful balancing act; similarly, despite the obvious presence of the Discworld's more overt agendas of comedy, parody, and entertainment, narrative explorations are never quite subordinated to the demands of the popular market. In this, Pratchett represents the more accomplished and thoughtful end of the fantasy/sf spectrum, as well as the more self-aware. The Discworld is perhaps so appealing because Pratchett retains throughout a joyful sense of the status of his writing *as writing*, as the playful fictional act which comments continually on reality, but consistently problematizes its ability to represent that reality. His knowing awareness of narrative, and its postmodern invocation throughout the Discworld novels, makes his use of fairy tale inevitable, but he extends that narrative awareness to offer a profound sense of the form in both its literary and its folkloric implications.

REVISIONS: SHERI S. TEPPER

Peter Nicholls, in *The Encyclopaedia of Science Fiction*, identifies Sheri S. Tepper as "one of the most significant new—and new feminist—voices to enter 1980s sf." Since her early fantasy works, the aimed-at-adolescents True Game series, Tepper has combined a growing popularity within the sf and fantasy market with a sustained and passionate exposition of social theme. Across all her novels she is characteristically concerned with the prospect of ecological disaster resulting from our sophisticated but uncontrolled technological culture, and she largely uses the science fiction framework to provide radical solutions to the problem. She also has a strongly feminist awareness of the position of women within our society; novels such as *The Gate to Women's Country* and *Gibbon's Decline and Fall* are almost entirely feminist polemic, which at times is entwined with problems of technological destruction. At the same time, her books have a definite popular appeal based in fast-paced narratives, upbeat endings, considerable humor, and an ability to create whimsically attractive races, cultures, and people. This popular aspect to her narratives is often misleading; Nicholls has noted that Tepper "requires the engine of story to provide impulsion for the other things she can do, which tends to tilt her work towards melodrama and excess, and thus to obscure a little her remarkable sophistication" (1212). The novel with which I am concerned here, *Beauty*, is her only serious incursion into fairy-tale territory, and its metafictional use of the form throws into strong relief the recurring interests and techniques of the writer. Published in 1991, *Beauty* won the Locus Award for Best Fantasy Novel, although Tepper's work has largely gone unrecognized by the more prestigious Hugo or Nebula nominations—perhaps a result of her writing's uncomfortable polemical content and uneasy shift between the popular and the issue-driven. The novel certainly represents something of a departure for Tepper, whose science fiction is most often straightforwardly postapocalyptic, focused on alien intervention, or based in the multiplanetary societies of space opera.

The intersection of Tepper's basically science fiction writing with the structures of fairy tale is logical and extremely fruitful. The closure and utopian impulse provided by the classic fairy-tale narrative works very similarly to Tepper's narrative structures, coinciding with the romance elements found in the formulaic adventure narratives of science fiction, and operating in some ways against the serious social exploration of which the form is capable. From its earliest days science fiction has offered a frequently uneasy meld between popular adventure, the excitement and easy resolution of an essentially romance form, and the more strenuous demands of what Le Guin calls the "thought experiment" (130–31)—the realistic extrapolation and investigation of other societies, other worlds, from elements in our own. In Tepper's works, serious concerns (she insists that "books have to come from what bothers you" ["Rare Breeds" 4]) are expressed side by side with an insistence on ultimate redemption, the eventual rescue both of individual and of human society despite apparent disaster and considerable resistance to change. *Beauty* is an unusual and particularly interesting example of her work in that the presence of fairy-tale closure operates in almost exact reversal to Thurber's discovery of reconciliation; instead, Tepper uses it to self-consciously critique the expectation of a "happy ending." This is a sharp contrast to her tendencies toward upbeat closure in most of her other work, and renders *Beauty* one of the more complex and challenging of her narratives.

In this tension between the romance elements and desperately real concerns in these narratives, the interplay between popular/fairy-tale form and social commentary becomes problematical, even recursive. Indeed, the nature of Tepper's work as popular narrative may offer an entry into the precise nature of the problem which hinders social reform to the point of requiring resolution only through disaster: the belief that "everything will be all right in the end," that the happy ending will happen anyway—the romance resolution of a thousand popular adventure stories, or of a thousand fairy tales. Tepper provides the outside force, the hero or heroine who will resolve humanity's conflicts, precisely because that is what technological society, comfortably ensconced in its unrealistic fictions, has come to expect. Significantly, many of the fairy-tale patterns she invokes, in the novel's framing "Sleeping Beauty" structure and in the other tales ("Snow White," "Cinderella," "The Frog Prince") visited as subsets of the narrative, are explicitly those of twentieth-century popular culture rather than earlier literary or folklore versions. As the heroine, Beauty, comments, "I've seen Disney, for the love of God. I know the Cinderella story" (261). The novel offers a witch queen straight out of the Disney *Sleeping Beauty*—dark hair, widow's peak, a "close-fitting gown of blood-coloured damask" (340), and a Snow White figure clad in "a full white shift with puffy sleeves and a kind of laced bodice over it. Disney had got that part right" (353). Tepper's use of consumer culture images is ironic and self-aware, but it is also ironic that she expresses her frustration with the dominant consumer-culture's resistance to social change via a participation in that same culture, in the romantic and melodramatic aspects which mark the popular component to her work.

At the same time, fairy-tale structures allow Tepper to express more fully a tendency found in her other works, toward the symbolic structures of fantasy. In many of her works the surface of Tepper's writing seems more magical than science fictional, an effect particularly true of the early True Game series or of later works such as *The Family Tree;* often, the science that animates meteorites or rationalizes talking animals and telepathic abilities is revealed only gradually or at the last minute. As a result of her drift toward the romance end of the science fiction spectrum, her narratives tend to employ archetypal characters who are useful for her polemical ends, whether ecological or feminist. This reaches its logical conclusion in *Plague of Angels,* in which a postapocalyptic landscape with high-tech enclaves makes use of "archetypal villages," spaces in which social misfits operate under rigid archetypal definitions. More than this, however, the characteristic accepting wonder of fantasy allows for a use of the marvelous which is far freer than the rigorous logical and intellectual demands of science fiction. Given these tendencies, it is inevitable that she should choose to use fairy-tale structures sooner or later; also, given her polemical approach, it is not surprising that her use of the form should be complex and self-conscious.

Tepper's interest in form is also very much behind her employment of the fairy tale. While not as strongly an intertextual writer as someone like Carter—and, after all, Tepper's market is popular rather than literary—Tepper is capable of some sophistication in her invocation of other texts. Perhaps the best example of this is *The Gate to Women's Country*, a hard-hitting feminist narrative in which postapocalyptic society offers a critique of women's power under patriarchy, seen through the lens of Greek tragedy, specifically the powerful intertext of the Iphigenia tragedies of Euripides. The classic texts provide a monolithic sense of the patriarchal ideals of war, against which women's experience is seen as marginal and futile; ultimately, social and gender imbalances are provocative of the extreme social solution the postapocalyptic setting enables. A similar awareness of the power of narratives drifts through the True Game series, in which folkloric retellings encode important social and ecological knowledge. In *Beauty*, however, Tepper's narrative awareness becomes postmodern, problematizing the notion of objective reality to the point where realism dissolves and narrative is the only given. In the indeterminate shifting of realities within the novel, fairy tale remains the only reliable or predictable framework, a tendency which recalls both Propp's comments on fairy-tale resistance and the postmodern fascination with strong narrative shape.

In terms of narrative structure *Beauty* is a complex novel, interleaving the Sleeping Beauty framework with an almost magical-realist awareness which deals variously with fairy tale, fairyland, science fiction, time travel, magical dream worlds, and Hell. Like the authors in Windling's Fairy Tale series, Tepper conflates the folkloric world of faerie with the structures of fairy-tale narrative, but her use of narrative pattern to impel, inform, and energize her story and themes is strong and self-aware. The novel exists at the extreme range of acceptability for my criteria of fairy-tale context, since its social awareness is resolutely historical and its alternative narratives far removed from fairy-tale sparseness. However, Tepper's return, again and again, to fairy-tale narratives jolts the historical back into timeless, archetypal meaning; rather than compromising fairy-tale ahistoricity, this insists on stressing the pitfalls in fairy-tale simplification of present and future realities. The novel is unavoidably metafictional, its characters, like Byatt's, aware of and railing against their entrapping predestinations. Like Carter and Lee, Tepper is a feminist writer alert to the nuances of sexuality in the tales she uses, and all too aware of narrative as a tool of patriarchy. Interestingly, given her tendencies toward upbeat closure, she sees little hope for a happy heterosexual ending within the confines of the traditional tales. In both the feminist and ecological polemics, resolution is withheld from the fairy-tale heroine, deferred to be only a possibility for the future given the unrelieved bleakness of the present.

The "Beauty" of the novel's title is not that of Beauty and the Beast, but of the Sleeping Beauty, and the Sleeping Beauty structure forms the overarching plot of the novel. Sexuality and ecology are equal and codependent issues in this use of the tale, as Tepper explores the notion of beauty itself, both its implications for the heroine, and its implications on a more global scale. Tepper comments:

> I had been depressed by seeing the natural places I had loved as a child—the river bottoms and woods—destroyed, and uglification taking their place, and sometimes I felt that all beauty was dying. This, by an association of ideas, led me to the idea of the Sleeping Beauty, and the hope that maybe she wasn't dead but only sleeping, that maybe it would come back. . . . I hope it's not dead, I hope it's only sleeping, and through magic and love it will wake up some day—or we will wake up some day. ("Aspiring Up" 4)

Fairy tales traditionally demand a beautiful heroine, usually, as Marina Warner has noted, golden-haired—in *Beauty,* the heroine's hair is "silver-gilt" (43) and her beauty inherited from a fairy mother. The fair-haired fairy-tale princess carries connotations of perfection, freedom from blemish, and, most importantly, innocence. Warner's argument explores fair hair as "a guarantee of quality" as well as "the imaginary opposite of foul, [connoting] all that was pure, good, clean" (*Beast to the Blonde* 363–64). It is also an emblem of physical desirability, the "problematic fleshly envelope," which causes the heroines of fairy tale, as Warner points out, to flee, change shape, or hide behind dirt and ugliness (353)—paralleled in the novel by the heroine's deceptive boy-clothes, and later in the sullying of that beauty by rape and aging. (Rather entertainingly, Tepper attacks the assumptions behind beauty and purity for women by having virginity, at least for Beauty's fey mother Elladine, more or less optional; it regenerates once lost, neatly debunking its semisacred status in fairy-tale archetype.) In the Sleeping Beauty tale, particularly, the heroine is an abstraction rather than an individual, a body operating as a locus of desirability in the structure of the prince's quest. The most passive of fairy-tale archetypes, her only purpose is to wait for the awakening touch of the more active masculine force.

Tepper's use of these fairy-tale resonances is complex. Her transposition of the ideal of beauty onto the environment relies heavily on the notion of that which is desirable because it is unspoiled and without flaw. At the same time, she rejects utterly the notion of physical beauty and purity as a defining feature of the fairy-tale woman. However, there are strong conflicts here: the essential passivity of the Sleeping Beauty archetype is all too appropriate to Tepper's deterministic tendencies in her ecological agendas. As in many of her other novels, Tepper's real and desperate sense of outrage at current trends toward ecological disaster is also profoundly pessimistic: we will not stop the disaster, we can only hope to recreate lost beauty after it has been completely destroyed. The novel works to preserve a notion of natural diversity and cultural heritage, carried within the heroine in symbolic form as a spark of light, and echoed in the transformation of the Sleeping Beauty's enchanted and thorn-circled castle into an ark which carries sleeping animals, plants, and artifacts forward through time into a more receptive future. Such beauty is preserved to "sleep" through inevitable environmental destruction, until the destroyers are dead and beauty can be reawakened. This is an acceptance of fairy tale's symbolic structures which connote beauty as unspoiled and desirable, an assumption which exists in considerable tension with the feminist deconstruction of the passive beauty. Tepper manages, somehow, to embody these contradictory issues through the novel's postmodern awareness of the tale's structures; beauty remains beautiful and pure, asleep in the castle, but Beauty herself does *not* sleep through time, diverging from the tale's preordained structures in order to carve out her own destiny and identity. The self-determined feminist heroine coexists self-consciously with the passive ecological beauty symbolized by the sleeping girl who takes the heroine's place.

The novel is thus interestingly postmodern in that the heroine is and is not the sleeping fairy-tale princess; the only space open through the narrative's predestinations is that *outside* the narrative, an escape from the story similar to that of Byatt's Eldest Princess. Behind her, Beauty leaves the narrative to continue essentially unchecked, the finger-pricking and enchanted sleep falling instead on a scapegoat double. From outside that predetermined fairy-tale space Tepper is remarkably free to comment on the tale and on its political implications. During the course of Beauty's career Tepper manages to overturn almost every association of the beautiful blonde heroine. Beauty is raped, becomes pregnant, and gives birth to an unwanted daughter; in the best tradition of the fairy-tale witch, she achieves a certain amount of her own magical power, manipulates her children's futures, and, most importantly, grows old. She becomes an active figure of intervention and rescue, to her hapless female descendants and to the ideal of diverse natural and cultural beauty the novel seeks to preserve. The pure, unblemished, passive, youthful Sleeping Beauty is disintegrated on all fronts, replaced by a far more complex and realistic heroine whom Tepper intends as "Everywoman . . . Beauty stands as a sort of surrogate for all of us" ("Aspiring Up" 4). At the same time the structures of the original fairy tale remain in place despite Beauty's abdication, since her half-sister Beloved has taken her place. Like Byatt's heroines, Beauty recognizes the inherent trap in the fairy-tale structure and escapes. However, Byatt is unconfined by the demands of a popular market and can tinker more radically with structure. Tepper, like Pratchett, insists on the reassuring power of the expected, familiar narrative to assert itself despite the actions of its self-aware protagonists. In a sense, that narrative power is part of the problem the novel seeks to solve.

Within the metanarrative of the Sleeping Beauty tale, Tepper, like Pratchett, plays with various other fairy-tale narratives—possibly an inevitable structural technique given a novel's length. On the level of the popular readership, such subpatterns have powerful appeal in terms of recognition; like much postmodern writing, they offer the reader a self-congratulatory moment of identification with the narrative games of the writer. Here they are more accessible, and hence in some ways more immediately powerful, since the stories they evoke are Disney rather than Grimm. Tepper's subtales are developed mostly around the figures of Beauty's various descendants, as she moves through time to operate as a fairy godmother figure to all of them. The motivating power of almost all the tales is, quite simply, sex. Carter's narrative games are similar in that she plays with the erotic potential of fairy-tale narrative, but Tepper's awareness is far more brutal—within the familiar patterns of the tale, she identifies a common aspect of mindless, unthinking lust. This is akin to Tatar's characterization of violent folkloric patterns in Grimm, and provides a particularly savage vision of fairy tale as cultural code and patriarchal entrapment. The protagonists in Tepper's subtales are incomplete as individuals; they fall in with the fairy-tale plots because they are too blinded by lust or too unintelligent to recognize the fairy tale's essential artificiality.

Most powerfully, patriarchy is embodied in the tale as sexual violence, rendered the more horrific by its contrast with the assumptions attached to the fairy-tale heroine as pure and virginal; it echoes throughout the novel's emblematic use of other fairy tales. Characteristically for Tepper, sexuality—and thus its encoding in fairy-tale structures—is most condemned when it is unthinking, divorced from its consequences to be the act for its own, often perverse sake. Beauty, pregnant with the psychotic Jaybee's child after his rape of her, is forced to ensure the child's future by seducing and marrying Ned. She does this via a deliberate enactment of the Cinderella tale in which the classic pattern of mysterious appearances in beautiful clothes becomes an obvious exercise in titillation and delayed gratification, so that Ned is completely at the mercy of his desire for her. Beauty's child, Elly, is the "ravishingly beautiful" girl of fairy tale (257) but also carries the heritage of her psychotic father; she, too, re-enacts the Cinderella tale, this time with the more familiar aspects of prince, ball, and glass slipper. The tale is guided by Beauty, who recognizes the tale for what it is: "I've been in the Twentieth . . . I've read books. I've seen Disney" (261). Elly's engagement with the situation is entirely in sexual terms: "lust, the lubricious waves she swam upon, the elegant titillation she was prey to" (279). The fairy-tale three-night attraction ending in marriage is reduced to its simplest and most logical terms—Cinderella wants her prince because "I want to go to bed with him . . . over and over again" (281). Tepper recognizes, as Pratchett does, that fairy-tale unions have nothing to do with actual emotional involvement, but where Pratchett attributes the impetus to the narrative, Tepper suggests that the familiar tales conceal both primitive impulses and reactionary ideologies. Fairy-tale marriage becomes simply the sanctioned social veneer over the gratification of lust. Elly's daughter Galantha enacts a similar fate; her tale is that of Snow White, her dwarves little Basque men. Galantha is "a sweet, pretty girl. Not much sense, but sweet" (354); she lacks Jaybee's psychotic heritage, but she is singularly lacking in intelligence. Her prince is a single-minded young sex maniac whose response is distilled to its most basic: "I want her . . . buy her for me" (360). While Jaybee's taint is diluted, the couple is likewise destined to unhappiness. This tendency can be traced to one of Tepper's consuming concerns, that of overpopulation and hence unplanned pregnancy; across her writing, unwanted children are monstrous, inhuman, incomplete.

The use of fairy-tale patterns to point to artificial and irrational sexual gratification is linked to the profoundly dystopian view of the future found in *Beauty*. The future has nothing of the technological glamour of Lee's futuristic Earth; rather, it is a crowded and ugly society defined solely in terms of overpopulation. Tepper's background in Planned Parenthood has obviously influenced her writing in this regard; admitting her lifelong preoccupation with overpopulation, she comments: "I am appalled when I hear . . . a pronouncement that . . . we can agriculturally keep up with a doubled population in the world—as though that was the only thing that was important, paying no attention to what else is going to have to be lost along the way" ("Rare Breeds" 4). The future scenario of *Beauty* explores precisely this problem in its depiction of the complete loss of quality of life and global biodiversity in order to feed huge human populations. Fairy-tale magic is used as a profound contrast to this situation, and, with the exception of time-traveling machines capable of a limited version of the boots' travel powers, no attempt is made, as Lee does, to find parallels between fairy tale and technological wonder. Instead, Tepper sets up the ideal of beauty as inherent in the fourteenth-century fairy-tale world, and portrays a society which gradually and inexorably loses access to magic and beauty as time progresses. In the twentieth century, Beauty's magical cloak and boots hardly work—there is little magic left in the world, and none at all in the overcrowded future. Thus for Tepper fairy-tale narrative does offer, despite its encoding of unthinking sexuality, a deeply desirable ideal of beauty, magic, and wonder and the potential loss of which is seen as tragic.

Beauty's conclusion is strangely provisional: the novel ends in limbo, the tales' various conclusions deferred indefinitely in a postmodern open-endedness. Beauty's "happy ending" has in a sense *already* happened, in her partnership with Giles. Likewise the working out of the sexual motifs has led, through several generations, to the character of Beauty's great-grandson Giles, whose urbane (and slightly satirically excessive) knowledge and courtesy hold out considerable hopes for an equal and intelligent partner for Beloved. However, circumstances dictate that these positive conclusions cannot be enjoyed, but must be postponed indefinitely: if the individuals deserve them, the world itself, sexist and technologically doomed, does not. The anger and despair in Tepper's narratives thus come to exist in significant tension with the more popular and market-related aspects of her writing, and to radically undermine and disrupt the familiar structures of the fairy tales she uses. Despite this, the whimsy, humor, and innovation of the novel does partially disguise its savage polemic; as Nicholls comments, "the kindly spellbinder, who tells romantic tales around the campfire, has jaws that bite and claws that snatch" (1212). *Beauty* is perhaps one of the less beguilingly comfortable of Tepper's narratives, precisely because the familiarity of fairy-tale patterns is so brutally disrupted. However, it is an enjoyable read which plays entertainingly on the reader's recognition and expectation, while remaining an innovative and in many ways radical fairy-tale text.

6

MAGICAL ILLUSION: FAIRY-TALE FILM

Film versions of fairy tale are inevitable, given the extreme adaptability shown by fairy-tale structures across the centuries, and its ability to continually reinvent its voices, settings, and message as well as its medium of expression. As with the adaptation of oral folktale into written literature, the adaptation of written literature into film brings with it the possibilities and the constraints of the new medium: if writing and the printed book reinvented the oral tale, cinema's impact on literary storytelling is perhaps even more profound. Film is a vitally different form of expression from the book, and its creation—technical, massively expensive, requiring the input and skills of a large and diverse body of contributors—hugely exaggerates the importance of technology in the transmission of cultural artifacts. This leap in the complexity of the process is enabled by the concomitant leap in audience: the twentieth century saw the development of the mass market, the ability of texts to reach more people more easily than ever before. The distance from the cozy oral storyteller in a small circle of listeners could not be greater. With the new costs and new audience naturally come new constraints on the narrative, which must be adapted to its viewers on a far broader and less personal scale to provide the necessary mass appeal which will recoup the enormous costs of production. Film thus has a dual nature as an exciting and powerfully visual form of artistic expression but also as a medium operating within the consumerist paradigm of modern mass culture. Both film-as-art and film-as-product retain the potential to offer an essentially self-reflexive notion of narrative, metafiction given new expression by a new technology.

From the earliest days of cinema, in texts such as the experimental fairy-tale films of Georges Méliès, fairy-tale film has been extremely successful. Fairy-tale motifs adapt easily to the visual, and fairy tale's clear, simplified narratives are also far more conveniently adaptable to the time-scale of a film than are the detailed textures and events of a novel. This thematic simplicity also possibly explains why fairy-tale film has become strongly associated with the particular film medium of animation, a form which similarly refuses to reflect a realistically textured world. On the narrative level, fairy-tale film offers an obvious articulation of the classic Hollywood "fairy-tale" plot, which relies heavily on the comedic marriage resolution and on wish fulfillment and utopian impulses that empower the underdog. The close fit between film and fairy tale is also in some ways inevitable given folkloric narrative's long history of happy interaction with theatrical as well as literary forms. Following the adaptation of folklore into the French aristocratic pursuits of the eighteenth century, fairy-tale motifs seem to have spread rapidly to the theater, ballet, and opera. The heyday of fairy-tale ballet in the nineteenth century saw the creation of such classics as *Sleeping Beauty, Swan Lake,* and *The Nutcracker,* all with recognizable fairy-tale themes. In opera, fairy-tale awareness, although expanded into a more complex narrative, informs operas such as Mozart's *The Magic Flute,* Verdi's *Vakula the Smith,* and Puccini's *Turandot.*

As a symbolic genre, fairy tale has strong visual and dramatic potential. It is also obvious that the simple, ritualistic formulae of fairy tale would work well in ritualistic traditions, most notably ballet and opera, which are artistic productions whose meaning is expressed via a powerful system of structural codes (song, movement) rather than a process of realistic representation. Suzanne Rahn writes, "Like fairy tales, ballets are constructed as highly formalized narratives which make extensive use of repetition and tell their stories primarily through the physical actions of their characters" (in Zipes, *Oxford Companion* 34). In the twentieth century, the successful use of fairy tale in the Broadway musical follows a similar pattern; Stephen Sondheim's 1986 musical *Into the Woods,* for example, explores the dangerous gap between fairy tale and real life in a manner similar to Pratchett's *Witches Abroad.* Again, the musical is an artificial form whose encodings—the stock romantic characters, the likelihood of any character to break into song or dance at any moment—have very little to do with reality. Disney's characteristic blending of the fairy tale and the musical is a good illustration of these similarities; films such as *Beauty and the Beast* not only use the musical format but also refer constantly to the Hollywood musical.

However, theater, ballet, and other live art forms face an inherent logical problem in visually representing the marvelous, relying on stylization or at times unconvincing mechanisms to pretend to the magical; Tolkien, typically, claims that "Fantasy . . . hardly ever succeeds in Drama. . . . Fantastic forms are not to be counterfeited" (49). This is in many ways an anachronistic view in the age of CGI (computer-generated imagery), and the verisimilitude of magical spectacle in film has seen a steady increase over the last hundred years, culminating in the giant leaps made by computer imagery in influential films such as Peter Jackson's three-film version of *The Lord of the Rings*. Cinema's tricky camera is thus ultimately able to overcome the difficulties of nonreal representation, harnessing fairy tale's symbolic qualities to provide a rich visual texture. The contributions of special effects and CGI have made possible visual enchantments Tolkien could not have imagined, but the film/fairy tale fit is more profound than that; even in the early days of the medium, cinema has always been the site of magic. While apparently offering the real, it is a fertile ground for trickery, in which apparently real objects may disappear, reappear, change size or orientation, change shape—in fact, the whole of the special effects man's box of tricks; David Galef's discussion of Jean Cocteau's *La Belle et la Bête* offers a detailed and interesting analysis of this kind of magical cinematic function. The authority of the camera is such that the impossible takes on the same status as the realistic, which is in any case a good working definition of magic.

On a more fundamental level, the magical paradigm of fairy tale finds echoes in the magic of the film experience even without special effects, in film's ability to create the apparent three-dimensionality of the real on a flat, unmoving screen, through the trickery of light and image. Film powerfully realizes the transcendence over reality with which magical narrative is intrinsically concerned. This is, of course, another aspect of the debate André Bazin has called "the quarrel over realism in art" that arises from ongoing technical refinement; he suggests that the eye of the camera has the power to satisfy "our obsession with realism" and "our appetite for illusion" (12). Photography and film are particularly suited to the depiction of the fantastic because they are able to produce "a hallucination that is also a fact" (16); to blur, in fact, the boundaries between fiction and mimesis, although in a way which seldom denies its own illusion to produce the frame break which would signal metafictional play.

In addition to this, the absorbing effect of the film experience—the immersion of the viewer in a constructed reality—parallels the more traditional folk storytelling experience. Jack Zipes formulates a general theory of fairy-tale film, commenting on the importance of the storyteller's ability to create a new, removed, and absorbing reality for his or her audience. He suggests, "A magic folk tale concerned not only the miraculous turn of events in the story, but also the magical play of words by the teller as performer. . . . Telling a magic folk tale was and is not unlike performing a magic trick, and depending on the art of the storyteller, listeners are placed under a spell. They are . . . transcending reality for a brief moment, to be transported to extraordinary realms of experience" (*Happily Ever After* 63). In this characterization, cinema, like fairy tale, is a form of illusion, its viewers willingly suspending disbelief in order to surpass reality and experience the magical. Zipes notes the association between early filmmakers and stage magic—"magic lantern shows, magician's tricks, shadow theatres, animation devices . . ." (68). The filmmaker becomes the magician, the showman with the power of technological marvels, exerting the same spell as the storyteller, but with new, spectacular special effects.

The interaction of film and fairy tale does not, however, constitute an unproblematical romance. While the magic of film may parallel some aspects of fairy tale, at the same time a visual medium can be crippling to the kind of imaginative exercise usually required of the reader by almost any magical narrative. Tolkien goes as far as to deny the validity even of illustrated literary fairy tale: "The radical distinction between all art (including drama) that offers a *visible* presentation and true literature is that it imposes one visible form. Literature works from mind to mind and is thus more progenitive" (80). In this context, film's presentation of realism is a problem as well as a strength. The recording eye of the camera intrinsically designates its objects as real, and the effect of watching a film is that of immersion in a highly detailed reality. In contrast, most forms of fantasy, fairy tale included, work on evocation, rather than being explicit; the process of imaginative interaction with the fantasy requires a tailoring of the fantasy world to the psychological reality of the individual. Film, in its extreme visuality, operates directly against this; a fairy-tale medium, in its metafictional awareness of craftedness, is specifically not realistic, and it may be jarring to have realistic representation on screen. Donald P. Haase's discussion of Neil Jordan's *The Company of Wolves* raises the same point: "The one-dimensionality, the depthlessness, and the abstract style (Lüthi 4–36) of the fairy tale do not require the auditor or reader to envision a specific reality, and thereby they encourage imaginative belief in an unreal world. In the fairy tale, then, *not seeing* is believing" (90). Yet film paradoxically offers the potential for sending strong signals through visual details of setting and costume—the presence of self-conscious medievalism in a fairy-tale film, together with details of fairy-tale landscapes (forests, mountains, castles) may effectively signal the unreality of long ago and far away. Thus fairy-tale films such as *The Company of Wolves* and *The Grimm Brothers' Snow White* feature particularly vast and Gothic stretches of forest, while *Ever After* makes effective use of medieval castles, sweeping landscapes, and beautiful costumes. Cocteau's unexplained surrealist images in the Beast's castle, and Jordan's dense use of apparently disconnected symbol (animals, roses, etc.) fulfill the same function. In this deliberate symbolic texturing, once again, fairy-tale film has the potential to realize visually the metafictional strategy at the heart of its structures, despite its illusory offering of realism.

FILM AND THE FOLK VOICE

A real fairy tale, a tale in its true function, is a tale within a circle

of listeners. —KAREL CAPEK in Warner, *Beast to the Blonde* 17

There are various thematic matches between film and fairy-tale narrative, but cinematic versions of fairy tale can be seen to offer their own pitfalls and drawbacks. While the power of the film medium in modern society has provided a fertile new ground for fairy-tale cultural and ideological production, the medium of film offers problems as well as possibilities for fairy tale. One of the most insidious tendencies has been that of the powerful new visual medium, rooted firmly in modern technological popular culture, to supplant all other versions, and in so doing, to deliberately claim the folk voice originally excluded by the adaptation of fairy tale into a literary form. While parallel in many ways to the process by which oral folktale became written fairy tale, the adaptation from written fairy tale into fairy-tale film is more problematical precisely because of the power of the film medium, and the striking fit between some narrative aspects of fairy tale and the narrative function of film. To unwrap the dangers of this process will require examination of the uneasy, contested spaces of folk culture, popular culture, and mass culture.

As one of the more powerful and pervasive forms of popular culture in the twentieth and twenty-first century, film offers an interesting context for the folk voice of fairy tale. Although the folktale has been replaced gradually with the literary fairy tale in the last few centuries, film versions of fairy tale tend to flirt superficially and self-consciously with the folk voice. As the most prevalent cinematic experience in Western culture, Hollywood film caters to a popular market, offering both entertainment and the opportunity to participate in a popular awareness of actors and film which centers on the Hollywood star system. Although a form of mass culture in its reliance on the budgets of wealthy studios, and the resulting need to commodify film in order to fill cinema seats, film functions in modern Western culture as a group and social activity whose audience participates in an essentially nonliterary popular culture. Walter Ong argues for a modern notion of "secondary orality," a development through literacy into a kind of postliteracy under technology; he points out that "the drive towards group sense and towards participatory activities, towards 'happenings,' which mysteriously emerges out of modern electronic technological cultures is strikingly similar to certain drives in preliterate cultures" (*Rhetoric, Romance, and Technology* 284). The cinema experience offers far more of group participation than reading a written text. This inheres not only in the simultaneous experience of the film text, with shared reactions such as laughter, but also in the social activity around a common interest in film genres or specific stars, meeting to view a film, the discussion which often takes place either before or afterward over drinks or a meal. The experience of a home viewing of the video or DVD version of a film is an even more pronounced version of this communality. This is in many ways a superficial restoration of the communal folk experience of storytelling, in some senses reversing the historical translation of the oral folk voice into a written form experienced only by the individual, and reinstating it as shared cultural artifact. It also underlines the restitution offered the form after its appropriation by written narrative, and thus a social elite; Zipes comments that popular fairy-tale film "actually returns the fairy tale to the majority of people" (*Fairy Tale as Myth*, 83).

However, while a film is certainly more communal than a single individual reading a book, it is not a true folk culture. The group may share the experience, but it is not *produced* from within the group, nor does the production come from a source which has the same status— here defined economically—as group members. Likewise, interaction with the film narrative cannot equal the folk experience since film is a one-way process. The film modifies the experience of the viewer, but the film is not a genuine oral voice and cannot in its turn be modified in response to the audience, other than on the macrolevel represented by the research done by a studio's marketing arm before the next film is made. Walter Benjamin suggests, in fact, that the reproduction of mass images ultimately denies the authenticity of the artistic object, its ability to transfer value, and that film "is inconceivable without its destructive, cathartic effect, that is, the liquidation of the traditional value of the cultural heritage" (II); the denial of tradition in this formulation speaks directly to the divide between folk and mass culture. Film may imitate folk culture, but if it functions as a true form of modern folk culture, it is within a somewhat radically restructured notion of "folk," and, indeed, of "culture."

In keeping with film's apparently transparent offer of itself as a substitute oral and folk tradition, many fairy-tale films rely heavily on an explicit evocation of the folk voice in order to frame and contextualize their narratives. In apparently receiving the story from the physical presence or voice of an onscreen narrator, the viewer is able to participate in the removal of the tale from literary capture, placing him or herself in the position of audience to an oral storyteller. The self-conscious recognition of viewer as "listener" taps into a notion of orality which is both artificial and idealized. The purpose here is only partially to participate in the metafictional play of crafted tale and its self-conscious pleasures; it is also to access the notions of communality and trust which inhere in modern notions of orality. Thus many Disney films begin with a voice-over giving the initial scenario of the tale in traditional fairy-tale form: "Once upon a time." This is usually accompanied by static images that characterize tale as artifact—*Sleeping Beauty*'s medieval stills, *Beauty and the Beast*'s stained-glass windows, the Grecian vases of *Hercules*. At the same time, many of Disney's films characteristically hedge their bets: the voice-over may well be associated with stills that strongly associate the tale with the written tradition, in the form of a beautifully calligraphed and illuminated book whose pages are turned as the voice-over progresses (*Sleeping Beauty, Snow White*). As well as invoking the nostalgic memory of the parent-to-child oral voice and the familiar form of the literary fairy tale, this also claims the historical status of literature—generally, in its association with literacy and education, *higher* than that of the oral tale—for the film. The use of this motif in Dreamworks' *Shrek* was notable for its acute and cynical insight into the actual status of the original tale as written narrative—Shrek's voice reads out the dragon-slaying fairy tale, after which the camera pulls back to reveal that the book is being used as toilet paper. This nods ironically to the fact that film versions of fairy tale have all but replaced the written, but the film's ideological project affirms the status of the film version in its suggestion that they *should* replace the written, which entrenches the outdated and reactionary social assumptions the film sets out to upset.

It is important to note, however, that invocation of the oral and literary are not sustained through most fairy-tale films, which quickly give way to the immersing experience of the moving image. The result is effectively to overwrite the literary and the oral with the cinematic. Jack Zipes picks up on this erasure in readings of fairy-tale film which generally rely on the characterization of modern fairy tale within a somewhat totalitarian sense of the culture industry. He argues that film has "silenced the personal and communal voice of the oral magic tales and obfuscated the personal voice of literary fairy-tale narratives"; it focuses on image rather than text, distances its audience, and transforms traditional tales into standardized units of mass production (*Happily Ever After* 69). In this characterization, rather as the upper classes appropriated folk narrative in the seventeenth and eighteenth centuries, the folk voice in the twentieth and twenty-first centuries is colonized by a ruling monolith, although one that is commercial rather than aristocratic. Such a colonization entails, in Baudrillard's terms, an actual *re-creation* of a spurious notion of orality; simultaneously, its commercial aspect redefines the awareness of artifact central to metafictional storytelling as, effectively, awareness of *product*. Zipes's characterization of fairy tale as "secular instructive narratives" offering "strategies of intervention within the civilising process" (*Happily Ever After* 65) becomes more sinister when, rather than reflecting the mores and beliefs of the folk culture, fairy tales are used to reflect the conservative and market-driven ideologies of large companies marketing consumer culture. Such characterizations of mass cultural productions sound a note of alarm in their sense of a production elite which seeks to duplicate and usurp the popular or folk voice. Zipes's argument implies that any claim of nostalgic orality or literariness in fairy-tale film is entirely spurious; logically, the elements of self-conscious play that I suggest are present become in his terms a cynical appropriation of fairy tale's metafictional project by what are effectively market forces. He is, of course, engaging in cultural criticism firmly in the mode of the Frankfurt School, and more specifically Adorno and Horkheimer, who suggest that modern consumer culture is a process of the deliberate discouragement of imaginative or intellectual response to the cultural products of the mass market. Instead, the receiver of such artifacts is lulled, via strategies such as nostalgia, familiarity, and superficial novelty, into the passive acceptance of a standardized cultural product. This logically suggests that the essentially reciprocal functioning of a folk culture is completely erased, as is its ability to mirror in any immediate or vital sense the day-to-day experiences and desires of its listeners. Adorno and Horkheimer stress the absolute lack of true participation by the public in mass cultural production:

> The attitude of the public, which ostensibly and actually favours the system of the culture industry, is a part of the system and not an excuse for it. If one branch of art follows the same formula as one with a very different medium and content . . . if a movement from a Beethoven symphony is crudely "adapted" for a film sound-track in the same way that a Tolstoy novel is garbled in a film script; then the claim that this is done to sat-

isfy the spontaneous wishes of the public is no more than hot air. We are closer to the facts if we explain these phenomena as inherent in the technical and personnel apparatus which, down to its last cog, itself forms part of the economic mechanism of selection. . . . In our age the objective social tendency is incarnate in the hidden subjective purposes of company directors. (32)

By this definition, mass culture and folk culture are mutually exclusive; there can be no true "objective social tendency," in Adorno and Horkheimer's words, because original and spontaneous cultural impulses are modified by the purposes of mass-cultural monoliths. There can therefore be no folk voice in mass culture. This means that the pretensions to the folk voice in many fairy-tale films are, as suggested above, "hot air"—their purpose is solely to conceal their commercial manipulations.

This is perhaps too sweeping a judgment, and more recent perceptions of popular culture as a site of struggle suggest that Adorno and Horkheimer represent only one end of the popular theory spectrum. Noël Carroll offers an opposing voice which explicitly denies the truth of such claims; he maintains that numerous examples of popular art demonstrate clearly the lack of "necessary connection between accessibility and a passive audience response," and that indeed, "in some cases, the very success of the mass artwork presupposes active spectatorship" (38–39). This line of thought is certainly appropriate to the sf/fantasy ghetto, in which the highly specific readership may well require active participation in the text—or, indeed, to written narratives generally, as Carroll demonstrates (40–41); nonetheless, it is also true, to a greater or lesser extent, of film. The self-conscious narrative play found in texts such as Disney fairy tales or Dreamworks' *Shrek* may empower a mass-market text, but it is equally able to give the artistic and intellectual pleasure of active reading to the viewer, and indeed would not be successful *without* such narrative pleasures. Theories of a mass-cultural monolith also deny the possibilities offered by the art-house end of the film spectrum, in which films are generally made on a far lower budget, and may be more able to balance their artistic requirements against the need to recoup their costs. A good example of film's potential for self-conscious use of fairy tale is Jordan's *The Company of Wolves,* in which frame narratives and tale-within-tale represent a sustained effort to reproduce the folk voice, and thus allow ongoing metafictional awareness. This is strengthened by the film's attention to the character of the oral storytellers (unlike Disney's disembodied voices), and their association of that oral voice with the readily identifiable grandmother archetype.

However, despite innovative uses such as Jordan's of the folk voice in film, Zipes's characterization is valid in that many fairy-tale films seem to represent an appropriation as much as an exploration or celebration of folk narrative. This exemplifies the uneasy and problematical intersections between popular or folk cultures, and the mass culture of consumerism. Film narrative is dominated by Hollywood, and particularly by big-budget studio films whose economies of scale require appeal to a broad demographic; many recent fairy-tale films represent a process of identifying the kinds of narrative which are currently selling, and reproducing them as closely as possible. Disney's huge successes with fairy tale in the late 1980s and early 1990s could be seen to have prompted later films such as *Ever After* and *The Grimm Brothers' Snow White,* and ultimately *Shrek,* which has itself spawned two sequels and a host of imitators in the knowing fairy-tale parody mode, including *Hoodwinked* and *Happily N'Ever After.* At the same time, the production-by-committee effect of financial oversight on films exists in palpable tension with the impulses of particular directors or screenwriters, who may well see the artistic rather than the commercial potential in recreating a familiar folkloric text. In addition, the construction of a particular text in terms favoring commercial success does not in any way prevent countercultural readings of such a text, representing a very different notion of narrative pleasure from that intended by the producers. Audience-generated responses such as fan fiction demonstrate precisely the kind of active, potentially subversive receptions of mass-cultural texts described by critics such as John Fiske and Henry Jenkins. Even Disney films, perhaps the strongest example of deliberate mass-cultural packaging, are capable of being read on multiple levels which address child and adult audiences separately. Thus, like much of mass culture, fairy-tale film is a site of contestation, with the warping of metafictional play to commercial ends balanced by a wresting back of commercial requirements to artistic and individual purposes. The postmodern cultural environment of modern film also means that at times the two impulses are one: self-consciousness, irony, and the pleasures of recognition are highly saleable commodities.

LIVE-ACTION FAIRY-TALE FILM: NARRATIVE EXPLORATIONS

At one end of the wide spectrum of film's purposes and effects, fairy-tale films have precisely the same potential to offer self-conscious intellectual play with form and expectation as do the "high-culture" literary texts of the postmodern writers. To the wealth of potential reference and shared generic understanding of fairy tale is added another dimension, that of film and film genre, after a hundred years a dense and colorful repository of exemplar, tradition, and textual expectation. Interestingly, while fairy-tale film has been equally successful in live-action and animated forms, live-action filmmaking has tended to offer the most serious and interesting fairy-tale explorations. This perhaps reflects the general tendency in Western cinema to associate animation fairly strongly with children's films; live-action fairy tale suffers the equal and opposing association with the fluffy and formulaic genre of Hollywood romance, equally the arena of stock characters, formulaic plot lines and the much-vaunted "Hollywood happy ending," but live-action film also has the strongest tradition of "art" cinema. In some ways this is once again a commercial issue, since animation is considerably more expensive to make than live-action film; experimental animation, comparatively less accessible and lacking in broader popular appeal, tends to be confined to festival-circuit film shorts.

An early and particularly interesting exploration of fairy tale in the live-action film medium is offered by Jean Cocteau's self-consciously artistic use of Mme. Leprince de Beaumont's "Beauty and the Beast" in his 1946 film, *La Belle et la Bête,* a text which has influenced and informed many subsequent fairy-tale films. Rebecca Pauley has commented on Cocteau's film as a deliberately nostalgic and utopian use of fairy-tale structures as a response to the horrors of the war years: "his wish to return to the world of creative freedom and vitality which had been so crushed by World War Two and the German occupation" (86). On another, more individual level, the film provides a site for the exploration of Cocteau's sense of the filmmaker as artist or poet, which is possible through his status as auteur and his complete artistic control over the production, direction, and script (Hayward 47). Here, film as artifact becomes stylized, even aestheticized, presenting film as individual artwork rather than as either popular film or as simple reiteration of a traditional tale. Most strikingly, however, the film offers a particularly individual response to the problem of fairy-tale narrative in live-action cinema, in Cocteau's use of near-surrealist visual and narrative effects which echo and reinvent fairy tale's problematical relationship with reality.

To identify Cocteau with the surrealist movement is a thorny issue, but a useful link for my investigation of fairy-tale film's strategies to overcome the clash between the unreality of fairy tale and the realism of the camera. Critical responses to Cocteau's works often invoke surrealism; Pauley, for example, comments on the film as "an illustration of the dangerous yet necessary sexual journey into the realm of the surreal" (89), and Arthur Evans comments that Cocteau's films are "strangely reminiscent of the surrealists' dreamworlds" (87). André Breton's definitions of surrealism include an awareness of "interior reality and exterior reality as two elements in process of unification, of finally becoming *one*" (116). Cocteau shares with the surrealists an interest in the unconscious, in dreams and images which are an end in themselves, and which do not need to be connected by reason or logic; what Breton has called "the omnipotence of the dream and . . . the disinterested play of thought" (122). Where Cocteau diverges from this, however, is in his awareness of aesthetics, structure, system: Breton calls for "thought in the absence of all control exercised by reason and outside all aesthetic or moral preoccupations" (122), while Cocteau freely uses the strong structures and systems of fairy tale and myth, and has a dedication to beauty which has led to his films being described as "painterly" and "picturesque" (Hayward 47).

Where Cocteau's common concerns with surrealism are interesting is in precisely this clash between structure and the free play of thought. Both fairy tale and surrealism reject the conventional, realist representations of most art and literature, but they also have different attitudes from realism, related but distinct. Surrealism entails a process of disconnection between elements, whereas fairy tale presupposes some kind of intrinsic connection, even if it is a never-explained magical connection; picking a rose has the direct causal effect of angering the Beast and leading to his demand for the merchant's daughter, even if you never know why the rose is so important. In Cocteau's film, the presence of living statues is never explained; the statues and living human arms of the Beast's castle provide a surreal interpretation of Mme. de Beaumont's invisible, magical servants, in a similar fashion to Disney's transformation of invisible servants into animated domestic items. (Invisible servants are a terrible idea for film; a visual medium makes heavy work of the unseen). Essentially, fairy tale depends on the familiar, where surrealism insists on defamiliarizing it. Nonetheless, they share the metafictional quality of problematizing the real, a tendency Cocteau develops in various ways in the film, developing and intensifying the atmosphere of otherworldly strangeness which pervades *La Belle et la Bête*: the visual representation of the magical as a dislocation of the real. Thus gates open invisibly, statues have living eyes, living arms hold candlesticks or serve a meal, and Belle drifts down the corridor in a magical, dreamlike glide which gives, in Hayward's words, "the illusion that she [is] floating into her unconscious" (45). Their dreamlike unreality underlines fairy-tale's coding as antimimetic space, a world far removed from the real. The film's conclusion, shorn of the French tale's triumphal journey to a restored kingdom, and the celebratory presence of the families of both Belle and the transformed prince, offers a similar sense of dislocation. The couple rises into the air in a vivid symbolic gesture which removes them from narrative causation as much as visually celebrating the happy conclusion to the tale.

Not all aspects of the film counteract film realism by surreal elements; Cocteau's techniques are more varied than this. One of the best examples is the extreme stylization of acting technique in the film. The actors' exaggerated gestures, carefully posed static quality, and choreographed movements operate similarly to the frame narrative in other fairy-tale films—to heighten, highlight, and draw attention to the fairy tale's essential unreality. The film offers a system of encoding similar to that of ballet or opera, one of ritualized gesture rather than realistic emotion. This, together with the film's framing by blackboard messages which insist on its imaginative and constructed nature, goes some way toward metafictional awareness, counteracting the visual realism of the film genre. In addition, like more recent films such as *Ever After,* the film makes use of the visual in its careful seventeenth-century costuming, which explicitly invokes the distant unreality of the original French tale for the film's viewers. This is paralleled by the film's recurring interest in artifact: Cocteau expands the rose of the original tale into a series of magical symbols—rose, key, glove, mirror, and horse—all of which invoke fairy-tale traditions as well as rendering visual and concrete the Beast's magical power.

The choice of the "Beauty and the Beast" tale is interesting for Cocteau's surrealist quality. Many versions of "Beauty and the Beast," including the Disney version, suffer from a strange moment of regret at the transformation of Beast into handsome prince. Both Beauty and the audience find themselves mourning the loss of the Beast, with whom they have identified during the course of the film. Michael Popkin reports the classic response of Greta Garbo to Cocteau's film—"Give me back my Beast" (101, quoting Pauline Kael's study), and draws interesting parallels with *King Kong,* finding a similar process of audience identification with the Beast (101ff.). In Cocteau's version, the transformation of Beast into prince is utilized and highlighted as another moment of surrealist dislocation—the causal process of Belle's attraction to the Beast is disrupted, replaced by the necessary fairy-tale denouement which overturns the causal relationship already set up. This is complicated by the adaptations Cocteau has made to the original tale, in the form of Avenant, Belle's rejected suitor, played by Jean Marais, the same actor who plays Beast and Prince. There is no real reason why the Prince should be physically identical to Avenant, who is identified as a complete cad despite his handsome exterior, and who brings about his own downfall by desecrating the Temple of Diana. The transformation attempts to render neatly symmetrical and obviously visual the theme of exterior versus interior value—the Beast looks ugly but is good, Avenant looks good but is worthless, and the transformation relocates all value in a strictly binary sense, with interior worth mirrored absolutely by exterior appearance. The stylized structures of fairy tale are here exaggerated, motifs of reflection and repetition taken to self-conscious extremes; however, this overly tidy self-consciousness is partially undercut by the processes through which the audience becomes identified with the visual presence of the Beast.

Cocteau's script calls for the Beast to have "the appearance of a werewolf, with long fangs and grotesque features" (209). This makes for notable parallels with the other twentieth-century film offering serious treatment of fairy-tale motifs, Neil Jordan's *The Company of Wolves* (1984). This is a particularly interesting work given that the film was based on several stories from Angela Carter's *Bloody Chamber* collection, and Carter herself co-wrote the script with Jordan. While following Carter's interest in the development of female sexuality under patriarchy through the self-conscious rewriting of fairy tales, the film offers a stunning visual reinterpretation of Carter's Gothic-flavored tales, as well as a creative use of framing narrative, embedded tales, and the oral voice. Given that Jordan uses the framing narrative of the dream to both highlight and justify his use of disconnected and nightmarish visual images (unlike Cocteau, who simply includes them and leaves his viewers to deal with the resulting illogic), the self-possessed heroine Rosaleen could be seen as a twentieth-century Alice, moving through the potential threat of the dreamworld with unimpaired calm. (The name is explicitly given to her older sister, who is the frame dreamer in Carter's original script.) Rosaleen evokes beautifully the child in Carter's tale "The Company of Wolves," who "stands and moves within the invisible pentacle of her own virginity . . . she is a closed system, she does not know how to shiver" (114). The closed system is also that of fairy tale, each self-contained narrative an investigation not only of sexual subjectivity but also of narrative.

Carter seems to have been aware of the problems of film for fairy tale: Susannah Clapp's introduction to a collection of Carter's radio scripts and screenplays quotes her as saying, in an echo of Tolkien, that radio is "the most visual of mediums because you cannot see it" (in Carter, *Curious Room* ix). *Company of Wolves*, however, rises triumphantly above the dangers of the visual, since its visual texture is ambiguously symbolic enough to offer even more imaginative potential than it does imaginative realization. Like Cocteau, Jordan's techniques are many and various, but he is able to make use of more developed cinematic technology—special effects, color, a larger cast and budget, an audience more familiar with cinema and Freud—to achieve an absorbing and visually compelling film. Frame tale and embedded narrative allow for a self-conscious flaunting of narrative constructedness as well as an authentic sense of the folk voice. Numerous folktales—the wedding night werewolf, the wronged village witch, the young man meeting the devil in the forest—are told in voice-over by Rosaleen's grandmother or Rosaleen herself, and are given added impact by their rather sumptuous visual realization; the aristocratic wedding banquet, interrupted by witchcraft and general werewolf mayhem, is a visual tour de force. Such folkloric elements give depth and significance to the fairly straightforward tale of Rosaleen and her village, the site of the Red Riding Hood story; the folk voice, together with the use of visual symbol, diversify the narratives so that their visual realization is not restrictive. At the same time the oral framing insists on tale as craft, narrative as construction, intertextual resonances between the tales, and thus, visual reality as an illustration of structures more profound than the simple image.

Jordan's Gothic forest and the village itself, a peasant seventeenth-century setting, are another example of the power of live-action film to create the "long ago and far away" feel of fairy tale, an essential unreality despite the realism of the setting. Carter's script interestingly describes the forest as both "the mysterious forest of the European imagination" and "a brooding, Disney forest" (*Curious Room* 187): the film invokes modern visual intertexts as well as traditional, to add depth and texture. In addition the film is packed with images of nightmare and the unconscious which operate with metafictional and Freudian implication—animated childhood toys, a forest filled with snakes, toads and ravens, and apparently random cuts to, for example, white roses turning slowly red. Jordan manages the seemingly impossible feat of translating into visual terms the richness of Carter's Gothic prose. His special effects also access the element of brutal violence which critics such as Maria Tatar have found in fairy tale—the werewolf transformations in *Company of Wolves* are horrific even by the standards of the modern horror film, with heaving, warping bodies and splitting flesh. In Carter's exploration, this comes to represent the fear the inexperienced adolescent has for the purely physical—and potentially painful—aspects of the sexual act. In its translation to the constructedness of story, however, such pubescent anxieties are distanced, their removal into the realm of unreality allowing them to be examined as fiction rather than mimesis. (One could make a similar case for teenage angst and the distancing effect of symbol in modern texts such as Joss Whedon's *Buffy the Vampire Slayer,* a TV series which frequently plays self-consciously with its own status as television narrative and as horror text.) Jordan's film invokes something of the violence of the Hollywood horror genre, but its images, while being the standard forests, wolves, and transformation scenes of the Gothic, are more self-consciously aware of symbolism. In one particularly memorable example the bloody severed head of a werewolf lands in a bucket of milk, inviting comparisons with the film's running use of white and red to suggest innocence and sexual experience, or virginity and deflowerment. Violence is never gratuitous, always carefully judged within the film's symbolic structures; such structures are never allowed to stand alone, requiring constant decoding so that the viewer must acknowledge the act of reception, and thus, of storytelling.

The dream-sequence framing of the film obviously allows Jordan free play with the kind of unreality necessary to overcome live action film's reproduction of realistic scenes, although in some ways its formless, nightmare qualities work against the structuredness of tale. Tolkien denies narratives framed as dream the status of fairy tale; he argues, "If a waking writer tells you that his tale is only a thing imagined in his sleep, he cheats deliberately on the primal desire at the heart of Faërie: the realisation, independent of the conceiving mind, of imagined wonder" (14). Jordan's film seems to avoid this trap because of the substantial reality of Rosaleen's fairy-tale village setting, which allows the dream narrative to access the "long ago and far away" of fairy tale as a vivid *psychological* reality. This greatly empowers Carter's feminist explorations in psychological terms; while we explore Rosaleen's adolescent dream, we are encouraged to move more deeply into her unconscious, away from normal reality. Jordan's awareness of the marvelous apparently conflates the unconscious and dream with fairy-tale symbol, a particularly Jungian framework recalling the work of Marie-Louise von Franz. Unstructured dream narrative (Rosaleen's sister attacked by toys/wolves) gives way to a deeper, more structured dream (Red Riding Hood's village), which in turn moves deeper into embedded narratives (Granny's tales, and later Rosaleen's). While, paradoxically, structure intensifies the deeper we go, so too does psychological significance, as Jordan tempers the fairly standard revenge fantasies of a younger sibling with a more complex interaction between desire and social conditioning. As is appropriate to any reworking of Carter, the film explores the effect of social structures—the village, the folktales of the grandmother—on the adolescent sexual development of Rosaleen. Like Carter's other heroines, she must escape the narratives imposed by her society if she is to function autonomously as a woman and a sexual being in her own right.

Women are the tellers of tales in the film, a characterization appropriate for Carter's feminist intentions, but which also recalls Marina Warner's identification of the female voice as the original purveyor of folklore. She argues that women's folktale narratives "reveal possibilities ... map out a different way and a new perception of love, marriage, women's skills, thus advocating a means of escaping imposed limits and prescribed destiny" (*Beast to the Blonde* 24). Carter and Jordan would argue otherwise. Rosaleen's Granny is an archetypal tale-telling figure, the repository of experience and social wisdom, yet in Jordan's film she is the most reactionary figure. Her strictures ("Don't stray from the path!") and her social awareness are constructed entirely around warning and threat, the awareness of male sexuality as violence, and any female sexual impulse as transgressive and inviting disaster. Thus men are "nice as pie until they've had their way with you. But once the bloom is gone, the beast comes out." Her narratives, which are repeated either to or by Rosaleen in the film, are cautionary frameworks which insist on the dangers of untrammeled sexuality, of the deserved fate of a woman who chooses a "traveling man" whose eyebrows meet, rather than the known safety of a village man "not too shy to piss in a pot." This parallels the tension between Rosaleen's suitors, the Amorous Boy who stands for socially sanctioned sexuality ("A walk ... in the woods, on Sunday, after service ... Tell your mother I'll be with you"), and the more powerful and dangerous sexual presence of the Hunter.

Granny is a strangely ambiguous figure, though—she is at once protective and threatening, reassuring Rosaleen of her safety within the web of Granny's knowledge and experience, even while the old woman's spectacles catch the light to silver over eerily, like a wolf's eyes. Her animated fox-fur is another association between the old woman and the life of the wild predator. She represents an absolutely ideological investigation of tale-telling and cultural structure, to no degree compromised by the cinematic format. While Rosaleen's experiences with the werewolf Hunter ultimately deny everything Granny has told her, Granny is nonetheless a figure of female power in the text, and presumably, since she is Rosaleen's father's mother, one of sexual experience. She has moved through the processes of socially sanctioned sexuality and now stands outside them, isolated in her hut in the forest—and, similarly, isolated but powerful in the position of teller rather than participant in tales, her metafictional awareness embracing her society as text as much as the tales she tells. However, while apart, she is still very much a product of such structures: the female patterns she offers Rosaleen are those of patriarchy, either the submissive woman of the wedding-night werewolf tale, or the demonized witch-figure of the aristocratic banquet. In Carter's original tale, "The Werewolf," the grandmother *is* the werewolf; the girl-child, besting the wolf, is also heir to her grandmother's house and, presumably, demonic female powers. Jordan's film chooses rather to play on the grandmother figure as a reactionary social force, attempting to indoctrinate successive generations into a limited rather than a powerful female sexuality, competing with her daughter-in-law for the attentions of her son in the classic patriarchal pattern. Ultimately she is reduced to a china doll, an image of fragile constructedness which shatters, as do her tales. The undercutting of her narratives brings into play a metafictional falling-domino effect as we are forced to acknowledge and distrust the Chinese-box tale-telling of the film.

Whatever Granny's intentions in the warning folklore she imparts to Rosaleen, the effect on Rosaleen is empowering; the lessons Rosaleen learns from the folktales are not those intended by their teller. Rather than being warned, Rosaleen's response to the tales is one of aroused curiosity. The folk patterns of wolf/man/woman are reinterpreted, not only through the lens of Rosaleen's adolescent sexual curiosity and the images offered by the horror film tradition but also through the motif of tale-telling and its exposure of the weakening patriarchal bonds in each succeeding generation. Rosaleen's mother offers an antidote to the superstitious fears of the grandmother: where Granny believes that men are beasts and girls who stray will be eaten, the mother has a strong sense of Carteresque equality: "your granny . . . knows a lot, but she doesn't know everything. If there's a beast in men it meets its match in women too." This, and the conclusion to Rosaleen's Red Riding Hood tale, parallels the conclusion to Carter's "The Tiger's Bride," where, at the moment of transformation, Beauty becomes Beast rather than Beast becoming Prince. In her analysis of the film, Carole Zucker notes that "it is only [Rosaleen's] mother, the character closest to the natural world, who recognises the wolf as her daughter and implores the group of gathered hunters not to shoot" (69). Like Carter's progression of stories in *The Bloody Chamber,* the film offers a successive sense of female sexual identity, each generation less entrapped than the one before. Self-conscious employment of narrative is central to this process; cultural critique is only possible from outside the tale, looking in.

In this investigation of female sexuality, Red Riding Hood's narrative is at the heart of the film, and awareness of its cultural history allows the invocation of powerful intertexts, an echo of Carter's metafictional project. The tale has always seemed inherently concerned with sexual relations, even before Carter's feminist rewrites. Carter's script for the film specifically invokes the Gustav Doré illustrations to the Red Riding Hood story (*Curious Room* 187); Doré gives an essentially sexualized interpretation which tends to focus on the girl's horrified fascination with the wolf, depicted as a dark, voracious presence considerably larger than the child. Doré's illustrations pick up on essential undercurrents in the tale. The familiar Perrault elements—forest, animal, innocently straying girl, bedroom striptease, and symbolic rape—cast woman as victim and as transgressor who invites her own destruction. Zipes, in his introduction to a collection of Red Riding Hood retellings, argues that this is a distortion of the tale's original import. He traces the development of the tale from the original folk form, an adolescent initiatory scenario where the girl outwits the beast and escapes, through Perrault's adaptations into a patriarchal fable which transforms the girl into an object of sadistic exploitation (*Trials and Tribulations* 23–27). Carter and Jordan's self-aware heroine is in some ways an antidote to this patriarchal retelling; with a knife in her basket, she is unafraid of the forests, and even in the confrontation with the werewolf, uses the Hunter's shotgun against him rather than passively awaiting rescue. Her relationship to the original tales is thus that of her relationship with her grandmother's stories: critical onlooker selecting and rejecting from the proffered work of art.

At the same time, Rosaleen's interpretation of her granny's tales makes her perfectly aware of the sexual initiation she is being offered. This also echoes aspects of Red Riding Hood in popular culture, as noted by Zipes: "Almost all the commodified forms of Little Red Riding Hood as sex object portray her as thoroughly grown-up and desirous of some kind of sexual assignation with the wolf" (*Trials and Tribulations* 8–9). Thus, while the film attempts to address Red Riding Hood as victim, it perhaps fails to elude the process of film itself, both patriarchal and commodifying: the camera's association with a male gaze, and the female's inevitable designation as object. In fact, this also reflects entrapment within the structures of fairy tale. The picnic scene is an extended flirtation between Rosaleen and the Hunter, with what Carter's script describes as a "terrific erotic charge between them" (234); they tussle, exchange suggestive quips about the magic object the Hunter has in his trousers, and part with Rosaleen's suggestion that her reward for winning their bet should be the compass, the phallic object they have been discussing. Jordan's Hunter, urbane, foreign, and definitely upper class, is an icon of male sexual experience, set up in contrast to the callow village lad who most resembles the sailor doll of the frame narrative—"They're clowns, the village boys." The figure of Rosaleen thus becomes ambiguous, moving between the two competing narratives. On the one hand, the objectifying male gaze of the camera highlights the tale's inherent interest in a transgressive female figure who responds to a promise of male skill that is also symbolized as male power—as Zipes has noted, this "reinforces the notion that 'women want to be raped.'" (*Trials and Tribulations* 11). On the other, Carter attempts to revive the passive girl of Perrault's tale and to give her an awareness of her choices and access to genuine desire, although, like "The Tiger's Bride," at the price of rejecting her society—and thus its narratives—completely.

It is possible to see some of this ambiguity and unease around the film's sexual politics as a direct result of film narrative as a process of multiple authorship. The film operates firmly within the modern film production system, which entails potentially enormous divisions between the script on one hand and the interpretations of the director on the other. Unlike Cocteau's *La Belle et la Bête*, where the hand of Cocteau the auteur is discernible in the film's artistic integrity, *The Company of Wolves* represents Carter's script under Jordan's direction, and the differences between the original script and the final film product are striking. While Carter may be a feminist scriptwriter rewriting fairy tale, Jordan is a male director, and the gaze of the camera is his, not Carter's. The changes are most apparent in the ending of both the Red Riding Hood narrative and the frame narrative. Carter's script reproduces the strong female assertion of the child faced with the male monster: "I'm nobody's meat, not I!" Jordan's film omits this, and Rosaleen's admonishing tone as she instructs the transformed Hunter, "You must be a wolf for good and all. . . . Not a gentleman or a prince of darkness. But an honest, good wolf . . ." (241). Her scripted words acknowledge the dangers of the Hunter's seductive human identity; unlike the film version of Rosaleen, she can see through the facade of sexual experience. Rosaleen's concluding story, from the same scene in the script, is of "love between wolves," not of a naked wolf-girl; the objectifying gaze of the camera is particularly evident in the largely pointless fragment of wolf-girl narrative and her problematical association with "the world below" and the demonic female.

The clash between Jordan and Carter's approaches here is possibly more extreme because of the tradition of horror film in which *The Company of Wolves* operates—fairy tale is not the only structural tradition at work. The classic horror movie is a particularly male tradition, based on the stereotype of a passive female victim under threat from forces that often represent exaggerated male sexuality (the vampire, the monster, the stalker of films such as *Friday the 13th* and *Nightmare on Elm Street*). Thus, despite Rosaleen's triumphant transformation at the end of the Red Riding Hood narrative, the ending of the actual film is far from upbeat from a feminist point of view. In the frame narrative of Rosaleen dreaming, her dream is interrupted by the intrusion of wolves into her bedroom, to crash first through a portrait of a girl in the passage outside her bedroom, and then in through the bedroom window. This blurring of dream and reality effectively undoes all the resolution of the dream narrative; despite having come to terms with adult sexuality through the wolf-symbols of the dream, Rosaleen still undergoes metaphorical rape as she awakens to the sound of shattering glass. While she may celebrate metafictional awareness of tale within her story, she is revealed, in the end, to be no more than a figure in a larger narrative, the power ultimately not her own. The voice-over which concludes the film is a Perrault-style and patriarchalist warning not to stray, since "sweetest tongue has sharpest tooth." Zucker comments, "The sweet tongue is Rosaleen's dream of a mellifluous fusion of nature and culture, of powerful femininity and desire without reproach. The sharp tooth must then surely be the more painful reality into which Rosaleen must grow up. It is not a happy ending." (70). The film's ending thus extends fairy tale's classic problematization of the borders between fantasy and reality, here blurring them to anxiety-causing effect. I would argue that the ending has much to do with the expectations of the horror film, which tend toward one last, unexpected scream from the passive female, one last resurgence of the evil (male) threat. Many horror films similarly refuse to completely destroy the monster, leaving an ambiguous and open-ended sense of menace, a lingering intrusion of the fantasy into the mundane (and, of course, the potential for a sequel). In Carter's original script, the concluding image is very different:

> ALICE is sitting on her bed. . . . The door is still open and the tangle of the forest can be seen sprouting through it.
> ALICE suddenly springs off the bed, up into the air, as if off a diving board. She curls, in a graceful jack-knife and plummets towards the floor. The floor parts. It is in fact water. She vanishes beneath it.
> The floor ripples, with the aftermath of her dive. Gradually it settles back into plain floor again.
> We see the room, for a beat, half-forest, half-girl's bedroom. There is a whining at the door. It opens, under the pressure of one wolf's snout. First the he-wolf enters, then the she-wolf. They nose their way around ALICE's things. (Curious Room 244)

This beautifully reversed image of female rather than male penetration provides a triumphant and transcendent moment in which the adolescent girl is transformed into the sexually mature adult, equal to the male, and in which the girl chooses to abdicate her innocence in an act which celebrates as well as relinquishes it. The moment is also ultimately metafictional, the girl choosing to break the frame of her narrative reality, rejecting it as spurious construct, and choosing simply to go elsewhere. It is a great pity that Jordan could not have used this final image, since his choice of conclusion plunges Carter's script back into the darkness and male threat of Perrault's version, while also succumbing to the pressures of the horror film genre. Thus, although offering a powerful and complex use of film's visual capacity, *Company of Wolves* is ultimately a flawed artwork, its cinematic format the site of the familiar tension, and its treatment of fairy-tale narrative reactionary as well as innovative.

LIVE-ACTION FAIRY TALE: THE HOLLYWOOD MOVIE

Quite apart from the narrative explorations of filmmakers such as Cocteau and Jordan, the fairy tale occupies a fairly prominent place in the commodity arsenal of the popular Hollywood movie. The classic happy-ever-after conclusion of the fairy tale, together with its recurring theme of the rise to success and happiness of a disadvantaged protagonist, is a fertile ground for commercial cinema. The American Dream so beloved by Hollywood is itself a fairy-tale narrative—hard work and obeying the rules is all that is needed for wealth and the happily-ever-after of marriage and a family. The use of fairy tale also provides an interesting counterpoint to the decline of the importance of story or script in popular Hollywood film. Fairy tale provides strong and recognizable narrative which is not too demanding or complex, and which fills the painful gap left in commercial film by the diminishing importance of the actual script against big-name stars, high production values, and special effects.

The late twentieth and early twenty-first centuries have seen a run of fairy-tale films, most notably *Ever After* (1998) and *The Grimm Brothers' Snow White* (1997), but also productions such as *Freeway* (1996) and the recent slew of films including *Ella Enchanted* culminating in *Enchanted* (2007). In some senses this trend looks back to Gary Marshall's 1990 production, *Pretty Woman* or even to the Richard Chamberlain vehicle *The Slipper and the Rose* (1976), which retold the Cinderella tale as romanticized social comedy. Marshall's self-conscious use of the Cinderella tale was highly successful: the structure of the Hollywood romantic comedy merged seamlessly with the rags-to-riches tale of Cinderella, rendered contemporary by the modern setting and innovative use of recognizable modern archetypes which simultaneously echo fairy-tale antecedents—the whore-with-the-heart-of-gold redeems the soulless big businessman in a direct parallel to Beauty's civilizing of the Beast. While successful, the film's use of fairy tale was also intrinsically uncritical, relying on an audience response of nostalgia for the familiar fairy-tale motifs, and ignoring their more unpleasant patriarchalist implications. This, together with the film's modern setting, allowed *Pretty Woman* to negotiate the familiarity/novelty tension Cawelti argues is such an important feature of popular cultural productions. Later films such as *Freeway* and *Ever After* followed the same, highly successful formula, although *Freeway* explored a far darker aspect of Red Riding Hood than *Ever After* does with Cinderella. Both *Freeway* and *Pretty Woman* function as contemporary films which use fairy-tale motifs, rather than being fairy-tale films; I am thus more interested in the more explicitly fairy-tale texts of *Ever After,* despite its quasi-historical feel, and *The Grimm Brothers' Snow White.*

Andy Tennant, the director of *Ever After,* insists that the film "is not a cartoon or fairy tale—it's an adventure with completely unexpected attitude" (in "Ever After" production notes). This is not entirely true. While the film's approach to the Cinderella story is in some ways innovative, its basic structure—the despised stepdaughter, unpleasant stepmother, prince in search of a wife, and grand denouement at a glittering ball—remain intact. Where *Ever After* is interesting is in its use of realism, since fairy-tale story and setting are completely denuded of their magical elements, and the film attempts to present some kind of historical narrative (albeit, as John Stephens and Robyn McCallum argue, one that is "tongue-in-cheek" [202]), framed by the storyteller who claims to be a descendant of the "real Cinderella." The film's insistence that it is offering the "real story" is an acute narrative play that highlights the constructedness of the fairy tale by contrasting the film's reality with the more unrealistic expectations attached to fairy tale. Cathy Preston's review of the film makes valid points about the translation of the tale from the folkloric to the legendary, with its assumptions of possible reality rather than a resolutely marvelous space (175); however, the viewer's awareness of the Cinderella story is strong enough that it exists in tension with the claim of realism in a rather enjoyable narrative clash. The traditional "long ago and far away" narrative of fairy tale is anchored in specific figures such as Thomas More and Leonardo da Vinci, while Prince Henry is probably Henry II of France. The film uses some historical details: problems with Spain, Francis's fascination with Italian artists, including da Vinci (Duruy 479), and the establishment of the College of France, although historically this was by his father Francis, not Henry (522). As Stephens and McCallum point out, this is a chronologically impossible mixture of elements; the awareness of the clash, ultimately, "might only reinforce the power of a metanarrative to impose teleology on culture" (204). This renders the elements of historicism and the "real" ultimately false, an effect supported by the film's haziness on historical detail, the conglomeration of medieval styles in its costuming, and the sweeping grandeur of its landscapes—mountains, woods and castles—which explicitly invoke a timeless and essentially fairy-tale experience. In addition, the imposition of the Cinderella narrative onto actual history moves the entire story into ahistorical space: in reality, marriages of the time were political, not personal, and Henry II married Catherine de Medici, not a commoner. The film thus uses a superficial gloss of historical accuracy to lend credence to its attempt at realism, but historical elements in no way disrupt the workings of the fairy-tale plot, and serve in many ways to highlight them. Something similar is seen in Disney's *Sleeping Beauty*, where the costumes and visual feel are medieval, and the Prince admonishes his father with a reminder that "This is the fourteenth century!" while in fact, the film's costuming and sense of medieval pageantry are largely fifteenth-century.

Ever After's invocation of fairy tale is thus quite deliberate, whatever its director might claim. Like many fairy-tale films it makes use of the frame narrative and oral voice, in the nineteenth-century frame which presents the tale as oral history told by the Grande Dame of France to the Brothers Grimm—an aging, female, oral voice, corresponding to Marina Warner's analysis in which she comments that "the connection of old women's speech and the consolatory, erotic, often fanciful fable appears deeply entwined in language itself, and with women's speaking roles" (*Beast to the Blonde* 14). This becomes the site for metafictional play as reality, fairy tale and film blur and shift status. In a process similar to that followed by Disney's fairy-tale features, the film in effect claims *higher* status than the literary or folk narrative: the old woman maintains that she intends "to set the record straight," thus characterizing the Grimms' Cinderella story as a distortion of the reality represented by the film, rather than the film as a version of the story. Nonetheless, the film's fairy-tale narrative is explicitly that: apart from the film's title, the old woman begins "Once upon a time," and the Cinderella tale ends on an interchange between Danielle and the Prince in which they play in a particularly self-aware fashion with the fairy-tale stereotypes and the idea of "living happily ever after":

DANIELLE: You, sir, are supposed to be charming!
PRINCE: And we, princess, are supposed to live happily ever after.

DANIELLE: Says who?
PRINCE: Do you know . . . I don't know?

Despite the director's desire to repudiate it, the invocation of the fairy-tale narrative is perfectly explicit, although less accomplished than similar occurrences in Byatt or Pratchett, and problematized by the fact that they do not know *what* dictates the pattern. The film's dispute is also not with the pattern, but with its status as folklore/unreality, so that the characters' self-awareness lacks instrumentality; while aware of pattern, they leave it uninterrupted. Stephens and McCallum argue that the film "opposes postmodern ideology through its reaffirmation of the agency of the subject, its thematization of discourses of 'identity'" (202), but in fact I find the opposite to be true: while the film may indeed deny postmodern dissolution, it does this through the affirmation of structures which ultimately deny individual agency in favor of a reactionary utopianism.

This becomes interesting given Preston's argument for the feminist potential in the film's rewriting of characters; Danielle is an intelligent young woman with a strong personality, her qualities set up to counteract the passivity of the original Cinderella, but, unlike Byatt's or Carter's heroines, she does not actually escape the narrative to achieve anything other than marriage to the prince. Rather like Disney's Belle or Byatt's Eldest Princess, Danielle is a heroine who reads—a recurring archetype in the modern fairy tale, which underlines the self-aware sense of narrative in both characters and creators. She is also far from the gentle sweetness of Cinderella's acceptance of her role: perhaps the most effective scene in the film is Danielle's rescue of the stunned and unresisting Prince by picking him up and slinging him over her shoulder. As well as giving the odious Marguerite a black eye, Danielle, once she has triumphed and wed the prince, punishes her stepmother and sister in the antithesis of meek forgiveness. A further self-conscious play with fairy-tale expectation is in the characterizing of the stepmother and at least one of the two stepsisters, whose nastiness is rounded out by psychological victimization of Danielle and by their own motivations (lack of money and hopeless social climbing). The casting of Angelica Huston, a noted character actress, as Baroness Rodmilla assists materially with the three-dimensionality of the character. The film thus takes advantage of the metanarratives of the star system to access a kind of character depth by association, relating the character to other, equally recognizable stereotypes and to a certain kind of cinema entertainment—offbeat, amusing, and slightly dark. Despite its naive delight in oversetting the traditional fairy-tale stereotypes, however, the film must necessarily remain aware of those stereotypes at all times for their effect to be felt, and in the end they are not actually transcended. This is fairy-tale film packaged as Hollywood romance and, despite its play with fairy-tale expectation, it ultimately celebrates a fairy-tale romance which ends in the heroine's acquisition of wealth and social position through marriage. Tennant may argue that he "did not want [his daughters] growing up believing you have to marry a rich guy with a big house in order to live happily ever after" ("Ever After"), but in the end this is exactly what Danielle does. The play with archetypes is superficial, and fairy tale's basically reactionary principles remain undisturbed.

The film's focus on psychological motivation gives added dimension to Prince Henry as a character who, while "supposed to be charming," is humanly flawed and uncertain. The contrast between the apathetic prince and Danielle's passionate engagement in her life reinforces the feminist subtext (worthless man made acceptable by spirited woman) but also speaks to the film's nascent awareness of structure as confinement, its insistence on itself as reality rather than fairy tale. Trapped in his social role as prince, Henry's life is robbed of meaning and zest. Danielle, who might be expected to be passive under the daily grind of her truly awful life, has the character to rise above the role (abused stepdaughter) which defines her. The message, while less explicitly developed, is curiously similar to that of Pratchett in *Witches Abroad*: to define anyone by their function is dehumanizing. The film comes closest to articulating this metafictional awareness of fairy-tale function in the closing comments of the Grande Dame, when she insists that "while Cinderella and her prince did live happily ever after, the point, gentlemen, is that they *lived*." The point of recasting fairy tale as history is to insist that the figures in the tale should be real human beings, not simply symbols in the narrative. However, this message is largely masked by the overwhelming feel-good effect of the film; while the play with fairy tale is a valiant attempt at innovation, in the end the characters escape fairy-tale stereotype only to become equally predestined symbols in the powerful romantic narrative of the Hollywood film.

As a complete contrast to the somewhat saccharine Hollywood romance of *Ever After*, Michael Cohn's *The Grimm Brothers' Snow White* (also variously released as *Snow White in the Black Forest* and *Snow White: A Tale of Terror*) is in many ways a deliberately nasty piece of cinema. Where *Ever After* plays with the perfect, fated romance of fairy tale, *Snow White* is an exercise in self-conscious Gothic, a return to the dark, sexy, and violent roots of fairy tale, à la Angela Carter, Tanith Lee, or Maria Tatar. Like *Ever After*, the film is motivated by psychological undercurrents, but here they represent a rediscovery of the metaphorical power of fairy tale to depict an explicitly post-Freudian awareness of individuality and desire. At the same time, it partakes wholeheartedly of the trappings of the modern horror film, to a far greater extent than does *The Company of Wolves;* as well as bloody violence, *Snow White* flirts with black magic, sex magic, mass murder, and psychosis. The "Grimm Brothers" rider on the title is entirely necessary in order to distance the film from the sugary sweetness of Disney's more famous *Snow White*. While the film is aware of the Disney version, it invokes it ironically (Lily's terrified dash through a threatening forest, the fact that the "dwarves" call her "Princess"), or sets out to invert it completely (sexualized members of the underclass rather than childlike little old men).

The film is very aware of fairy-tale narrative, not only in its title but also in the Gothic forests and castle of its setting, and in its deliberate invocation of Grimm through use of German names—Baron Hoffman, Dr. Gutenberg, Lady Claudia. The symbolic import of the Snow White figure is carried through not only in Lily's name—constructed similarly to Lee's Bianca—but also in the motif of snow, the snowy woods into which Lily is born, and the film's climax with Lily, her lover and her father reunited as snow begins to fall. The standard associations of snow with chill purity are a sharp and ironic contrast to the bloody sexuality with which the film is actually concerned. The film also plays rather vaguely with the folk voice, in the child Lily asking for the tale of her birth from her nurse, the standard old woman figure of folklore. The tale the nurse begins is almost word for word from the opening of the Grimm version.

The film makes full use of the visual medium to dramatize the classic elements of the story, but in a manner that takes symbol to excess. Thus the blood-on-the-snow motif from the Grimm original, where "three drops of blood fell upon the snow," becomes a disturbing flood of red on white as the Baron uses a dagger to deliver his daughter from the body of his dying wife. The pig's heart which represents Snow White's, seen as a discreet box with a dagger and heart motif in the Disney version, is here a rather disgusting raw lump of meat, eventually eaten by Lily's dog after a bloodstained Claudia has been gloating over it. No cheerful popular feminism motivates this production; the tale revolves, simply and uncomplicatedly, around the very primitive roots of the Snow White tale in incestuous sexuality and jealousy between women. Sigourney Weaver as Lady Claudia is the film's central figure, her tormented awareness of her fading beauty providing the impetus for events. Her black magic is deliberately stagy and self-indulgent, a creative reinterpretation of the three attempts the stepmother makes on Snow White's life in the Grimm version.

The magic mirror is a legacy from her mother, in the classic fairy-tale motif of a dead mother assisting her daughter seen in tales such as "Cinderella" and "The Juniper Tree." Lady Claudia's interactions with her idealized self in the mirror provide an effective visual metaphor for female beauty as power in fairy tale's patriarchal system. In the final scenes of the film, Lady Claudia's existence is seen to be intrinsically and narcissistically bound up with her beauty—when Lily stabs the image in the mirror, Claudia dies.

While both films are enjoyable artifacts of popular cinema, one cannot help feeling that both are essentially self-indulgent responses to fairy-tale narrative: *Ever After* in the sense of fairy-tale romance, *Snow White* in its use of horror. While the films are aware of the structures of fairy-tale narrative, their explorations and rewritings are limited by the popular arena in which they play; as I have discussed in a previous chapter, popular narratives cannot disrupt their popular genres, however much they may play with fairy tales. Thus the films are essentially using fairy tale as a basis for creating undisturbed genre films, either romance or horror; social comment, particularly around issues of gender, becomes subordinate to the expectations of the popular form, either marriage, or the demonic female. While the films are visually clever and appealing, the visual encodings speak more to the modern popular genre than to the fairy tale, and thus tend to obscure rather than illuminate fairy-tale structures.

ANIMATED FAIRY TALE: THE DISNEY PRODUCT

Animation and fairy tale have had a long and distinguished association. In the earliest days of film, Lotte Reiniger's silhouette fairy tales pioneered visual techniques and the use of fairy tale's narrative structures to add coherence to film. Charles Solomon's *History of Animation* gives recurring examples of fairy-tale themes in early animated works: Disney's series of fairy-tale films in the 1930s, including *Three Little Pigs, Red Riding Hood,* and *The Four Musicians of Bremen;* the Fleischer studio's Betty Boop version of "Snow White," and Popeye shorts with Sinbad the Sailor, Ali Baba, and Aladdin; and the Mintz studio's *Little Match Girl* (37–98). Despite the long history of animated fairy tales, however, the second half of the twentieth century saw Disney animated fairy tales rising to replace most other kinds of fairy-tale narrative in the popular consciousness. This grasp on the genre reached its height with the extreme success of the flagship fairy tales in the early 1990s, most notably *Aladdin* and *Beauty and the Beast*. Only recently has Disney's monopolistic association with fairy tale begun to wane, with the rise of other animation studios such as Dreamworks and Pixar. These companies could be seen as taking full advantage of the waning artistic and commercial success of Disney films, a decline interestingly correlated with their tendency to abandon the fairy-tale format in favor of more contemporary, historical, or vaguely folkloric narratives. Disney's recent acquisition of the Pixar company seems to suggest an attempt to sustain the monopoly, and to ensure that animation and fairy tale, in the broadest possible sense, remain synonymous with Disney to the bulk of the moviegoing public.

While the generic conflation of animation with fairy tale is partially a result of the power of the Disney marketing machine, there are also some sound structural reasons for the successful alliance of fairy tale with the animated form. In the case of fairy tale, the potential of film to offer a dizzyingly full visual canvas in some ways works directly against the characteristic textual sparseness of the fairy-tale narrative. However, in the marrying of the fairy tale to the animated feature form, these problems have been at least partially overcome. Animation as a medium shadows the features of metafictional writing as defined by Waugh, and thus those metafictional features I have attributed to fairy tale; like fairy tale, animation continually signals its own problematized relationship with reality, offering no attempt at a realistic mirror, but rather a ritualized, simplified, and antirealist process. Animation signals *constructedness* as strongly as fairy tale's classic opening of "once upon a time." Like fairy tale, it operates in a framework composed of smooth, simple lines and bright colors which visually echo the characteristic symbolic compression of fairy-tale narrative. Both fairy tale and animation deal in stereotypes, archetypes, and clichés, the stock characters of metaphorical writing, magical narrative—and, most importantly, of the formula fiction which makes up the bulk of the popular market. In addition, animation is perhaps the most perfect site of the magical; the power of animation is to represent figures that can *change* completely outside the bounds of reality in precisely the same way that magical transformations occur in fairy tales. Paul Wells discusses the overlap of fairy tale and animation in this context, quoting Marina Warner—"metamorphosis defines the fairy tale" (*Beast to the Blonde* xvi) and continuing:

> Clearly, here "metamorphosis" is about changes in characters and situations that may be termed "magical" or impossible within the concept of a real world served by physiological, gravitational, or functionalist norms. Virtually all animated films play out this definition of metamorphosis as a technical and narrational orthodoxy, thus rendering the adaptation of fairy tale on this basis, a matter of relative ease. (Wells 201)

The plasticity of the animated figure—its ability to stretch, compress, fragment, transform, defy gravity—is magical, unreal, and a prime site for magical narrative. This aspect of marvelous visual play is underlined by the tendency of the Disney studios to focus on the technical rather than the artistic aspects of the animation process: Disney films pushed the boundaries of new techniques and effects (as discussed by both Solomon and Richard Schickel), focusing on this far more than on the requirements of script or story.

Another important feature of Disney fairy tale is in the extent to which the animated feature film has come to have an accepted and powerful association with children. Like fairy tale, which Tolkien characterizes as having been relegated to the nursery, along with other worn-out and unwanted furniture, in the nineteenth century (34), animation is seen as a children's medium, an identification broken only by a fringe of serious films or, more recently, by the rise of the Japanese tradition of adult animation in anime. In Western cinema, in both fairy tale and animation, an initial artistic seriousness—oral folktale, the experimental films of Georges Méliès—has given way to a mainstream nonadult intention with the progression of the twentieth century. The tendency has been exaggerated by the prevalence of the animated series on children's daytime television, many of them distinguished by poor technical animation, violence, and lack of innovation (Solomon 285). This has been alleviated only in the late twentieth century with the reclamation of the form in both mediums—fairy tale's adaptation to adult concerns such as erotic, feminist, or self-aware narrative, and animation's development into the adult sex and violence of anime, adult films such as Ralph Bakshi's *Fritz the Cat* or *Heavy Traffic*, or the self-conscious artistry of experimental forms. However, it is possible to identify a mutual unease around the status of animated and fairy-tale narratives, a feeling that both animation and fairy tale ought really to be clean, innocent, suitable for children. If there is an awareness of animation as a children's medium, Disney's animated fairy tales play deliberately straight into this, creating an association which has defined their products from the start, as Brenda Ayres demonstrates (3); the occasional furor around the apparent discovery of obscene motifs in various Disney films, such as that chronicled by Ronald E. Ostman, underlines the power of this association. In the formulation of Elizabeth Bell, Lynda Haas, and Laura Sells in their influential collection *From Mouse to Mermaid,* whatever popular cultural debates might rage around the Disney product, this assumption of child-friendly values is both a defining feature of Disney texts and an uncontested area in Disney studies. It becomes an "ideological center that *does* hold, against both metonymic and monolithic constructions" and a " 'trademark' of Disney innocence that masks the personal, historical, and material relationship between Disney film and politics" (5). Critics such as Henry Giroux extend this notion of "family values" to express their concern with Disney's appropriation of childhood innocence and the ideological power of the corporation over children. Giroux's consumer-culture sense of Disney's functioning echoes that of the Frankfurt School and Zipes, and serves to highlight the extent to which associations with folk culture, with its status as a universal and trustworthy expression in the popular consciousness, can be twisted to serve the ends of marketing.

Giroux and Bell, Haas, and Sells represent earlier documents in the growing area of modern Disney studies, but already the ideological lines are drawn, demonstrating a critical tendency to assess Disney's films in terms of their identity as ideological and consumer artifacts before their operation as works of art. This propensity to identify the Disney product as having a commercial purpose inextricable from its artistic status reflects to some extent the nature of the Disney corporation, which self-consciously and unambiguously treats its animated images as products. Their consumerist treatment not only inheres in the deliberate construction of a consistent and recognizable Disney film formula and the tireless marketing of spin-off products, merchandise, and theme park experiences but also in the company's extreme protectiveness of trademark and image. Bell and coauthors report the difficulties they faced in publishing a critical volume on Disney, which was ultimately not permitted to use Disney's name in the title (1); while this restriction has clearly relaxed in later years, as seen in the titles of the works by Ayres and by Eleanor Byrne and Martin McQuillan, Disney remains famously litigious. Again, this demonstrates the distance between the communal nature of genuine folk texts and the ownership-slanted operation of the mass media. It also suggests the existence of a new level of potentially metafictional awareness: artifact not only as crafted work, with particular reference to technical proficiency, but film narrative as a specifically *commercial* product rather than artistic construction. Thus, while the visual spectacle of a Disney animated film successfully submerges the viewer in a noisy, vivid world, an element of self-consciousness inheres in the construction of the characters and images as trademarks, already familiar from merchandise and fast-food packaging. Their independent existence outside the text irresistibly embodies the film text as artificial construct.

An essential component of this focus on commercial purpose is ideological, in some ways related to the Frankfurt School's sense of mass culture as entrenching reactionary ideologies in order to pacify their markets, but on a broader level relating simply to the need for mass-market texts to appeal to the widest possible demographic. Given the genesis and nature of the Disney corporation, the ideological values entrenched in its product tend to be those of a white, American, conservative middle class, which also resonate particularly well with the fairy-tale forms emerging from the eighteenth and nineteenth centuries, appropriated from oral tradition by French aristocrats or the German bourgeoisie. This element is largely taken for granted in recent critical accounts of Disney films, as exemplified, for example, in Ayres's collection of postcolonial accounts of Disney, which offers sustained interrogation of gender, racial, and cultural stereotypes in the films. Byrne and McQuillan acknowledge the general tendency throughout the critical history of Disney to attack it as being "synonymous with a certain conservative, patriarchal, heterosexual ideology which is loosely associated with American cultural imperialism" (1–2); importantly, however, they also suggest that it is precisely the ongoing attacks of the critical/intellectual/left-wing strata which allow Disney to deliberately define its ideological nature in conservative terms. This opposition is also what allows Disney texts to construct themselves as truly representative and democratic institutions in the face of elitist criticism. At the same time, such critical approaches echo the broader issues of popular culture criticism in their tendency to entrench an absolutist view of culture. Miriam Hansen's discussion of Benjamin and Adorno's responses to Disney is interesting in its treatment of the more antistructuralist possibilities of Disney criticism; she suggests that the debates sparked by early Disney texts represent a broader attempt to come to terms with the new mass culture, to identify "which role the technical media were playing in the historical demolition and restructuring of subjectivity: whether they were giving rise to new forms of imagination, expression and collectivity, or whether they were merely perfecting techniques of total subjection and domination" (28). The debate has continued to rage, and contemporary theory suggests that mass texts can, indeed, do both.

Benjamin's characterization of film insists on its ability to democratize art, to, in Hansen's terms, "[destroy] the fixed perspectives that have naturalised social and economical arrangements"; she quotes Benjamin's comments on the identity of film as an absolutely new form of expression which "exploded this prison-world with the dynamite of one-tenth seconds, so that now, in the midst of its far-flung ruins and debris, we calmly advance on adventurous travels" (Benjamin, in Hansen 30). In tension with the limitations of the mass market, Disney animated films also represent a kind of freedom from realism as well as a sense of energetic enjoyment. Few critical approaches to

Disney seem to address the ability of the animated feature to mine the form for its sheer fantasy, its ability to produce screen magic on a level far above that of the live-action film. This offers an intensification of the idea discussed above, of filmmaker as magician. More than any other filmmaker, the animator is an enchanter manipulating a magical medium, and thus a self-aware producer of crafted, metafictional artifact (Zipes, *Happily Ever After* 68). In keeping with the notion of commercialized metafiction, technical wizardry is part of Disney's extreme narrative self-consciousness, offering a sort of "look at me" sense of its own cleverness that spills over into narrative games and cultural reference, becoming a potentially comic and ironic awareness which sells enjoyment on an intellectual level as well as on the level of technical spectacle. However, this exuberance is generally expressed only in subjection to the overall Disney formula, with its associations of child-friendly ideological safety and predictable content. Effectively, the partial adaptation to a popular sense of contemporary postmodern irony has left Disney films slightly behind in the market; the success of *Shrek* and its sequels demonstrates Dreamworks' more sophisticated ability to balance the needs of mass marketing with a sense of subversive narrative play. The uniformity of the Disney product, originally a selling point, has thus ceased to function given its comparative resistance to adaptation with time; in a sense, innocence has become outdated to a certain segment of its previous market.

This uniformity is an important technique in negotiating the tension between the novelty and color of the animated format, and the familiarity of the fairy-tale forms. Disney fairy-tale films have developed their own, distinctive and instantly recognizable formula, which works in deliberate concord or, at times, dissonance, with the structures of fairy tale. The extent to which a promise of a particular experience and ideological content inheres in Walt Disney's signature on each film, is a powerful marketing tool. Janet Wasko refers to this as "classic Disney" (110), the film format established under the rule of Walt Disney himself, which remains relatively undisrupted in contemporary Disney animated features. From the early success of *Snow White*, the Disney formula has refined its original components—the musical format, the presence of cute animals in interaction with the main characters, an easily recognizable antagonist, the elements of slapstick comedy, the romantic conclusion—but has not materially changed them. The Disney formula intersects with and overwrites any kind of narrative its films use, whether popular children's literature (*101 Dalmatians, Peter Pan*), folklore (*Robin Hood*), history (*Pocahontas*), or fairy tale. More than the tales themselves, the familiar Disney format is reassuring to children as well as to their parents, who can send children to see

Disney films secure in the knowledge that sex and realistic violence will not be on the menu. In some senses this formulaic function parodies the nostalgic certainty associated with fairy tale, and lays claim to an equal status as a given of Western culture. Nonetheless, as Byrne and McQuillan note, contemporary poststructuralist analysis dictates that the Disney formula suffers an inevitable shift in meaning: "On every occasion the Disney signature does not signify the same thing" (6). In this the formula shares with folkloric structures not only the status of a legitimate cultural tradition but also the appearance, rather than the reality, of an unassailable, monolithic authority.

The history of Disney fairy-tale features occupies a trajectory from the initial success of *Snow White* (1937), one of the earliest animated features, through similar adaptations of *Cinderella* (1950), and *Sleeping Beauty* (1959). After a break of some thirty years, during which adaptations were made from literature rather than fairy tale, Disney moved back into fairy tale—and into a reclamation of blockbuster success—with their rather mutilated version of Anderson's "Little Mermaid" in 1989. The peak of their fairy-tale production is with the two great successes of the early 1990s, *Beauty and the Beast* (1991) and *Aladdin* (1992), which represent a pinnacle of Disney achievement in terms of commercial success and in successful adaptation and technical innovation. It would appear that the combination of fairy-tale narrative with Disney formula is a winning one that has not been equaled since by other generic frameworks used by the studio; subsequent semi-folkloric offerings such as *The Emperor's New Groove* and *Brother Bear* were fairly damp squibs, and *Lilo and Stitch*, while successful, did not reach the heights of the great fairy-tale films.

Made in successive years, *Beauty and the Beast* and *Aladdin* are nonetheless very different films, at least partially because of the divergent nature of their sources; the feel and texture of Mme. Leprince de Beaumont's "Beauty and the Beast" are very different from the *Arabian Nights'* "Aladdin," a difference exaggerated by Disney's disparate approaches in the two films. However, both films rely centrally on the familiarity of the tales they rework; "Beauty and the Beast" is a staple of the child's fairy-tale collection, while "Aladdin," although Eastern in flavor, has been long adopted into the corpus of Western fairy tale, and in fact, as Ulrich Marzolph intimates, has a somewhat vexed origin which suggests it was not actually an authentic part of the *Arabian Nights*. The films thus reflect the standard Disney fairy-tale practice, following *Snow White, Cinderella,* and *The Sleeping Beauty* in the tradition which allows the studio self-consciously to assume the mantle of storyteller, inheritor of fairy tale. Both films retell their original story only in the loosest sense, retaining sufficient features for recognition while adapting to the demands of the formula and of contemporary culture. The reassuring predictability of the action—the self-conscious investment of the audience in the structures of fairy tale—provides a firm base for technical innovation, formula characters, and peripheral disturbances of the familiar plot. At the same time, Disney's formula in these films works slightly differently from its earlier incarnations, offering some familiar figures with a slightly ironic slant: the Genie's stand-up-comic intertextuality, for example, or Gaston's construction as an antifeminist villain, not only play against the assumptions of classic fairy tale but also invite the audience to make ironic comparisons with early versions of the Disney formula.

Beauty and the Beast uses only the barest bones of de Beaumont's tale, but focuses on the figure of Belle, another Byatt-style "reading princess" whose yearning for "more than this provincial life" demands comparison with the passive heroine of both Disney and classic fairy tale. Narrative impetus is gained by imposition of a time limit (the rewriting of the rose's significance), and the addition of Gaston as the villain serves a similar function as Avenant in Cocteau's *La Belle et la Bête;* the film medium seems to require some visual realization of the Beast's antithesis, all surface looks and character flaw. The overall visual feel of the film is textured and slightly cluttered, often achieving an effective Gothic atmosphere; the muted colors and heavy shadows are a strong contrast to *Aladdin*'s clean lines and bright, rich colors just a year later. *Beauty and the Beast* appears to be nostalgic rather than contemporary in overall tone, accessing the same "old European storybook" feel of *Snow White* (Solomon 59) and, to a lesser extent, *Sleeping Beauty.* This is underlined by its particularly self-conscious use of the musical format, another familiar popular formula whose stylization suitably reinforces fairy-tale essentialism. Sequences in the village invoke the ensemble vocals of operetta such as Lehar's *Merry Widow,* enhanced by the opera-trained voices of the villagers and, particularly, Gaston. Other intertextual references include Belle doing a *Sound of Music* routine in the golden fields around her house, and of course the rousing Busby Berkeley–style "Be Our Guest" routine headed by Lumière. The audience is continually prodded to admire the film's achievements as musical in a long tradition of musical cinema. Despite this, the film also lays claim to the status of authentic fairy tale, through the opening voice-overs and reverential stained-glass windows as much as through the song lyrics which proclaim the film a "Tale as old as time / True as it can be . . ." Overall, the film plays self-consciously with its identity as fairy tale, with particular emphasis, through use of other formulae, on its unrealistic qualities of naive romance.

Aladdin is, by contrast, a more superficial film, its prevailing mode the comic rather than the Gothic or melodramatic. Its adaptation of a story traditionally regarded as Eastern offers a notable departure from Disney's hitherto unvarying use of Western cultural classics. The position of Middle Eastern culture in *Aladdin* is very similar to that of French culture in *Beauty and the Beast*—the films present an essentially superficial and patronizing view of a culture effectively defined in terms of being non-American, and therefore exotic and interesting, if not to be taken seriously. The film's view of Eastern culture is basically Orientalist: the outcry among the Islamic community when *Aladdin* was released was sufficient for Disney to recall the prints and excise an offending lyric in the opening song: "Where they cut off your nose if they don't like your face / It's barbaric, but hey, it's home." (Timothy White and J. E. Winn in their *Kinema* article summarize the Islamic point of view.) *Aladdin*'s fairy-tale structure—poor boy, evil magician, lamp, genie, princess—is familiar from fairy tale, but is rendered even more familiar by the imposition of Western fairy-tale motifs onto the Eastern tale; thus the limitless power of the genie is reduced to three wishes, in the style of the Grimm tale, adding narrative impetus and closure. This familiarity is strengthened by the film's play with the trope of "poor boy makes good" associated with the American Dream, and Aladdin himself is a trickster archetype in the Puss-in-Boots mold, using cunning to persuade the villain to his own destruction through the use of his power. Jafar being persuaded to wish himself a genie is a pattern found in many fairy tales, most notably "Puss in Boots," where the ogre turns himself into a mouse, only to be pounced on and destroyed.

Aladdin offers a particularly interesting example of Disney's adaptation of fairy-tale narrative to the rather different demands of film; as well as limiting the wishes, the film makes various changes to the details of the original, which is in many ways a sprawling narrative unsuited to a dramatic or visual medium. Thus the Moorish magician, the Wazir, and the Wazir's son become one in the figure of Jafar, who neatly encapsulates the magician's sorcerous power and abuse of Aladdin, the Wazir's scheming, and the Wazir's son's lust for the Sultan's daughter. This gives the necessary single villain figure of the Disney formula, and a visual focus for the dangers besetting the hero. Likewise, the two genies are conflated in the Robin Williams character while the ring, a boring object offering little scope for animation, becomes the carpet, a familiar visual icon of the East and a fertile ground for the computer animations which distinguish this film. The carpet's computer animation is groundbreaking and innovative, a superb and magical creation of character and emotion for an essentially two-dimensional object. Other elements of the tale—the Cave of Wonders and Aladdin's grand processional entrance—are simply elaborate visual renditions of elements already in the tale. In fact, the structure of the film seems to owe as much to the plot of Alexander Korda's 1939 film *The Thief of Bagdad*, as to the *Arabian Nights* original, with similarities including a villain named Jafar, a thief called Abu, a djinn of personality, and a flying carpet. The clichés of the classic film narrative are as importantly nostalgic as are the fairy-tale elements.

Both films engage in the classic Disney oral invocation at their opening. *Beauty and the Beast*'s stained-glass windows invoke tale as artifact as well as claiming oral status through the initial voice-over which gives background to the Beast's curse. This is a novel rearrangement of de Beaumont's use of flashback; here, the audience has events explained unambiguously from the start. Belle's interest in reading fairy tales also confirms the film's claim to storybook authenticity. However, these techniques pale to insignificance besides *Aladdin*'s adept framing of film as oral narrative. The disembodied voice-over gives way to an actual figure, whose direct interaction with the film audience parallels the realization of the folk voice through Granny in *Company of Wolves*, although gaining comic vitality through its obvious distance from the archetype of the old Western female storyteller. The figure of the Middle Eastern salesman, together with his camel, the "Arabian Nights" song, and the magnificent sweeping deserts of the opening sequence, sets the cultural tone, allowing the film to lay claim to the status of a genuine Middle Eastern oral voice, while also playfully satirizing the film's commercial purpose. The oral voice is cleverly counterfeited; the salesman's interaction with us, the audience, evokes an involuntary response as the camera, losing interest, starts to slide away from the speaker—we are, the film intimates, too discerning an audience to be taken in by spurious junk. The salesman must run after us to regain our attention, and our illusion of power and control in the oral interaction is further reinforced when his invitation to come a little closer—and thus partake in the intimate relationship between storyteller and audience—is taken too literally, plastering the camera against his face. The sequence plays equally on our awareness of the oral storytelling tradition and on the audience familiarity with film conventions, once more equating the film version with the original, and effectively replacing and erasing the original, but also inviting the audience's enjoyment of the comic clash of modes.

The viewer's self-conscious participation in the conventions of the film medium highlights the film's metafictional qualities. At the same time, the storyteller's status as *salesman* rather than actual storyteller underlines that aspect of Disney narrative which goes right through metafiction and out the other side—awareness of the tale's nature as artifact, certainly, but artifact as *product*. Having attempted to sell us spurious merchandise (a combination hookah and coffee grinder that also slices and dices, and an example of the Dead Sea Tupperware), the salesman moves on to the genuine product, the lamp which embodies the tale—and, by extension, the Disney film. The encapsulation of tale in static artifact parallels similar Disney characterizations of tale as book (*Snow White, Cinderella, Sleeping Beauty*) or stained-glass window (*Beauty and the Beast*); as in these cases, the point is the dramatic juxtaposition of the lively, dynamic Disney film version with the static original. It becomes evident that Disney's *Aladdin* is firmly rooted in contemporary culture, far more so than in the Eastern culture it professes to depict. The film assumes the audience's familiarity with cinematographic conventions such as the camera's point of view, but it also takes for granted the viewer's essential situation within modern commodity culture. *Beauty and the Beast* contained its fair share of consumer reference—Belle's "I want much more," the voice-over's regret that the Prince, before his transformation, "although he had everything his heart could desire, was spoiled and selfish"—but it is in *Aladdin,* and in subsequent productions such as *The Lion King,* that this becomes overt. The choice of "Aladdin" as a basis for Disney fairy-tale film is thus relevant, since the original tale is more than a little preoccupied with the desire for wealth, and with fabulous riches in the form of the cave of the lamp, the sumptuous processions with which Aladdin dazzles the Sultan, and Aladdin's miraculously constructed and glittering palace. Robin Williams's Genie is literally a genie of commodity culture, able to offer a dizzying array of consumer artifact to the stunned Aladdin, and to flaunt his power as synonymous with Disney's: "You ain't never had a friend like me!" Thus, to Aladdin and the consumer, "Life is your restaurant / And I'm your maitre d' . . . Say what you wish / It's yours!" As with many forms of cultural commodification, the product is presented as a matter of choice, and the consumer as an empowered individual who chooses with discernment and is above the blandishments of the commercial process. *Aladdin* represents the consumerist approach—the desire for wealth, a palace, a trophy woman—as natural and inevitable; Aladdin claims, "I steal only what I can't afford—and that's everything," suggesting that the consumer has some kind of a *right* to everything he or she desires. The classic empowerment process of fairy tale—the poor boy, youngest son, or despised stepdaughter making good to marry the wealthy prince or princess—is close enough to the consumer process to make for a strong message, but the message hinges ultimately on the tale's self-conscious status as product. Rather than being the passive dupes of the consumerist process, however, the audience is invited to enjoy an ironic and self-conscious awareness of the culture in which both they and the film exist.

If *Aladdin* offers tale as commodity artifact, it extends this even further to conflate the tale with the experience of Disney, and thus to claim to sell experience as commodity. The lamp stands for the Disney experience of the tale, complete with music, image, and color. By extension, what *Aladdin* (and *Beauty and the Beast*) offers to the viewer is also culture as commodity. In packaging and selling story, the film also packages and sells the idea of a foreign culture, presenting it to a gaze that is essentially that of the American tourist. This is seen in the opening sequence of *Aladdin,* where Aladdin leads the city guard on a merry chase through the streets of Agrabah, passing sword swallowers, fakirs on beds of nails, fire walkers, rope tricks, and snake charmers—all the unthinking stereotypes of a generalized "Eastern" culture that does not care to distinguish Indian from Arabian traditions, but which immerses the viewer in a sense of non-specific participation in a broader sense of "folk culture." Disney claims, "I can show you the world," and proceeds to do so, in a process paralleled in *Beauty and the Beast's* view of French culture, all baguettes, berets, and the salacious womanizing of Lumière. Later in *Aladdin,* momentary vignettes of Grecian temples and Chinese dragon dances encapsulate the tourist viewpoint, equating the Disney experience with Aladdin's "magic carpet ride," and entrenching the studio in the position of the controlling wizard/storyteller. The folkloric status of the narratives is thus shored up by the film's authoritative control over folk *culture,* in the more superficial sense of the word.

While the sheer spectacle and visual entertainment of the Disney animated fairy tale cannot be denied, there are ways in which the constraints of the animated format work directly against inherent aspects of fairy tale—most strongly, its elements of wonder, beauty, and seriousness. What sinks the otherwise interesting potential of these films is, ultimately, Disneyfication—the problem so pilloried by Pratchett, the paralyzing of the narrative by sheer cuteness. *Aladdin* is perhaps a more successful film because, paradoxically, it most completely loses sight of the elements of beauty and threat in the original tale. Its comic framing cheerfully accommodates anachronistic references and slapstick interactions where *Beauty and the Beast's* storybook Gothic produces some uncomfortable clashes with the animated formula. The accomplished craft of the animators gives perky character to the castle's furniture and utensils, emphasizing the marvelous unreality of animation and the absolute awareness of artifact which characterizes fairy tale and consumer text. However, the potentially real Gothic threat of the Beast's castle is effectively undercut—no one can take seriously the looming gargoyles, shadows, and marks of violence when ridiculous cultural caricatures of a French candlestick and British clock are conducting the tour. This is, of course, deliberate to some extent: the Disney formula's comforting provision of unthreatening entertainment works to mitigate the Gothic undertones, rendering them controlled and slightly sanitized. In the competing frameworks of the real and the unreal, the film also succumbs even more completely than Cocteau's does to the lure of visual identification, here exaggerated by the essential unreality of the animated format. The moment of the Beast's transformation is a complete anticlimax despite its excessive effects, partially because of the cardboard cut-out prince, but mainly because of the visual cues attached to the Beast—his animated figure is simultaneously masculine and comic, idealized and endearing, having more in common with the animated beast-fable of children's Sunday morning cartoons than with the underlying violence and eroticism of the classic fairy tale.

In discussing Disney as an example of metafictional fairy tale, it becomes evident that self-awareness in this context cannot be separated from commercial appeal. Disney's self-consciousness about tale as artifact is playfully entertaining, but like popular literary forms, tends to sacrifice genuinely innovative narrative play to the demands of marketability. The result is to trivialize fairy tale, losing the potential depth of the form, and to somewhat unreflectively perpetuate the stereotype of fairy tale as monolithic ideological entity whose structures permit only reactionary concepts of culture. At the same time, however, Disney films also powerfully display cinema's potential to mimic oral function in its ability to adapt to and to shape the culture within which it is retold, and to recreate itself as an unquestioned cultural given. The films remain sufficiently acute, relevant, and entertaining to have almost usurped the role of fairy tale in the lives of many Western children.

7

"HAPPILY EVER AFTER": FAIRY TALE AS POPULAR PARODY

> Now that the book is finished, I know that this was not a
> hallucination, a sort of professional malady, but the con-
> firmation of something I already suspected—folktales are
> real. —ITALO CALVINO, *Italian Folk Tales* xviii

I hope this survey across the marvelous geometry of
modern fairy tale has served to demonstrate the vitality and the proliferation of fairy-tale forms in twentieth-century literature and film.
The huge range of contexts in which fairy-tale structures are self-
consciously employed suggests that in recent expressions the form
preserves its power and profundity as a narrative whose encoded structures are widely meaningful. In this sense, despite the translation of
fairy tale into different mediums, fairy tale retains some aspects of
its original identity as a folk expression, endlessly adaptable and continually mutating as it is reflected across cultures and time. The twentieth century's tendency toward commercial appropriation of fairy
tale has perhaps blunted its aspect of communal *ownership*, despite
its adoption of the mock-oral voice at times, but it has simultaneously
ensured that the process of communal *experience* is enabled by the
new technologies of mass culture and mass production.

At the same time, the popularity of fairy tale in contemporary literature is interesting in terms of the central focus of this study: the highly
structured and self-consciously nonrealist nature of fairy tale. In a technological age the increasing popularity of magical narratives—not only
popular narratives such as fantasy romance but also the flourishing
presence of the unreal in postmodern and experimental texts—surely

represents some strong cultural imperative. This is perhaps a response to the growing complexity of our society, and the stresses and demands of a fast-moving technological existence. Antirealist fiction in some ways represents the failure of the finite and ordered world of realism; as Ursula Le Guin suggests, "Sophisticated readers are accepting the fact that an improbable and unmanageable world is going to produce an improbable and hypothetical art" (47). More than this, the magical structures of fairy tale are beguilingly simple, a symbolic and, in Baudrillard's terms, essentially unrealist access to a lost feudal age. If this century and the last are bewilderingly complex, then fantasy is, as Tolkien suggests, a consolation and an escape, allowing access to the past and its "transfer and reorganization," as identified by Hutcheon (*Parody* 4). At the same time, in a century whose most recent and defining intellectual movement is the indeterminacy of postmodernism, the ongoing fascination with fairy-tale structuredness is particularly interesting. Structure offers security and predictability, both increasingly rare in our complex modern times. Through these structures fairy tale has the potential to reflect, in an encapsulated and simplified form, the key issues of human existence. As Byatt suggests, "stories and tales [are] intimately to do with death" (*Histories and Stories* 132), not only enacting for us the realities of life but also imposing a structured narrative on the chaos of existence. In its very explicit structuring fairy tale illustrates and emphasizes the terms on which we interact with literature, the complex tension between the multiplicity of reality and the order of the artifact.

In this exploration of relevance and literary function, the tension between escape and investigation in modern fairy tale becomes particularly interesting. In his chapter "The Contemporary American Fairy Tale" (*Fairy Tale as Myth*), Zipes queries whether the cultural purposes of fairy tale have been subverted in the majority of its modern expressions to redefine it simply as a commodity, impoverished in its imaginative power and cultural relevance. His argument quotes Friedmar Apel in questioning whether fairy tale has come to function primarily as consolatory utopian narrative, its status that of distraction or ornament which, in Apel's words, serves only to "amuse the imagination" rather than "fulfill the old functions of conveying a sublime interpretation of life and a way of putting the meaning into practice" (in Zipes 140). The argument recalls Tolkien's distinction between "the Escape of the Prisoner [and] the Flight of the Deserter" (60). Zipes, as always, is concerned with the sociological and ideological function of fairy tale and the extent to which its current incarnations tend to represent reactionary middle-class and conservative values which badly need to be replaced in a "postmodern endeavor to go beyond the traditional boundaries of the fairy tale and generate new worlds" (143). Here utopian function becomes redefined in different ideological terms, in a way which performs, as Zipes argues, the vital purpose of adapting fairy tale continually to its social context, and thus to a continually shifting notion of utopian outcome. In the light both of Zipes's argument and of the central concerns of my own discussion, the self-conscious metafictional quality of fairy tale becomes essential to its functioning as something other than entertainment or reinforcement of the status quo. While examples of fairy tale as reactionary consumer artifact abound, in fact many of the twentieth-and twenty-first-century popular versions go out of their way to exploit the self-conscious unreality of the narrative, many of them finding in this metafictional awareness the necessary distance for critique. As I have earlier discussed, so-called low and high art are fluid, flexible categories under the contemporary gaze.

Thus, for example, while A. S. Byatt's purposes in employing *Arabian Nights* motifs in her stories are very different from those of Disney, both forms of usage rely intrinsically on the notion of self-consciousness; the effect of the narratives lie in their metafictional operation. A more extended analysis is revealing not only for the differences it reveals but also for the similarities—both texts are, as Hutcheon would suggest, ultimately didactic in function. Disney's *Aladdin* and Byatt's "The Djinn in the Nightingale's Eye" have in common their assumption of *Arabian Nights* tales—"Aladdin" and "The Fisherman and the Jinni"—as texts familiar in the Western fairy-tale corpus, and their readers' or viewers' awareness, not only of that specific text but also of the tradition of fairy-tale texts as a whole. Byatt, however, seems to draw on the *Arabian Nights* structure to highlight narrative embedding and the strategic use of tale-telling. Disney, one feels, is drawn to "Aladdin" not only because of its familiarity but also because it focuses on the desire for wealth and includes very visual treasures which speak to Disney's visual nature and to their commodity function. Tellingly, Disney's version makes full use of the qualities of exoticism and otherness in "Aladdin," blandly smoothing over the tale's somewhat vexed genesis, more Western than Eastern. Both works, however, employ familiar Western fairy-tale motifs to render the Eastern elements more familiar; both are fascinated by the changes wrought in the tale when the possible wishes are limited to three. It is also striking how both Byatt and Disney insist on the idea of freedom as integral to the choice of the third wish, a rather more concentrated version of fairy-tale's classic insistence on the need for courtesy to chance-met magical helpers. Byatt, however, uses this limitation as the basis for a profound investigation of human values, where Disney's rather facile moral point in fact masks the use of the motif for narrative tension and impetus, and for the basic middle-class "civilizing" function noted by Zipes. At the same time Disney's retelling of a complete and recognizable Aladdin tale, despite its adaptation to formula and to visual narrative, speaks to the necessity for familiarity and acceptance in its audiences. Byatt, meanwhile, is able to use motifs from the familiar tale in a completely different context, invoking without actually retelling the original story, and challenging her readers to make the necessary intertextual connections.

Perhaps the strongest contrast is in the two texts' very different treatment of the genie, which functions as a paradigm for the widely divergent attitudes Byatt and Disney have to the tradition on which they draw. Disney's genie is a (visually necessary) compression of two figures from the original "Aladdin," and abandons all sense of an awe-inspiring, otherworldly power in to represent instead a cuddly commodity impresario. The genie is cleansed of much of his possible otherness both through his very obvious Robin Williams characteristics and through his safe appropriation of Western consumer motifs in his bewildering and ongoing comic transformations. This is a sharp contrast to Byatt's genie, whose otherness is explored and emphasized by his placing within the context of a Western-style hotel, his visible difference in terms of size and culture also underlined by Gillian's fascination with it. Byatt thus insists on the existence and importance of a non-Western tradition of tale-telling; Disney instead marginalizes the other culture, claiming through motifs of familiarity and the Americanization of key characters, that all fairy-tale traditions are, in fact, the Western tradition. Where Byatt's tale requires that the reader consider both the universality of fairy tales and their specific cultural natures, Disney's film encourages viewers to accept and enjoy the witty cultural clashes in Disney's version of fairy-tale functioning. Both texts offer a version of self-awareness about their fairy-tale project, but the framing of *Aladdin* as both oral narrative and commodity, while clever, points to a very different form of self-awareness from Byatt's sophisticated and sensitive use of embedded tale and a simulated oral voice.

The Byatt/Disney comparison suggests that employment of meta-fictional properties in fairy-tale retellings is very different in literary and consumer artifacts; however, my sense is that, as self-reflexiveness develops in contemporary popular culture, in fact the two extremes tend to converge. The proliferation of cultural signage in a postmodern media age has granted bewilderingly easy access to a vast array of cultural productions, and even popular texts must resort to layering, intertextuality, and self-awareness in order to adequately reflect their context. This process is easily adaptable to the constraints of mass-market production to an extent which, as we have seen, mirrors some aspects of folkloric communality, and is thus particularly pertinent to the fairy tale. Perhaps more strongly than at any other point in the development of the form, modern fairy tales function as a celebration of the mutual understanding of writer and reader, the re-establishment of a new sense of somewhat abstract community based in shared awareness of cultural capital. This effect lies not only in reiteration of the tales as in their original, oral retelling but also in development and play based on that mutual sense of what the form is and how it works, from its myriad reflections in literature, film, and popular culture. Whether for fun, profit, or intellectual exercise, contemporary metafictional fairy tale invokes and exposes as well as develops the form.

With exposure, necessarily, comes distance; effectively, given the sense of irony intrinsic to postmodern culture, modern versions cannot simply accept the geometry of the marvelous, but must highlight their self-conscious use of it in a way that suggests their celebration is not naive. The intrinsic metafictional elements thus hover on the edge of parody or spill over completely into it, their self-consciousness simultaneously celebrating and undercutting the functioning of the form. The process is similar to that noted by Umberto Eco as the defining feature of the postmodern age:

> The postmodern reply to the modern consists of recognizing that the past, since it cannot really be destroyed, because its destruction leads to silence, must be revisited: but with irony, not innocently. I think of the postmodern attitude as that of a man who loves a very cultivated woman and knows he cannot say to her, "I love you madly," because he knows that she knows (and that she knows that he knows) that these words have already been written by Barbara Cartland. Still, there is a solution. He can say, "As Barbara Cartland would put it, I love you madly." (*Reflections* 19)

In the same way that Eco's lover cannot say "I love you," the modern fairy tale cannot say "happily ever after"; its use, as is mine in this chapter's title, must be ironic. The *only* possible way to express that structured and unrealistic closure is in the metafictional mode, to stress that this fairy tale is, after all, an artificial construction, and that both writer and reader are ironically complicit in this awareness. Linda Hutcheon makes the same point: in the late twentieth century, the tendency is for all cultural forms to be self-reflexive, and "Parody is one of the major forms of modern self-reflexivity" (*Parody* 1–2). This awareness also informs political rewriting such as feminist fairy tale, where the pitfalls of acculturation inherent in the form can only be acceptable if they are accessed and reused parodically or investigatively. Self-awareness of structure and unreality allows for profound social comment in fairy-tale adaptations. In Hutcheon's words, "the art forms of [the twentieth] century have been extremely and self-consciously didactic, and seem to be getting more so" (3). Parody is, in her terms, necessarily both investigation and critique.

The particular power of parody as a framework for considering fairy-tale rewrites is that it embraces, strangely, both possible ends of the spectrum in terms of fairy tale as entertainment and fairy tale as self-aware literary and ideological product. The proliferation of parodic forms in our time is a feature of so-called high art as well as the equally so-called popular; ideological content and purpose may differ wildly, but techniques are often similar. In a postmodern age the fashionable textual stance of ironic distance has, perhaps, some side effects in causing even the consumer dupes identified by Adorno and Horkheimer to take cultural productions with a pinch of salt. Parody, even if heavy-handed in the popular context, is becoming increasingly marketable, as evidenced by the success of film franchises such as the *Scream* and *Scary Movie* series, which evince an ongoing deconstruction of generic expectation and cliché. In the context of fairy tale the popular tendency to self-consciousness in Hollywood film has risen to new extremes following the success of the *Shrek* franchise, leading to a hyper-developed parodic consciousness I wish to explore in more depth, offering as it does a snapshot of the prevailing state of fairy tale as cultural artifact.

Dreamworks' animated feature *Shrek* erupted into popular cinematic consciousness in 2001, offering a paradigm for the kind of ironic and parodic functioning I have outlined above. A highly successful fairy-tale work, it exemplified both popular narrative, in the sense of popular film, and parodic critique of form in terms not only of the functioning of cliché but also of ideological content. Its sequels, *Shrek 2* (2004) and *Shrek the Third* (2007) provided more of the same, although I wish to argue that there is a shift in consciousness between the original film and its subsequent sequels and imitators. *Shrek* represents a huge step away from the straightforward adaptations of Disney; its animated format suggests the same self-aware accessing of unreality and the magical as we see in Disney animations, but its self-consciousness and deliberately parodic and inverted elements add a new critical distance to fairy tale. Unlike Disney, and rather like the best of Victorian children's fairy tale (or

A. S. Byatt), this is not fairy-tale retelling, but the creation of a new artifact firmly rooted in the traditions of the form. The narrative of the first film, based on a children's book by William Steig, wanders waywardly through dragon killing in the style of Saint George, the traditional christening curse, a Snow-White-style magic mirror, and the Sleeping Beauty and Beauty/Beast motifs. References are not only to well-known fairy tales in the sense of children's storybook retellings but also to film versions such as Disney's, and to other films with fairy-tale or folkloric elements (*The Princess Bride, Ladyhawke, Zorro,* even the self-conscious unreality of *The Matrix*).

As in many contemporary fairy tales, in *Shrek* fairy-tale format becomes the flexible vehicle for contemporary cultural awareness, in this reflecting the fluid social adaptability of the original oral form. The film's cheerful hodgepodge of fairy-tale narrative elements is reinforced by its employment of popular cultural collage, in the style of Disney's genie, but with a more acute and sensitive awareness of genre and the animated film. Thus Shrek's initial happy, ogreish isolation is invaded by the combined cast of Mother Goose, Perrault, and Grimm—"three blind mice in his food and a big, bad wolf in his bed" ("*Shrek* [2001]"), the cast of subcharacters who later rescue Shrek from imprisonment toward the end of the second film. Where Disney's genie morphs rapidly into various pop cultural icons, however, comic effect in the *Shrek* films comes in the updating of classic fairy-tale and nursery-rhyme stereotypes with a shrewd and comic modern awareness which, unlike the genie, avoids breaking the generic frame. Motifs are thus parodically expanded in context, such as the torture scene where Farquaad threatens the Gingerbread Man with "crumbling." The landscape of the films' world is peopled with the familiar icons of magical narrative, who may refer to the contemporary tropes of consumer culture but are not replaced by them; it thus retains a more affectionate and respectful attitude to the genre than does Disney's wholesale appropriation and mixing. In many ways *Shrek*'s world is akin to Pratchett's Discworld, a comic but humane attempt to put a sense of realism into the fantasy stereotypes.

The film's narrative employs the same appropriation of fairy-tale structures for social comment as do many of the works I have investigated; here, the unreality of the animated format takes some of the sting from the satire. The first film sets up the primary fairy-tale parody both films use, namely a Carteresque take on the Beauty and the Beast motif which achieves equality and the happy ending through a beastly rather than a beautiful couple. The romance between an ugly ogre and a beautiful princess cursed to be ugly at night also manages to work simultaneously against the Disney cleanliness and the beauty myth of modern consumer culture, an opposition underlined in the second film by the equation of Fiona's parents' unwelcoming "Magic Kingdom" with Hollywood—palm trees, limousines, star homes, red carpets, and all. The message is curiously similar to that of any version of "Beauty and the Beast"—it is not appearance that counts, but internal worth. Here, however, it is presented with a subversive conviction that is far more convincing than Disney's lip service to inner worth while pushing the power and value of the visual with both hands. Shrek is not only ugly, he is also crude, earthy, and occasionally gross. Zipes has characterized fairy tale as a narrative designed to "reinforce patriarchal notions of civilization" (*Happily Ever After* 67)—a notion *Shrek* wholeheartedly and self-consciously overturns. *Shrek* opens with a bathing scene which satirizes the acculturated cleanliness norms of modern consumer culture, as Shrek baths in a mud hole and cleans his teeth by squeezing a caterpillar onto his toothbrush. Later he illuminates his candlelit dinner for one with a candle made from his own earwax in a rather gross satire on the romantic myth; in the second film, he and Fiona enjoy a spa-style mud bath whose bubbles are provided by flatulence. These elements would never be found in a Disney fairy-tale film. Zipes, discussing the first film in relation to the book which inspired it, finds that it has true subversive potential, not only in terms of cultural forms but also in its attack on the means of production: the film denies monolithic meaning, "the tyranny of symmetry and homogenization," but in fact, the narrative conflicts also "represent a real struggle within the film industry of cultural production" (*Magic Spell* 229).

The films' visual effect is, similarly, a denial of the clean-cut, the idealized unreal. Dreamworks' groundbreaking computer animation gives the film a rich, almost sensuous texture that has slightly more depth than the usual animated landscape; it also allows for nuances of expression and reaction in the characters, so that the film's expression of emotion feels more genuine than a Disney equivalent, or the idealized lines of the average children's illustration. The upshot is a far more realistic idea of body shape for Princess Fiona, who actually looks like a person rather than one of Disney's wasp-waisted physical impossibilities. The Dreamworks studio does not, however, forget the value of the animation format for their comic and satirical purposes: apart from the rich, fairy-tale landscapes, the film makes shrewd use of classic animated distortion, most notably in the three-foot-high Lord Farquaad. John Lithgow, who provided Farquaad's voice, describes the character as "the walking embodiment of over-compensation" ("*Shrek* (2001)"). The film relies not only on the ability of animation to present broad variation in bodily form and size but also on the audience's awareness of popular Freudian interpretation, a self-conscious subtext underlined by the enormous, phallic block of Farquaad's castle. The power of animation similarly glosses over the essential unreality of the romance between Eddie Murphy's tiny Donkey and the enormous, *very* feminine Dragon. The difference in size is a comic visual realization of the film's moral subtext, that appearance is not important, but most importantly, only the assumptions behind animated caricature, in tandem with the beast-fable unreality of the fairy-tale format, make the relationship possible at all. Their "little mutant babies!" in the second film are effective because, for a moment, they insist that the audience conceptualize the physical *reality* of the donkey/dragon relationship—and its consequences.

Shrek makes infinitely more use of its animation than Disney ever did; its unashamed invocation of Disney films, while affectionate, is often irresistibly comic precisely because it overlays its more daring effects onto the often saccharine idealizations of Disney and the children's storybook. The metafictional assumptions of the film thus embrace not only fairy tale in its traditional format but also fairy tale in the twentieth-century mold; self-awareness is centered not only in the pure structures of fairy tale but also in the most recent versions of the form. Perhaps the film's most effective scene is one involving Princess Fiona singing, Snow White style, with a random bluebird; her high notes cause the bird to swell up to the point where it simply explodes. The interchange underlines the fact that, mercifully, the films are not musicals and their characters do not generally sing, the attractive soundtrack occurring only in voice-over; a similar undercutting is achieved in *Shrek 2* when the Fairy Godmother does, in fact, sing, her Disney-style musical number serving to reinforce her villainess-role adherence to outdated structures. *Shrek* and *Shrek 2* thus offer a rather different understanding of unreality from that presented by Disney. The parody of the musical format suggests that, above all, *Shrek*'s awareness of genre is anything but naive. Other highly recognizably visual parodies include the storybook beginning, which I have analyzed above, and Farquaad's magic mirror, which has a mask-like face almost identical to the witch-queen's mirror in *Snow White*; the Fairy Godmother's attempt to provide Fiona with her "very own furniture friends" in the second film is an extremely wicked dig at Disney's *Beauty and the Beast*. Interestingly, the transformation scene in the cathedral at the close of the first film invokes the denouements of both *The Princess Bride* and *Ladyhawke*, well-known romantic fantasies whose beauty myth is pilloried by the film, but who add live-action fairy tale to *Shrek*'s assumption of cultural capital. To this could also be added the Robin Hood characters, who owe more to the Mel

Brooks *Men in Tights* version than to anything folkloric. In *Shrek 2*, similar moments parody the ring forging from *Lord of the Rings* and the inverted kiss from *Spiderman*.

I have dealt above mostly with *Shrek* and only minimally with *Shrek 2*; this reflects my sense of the important changes that emerged in the sensibility of the second film and, especially, the third, which suggest that fairy tale in popular culture is moving into a slightly different form of expression. *Shrek 2* and *Shrek the Third*, while using the same characters and format as the original film, take parody to new extremes on the levels of content and of narrative structure, and in fact have more in common with their later imitations, films such as *Hoodwinked* (2005) and *Happily N'Ever After* (2006), or with the recent Disney postanimation offering, *Enchanted* (2008). All these films offer a parodic version of fairy tale, representing self-consciousness about the artifact taken to extremes not found in *Shrek* or in any of the literary versions I have thus far investigated. *Shrek* might choose to undercut the beauty myth, the Disney fairy-tale tradition, and various other cultural motifs, but its narrative retains its identity as fairy tale, albeit an inverted one—it riffs on "Beauty and the Beast" in a similar sense to the revisions offered by Carter's "Tiger's Bride." Rather like the Victorian rewrites or Carter's revisions, the outcomes of the tale may be refigured or disrupted, but the fairy-tale project is deadly serious. A similar seriousness seems to be lacking from later fairy-tale parodies, which increasingly lose sight of the tale as an artifact with any integrity of its own. While taking for granted its existence as cultural capital, these recent films fragment and distort the tale, reducing its remnants to the same status as the collage of contemporary cultural motifs that lends these films their contemporary currency—*Hoodwinked* with its detective procedural and extreme sports motif, or the Hells Angel witches and militarized Seven Dwarves in *Happily N'Ever After*. This is the parodic process Hutcheon noted whereby "the works of the past become aesthetic models whose recasting in a modern work is frequently aimed at a satirical ridicule of contemporary customs or practices" (11). Ultimately the fairy tale, despite its strong presence, no longer provides either the framework or the focus for the film, which means that to a greater or lesser extent they are not concerned with the intrinsic power of fairy tale in any real narrative, emotional, or psychological sense. This is, perhaps, a reflection of commercial drives that require easy recognition without necessarily offering coherent ideological exploration, but in another sense the tendency also reflects postmodern irony taken to new and slightly frenetic extremes. Disney produced fairy tale; fairy-tale films after *Shrek* seem to suggest, while invoking it in pastiche, that fairy tale is impossible to produce.

The most obvious symptom of this denial is in the overall shape of the plot in these films. *Shrek 2* has not moved as far from tale as whole as have the other films, but it merely elaborates on the Beast/Beauty tension set up by the first film, and the struggle to assert actual fairy-tale narrative is not only external to Shrek and Fiona's central quest for identity, it also is the obstacle to such identity. By *Shrek the Third* the franchise has almost entirely lost sight of its fairy-tale roots in its concerns with parenthood and the theatrical frustrations of the marginalized Prince Charming; the potentially strong mythology of Prince Arthur, rescued from obscurity to rule as rightful heir, is an appendage to the story rather than a motivating force. *Hoodwinked* takes the Red Riding Hood story as its jumping-off point rather than its focus, being largely concerned with the multiple-viewpoint detective story focusing on the new element of the Goody Bandit. The fairy tale's identity is not simply obscured by the incongruities of extreme sports, laconic investigator, or clichéd evil genius which drive the plot, it is also rendered largely irrelevant in the continual redefinition of events which results from the different viewpoints. *Happily N'Ever After* likewise transcends any individual fairy tale in order to posit a breakdown of all of them, and to forge a new adventure quest from the fragments; while Cinderella is a central character and her prince a gender-inverted echo of her status as marginalized kitchen help, their adventures bear no actual resemblance to the Cinderella story. All these films suggest that fairy tale is not worth exploring from within, on its own terms; all of them achieve in their parody a quality of distance and, at times, of mockery which recalls Jameson's definitions of postmodernism in terms of its "new kind of flatness or depthlessness, a new kind of superficiality" (9). To return to my earlier point, if this is parody, it is closer to Jameson's sense of pastiche, "a neutral practice of . . . mimicry . . . devoid of laughter and of any conviction that alongside the abnormal tongue you have momentarily borrowed, some healthy linguistic normality still exists" (17). Hutcheon makes a similar point when she talks about parody's "ironic distance," which "might well come from a loss of that earlier humanist faith in cultural continuity and stability" (10); indeed, these films have lost sight of fairy tale as a meaningful cultural force, and their invocations of its motifs lack depth and resonance as well as coherence. *Shrek the Third* is most telling in its presentation of Shrek's story as Prince Charming's theatrical spectacle, two-dimensional and obviously stage-managed to the point where it lacks any actual meaning, exposing itself to the mockery rather than the sympathetic identification of the audience. Whatever its consumerist purposes, Disney fairy tale was at least complicit with its medium, buying wholeheartedly into the power of fairy tale and demanding that viewer do the same. The metafictional elements in these more recent films tend to lead, not only to the necessary critical distance but also to an emotional estrangement from the structures of fairy tale—not exploration of their significance, but mockery of their inadequacies.

If these examples of post-*Shrek* contemporary fairy-tale film share a certain ironic distance from their fairy-tale roots, they also have in common their awareness of narrative, or, more accurately, an insecurity about it. All these films demonstrate a self-consciousness about narrative which, rather than being exploratory in the sense of Byatt or even Pratchett, is ultimately paranoid; in their pervasive fear of *incorrect* narratives, the films tend to disrupt *all* fairy-tale narratives, the fragments of which contribute to the non-fairy-tale metaplot. Again, this could be linked to postmodernism's denial of master narrative, so that fairy tale in these films is fragmented and ultimately rejected precisely because its strong structures are seen as illegitimate. The seeds of this are already present in *Shrek*, in which Shrek's inverted narrative battles with fairy-tale "correctness"; it becomes more explicit in the second film with the notion of "happily ever after" which pervades the plot, its lack of realism shattered against post-fairy-tale in-law problems and Fiona's resolute refusal to transform. The film presents an ongoing clash between the actual desires of the tale's protagonists and the expectations of the plot which keep trying to enfold them. Rather than being fairy tale, *Shrek 2* is explicitly post–fairy tale, an exploration of the essential fascism of the "happy ending" which also achieves some Pratchettesque rewritings of the narrative function of the fairy godmother and a telling critique of the implausibly perfect Disney prince. The terrible Fairy Godmother and her son Prince Charming, his metrosexual unsuitability underlined by the voice provided by gay actor Rupert Everett, continually attempt to assert that the first film's narrative was the *wrong* one, and hence to validate the traditional fairy-tale narrative to which they both subscribe, which empowers them while identifying Shrek as unsuccessful villain. That this narrative is intrinsically artificial is also a constant reminder: it can be encapsulated in a bottle of "Happily Ever After," and its origin is not only constructed but also industrial, a threatening factory poking fun at the postindustrial concept of craft as de-individualized manufacture. The Fairy Godmother is a sister to Pratchett's Lilith, her nature as totalitarian power underlined by the motifs of corporate power and of criminal, Mafia-style activity which attach to her: answering machines, business cards, limousine with attendant strong-men, and threats to the hapless frog-King Harold. These motifs are important, and not just for the amusing incongruity of their clash with fairy-tale forms; where

Pratchett's investigations take place *within* fairy tale, disrupting particular narratives which are nonetheless contained inside a larger, fantastical reality with its own mythological underpinnings, *Shrek 2* instead demonstrates the spuriousness of fairy-tale structure by mixing it wholesale with modern motifs. This is not in itself problematical, as the modern elements in tales by Carter, Byatt, and Lee have shown; what becomes problematical is the exaggerated extent of the modern incursions, and the drift within the film toward a suggestion that *all* fairy-tale narrative is somehow spurious, since none are allowed to prevail over the modern elements, whether cultural reference or Shrek and Fiona's quest for identity.

A similar awareness of narrative insecurity pervades *Hoodwinked*, with its concern for the *correct* narrative version of "Red Riding Hood," and *Happily N'Ever After*, whose wizard in magical control of narrative predestination makes more obviously the points about control and dehumanization made by *Shrek 2* and Pratchett's *Witches Abroad*. Both films, however, insist on the ultimate failure of fairy-tale narrative, *Hoodwinked* by insistent reinterpretation which loses sight of the original tale's meaning, *Happily N'Ever After* through its lack of concern for actual fairy-tale structures, which are invoked superficially and without exploration. More importantly, these tendencies point to the other recurring feature of these recent films: their concern with the narrative role of villainy. Where *Hoodwinked* tries to apportion blame and ends up locating it outside the tale entirely, both *Shrek the Third* and *Happily N'Ever After* exploit the meta-fairy-tale environment first posited by *Shrek*, in which all fairy-tale characters occupy the same landscape, to posit a coalition of villainy which threatens the stable order of fairy tale. This detachment of fairy-tale villains from their correct contexts within the tales ultimately denudes them of their structural significance; they become floating signifiers, much of their meaning lost, and fairy-tale structures unravel in their wake. Despite their ongoing paranoia about the authority and correctness of narrative, these films end up denying the familiar shapes of fairy tale to instead provide the expected utopian closure within a *different* plot structure, one from outside fairy tale—the defeat of the mad scientist Goody Bandit or the power-hungry stepmother seizing control of narrative through theft of the wizard's staff, or in fact Shrek's overturning of the crazed Prince Charming's insane theatrics. All these films restore narrative order, but it is not the narrative order of fairy tale; they use fairy-tale motifs from outside, not inside, the tale, and it is in this external narrative structure that meaning and value are located.

I do not mean to suggest, in this identification of ironic distance as an intrinsic quality of recent contemporary fairy-tale films, that the films are consequently less valid representations of fairy-tale narrative than earlier versions. If anything, they demonstrate the extent to which fairy tale is a given in the cinematic tradition, its status that of cultural capital which can be invoked in fragmented motif because the whole is so familiar. The flatness and denial of value I have found in these films is, at least partially, a result of their existence at the commercial end of the cinematic spectrum—they are not artistically successful films, and they come closest to exemplifying the concerns expressed by Zipes in *Fairy Tale as Myth,* that fairy tale could become simple ornament to a consumerist product, devoid of meaning. Much of the functioning of these films relies on recognition of *Shrek*'s blockbuster status, and a more or less shameless attempt to leap on the bandwagon, resulting in a gesture at meaning rather than any coherent explorations. This points to a new position of fairy tale in contemporary film culture, as a viable set of tools for popular filmmaking, a recognition which once more circles back to fairy tale's original identity as folk culture, relevant to the concerns of a broad section of the population. The sense of fairy tale's *impossibility* in these films stems, perhaps, from the uneasy balancing act they undertake between exploitation of cultural capital and the need for contemporary relevance, with the ironic or even cynical stance such relevance currently dictates.

Nor do I wish to imply that the trajectory toward increased irony and fragmentation I have found in these examples is indicative of any irrevocable trend. While I retain my sense that *Shrek* functions as some kind of watershed in cinematic fairy-tale awareness, with subsequent films adopting and exaggerating the commercially successful ironic formula it presents, it is also true that Disney's recent film *Enchanted* (2007) presents some kind of compromise between a notion of the value of fairy tale, and the necessary postmodern sense of its impossibility I have identified above. *Enchanted* is certainly post–fairy tale, more particularly post–animated fairy tale, and points to a developing awareness in the Disney monolith of the outdatedness of its twentieth-century fairy-tale formulae. *Enchanted*'s mix of live action with animation is highly self-conscious, not only playing into the success of early Disney mixed-format films such as *Mary Poppins* but also highlighting the tensions between real and unreal generated by the animated format. The story's overall shape is closer to classic fairy tale than the other examples I have discussed, with the hapless princess Giselle threatened by the requisite evil stepmother and rescued by the cliché of "true love's kiss," albeit provided by a jaded New York divorce lawyer rather than the dashing—and obliviously unintelligent—Prince Edward. This structure is continually examined by the film's format, however. The initial animated sequences are highly parodic in tone, with the unreality of plot and saccharine musical format of the tale effectively pillorying Disney's own traditions, and they are thrown into sharp relief by their juxtaposition with real-life, live-action New York. The "real" setting provides the prince figure and emotional resolution which shadow the more two-dimensional animated versions; the eruption of animated stereotypes, singing, dancing, and performing impossible feats, into modern New York is comic, entertaining, and exceptionally self-conscious about narrative cliché.

At the same time, however, even while the stilted interactions of fairy tale and the musical are mocked, the emotional validity of the narrative is celebrated: Giselle's naïveté and optimism are inappropriate to the harsh realities of modern New York, but they have a lesson for the cynical lawyer which is equal and opposite to the lesson in genuine emotion she learns from him and from the city, denying the narrative short-cuts of fairy-tale love at first sight. The film's pervading theme is that of reality, pointed not just by the animated versus live-action format but also in the literal realization of fairy-tale tropes—impractical hoop skirt, love at first sight, and all. Much of the success of *Enchanted* is in its refusal to deny the integrity of the fairy tale it gently satirizes. Giselle's animal helpers, the stilted artificiality of her acting, and her infectious music-and-dance numbers spill out of their fairy-tale framework into the real city; in this decontextualized environment they nonetheless succeed where strict realism demands they should fail. This is most powerfully true in the film's denouement, in which "happily ever after" with the prince entails city life with a lawyer; at the same time, Prince Edward is permitted to return to his animated kingdom with his bride, in counterpoint to the central love story. This neatly frames Giselle's love story in a direct literalization of the ironic distance identified by Eco; she and her lawyer can say "I love you madly, as a Disney fairy tale would put it," because the Disney fairy tale is right there for comparison.

Enchanted thus recoups, in some senses, the extremes of post-*Shrek* irony in fairy tale films while simultaneously demonstrating the breadth of possibility presented by the ironic distance of fairy-tale parody. While consumerism can assault the integrity of tale and narrative fragmentation has the potential to fragment the meaning and resonance of the tale, this is an extreme. *Enchanted* demonstrates as much as *Shrek* that, whatever the frenetic exaggerations achieved by filmmakers in search of successful formulae, there is a cultural space for explorations of the value of fairy tale as well as more superficial invocations of its more recognizable features. At whichever end of the scale, these films represent, in many ways, the *only* possible format for fairy tale in our postmodern age, one in which the form is interrogated even as it is affectionately reproduced. They showcase the achievements not only of a fairy-tale film industry but also of the institution of fairy tale, as one that has developed to the point where it can afford to be both nostalgic and satirical: to simultaneously depict and undercut the tyranny of structure. *Shrek*'s producer argues that "these characters are ripe for parody because they're part of the cosmic consciousness, so to speak" ("*Shrek* (2001)"); the consciousness of which they are part of is fairy tale as a construct, not a given. These films embrace live-action fairy-tale film as well as animation in their affectionate or satirical inversions, not to mention the familiar figures of original fairy tale and folklore—Red Riding Hood, Snow White, and the rest. More broadly, however, they offer a consciousness of *cultural artifact,* an ironic distance which these days characterizes more than fairy tale, and which finds in fairy tale a particularly familiar and strongly structured ground for self-awareness. This, more than anything achieved by Disney, suggests that there is, in fact, hope for the fairy-tale film as an inheritor of the folk voice, as simply one more step in the ongoing process by which fairy tale and other narratives are transformed in our culture to reflect that culture's concerns. While fairy tale has become a tool of consumerism, at the same time many versions move through and beyond consumerism, suggesting that metafiction is not only the province of the intellectual writer; that popular fairy tale can be intelligently aware of its own postmodern status while simultaneously celebrating its structural and generic roots. Above all, this demonstrates the strength of fairy tale's marvelous geometry as more than simply magical form, but as self-aware artifact with the power to adapt, change, and reflect the needs and concerns of its age.

BIBLIOGRAPHY

PRIMARY SOURCES

Apuleius. *The Golden Ass; or, Metamorphoses.* Tr. E. J. Kenney. London: Penguin, 1998.

Armstrong, Anthony. *The Naughty Princess.* London: Macdonald, 1945.

Atwood, Margaret. *Bluebeard's Egg and Other Stories.* London: Jonathan Cape, 1987.

Barthelme, Donald. "The Glass Mountain." 1970. *The Oxford Book of Modern Fairy Tales.* Ed. Alison Lurie. Oxford: Oxford University Press, 1993. 367–71.

Boccaccio, Giovanni. *The Decameron; or, Ten Days' Entertainment.* Tr. John Payne. Cleveland: World Publishing, 1947.

Brahms, Carol, and S. J. Simon. *Titania Has a Mother.* London: Michael Joseph, 1944.

Brust, Steven. *The Sun, the Moon, and the Stars.* New York: Tor, 1987.

Burton, Sir Richard. *The Book of the Thousand and One Nights.* Ed. P. H. Newby. London: Arthur Barker, 1950.

Byatt, A. S. *Angels and Insects.* London: Chatto and Windus, 1992.

———. *Babel Tower.* London: Chatto and Windus, 1996.

———. *The Biographer's Tale.* London: Vintage, 2000.

———. *The Djinn in the Nightingale's Eye: Five Fairy Stories.* London: Vintage, 1994.

———. *Elementals: Stories of Fire and Ice.* London: Vintage, 1998.

———. *The Game.* London: Vintage, 1967.

———. *Little Black Book of Stories.* London: Chatto and Windus, 2003.

———. *The Matisse Stories.* London: Vintage, 1993.

———. *Possession: A Romance.* London: Vintage, 1990.

———. *Shadow of a Sun.* London: Vintage, 1964.

———. *Still Life.* London: Chatto and Windus, 1985.

———. *Sugar and Other Stories.* London: Penguin, 1987.

———. *The Virgin in the Garden.* London: Chatto and Windus, 1978.

———. *A Whistling Woman.* London: Alfred Knopf, 2002.

Carroll, Lewis. *The Hunting of the Snark.* 1876. *The Annotated Snark.* Ed. Martin Gardener. London: Penguin, 1962.

Carter, Angela. *The Bloody Chamber and Other Stories.* London: Penguin, 1979.

———. *Burning Your Boats: Stories.* London: Chatto and Windus, 1995.

———. *The Curious Room: Plays, Film Scripts, and an Opera.* London: Chatto and Windus, 1996.

Chaucer, Geoffrey. *The Riverside Chaucer.* Ed. Larry D. Benson. London: Houghton Mifflin, 1987.

Cocteau, Jean. *Three Screenplays: L'eternel retour, Orphée, La Belle et la Bête.* Tr. Carol Martin-Sperry. New York: Grossman, 1972.

Coover, Robert. *Briar Rose.* New York: Grove, 1996.

———. *Pricksongs and Descants.* London: Picador, 1969.

D'Arras, Jean. *A Chronicle of Melusine in olde Englishe. compyled by Ihon of Arras, and dedicated to the Duke of Berry and Auuergne, and translated. as yt shoulde seeme. out of Frenche into Englishe.* Early English Text Series 68. Ed. A. K. Donald. Millwood, NY: Kraus Reprint, 1981.

Datlow, Ellen, and Terri Windling, eds. *Snow White, Blood Red.* London: Signet, 1993.

De la Motte Fouqué, Friedrich. "Undine." 1811. *Romantic Fairy Tales.* Tr. and ed. Carol Tully. London: Penguin, 2000. 53–125.

De Lint, Charles. *Jack the Giant Killer.* 1987. *Drink Down the Moon.* 1990. *Jack of Kinrowan.* New York: Tor, 1995.

De Villeneuve, Gabrielle-Suzanne. "The Story of Beauty and the Beast." 1740. Zipes, *Beauties, Beasts* 153–232.

Dean, Pamela. *Tam Lin.* New York: Tor, 1991.

Del Rey, Lester. *Once Upon a Time: A Treasury of Fantasies and Fairy Tales.* London: Century, 1991.

Dickens, Charles. "The Magic Fishbone." 1868. Zipes, *Victorian Fairy Tales* 91–99.

Donoghue, Emma. *Kissing the Witch: Old Tales in New Skins.* New York: HarperCollins, 1997.

Eco, Umberto. *The Name of the Rose.* London: Picador, 1980.

Eliot, T. S. *Old Possum's Book of Practical Cats.* London: Faber and Faber, 1939.

Ewing, Juliana Horatia. "The Ogre Courting." 1871. Zipes, *Victorian Fairy Tales* 129–33.

Frost, Gregory. *Fitcher's Brides.* New York: Tor, 2002.

Gaiman, Neil. "Snow, Glass, Apples." *Smoke and Mirrors.* London: Headline, 1999.

Garner, James Finn. *Once Upon a More Enlightened Time.* London: Simon and Schuster, 1995.

———. *Politically Correct Bedtime Stories.* London: Macmillan, 1994.

Grahame, Kenneth. "The Reluctant Dragon." *Dream Days.* 1898. London: Wordsworth, 1995. 87–114.

Grimm, Jakob and Wilhelm. 1812. *The Complete Fairy Tales of the Brothers Grimm.* Tr. Jack Zipes. New York: Bantam, 1987.

Kushner, Ellen. *Thomas the Rhymer*. New York: Tor, 1990.

Lee, Tanith. *The Book of the Beast: The Secret Books of Paradys II*. London: Unwin, 1988.

———. *The Book of the Damned: The Secret Books of Paradys I*. London: Unwin, 1988.

———. *Heart-Beast*. London: Headline, 1992.

———. *Heroine of the World*. London: Headline, 1989.

———. *Red as Blood: Tales from the Sisters Grimmer*. New York: Daw, 1983.

———. *The Silver Metal Lover*. New York: Daw, 1981.

———. *White as Snow*. New York: Tor, 2000.

Léger, Louis, tr. "Snowflake." *The Pink Fairy Book*. Ed. Andrew Lang. London: Dover, 1967. 143–47.

Leprince de Beaumont, Jeanne-Marie. 1757. "Beauty and the Beast." Zipes, *Beauties, Beasts* 233–45.

Macdonald, George. "The Day Boy and the Night Girl." 1879. *The Light Princess and Other Tales*.

———. "The Golden Key." 1867. *The Light Princess and Other Tales*.

———. *The Light Princess and Other Tales*. Ed. Roger Lancelyn Green. Edinburgh: Canongate, 1961.

———. *The Princess and the Goblin*. 1872. London: Puffin, 1962.

Maitland, Sarah. *A Book of Spells*. London: Michael Joseph, 1987.

McKinley, Robin. *Beauty*. London: Futura, 1978.

———. *Deerskin*. New York: Ace, 1993.

———. *The Door in the Hedge*. London: Futura, 1981.

———. *Spindle's End*. London: Corgi, 2000.

Milne, A. A. *Once on a Time*. London: Kaye and Ward, 1917.

Nesbit, E. *E. Nesbit Fairy Stories*. Ed. Naomi Lewis. London: Hodder and Stoughton, 1977.

———. *The Last of the Dragons and Some Others*. London: Puffin, 1972.

Perrault, Charles. "The Master Cat, or Puss in Boots"; "Cinderella, or The Glass Slipper"; "Blue Beard"; "The Sleeping Beauty in the Woods"; "Little Red Riding Hood"; "The Foolish Wishes." 1697. Zipes, *Beauties, Beasts* 21–66.

Pratchett, Terry. *The Amazing Maurice and His Educated Rodents*. London: Corgi, 2001.

———. *Carpe Jugulum*. London: Corgi, 1998.

———. *Equal Rites*. London: Corgi, 1987.

———. *Hogfather*. London: Corgi, 1996.

———. *Lords and Ladies*. London: Corgi, 1992.

———. *Reaper Man*. London: Corgi, 1991.

———. *Soul Music*. London: Corgi, 1994.

———. *Thief of Time*. London: Corgi, 2001.

———. *Witches Abroad*. London: Corgi, 1991.

Ruskin, John. *The King of the Golden River; or, the Black Brothers*. 1841. London: Kaye and Ward, 1958.

Sharp, Evelyn. "The Spell of the Magician's Daughter." 1902. Zipes, *Beauties, Beasts* 361–72.
Sitwell, Osbert. *Fee, Fi, Fo, Fum! A Book of Fairy Stories.* London: Macmillan, 1959.
Stoker, Bram. *Dracula.* 1897. Oxford: Oxford University Press, 1983.
Tepper, Sheri S. *Beauty.* New York: Bantam, 1991.
———. *The Chronicles of Mavin Manyshaped.* London: Corgi, 1985.
———. *Dervish Daughter.* London: Corgi, 1986.
———. *The Family Tree.* London: HarperCollins, 1997.
———. *The Gate to Women's Country.* London: Corgi, 1988.
———. *Jinian Footseer.* London: Corgi, 1985.
———. *Jinian Stareye.* London: Corgi, 1986.
———. *A Plague of Angels.* London: HarperCollins, 1993.
———. *The True Game.* London: Corgi, 1985.
Thackeray, W. M. *The Rose and the Ring; or, The History of Prince Giglio and Prince Bulbo.* 1855. London: Penguin, 1964.
Thurber, James. *The Beast in Me and Other Animals.* London: Hamish Hamilton, 1949.
———. *Fables for Our Time.* London: Hamish Hamilton, 1940.
———. "The Great Quillow." 1944. *The Puffin Book of Modern Fairy Tales.* Ed. Sara and Stephen Corrin, Harmondsworth: Puffin, 1981. 203–24.
———. *Lanterns and Lances.* Harmondsworth: Penguin, 1961.
———. *Many Moons.* 1943. San Diego: Harcourt Brace. 1970.
———. *Men, Women, and Dogs.* London: Hamish Hamilton, 1943.
———. *My Life and Hard Times.* 1933. New York: Bantam, 1971.
———. *My World—And Welcome to It.* London: Hamish Hamilton, 1942.
———. *The 13 Clocks and The Wonderful O.* Harmondsworth: Penguin, 1951.
———. *The Thurber Album.* 1952. Harmondsworth: Penguin, 1961.
———. *The Thurber Carnival.* 1945. Harmondsworth: Penguin, 1953.
———. *Thurber Country.* 1953. London: Sphere, 1967.
———. *Thurber's Dogs.* Harmondsworth: Penguin, 1955.
———. *The White Deer.* Harmondsworth: Penguin, 1945.
Thurber, James, and E. B. White. *Is Sex Necessary?* 1929. Harmondsworth: Penguin, 1960.
White, E. B. *Charlotte's Web.* London: Hamish Hamilton, 1952.
Wilde, Oscar. *The Happy Prince and Other Tales.* 1888. *The Complete Works of Oscar Wilde.* Twickenham: Hamlyn, 1963.
Wrede, Patricia C. *Calling on Dragons.* New York: Scholastic, 1993.
———. *Dealing with Dragons.* New York: Scholastic, 1990.
———. *Searching for Dragons.* New York: Scholastic, 1991.
———. *Snow White and Rose Red.* New York: Tor, 1989.
———. *Talking to Dragons.* New York: Scholastic, 1985.
Yolen, Jane. *Briar Rose.* New York: Tor, 1992.
———. *Tales of Wonder.* London: Futura, 1983.
Zipes, Jack, ed. *The Trials and Tribulations of Little Red Riding Hood.* New York and London: Routledge and Kegan Paul, 1993.

————. *Victorian Fairy Tales: The Revolt of the Fairies and Elves*. New York: Methuen, 1987.

Zipes, Jack, tr. and ed. *Beauties, Beasts, and Enchantments: Classic French Fairy Tales*. New York: Meridian, 1989.

Filmography

101 Dalmatians. Dir. Hamilton Luske and Clyde Geronimi. Disney, 1961.

Aladdin. Dir. Ron Clements and John Musker. Disney, 1992.

Atlantis: The Lost Empire. Dir. Gary Trousdale and Kirk Wise. Disney, 2001.

Beauty and the Beast. Dir. Gary Trousdale and Kirk Wise. Disney, 1991.

Cinderella. Dir. Hamilton Luske and Wilfred Jackson. Disney, 1950.

The Company of Wolves. Dir. Neil Jordan. Cannon, 1984.

Ella Enchanted. Dir. Tommy O'Haver. Miramax, 2004.

The Emperor's New Groove. Dir. Mark Dindal. Disney, 2000.

The Empire Strikes Back. Dir. Irvin Kershner. Lucasfilm, 1980.

Enchanted. Dir. Kevin Lima. Disney, 2007.

Ever After. Dir. Andy Tennant. Fox, 1998.

Freeway. Dir. Matthew Bright. Lionsgate, 1996.

The Grimm Brothers' Snow White. Dir Michael Cohn. Polygram, 1997.

Happily N'Ever After. Dir. Paul J. Bolger and Yvette Kaplan. Lionsgate, 2006.

Hercules. Dir. Ron Clements and John Musker. Disney, 1997.

Hoodwinked. Dir. Cory and Todd Edwards. Blue Yonder, 2005.

La Belle et la Bête. Dir. Jean Cocteau. André Paulvé, 1946.

Ladyhawke. Dir. Richard Donner. 20th Century Fox/Warner Bros, 1985.

Lilo and Stitch. Dir. Dean DeBlois and Chris Sanders III. Disney, 2002.

The Little Mermaid. Dir. John Musker and Ron Clements. Disney, 1989.

The Lord of the Rings: The Fellowship of the Ring. Dir. Peter Jackson. New Line, 2001.

The Lord of the Rings: The Two Towers. Dir. Peter Jackson. New Line, 2002.

The Lord of the Rings: Return of the King. Dir. Peter Jackson. New Line, 2003.

Peter Pan. Dir. Wilfred Jackson and Clyde Geronimi. Disney, 1953.

Pocahontas. Dir. Mike Gabriel and Eric Goldberg. Disney, 1995.

Pretty Woman. Dir. Gary Marshall. Touchstone, 1990.

The Princess Bride. Dir. Rob Reiner. Act III Communications, 1987.

Return of the Jedi. Dir. Richard Marquand. Lucasfilm, 1983.

Robin Hood. Dir. Wolfgang Reitherman. Disney, 1973.

Robin Hood: Men in Tights. Dir. Mel Brooks. Brooksfilms/Gaumont, 1993.

Shrek. Dir. Andrew Adamson and Vicky Jenson. Dreamworks, 2001.

Shrek 2. Dir. Andrew Adamson, Kelly Asbury, and Conrad Vernon. Dreamworks, 2004.

Shrek the Third. Dir. Chris Miller and Raman Hui. Dreamworks, 2007

Sleeping Beauty. Disney, 1959.

The Slipper and the Rose. Dir. Bryan Forbes. Paradine, 1976.

Snow White. Disney, 1937.

Star Wars. Dir. George Lucas. Lucasfilm, 1977.

The Thief of Bagdad. Dir. Ludwig Berger and Michael Powell. London, 1940.

Secondary Sources

"A Glimpse inside the Fantasy Toolbox." *The Weekend Independent Arts and Entertainment Guide.* 8 July 1994. The L-Space Web. 28 August 1996. http://www.lspace.org/about-terry/interviews/index.html.

Adorno, Theodor, and Max Horkheimer. "The Culture Industry: Enlightenment as Mass Deception." *The Cultural Studies Reader.* Ed. Simon During. London: Routledge, 1993. 29–43.

Armitt, Lucie. "The Fragile Frames of *The Bloody Chamber*." *The Infernal Desires of Angela Carter: Fiction, Femininity, Feminism.* Ed. and Intro. Joseph Bristow and Trev Lynn Broughton. London and New York: Longman, 1997. 88–99.

Atwood, Margaret. "Running with the Tigers." Sage, *Flesh and the Mirror* 117–35.

Ayres, Brenda, ed. *The Emperor's Old Groove: Decolonizing Disney's Magic Kingdom.* New York: Peter Lang, 2003.

Bacchilega, Cristina. *Postmodern Fairy Tales: Gender and Narrative Strategies.* Philadelphia: University of Pennsylvania Press, 1997.

Bal, Mieke. "Notes on Narrative Embedding." *Poetics Today* 2.2 (1981): 41–59.

Barth, John. "The Literature of Replenishment: Postmodern Fiction." *The Post-Modern Reader.* Ed. Charles Jencks. London: Academy Editions, 1992. 172–80.

Baudrillard, Jean. "Simulacra and Simulation." *Jean Baudrillard: Selected Writings.* Ed. Mark Poster. Stanford: Stanford University Press, 1988. 166–84.

Bazin, André. *What Is Cinema?* Tr. Hugh Gray. Berkeley: University of California Press, 1967.

Bell, Elizabeth, Lynda Haas, and Laura Sells, eds. *From Mouse to Mermaid: The Politics of Film, Gender, and Culture.* Bloomington: Indiana University Press, 1995.

Benjamin, Walter. "The Storyteller." *Illuminations.* Ed. Hannah Arendt. London: Pimlico, 1999.

———. "The Work of Art in the Age of Mechanical Reproduction." *Illuminations.* Ed. Hannah Arendt. London: Pimlico, 1999.

Benson, Stephen. "Angela Carter and the Literary *Märchen:* A Review Essay." Roemer and Bacchilega 30–64.

———. *Cycles of Influence: Fiction, Folktale, Theory.* Detroit: Wayne State University Press, 2003.

Bettelheim, Bruno. *The Uses of Enchantment: The Meaning and Importance of Fairy Tales.* London: Thames and Hudson, 1976.

Black, Stephen A. *James Thurber: His Masquerades—A Critical Study*. The Hague: Mouton, 1970.

Breton, André. *What Is Surrealism? Selected Writings*. Ed. Franklin Rosemont. London: Pluto, 1978.

Brink, André. "Possessed by Language." *The Novel: Language and Narrative from Cervantes to Calvino*. Cape Town: University of Cape Town Press, 1998. 288–308.

Bristow, Joseph, and Trev Lynn Broughton. *The Infernal Desires of Angela Carter: Fiction, Femininity, Feminism*. London and New York: Longman, 1997.

Byatt, A. S. "Happy Ever After." *The Guardian*, Saturday, 3 January 2004. At http://books.guardian.co.uk/departments/generalfiction/story/0,6000,1115138,00.html. Accessed 2 December 2006.

———. *On Histories and Stories: Selected Essays*. London: Vintage, 2000.

———. *Passions of the Mind*. London: Vintage, 1991.

Byrne, Eleanor, and Martin McQuillan. *Deconstructing Disney*. London: Pluto, 1999.

Calvino, Italo. Introduction to *Italian Folk Tales*. Tr. George Martin. London: Penguin, 1956. xv–xxxii.

———. *The Literature Machine*. London: Secker and Warburg, 1982.

———. "Notes towards a Definition of the Narrative Form as a Combinative Process." *Twentieth Century Studies* 3 (1970): 93–101.

Campbell, Jane L. "Confecting *Sugar*: Narrative Theory and Practice in A. S. Byatt's Short Stories." *Critique* 38.2 (1997): 105–22.

Carroll, Noël. *A Philosophy of Mass Art*. Oxford: Clarendon, 1998.

Carter, Angela. *Expletives Deleted: Selected Writings*. London: Vintage, 1993.

———. "Notes from the Front Line." *On Gender and Writing*. Ed. Michelene Wandor. London: Pandora, 1983.

———. *The Sadeian Woman: An Exercise in Cultural History*. London: Virago, 1979.

Cawelti, John. *Adventure, Mystery and Romance: Formula Stories as Art and Popular Culture*. Chicago: University of Chicago Press, 1976.

Clark, Robert. "Angela Carter's Desire Machine." *Women's Studies* 14 (1987): 147–61.

Clarke, Arthur C. *Profiles of the Future*. Revised edition. New York: Harper, 1973.

Clarke, Gerald. "Great Galloping Galaxies!" *Time*, 23 May 1983. 74–80.

Clifford, Gay. *The Transformations of Allegory*. London: Routledge and Kegan Paul, 1974.

Clute, John. "Coming of Age." *Terry Pratchett: Guilty of Literature*. Ed. Andrew M. Butler, Edward James, and Farah Mendlesohn. Reading, UK: The Science Fiction Foundation, 2000. 7–20.

Coover, Robert. "A Passionate Remembrance." *Review of Contemporary Fiction* 14.3 (1994): 9–10.

Crunelle-Vanrigh, Anny. "The Logic of the Same and *Différance*: 'The Courtship of Mr Lyon.'" Roemer and Bacchilega 128–44.

De Caro, Frank, and Rosan Augusta Jordan. *Re-Situating Folklore: Folk Contexts and Twentieth-Century Literature and Art*. Knoxville: University of Tennessee Press, 2004.

de Saussure, Ferdinand. *Course in General Linguistics*. Tr. Wade Baskin. New York: McGraw-Hill, 1959.

Derrida, Jacques. "The Law of Genre." *Glyph: Textual Studies* 7 (1980): 202–32.

Duncker, Patricia. "Re-Imagining the Fairy Tales: Angela Carter's Bloody Chambers." *Literature and History* 10.1 (1984): 3–14.

Dundes, Alan. *Interpreting Folklore*. Bloomington: Indiana University Press, 1980.

Duruy, Victor. *A Short History of France*. Volumes 1 and 2. London: Dent, 1917.

Dworkin, Andrea. *Women Hating*. New York: E. P. Dutton, 1974.

Eco, Umberto. *Reflections on the Name of the Rose*. London: Secker and Warburg, 1983.

Eliade, Mircea. *Myth and Reality*. London: George Allen and Unwin, 1963.

Evans, Arthur B. *Jean Cocteau and His Films of Orphic Identity*. Philadelphia: Art Alliance Press, 1977.

"Ever After." *Fox Movies*. 1998. Twentieth Century Fox. 21 October 2001. http://www.foxmovies.com/everafter/themovie.html.

Fiske, John. *Reading the Popular*. Boston: Unwin, 1989.

Flegel, Monica. "Enchanted Readings and Fairy Tale Endings in A. S. Byatt's *Possession*." *English Studies in Canada* 24.4 (1998): 413–30.

Franken, Christien. *A. S. Byatt: Art, Authorship, Creativity*. Houndmills, UK: Palgrave, 2001.

Frye, Northrop. *Anatomy of Criticism: Four Essays*. Princeton: Princeton University Press, 1957.

———. *The Secular Scripture: A Study of the Nature of Romance*. Cambridge: Harvard University Press, 1976.

Galef, David. "A Sense of Magic: Reality and Illusion in Cocteau's *Beauty and the Beast*." *Literature/Film Quarterly* 12.2 (1984): 96–106.

Gilbert, Sandra M., and Susan Gubar. *The Madwoman in the Attic: The Woman Writer and the 19th Century Literary Imagination*. New Haven: Yale University Press, 1979.

Giroux, Henry A. *The Mouse That Roared: Disney and the End of Innocence*. Lanham, MD: Rowman and Littlefield, 1999.

Gitzen, Julian. "A. S. Byatt's Self-Mirroring Art." *Critique* 36.2 (1995): 83–95.

Haase, Donald P. "Is Seeing Believing? Proverbs and the Film Adaptation of a Fairy Tale." *Proverbium* 7 (1990): 89–104.

Hall, Stuart. "Notes on Deconstructing the Popular." *People's History and Socialist Theory*. London: Routledge, 1981. 227–49.

Hansen, Miriam. "Of Mice and Ducks: Benjamin and Adorno on Disney." *South Atlantic Quarterly* 92.1 (1993): 27–62.

Harries, Elizabeth Wanning. *Twice Upon a Time: Women Writers and the History of the Fairy Tale*. Princeton: Princeton University Press, 2001.

Hassan, Ihab. "Pluralism in Postmodern Perspective." *The Post-Modern Reader.* Ed. Charles Jencks. London: Academy Editions, 1992. 196–207.

Hayward, Susan. "Film in Context: *La Belle et la Bête.*" *History Today* 46.7 (1996): 43–48.

Henstra, Sarah M. "The Pressure of New Wine: Performative Reading in Angela Carter's *The Sadeian Woman.*" *Textual Practice* 13.1 (1999): 97–117.

Hills, Matthew. "Mapping Narrative Spaces." *Terry Pratchett: Guilty of Literature.* Ed. Andrew M. Butler, Edward James, and Farah Mendlesohn. Reading, UK: The Science Fiction Foundation, 2000. 128–44.

Holmes, Charles S. *The Clocks of Columbus: The Literary Career of James Thurber.* London: Secker and Warburg, 1973.

———. "James Thurber and the Art of Fantasy." *Yale Review* 55 (1965): 17–33.

Holmes, Charles S., ed. *Thurber: A Collection of Critical Essays.* Englewood Cliffs, NJ: Prentice-Hall, 1974.

Hutcheon, Linda. *A Poetics of Postmodernism: History, Theory, Fiction.* New York: Routledge, 1988.

———. *A Theory of Parody: The Teachings of Twentieth-Century Art Forms.* New York: Methuen, 1985.

Jackson, Rosemary. *Fantasy: The Literature of Subversion.* London: Methuen, 1981.

Jameson, Fredric. "The Cultural Logic of Late Capitalism." *Postmodernism; or, the Cultural Logic of Late Capitalism.* London: Verso, 1991. 1–54.

Jenkins, Henry. *Textual Poachers: Television Fans and Participatory Culture.* New York and London: Routledge, 1992.

Jordan, Elaine. "The Dangers of Angela Carter." *New Feminist Discourses: Critical Essays on Theories and Texts.* Ed. Isobel Armstrong. London: Routledge, 1992. 119–32.

———. 1994. "The Dangerous Edge." Sage, *Flesh and the Mirror* 189–215.

Jouve, Nicole Ward. 1994. "'Mother Is a Figure of Speech.'" Sage, *Flesh and the Mirror* 136–70.

Kaiser, Mary. "Fairy Tale as Sexual Allegory: Intertextuality in Angela Carter's *The Bloody Chamber.*" *Review of Contemporary Fiction* 14.3 (1994): 30–36.

Kappeler, Susanne. *The Pornography of Representation.* Cambridge, UK: Polity, 1986.

Kenney, Catherine McGehee. *Thurber's Anatomy of Confusion.* Hamden, CT: Archon, 1984.

Le Guin, Ursula K. *Dancing on the Edge of the World: Thoughts on Words, Women, Places.* New York: Harper and Row, 1990.

———. *The Language of the Night: Essays on Fantasy and Science Fiction.* Revised edition. London: The Women's Press, 1989.

Lefanu, Sarah. "Robots and Romance: The Science Fiction and Fantasy of Tanith Lee." *Sweet Dreams: Sexuality, Gender, and Popular Fiction.* Ed. Susannah Radstone. London: Lawrence and Wishart, 1988. 121–36.

Lévi-Strauss, Claude. "The Structural Study of Myth." *Journal of American Folklore* 68.270 (1955): 428–44.

Lewallen, Avis. "Wayward Girls but Wicked Women? Female Sexuality in Angela Carter's *The Bloody Chamber.*" *Perspectives on Pornography: Sexuality in Film and Literature.* Ed. Gary Day and Clive Bloom. New York: St. Martin's, 1988. 144–58.

Linkin, Harriet Kramer. "Isn't It Romantic? Angela Carter's Bloody Revision of the Romantic Aesthetic in *The Erl-King.*" *Contemporary Literature* 35.2 (1994): 305–23.

Lokke, Kari E. "*Bluebeard* and *The Bloody Chamber:* The Grotesque of Self-Parody and Self-Assertion." *Frontiers* 10.1 (1988): 7–12.

Lurie, Alison. *Don't Tell the Grown-Ups: Subversive Children's Literature.* London: Bloomsbury, 1990.

Lüthi, Max. *The Fairy Tale as Art Form and Portrait of Man.* Tr. Jon Erickson. Bloomington: Indiana University Press, 1975.

Macdonald, George. "The Fantastic Imagination." 1893. *Fantasists on Fantasy: A Collection of Critical Reflections by 18 Masters of the Art.* Ed. Robert H. Boyer and Kenneth J. Zahorski. New York: Avon, 1984. 14–21.

Maddocks, Melvin. "James Thurber and the Hazards of Humor." *Sewanee Review* 93.4 (1985): 597–601.

Marzolph, Ulrich. "Aladdin." Zipes, *Oxford Companion.*

Mendlesohn, Farah. "Faith and Ethics." *Terry Pratchett: Guilty of Literature.* Ed. Andrew M. Butler, Edward James, and Farah Mendlesohn. Reading, UK: The Science Fiction Foundation, 2000. 145–61.

Montenyohl, Eric L. "Oralities (and Literacies): Comments on the Relationships of Contemporary Folkloristics and Literary Studies." *Folklore, Literature, and Cultural Theory: Collected Essays.* Ed. Cathy Lynn Preston. New York: Garland, 1995.

Morsberger, Robert M. *James Thurber.* Boston: Twayne, 1964.

Nicholls, Peter. "Tepper, Sheri S." *The Encyclopaedia of Science Fiction.* Ed. John Clute and Peter Nicholls. London: Orbit, 1993.

Ong, Walter J. "From Mimesis to Irony: The Distancing of Voice." *Bulletin of the Midwest Modern Language Association* 9.1/2 (1976): 1–24.

———. *Rhetoric, Romance, and Technology: Studies in the Interaction of Expression and Culture.* Ithaca: Cornell University Press, 1971.

Ostman, Ronald E. "Disney and Its Conservative Critics." *Journal of Popular Film and Television* 24 (1996): 82–89.

Parker, Dorothy. "Unbaked Cookies." 1932. Holmes, *Clocks of Columbus* 56–61.

Pauley, Rebecca M. "*Beauty and the Beast:* From Fable to Film." *Literature/Film Quarterly* 17.2 (1989): 84–90.

Pawling, Christopher, ed. *Popular Fiction and Social Change.* London: Macmillan, 1984.

Plimpton, George, and Max Steele. "Thurber on Himself." 1957. Holmes, *Thurber* 106–16.

Pollin, Burton R. "James Thurber: A Humorist Haunted by Poe." *Southern Quarterly* 37.3–4 (1999): 139–58.

Popkin, Michael. "Jean Cocteau's *Beauty and the Beast:* The Poet as Monster." *Literature/Film Quarterly* 10.2 (1982): 100–109.

Pratchett, Terry. "From Terry." *TerryPratchettBooks.com.* 2001. HarperCollins. 18 March 2001. http://www.terrypratchettbooks.com.

———. "Interview. *Loose Ends,* BBC Radio 4, 27 Nov. 1993." The L-Space Web. 28 August 1996. http://www.lspace.org/about-terry/interviews/index.html.

Preston, Cathy. "*Ever After.* Directed by Andy Tennant. Twentieth Century Fox, 1998." Review. *Marvels & Tales* 14.1 (2000): 175–78.

Rabelais, François. *The Histories of Gargantua and Pantagruel.* 1532. Tr. J. M. Cohen. London: Penguin, 1955.

Propp, Vladimir. "Fairy Tale Transformations." 1928. *Readings in Russian Poetics: Formalist and Structuralist Views.* Ed. Ladislav Matejka and Krystyna Pomorska. Cambridge: MIT Press, 1971. 94–114.

———. *The Morphology of the Folktale.* Tr. Laurence Scott. Austin: University of Texas Press, 1968.

Rabkin, Eric S. "Fairy Tales and Science Fiction." *Bridges to Science Fiction.* Ed. George E. Slusser, George R. Guffey, and Mark Rose. Carbondale: Southern Illinois University Press, 1980. 78–90.

Richards, Linda. "Terry Pratchett's Discworld: On Soul Music; Dealing with Fame and Weaving Fantasies." *January* magazine, May 1998. The L-Space Web. 12 May 2005. http://www.lspace.org/about-terry/interviews/january.html.

Roemer, Danielle M., and Cristina Bacchilega, eds. *Angela Carter and the Fairy Tale.* Detroit: Wayne State University Press, 2001.

Rose, Ellen Cronan. "Through the Looking Glass: When Women Tell Fairy Tales." *The Voyage In: Fictions of Female Development.* Ed. Elizabeth Abel, Marianne Hirsch, Elizabeth Langland. Hanover: University Press of New England, 1983. 209–27.

Rubinson, Gregory J. "'On the Beach of Elsewhere': Angela Carter's Moral Pornography and the Critique of Gender Archetypes." *Women's Studies* 29 (2000): 717–40.

Rutledge, Amelia A. "Robin McKinley's *Deerskin:* Challenging Narcissisms." *Marvels & Tales* 15 (2002): 168–82.

Sage, Lorna. ed. "Angela Carter: The Fairy Tale." Roemer and Bacchilega 65–81.

———. *Flesh and the Mirror: Essays on the Art of Angela Carter.* London: Virago, 1994.

Sale, Roger. *Fairy Tales and After: From Snow White to E. B. White.* Cambridge: Harvard University Press, 1978.

Sanchez, Victoria. "A. S. Byatt's *Possession:* A Fairy Tale Romance." *Southern Folklore* 52.1 (1995): 33–52.

Sayre, Nora. "The Frog on the Typewriter and Other Literary Visitations." *New York Times Book Review* 24–27, January 1993.

Schickel, Richard. *The Disney Version: The Life, Times, Art, and Commerce of Walt Disney*. New York: Simon and Schuster, 1985.

Scholes, Robert. *Fabulation and Metafiction*. Urbana: University of Illinois Press, 1979.

Sewell, Elizabeth. *The Field of Nonsense*. 1952. London: Chatto and Windus, 1978.

Sheets, Robin Ann. "Pornography, Fairy Tales, and Feminism: Angela Carter's 'The Bloody Chamber.'" *Forbidden History: The State, Society, and the Regulation of Sexuality in Modern Europe*. Ed. John C. Fout. Chicago: University of Chicago Press, 1992. 335–59.

"Shrek (2001): Production Notes." *Cinema.com.* 2001. 12 May 2005. http://www.cinema.com/films/5025/shrek/production_notes.phtml.

Solomon, Charles. *Enchanted Drawings: The History of Animation*. New York: Alfred A. Knopf, 1989.

Stephens, John, and Robyn McCallum. "Utopia, Dystopia, and Cultural Controversy in *Ever After* and *The Grimm Brothers' Snow White*." *Marvels & Tales* 16.2 (2002): 201–13.

Sterling, Bruce, writing as Vincent Omniveritas. "RED AS BLOOD by Tanith Lee." *Cheap Truth* 1 (1983). 6 January 2001. http://www.doctort.org/adam/CheapTruth.

Strinati, Dominic. *An Introduction to Theories of Popular Culture*. Second edition. London and New York: Routledge, 1995, 2004.

Sturrock, John, ed. *Structuralism and Since: From Lévi-Strauss to Derrida*. Oxford: Oxford University Press, 1979.

Tatar, Maria. *The Hard Facts of the Grimms' Fairy Tales*. Princeton: Princeton University Press, 1987.

Tepper, Sheri S. "Fiction, Farming, and Other Rare Breeds." *Locus* 402 (July 1994): 4, 80–81.

———. "Sheri Tepper: Aspiring Up." *Locus* 367 (August 1991): 4, 69.

Tiffin, Jessica. "All the World's a Pizza: Postmodernism, Popular Culture, and Pshakespeare in Terry Pratchett's Discworld." *Inter Action* 5 (1997): 194–202.

———. "Digitally Remythicised: *Star Wars*, Modern Popular Mythology, and *Madam and Eve*." *Journal of Literary Studies* 15.1/2 (1999): 66–80.

———. "Ice, Glass, Snow: Fairy Tale as Art and Metafiction in the Writing of A. S. Byatt." *Marvels & Tales* 20.1 (2006): 47–66.

———. *Magical Land: Ecological Consciousness in Fantasy Romance*. Unpublished Master's thesis, University of Cape Town, 1995.

———. "'Nice and Neat and Formal': Entrapment, Transformation, and Narrative Convention in Thurber's Fairy Tales." *Fissions and Fusions: Proceedings of the First Conference of the Cape American Studies Association*. Ed. Lesley Marx, Loes Nas, and Lara Dunwell. Cape Town: University of the Western Cape Press, 1996. 124–30.

Todd, Richard. "The Retrieval of Unheard Voices in British Postmodernist Fiction: A. S. Byatt and Marina Warner." *Liminal Postmodernisms: The Postmodern, the (Post-)Colonial, and the (Post-)Feminist*. Ed.

Theo D'haen and Hans Bertens. Amsterdam, Atlanta: Rodopi, 1994. 99–114.

———. *Writers and Their Work: A. S. Byatt.* Plymouth, UK: Northcote House, 1997.

Todorov, Tzvetan. *The Fantastic: A Structural Approach to a Literary Genre.* Tr. Richard Howard. Ithaca: Cornell University Press, 1970.

———. "Fairy Tale Transformations." *Readings in Russian Poetics: Formalist and Structuralist Views.* Ed. Ladislav Matejka and Krystyna Pomorska. Cambridge: MIT Press, 1971. 94–114.

Tolkien, J. R. R. "On Fairy Stories." 1964. *The Tolkien Reader.* New York: Ballantine, 1966. 2–84.

Toombs, Sarah Eleanora. *James Thurber: An Annotated Bibliography of Criticism.* New York: Garland, 1987.

Trevenna, Joanne. "Gender as Performance: Questioning the 'Butlerification' of Angela Carter's Fiction." *Journal of Gender Studies* 11.3 (2002): 267–76.

Wachtel, Eleanor. "A. S. Byatt." *Writers and Company.* Toronto: Alfred A. Knopf, 1993. 77–89.

Warner, Marina. "Angela Carter: Bottle Blonde, Double Drag." Sage, *Flesh and the Mirror* 243–56.

———. *From the Beast to the Blonde: On Fairy Tales and Their Tellers.* London: Vintage, 1994.

———. *No Go the Bogeyman: Scaring, Lulling, and Making Mock.* London: Chatto and Windus, 1998.

Wasko, Janet. *Understanding Disney: The Manufacture of Fantasy.* Cambridge: Polity, 2004.

Waugh, Patricia. *Metafiction: The Theory and Practice of Self-Conscious Fiction.* London: Routledge, 1984.

Wells, Paul. " 'Thou Art Translated': Analysing Animated Adaptation." *Adaptations: From Text to Screen, Screen to Text.* Ed. Deborah Cartmell and Imelda Whelehan. London: Routledge, 1999. 199–225.

White, E. B. "James Thurber." 1961. Holmes, *Clocks of Columbus.* 171–72.

White, Timothy, and J. E. Winn. "Disney, Animation, and Money: The Reception of Disney's *Aladdin* in South-East Asia." *Kinema* (Spring 1995). University of Waterloo. 12 February 2005. http://www.arts. uwaterloo.ca/FINE/juhde/white951.htm.

Wignal, Brendan. "Throwing People to Stories—Terry Pratchett." *Million* 5 (1991). The L-Space Web. 29 January 2003. http://www.lspace.org/ about-terry/interviews/million.html.

Wilson, Robert Rawdon. "SLIP PAGE: Angela Carter, In/Out/In the Postmodern Nexus." *Past the Last Post: Theorizing Post-Colonialism and Post-Modernism.* Ed. Ian Adam and Helen Tiffin. Calgary: University of Calgary Press, 1990. 109–23.

Windling, Terri. "Artists without Borders." 2003. *Interstitial Arts: Artists without Borders.* The Interstitial Arts Foundation. 4 March 2005. http://www.interstitialarts.org/what/reflection_windling.html.

Wood, James. "England." *The Oxford Guide to Contemporary Writing*. Ed. John Sturrock. Oxford: Oxford University Press, 1996. 121–28.

Wynne, Patrick. "Bookhenge #12, *Possession*, by A. S. Byatt." *Butterbur's Woodshed*. 1 January 1996. The Rivendell Group of the Mythopoeic Society. 15 May 2005. http://www.tc.umn.edu/~d-lena/WynneOnByatt.html.

Young, Elizabeth. "Bestselling Fantasy Writer Who Hates Fantasy." *The Weekly Mail and Guardian*, 26 November to 2 December 1993.

Zipes, Jack. *Breaking the Magic Spell: Radical Theories of Folk and Fairy Tales*. Revised and expanded edition. Lexington: University Press of Kentucky, 2002.

———. "The Changing Function of the Fairy Tale." *The Lion and the Unicorn* 12.2 (1988): 7–31.

———. *Fairy Tale as Myth, Myth as Fairy Tale*. Lexington: University Press of Kentucky, 1994.

———. *Fairy Tales and the Art of Subversion*. London: Heinemann, 1983.

———. *Happily Ever After: Fairy Tales, Children, and the Culture Industry*. New York: Routledge, 1997.

———. *The Oxford Companion to Fairy Tales: The Western Fairy Tale Tradition from Medieval to Modern*. Oxford: Oxford University Press, 2000.

Zucker, Carole. "Sweetest Tongue Has Sharpest Tooth: The Dangers of Dreaming in Neil Jordan's *The Company of Wolves*." *Literature/Film Quarterly* 28.1 (2000): 66–71.

INDEX

10, 16–17, 22, 76–77, 85, 89–90, 102–3, 139–40, 172–73, 201–2; and the novel, 132–33, 143; parody of, 30, 32–33, 159–60, 223–24, 229; as popular literature, 4–5, 29–30, 39, 131–33, 135–37, 140–41; problematization of reality in, 4, 13–14, 16–18, 20–21, 22–24, 219–20; recognition of, 2–4, 5–8, 21, 24; texture of, 5–8, 123, 132; vampires in, 96–97, 150–52; Victorian, 4, 28, 45

fantasy. *See* romance, fantasy

film, fairy-tale, 30; adaptation from fairy tale, 179–80, 183–84; as folk culture, 181, 183–88; Hollywood, 136, 180, 183–84, 188, 200–206; the musical in, 180, 213, 227; and myth, 10–11, 17, 18, 76, 89; the oral voice in, 185–86, 187–88, 202, 215; status of reality in, 181–83, 189–94, 201–2; technology of, 179, 181. *See also* animation, Disney; *and specific titles*

folk culture, 4, 162, 219; film as, 181, 183–88; and mass culture, 131, 133, 140; as peasant culture, 66, 137–39, 149, 139–40; as popular culture, 135, 137, 141

folkloric voice, 25, 138–39, 183–84

folktale, 9–10, 26, 71, 85–87; adaptation into literary forms, 25, 66, 127–28, 131, 133, 137–41, 179, 183–86

formula fiction, 3, 19, 58, 131–33, 135, 142, 149, 211–13

Franken, Christien, 117–18

Frye, Northrop, 17–18

Gaiman, Neil, 151

Galef, David, 181

genre, 3, 7, 39, 79–82, 132–33, 135–37, 149; embedded, 124; generic marking, 142; conflict with fairy tale, 7, 35–36; horror, 132, 149, 150–51, 152–53, 193–94, 198–99, 204–205; science fiction, 142, 143–44, 155–56, 170, 171–72. *See also* fairy tale, Gothic literature, romance

geometry. *See* structure

ghetto, science fiction, 141–42, 148–49, 160, 187

Giroux, Henry, 209

Gitzen, Julian, 102

Gothic literature, 58–59, 80–81, 85, 96–98, 154–55, 204–5, 218

Grimm, Jakob and Wilhelm, 141, 149, 151; "Cinderella," 202; "The Glass Coffin," 108, 112, 113, 122; "The Golden Key," 109; "Snow White," 149–50, 205–6

Grimm Brothers' Snow White, The (Cohn), 182–83, 204–6

Haase, Donald P., 86, 182

Hall, Stuart, 134

Hansen, Miriam, 210

Happily N'Ever After (Bolger and Kaplan), 228–29

Harries, Elizabeth Wanning, 8, 23, 139

Holmes, Charles, 39, 41, 44

Hoodwinked (Edwards), 228–29

Horkheimer, Max, 165, 186–87

Hutcheon, Linda, 22, 24, 68, 139, 223–24, 228, 229

Jackson, Rosemary, 13, 18, 22–23, 99

Jameson, Fredric, 135, 161, 229

Jordan, Elaine, 68, 72

Jordan, Neil, 86, 128, 182–83, 187–88, 192–200

Jordan, Rosan Augusta, 26, 137, 140

Jouve, Nicole Ward, 73, 75, 89

Kaiser, Mary, 66, 95

Kenney, Catherine McGehee, 33, 34

Lee, Tanith, 29, 148–58; "Beauty," 155–58; Christian symbolism in, 151–52; feminism in, 87, 153–55, 156; horror elements in, 149, 150–51, 152–53, 154; "The Princess and her Future," 152–54; science fiction elements in, 149, 155–57; sexuality in, 153–54, 156–58; structural inversion in, 149, 150–51, 152, 154, 158; *Red as Blood*, 149, 150; "Red as Blood," 150–52, "Thorns," 150; *White as Snow*, 146; "Wolfland," 87, 154–55

Le Guin, Ursula K., 15, 142, 220

Levi-Strauss, Claude, 10
Linkin, Harriet Kramer, 83–84
Lüthi, Max, 12, 14, 15, 16–17, 19

Macdonald, George, 15–16, 18, 109, 118
magical narrative, 6–7, 11, 17–19,
    22, 27–28, 51, 88, 122, 177;
    and popular culture, 4–5;
    problematization of reality by,
    6, 17; visual representation of,
    180–82
marvelous. *See* magical narrative
mass culture, 131–33, 139–41, 165, 186–
    88, 209–10; and appropriation
    of the folk voice, 139–41, 186–87;
    communal aspects of, 133–34;
    and film, 179, 183–84; as folk
    culture, 131, 133–34, 183–85; self-
    consciousness in, 142–43, 187–88
McKinley, Robin, 144–45
metafiction, 3–4, 20–24, 74, 185,
    199–200; commercial use of,
    222–23; language in service of, 38,
    40, 80; and political awareness,
    72, 89; and the problematization
    of reality, 4, 16, 76, 90, 102–3
Montenyohl, Eric L., 138
Morsberger, Robert, 34–35
myth, 10–11, 17, 18, 76, 89

narrative, breakdown of, 230–31; fairy-
    tale (*see* fairy tale); embedding,
    103–5, 121–28, 193–94; magical
    (*see* magical narrative); oral
    (*see* oral narrative); pattern (*see*
    structure); relationship to reality
    of, 18, 21–23; structural accounts
    of, 2–4, 8–9

Ong, Walter, 135, 137–38, 140, 184
oral narrative, 137–40; adaptation
    of, 133, 135, 184–86; embedded,
    127–28; film's invocation of,
    184–85, 193, 202, 215

parody, 30, 32–33, 159–60, 223–24,
    229
Pauley, Rebecca, 189–90
Perrault, Charles, 71; "Little Red
    Riding Hood," 86, 153, 154, 197;

"Puss-in-Boots," 78; translated by
    Angela Carter, 65, 79–80
Pollin, Burton R., 58
popular culture, 4–5, 29–30, 39, 131–
    33, 140; folk culture as, 133–35,
    137, 141; as site of struggle, 132–
    34, 188; versus "high" culture,
    135, 142, 188–89; self-conscious
    narrative in, 133, 135, 141, 142–43,
    188–89; utopianism in, 136
postmodernism, in fairy tale, 20–25,
    74, 220, 222–24, 233–34; and
    historicity, 139–40; and
    structure, 2, 4, 10, 23–24, 65,
    68, 135–35
Pratchett, Terry, 29–30, 148, 158–69;
    *The Amazing Maurice and His
    Educated Rodents*, 33, 162, 163;
    Carpe Jugulum, 164; closure in,
    161; dehumanization in, 163–65,
    167–68; Discworld setting, 148,
    158–59, 160, 169; and fantasy,
    159–60; *Lords and Ladies*, 162–63;
    narrative self-consciousness in,
    162–66, 169; parody in, 159,
    160, 161; and postmodernism,
    159, 160–61; reality in, 159–160,
    162, 164, 167, 169; totalitarian
    narrative in, 166, 168; *Witches
    Abroad*, 26–27, 33, 152, 159,
    160–61, 163–69
Pretty Woman (Marshall), 200–201
Propp, Vladimir, 2, 7, 11–12, 110

Rabkin, Eric S., 144
Roemer, Danielle, 67, 71
romance, 17–18, 104, 144; fantasy,
    18, 137, 141–47, 159–60, 169;
    Hollywood, 189, 204; women's,
    81–82, 104, 135–37
Rubinson, Gregory J., 69, 76

Sage, Lorna, 85
Sale, Roger, 7
Saussure, Ferdinand de, 41–43
Scholes, Robert, 19, 20
science fiction, 142, 143–44, 155–56,
    170, 171–72; ghetto, 141–42,
    148–49, 160, 187
Sewell, Elizabeth, 40, 61

CPSIA information can be obtained
at www.ICGtesting.com
Printed in the USA
LVHW08s1258011018
592001LV00008B/81/P

9 780814 332627